鳥 山 明

This is my first time I've put my photo in this section. This is a photo of me with my son, Sasuke. I may seem like a "show-off" parent for including my son, but it does beat having to come up with something to draw for this page. Maybe I'll start doing this from now on. Or maybe I'm just getting lazy. Let's see, next time maybe I'll use a photo of my cat Koge, or my dog Mato. Hmmm…I think I'm onto something here…

—*Akira Toriyama, 1988*

Artist/writer Akira Toriyama burst onto the manga scene in 1980 with the wildly popular **Dr. Slump**, a science fiction comedy about the adventures of a mad scientist and his android "daughter." In 1984 he created his hit series **Dragon Ball**, which ran until 1995 in Shueisha's best-selling magazine **Weekly Shonen Jump**, and was translated into foreign languages around the world. Since **Dragon Ball**, he has worked on a variety of short series, including **Cowa!**, **Kajika**, **Sand Land**, and **Neko Majin**, as well as a children's book, **Toccio the Angel**. He is also known for his design work on video games, particularly the **Dragon Warrior** RPG series. He lives with his family in Japan.

DRAGON BALL VOL. 11
The SHONEN JUMP Graphic Novel Edition

This graphic novel is number 11 in a series of 42.

STORY AND ART BY
AKIRA TORIYAMA
ENGLISH ADAPTATION BY
GERARD JONES

Translation/Mari Morimoto
Touch-Up Art & Lettering/Wayne Truman
Cover Design/Sean Lee & Dan Ziegler
Graphics & Design/Sean Lee
Senior Editor/Jason Thompson

Managing Editor/Annette Roman
Editor in Chief/Hyoe Narita
Director, Licensing and Acquisitions/Rika Inouye
V.P. of Sales and Marketing/Liza Coppola
V.P. of Strategic Development/Yumi Hoashi
Publisher/Seiji Horibuchi

PARENTAL ADVISORY

Dragon Ball is rated "T" for Teen. It may contain violence, language, alcohol or tobacco use, or suggestive situations. It is recommended for ages 13 and up.

In the original Japanese edition, DRAGON BALL and DRAGON BALL Z are known collectively as the 42-volume series DRAGON BALL. The English DRAGON BALL Z was originally volumes 17-42 of the Japanese DRAGON BALL.

Published by VIZ, LLC
P.O. Box 77010 • San Francisco, CA 94107

SHONEN JUMP Graphic Novel Edition
10 9 8 7 6 5 4 3 2 1
First printing, May 2003

www.viz.com

THE WORLD'S MOST POPULAR MANGA

SHONEN JUMP GRAPHIC NOVEL

www.shonenjump.com

SHONEN JUMP GRAPHIC NOVEL

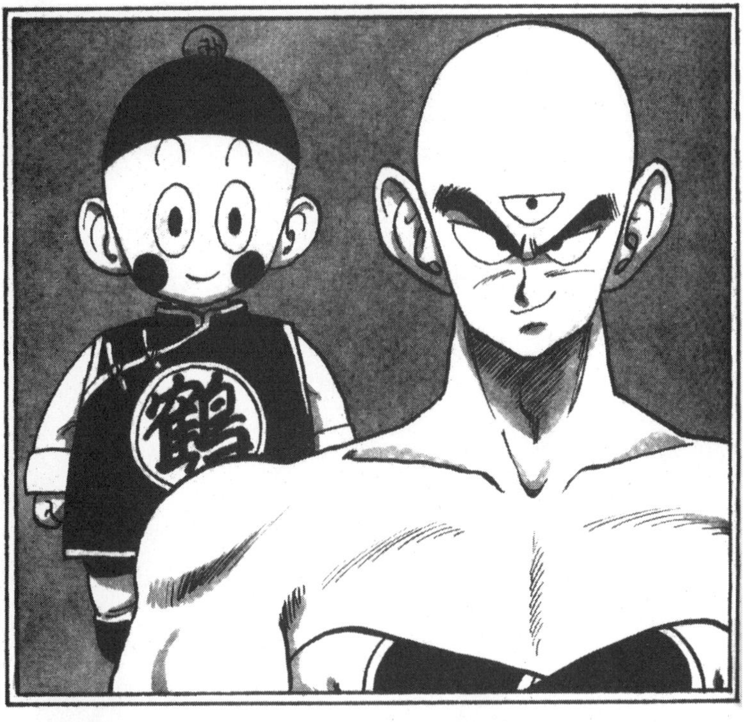
鶴

DRAGON BALL

Vol. 11

DB: 11 of 42

STORY AND ART BY
AKIRA TORIYAMA

THE MAIN CHARACTERS

Son Goku

Monkey-tailed young Goku has always been stronger than normal. His grandfather Gohan gave him the *nyoibô*, a magic staff, and Kame-Sen'nin gave him the *kinto'un*, a magic flying cloud.

Bulma

A genius inventor, Bulma met Goku on her quest for the seven magical Dragon Balls.

Yamcha

A student of Kame-Sen'nin, and Bulma's on-and-off boyfriend. He was seriously injured by Tenshinhan and taken to the hospital.

Lunch

A strange woman whose personality changes whenever she sneezes.

Kuririn

Goku's former martial arts schoolmate under Kame-Sen'nin.

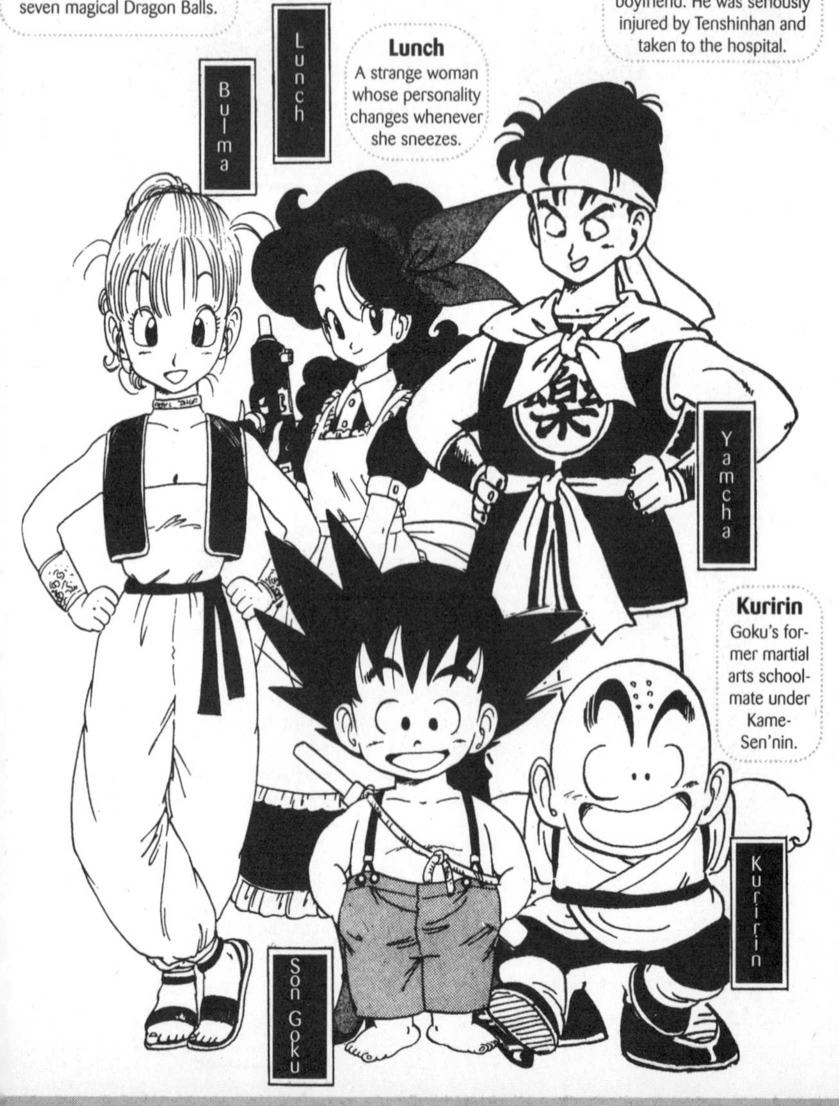

Lunch
Bulma
Yamcha
Kuririn
Son Goku

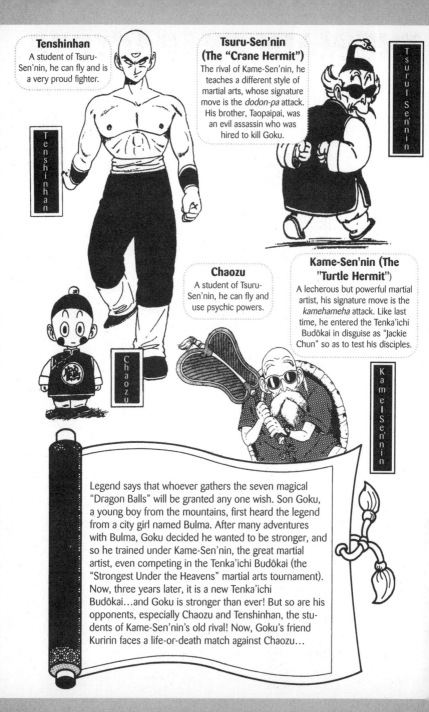

Tenshinhan

A student of Tsuru-Sen'nin, he can fly and is a very proud fighter.

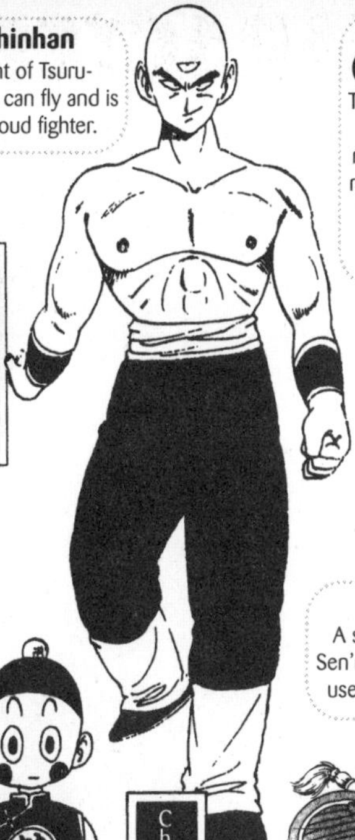
Tenshinhan

Tsuru-Sen'nin (The "Crane Hermit")

The rival of Kame-Sen'nin, he teaches a different style of martial arts, whose signature move is the *dodon-pa* attack. His brother, Taopaipai, was an evil assassin who was hired to kill Goku.

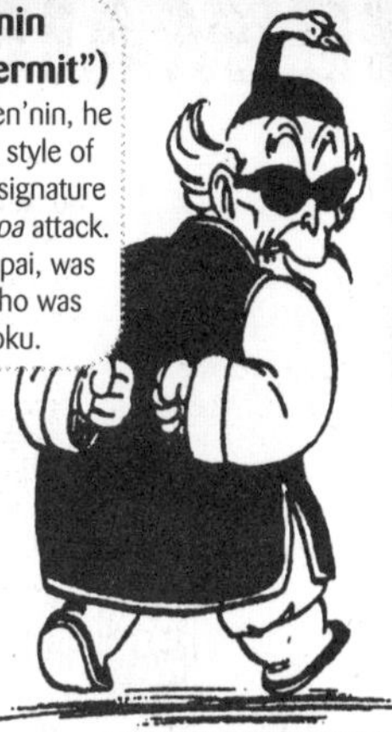
Tsuru-Sen'nin

Chaozu

A student of Tsuru-Sen'nin, he can fly and use psychic powers.

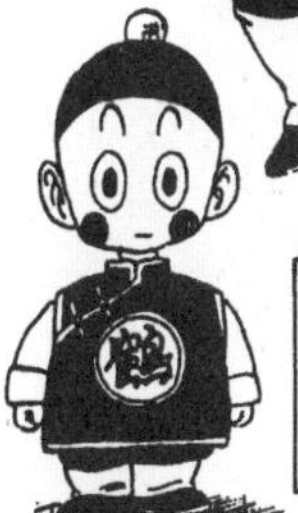
Chaozu

Kame-Sen'nin (The "Turtle Hermit")

A lecherous but powerful martial artist, his signature move is the *kamehameha* attack. Like last time, he entered the Tenka'ichi Budôkai in disguise as "Jackie Chun" so as to test his disciples.

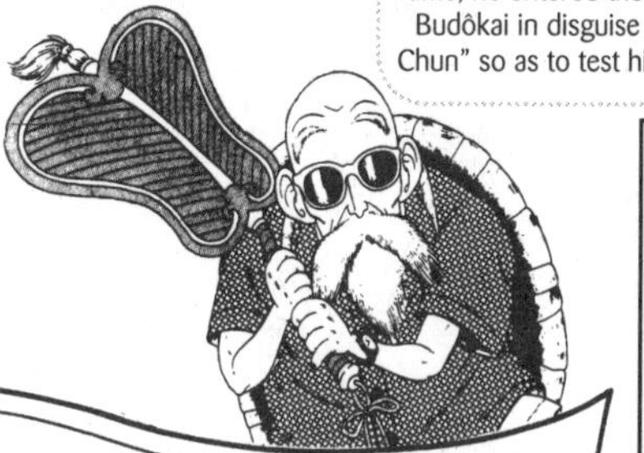
Kame-Sen'nin

Legend says that whoever gathers the seven magical "Dragon Balls" will be granted any one wish. Son Goku, a young boy from the mountains, first heard the legend from a city girl named Bulma. After many adventures with Bulma, Goku decided he wanted to be stronger, and so he trained under Kame-Sen'nin, the great martial artist, even competing in the Tenka'ichi Budôkai (the "Strongest Under the Heavens" martial arts tournament). Now, three years later, it is a new Tenka'ichi Budôkai...and Goku is stronger than ever! But so are his opponents, especially Chaozu and Tenshinhan, the students of Kame-Sen'nin's old rival! Now, Goku's friend Kuririn faces a life-or-death match against Chaozu...

DRAGON BALL 11

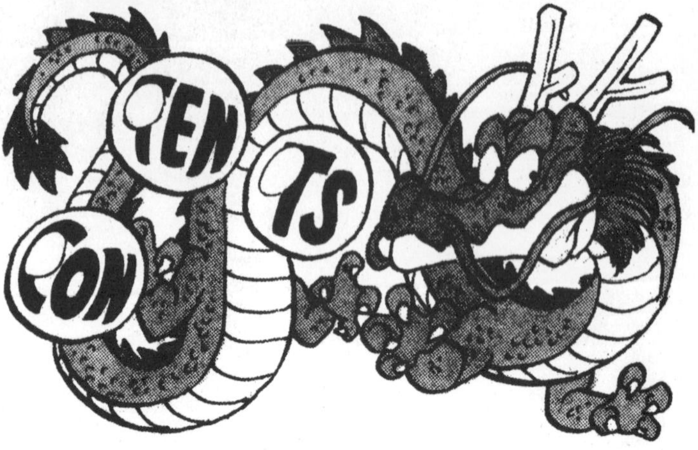
CON
TEN
TS

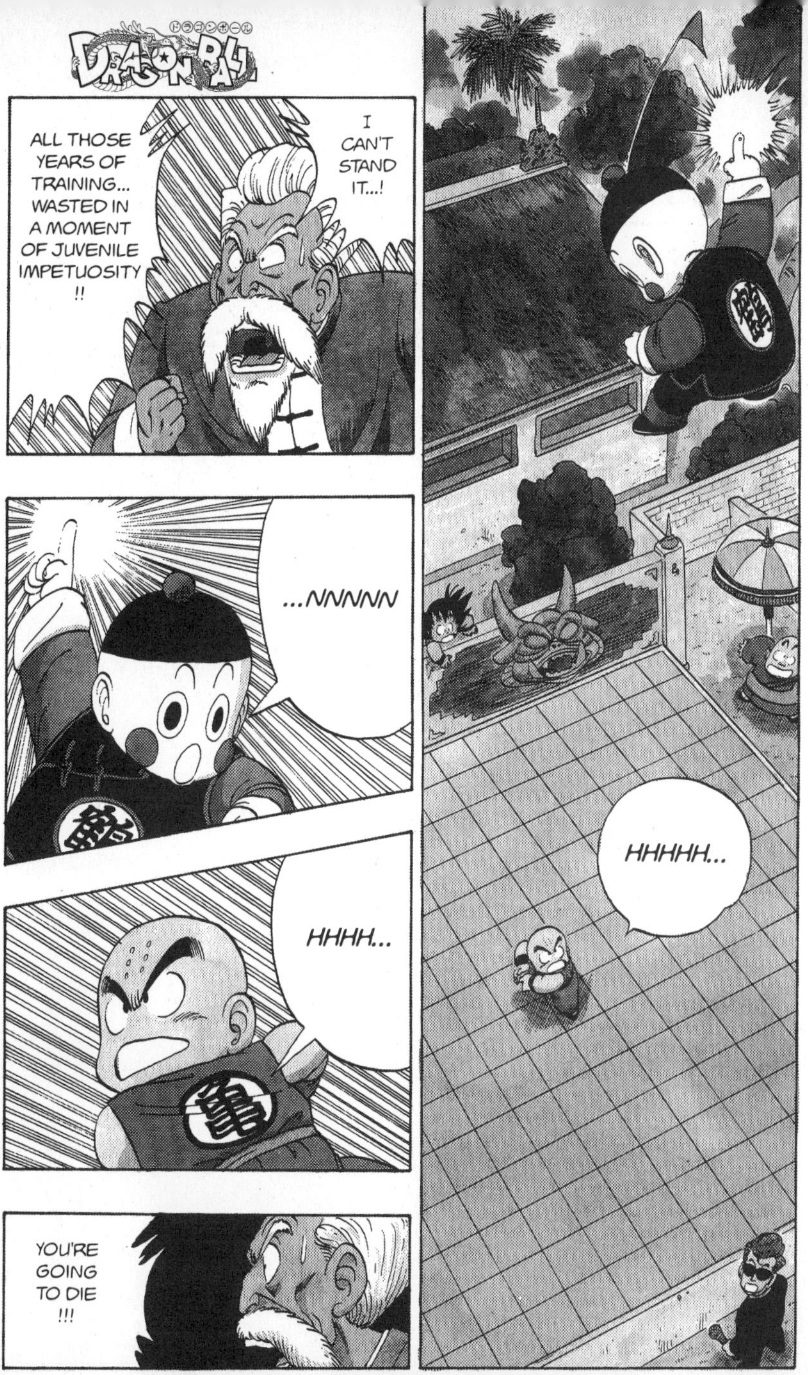
HHHHH...
I CAN'T STAND IT...!
ALL THOSE YEARS OF TRAINING... WASTED IN A MOMENT OF JUVENILE IMPETUOSITY !!
...NNNNN
HHHH...
YOU'RE GOING TO DIE !!!

Tale 121 • Kuririn's Master Plan

Tale 121 • Kuririn's Master Plan

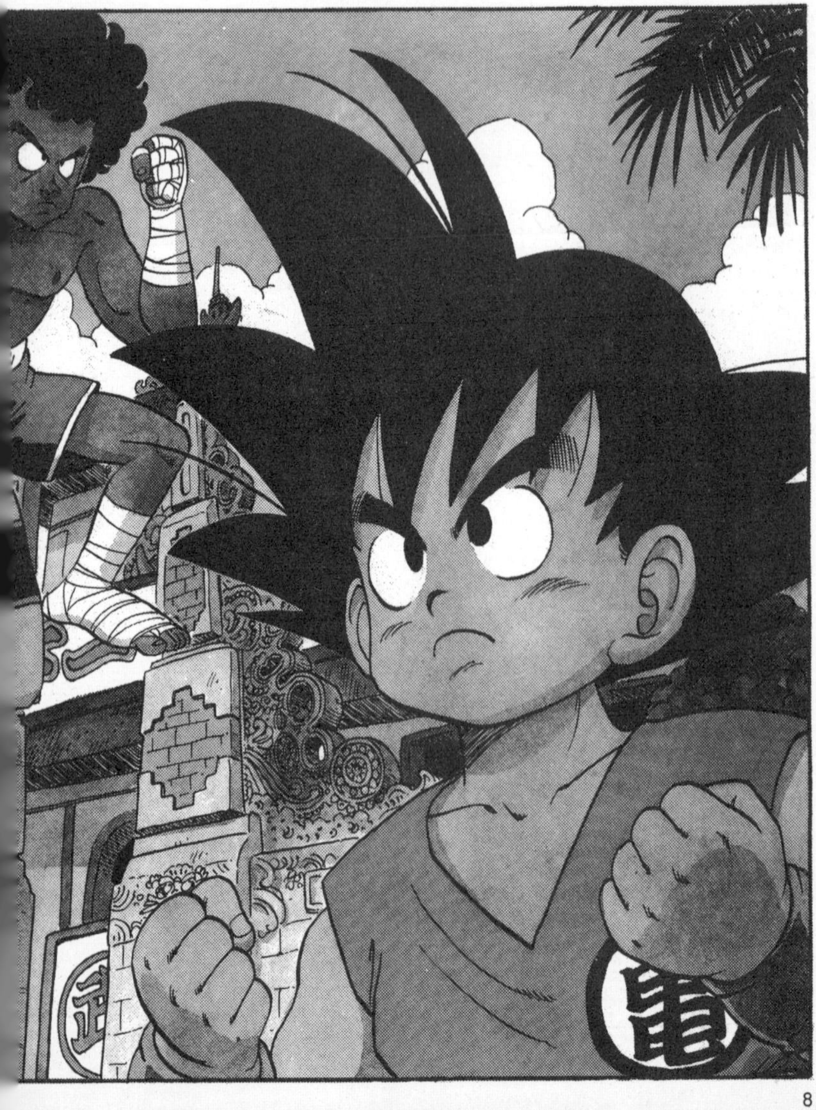

ドラゴンボール

DRAGON BALL

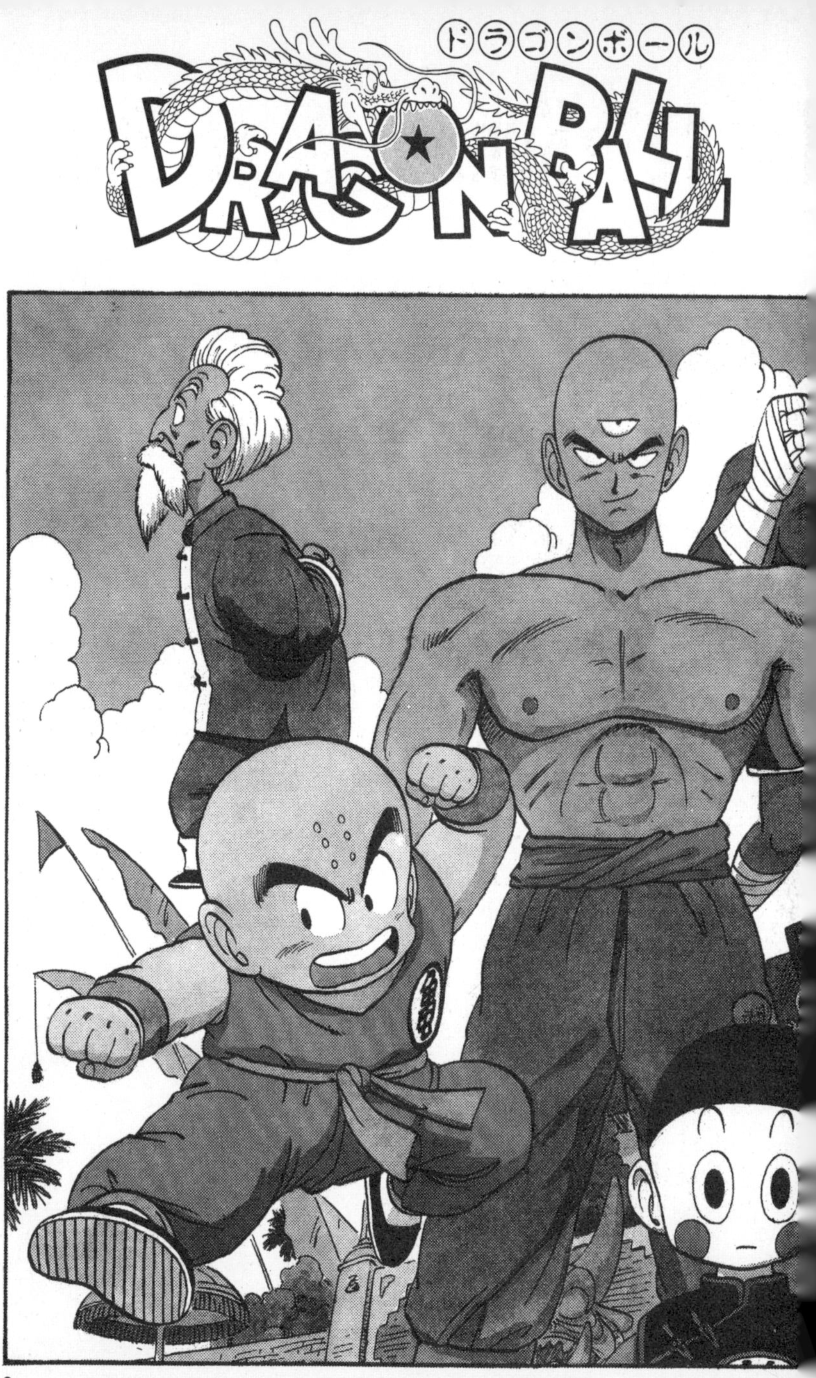

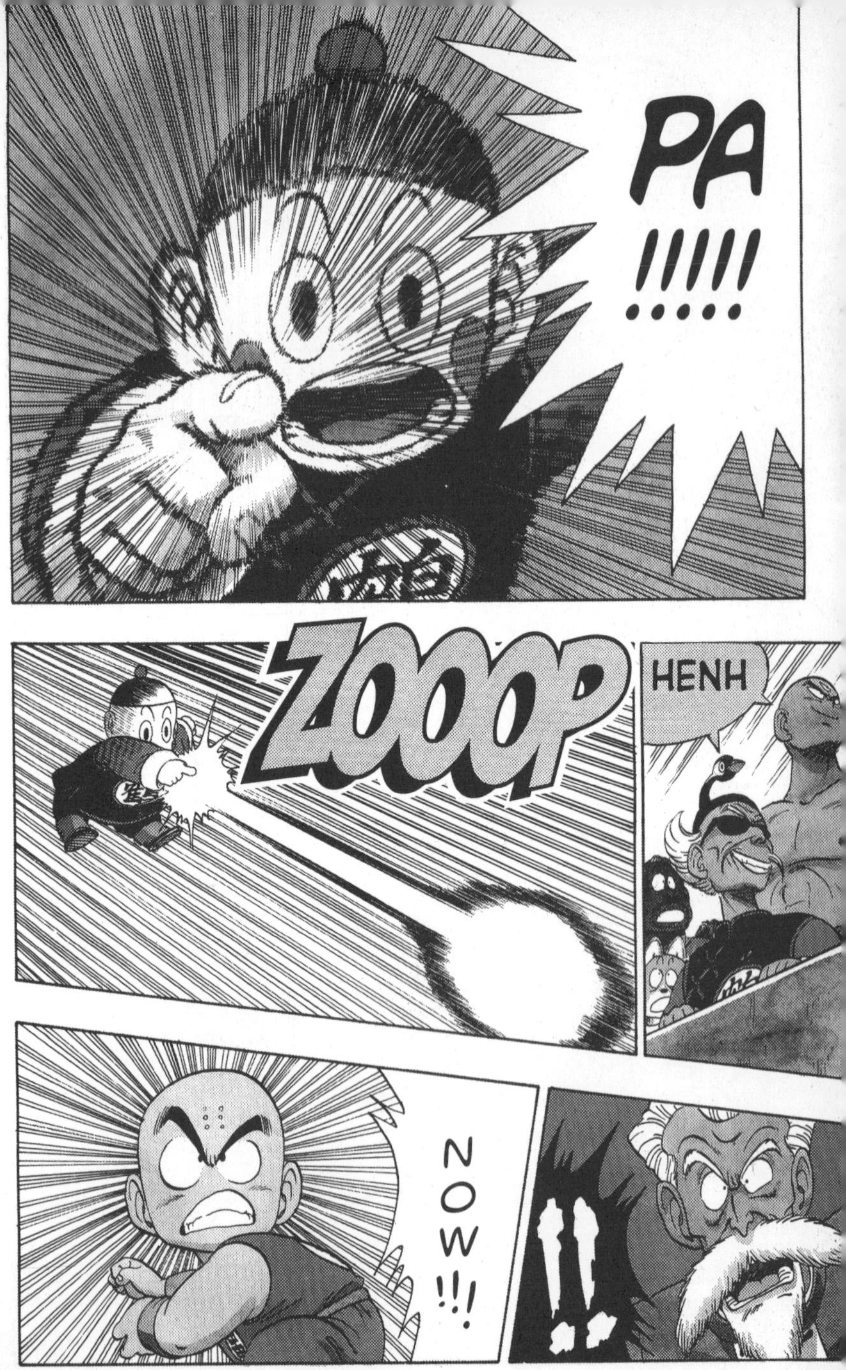
PA!!!!!
HENH
ZOOOP
!!
NOW!!!

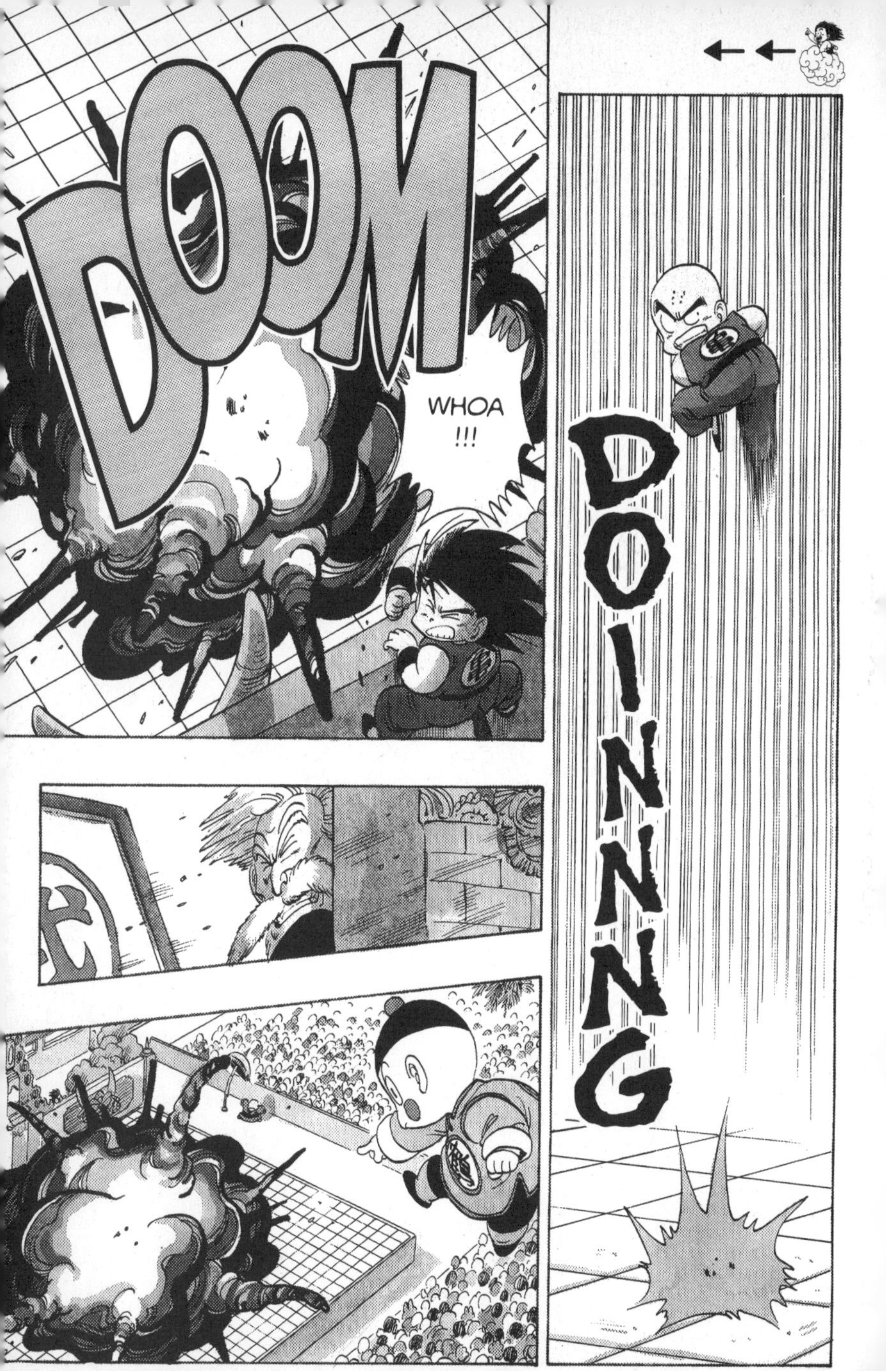
DOINNNG
DOOM
WHOA !!!

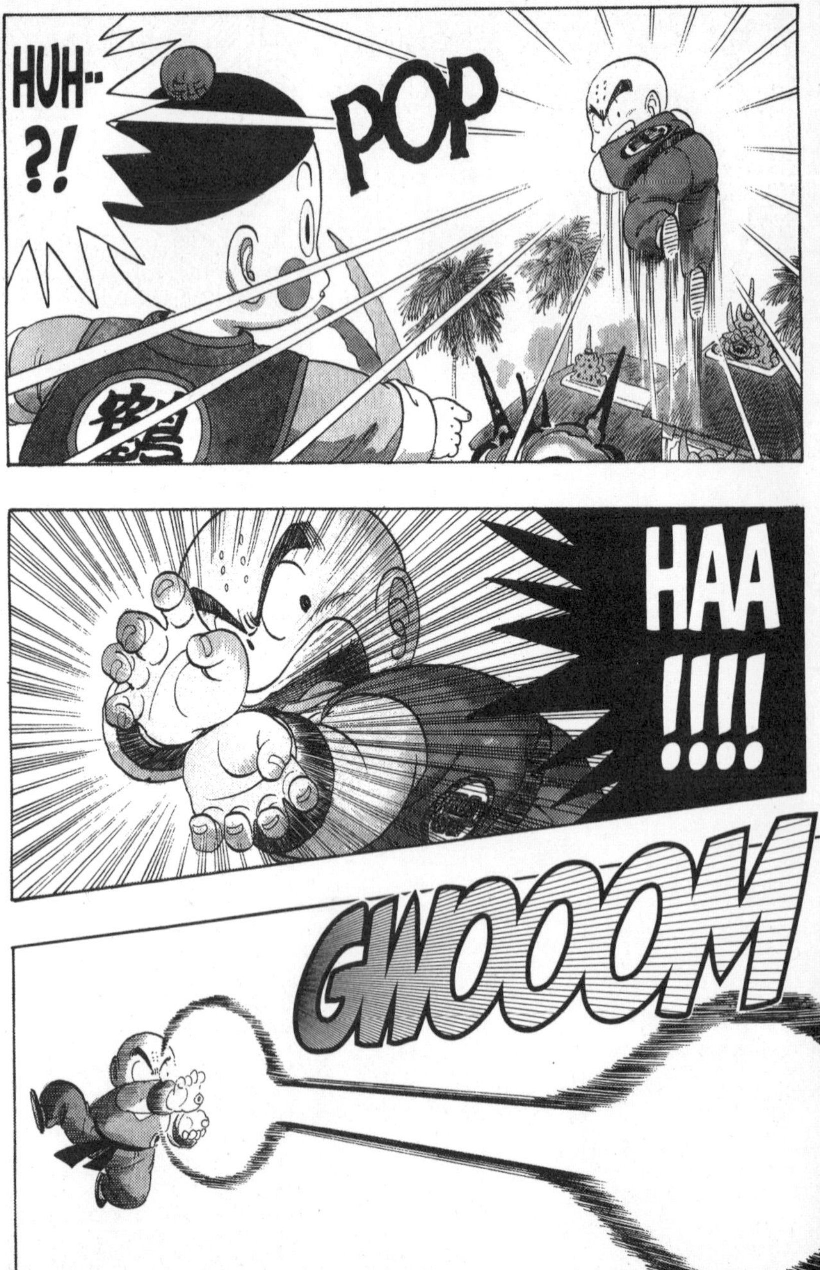
POP
HUH--?!
HAA!!!!
GWOOOM

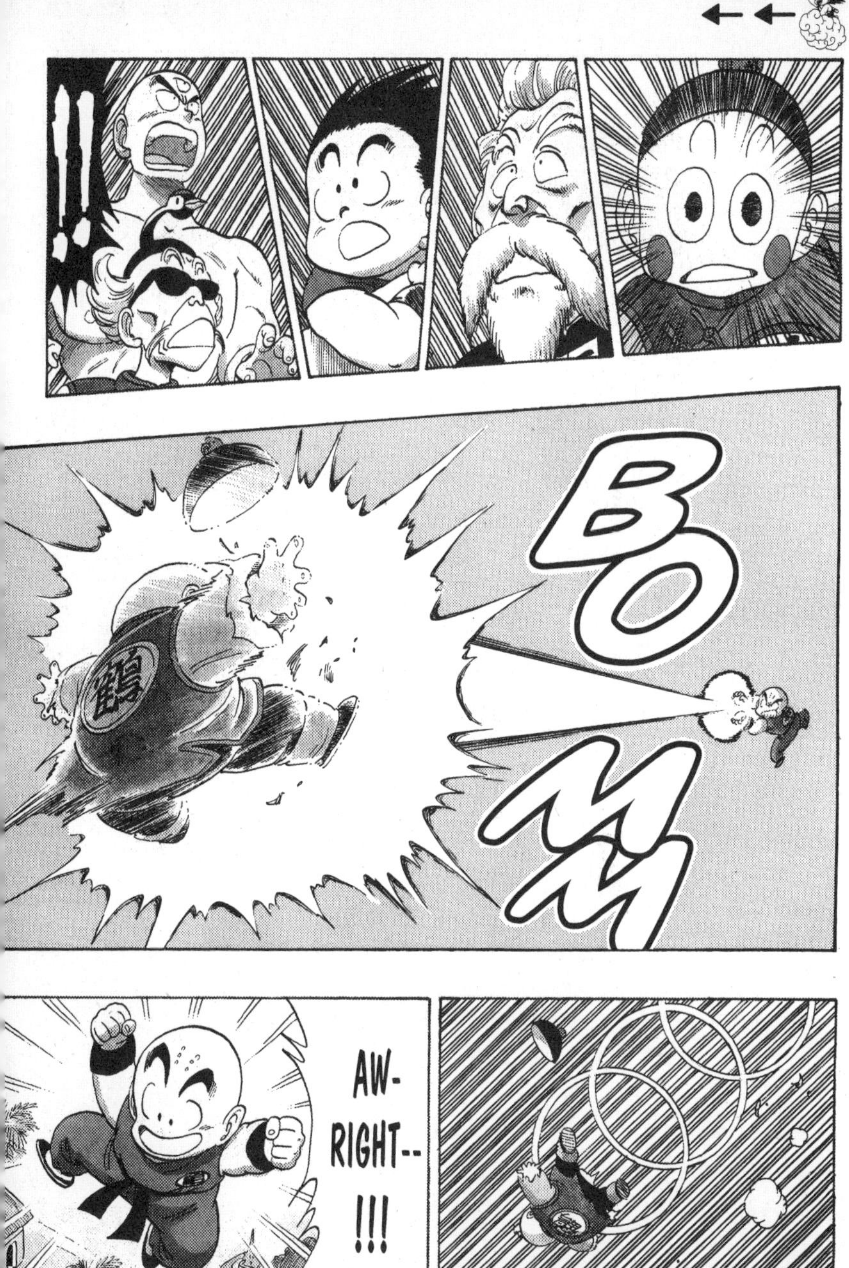
!!
BOMMM
AW- RIGHT-- !!!

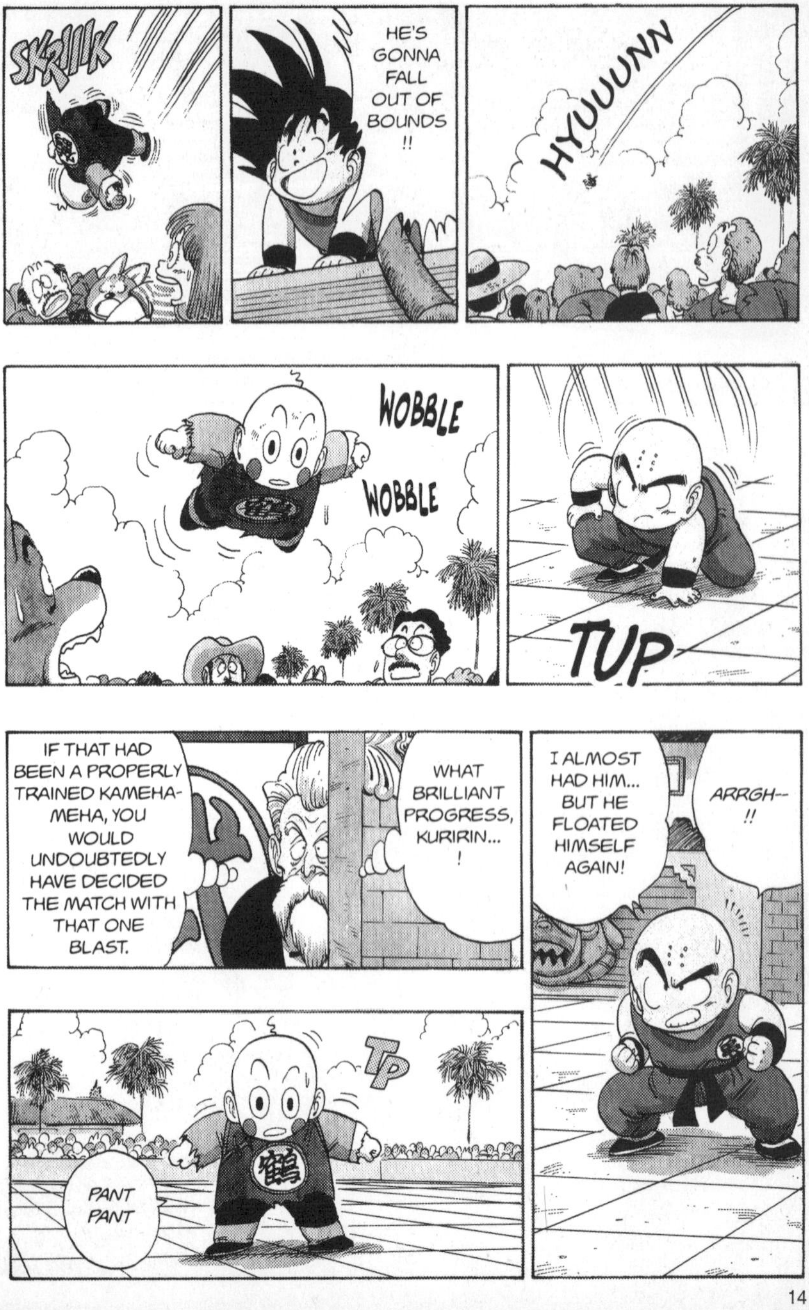
HYUUUNN
HE'S GONNA FALL OUT OF BOUNDS !!
SKRIIIK
TUP
WOBBLE
WOBBLE
ARRGH-- !!
I ALMOST HAD HIM... BUT HE FLOATED HIMSELF AGAIN!
WHAT BRILLIANT PROGRESS, KURIRIN... !
IF THAT HAD BEEN A PROPERLY TRAINED KAMEHA-MEHA, YOU WOULD UNDOUBTEDLY HAVE DECIDED THE MATCH WITH THAT ONE BLAST.
TP
PANT PANT

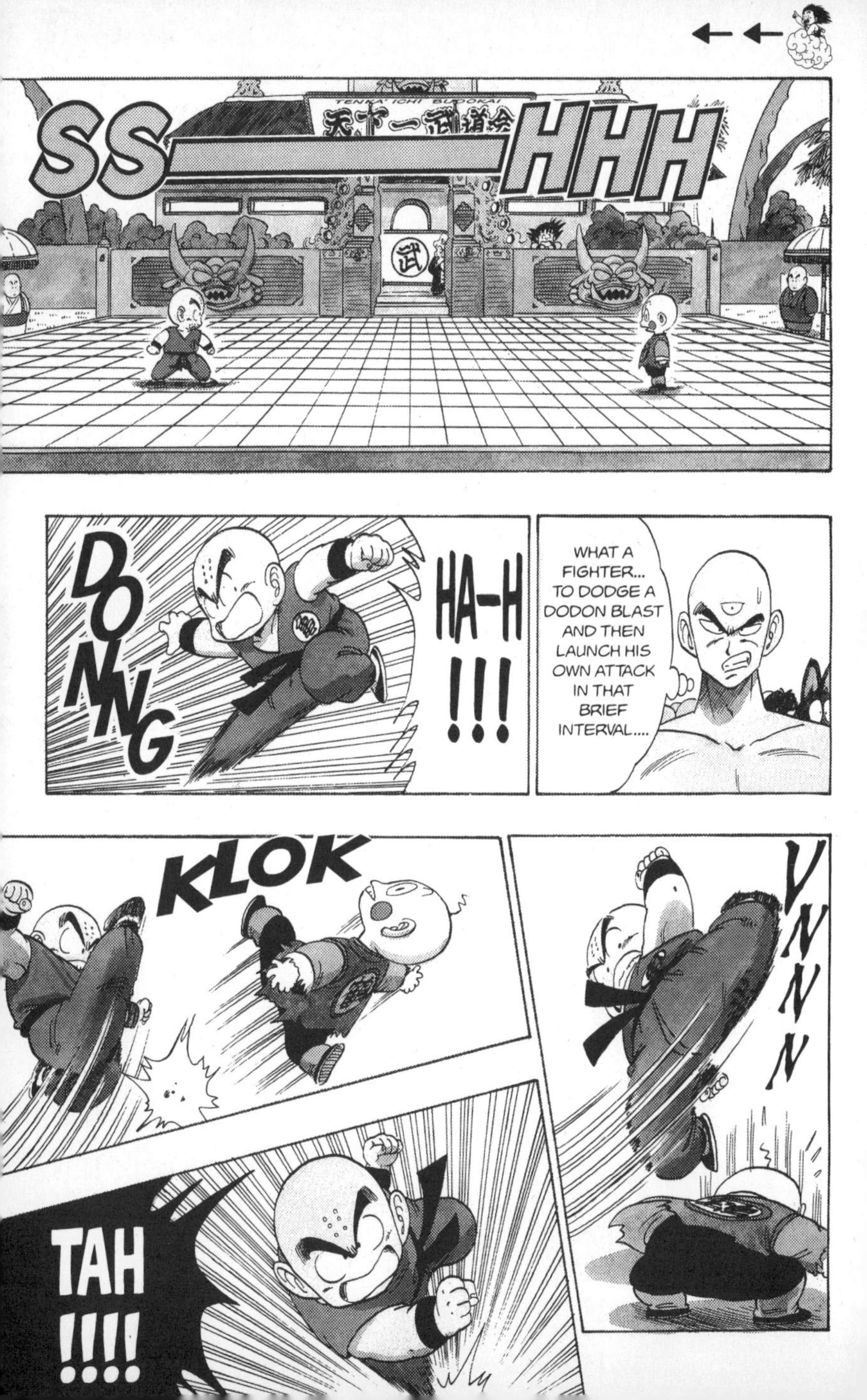
SS——HHH
天下一武道会
WHAT A FIGHTER... TO DODGE A DODON BLAST AND THEN LAUNCH HIS OWN ATTACK IN THAT BRIEF INTERVAL....
HA-H!!!
DONNG
VNNN
KLOK
TAH!!!!

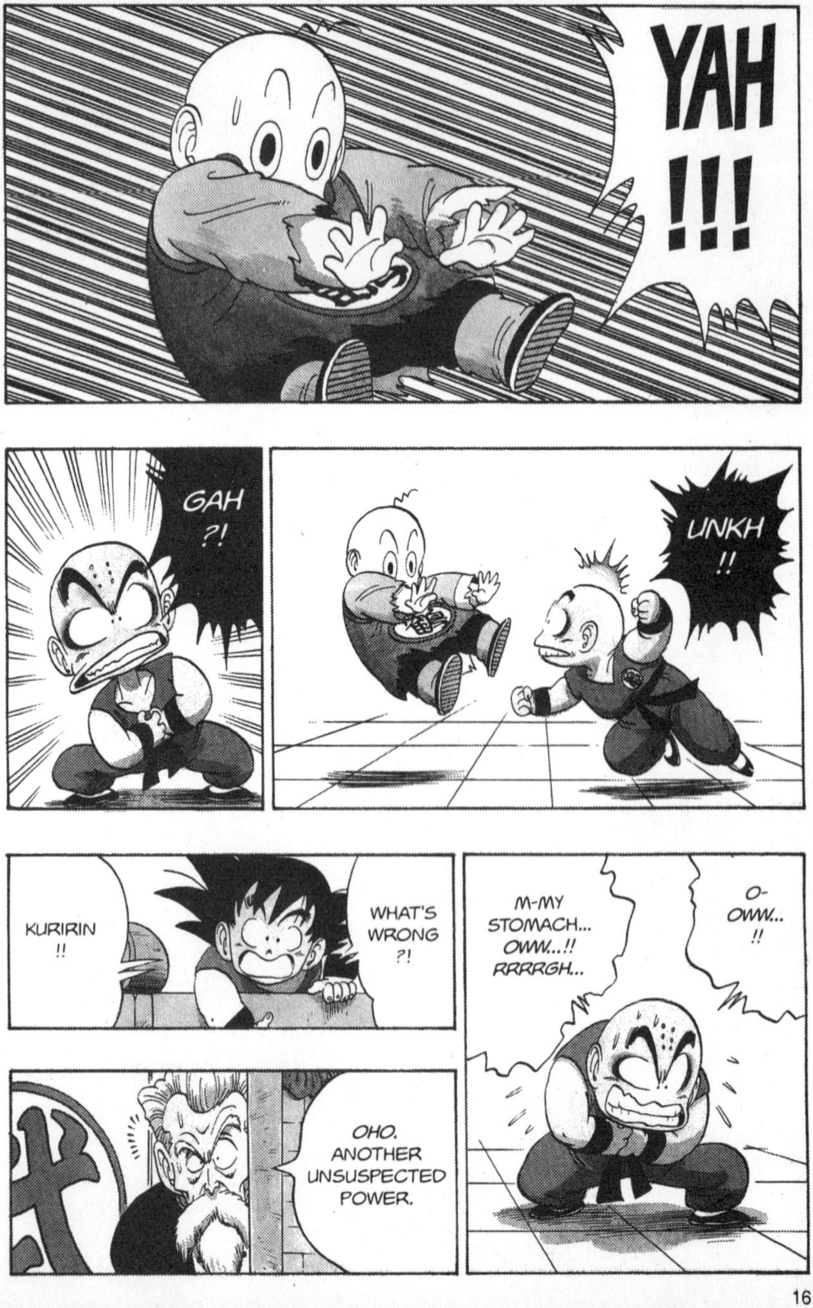
YAH !!!
UNKH !!
GAH ?!
O-OWW... !!
M-MY STOMACH... OWW...!! RRRRGH...
WHAT'S WRONG ?!
KURIRIN !!
OHO. ANOTHER UNSUSPECTED POWER.

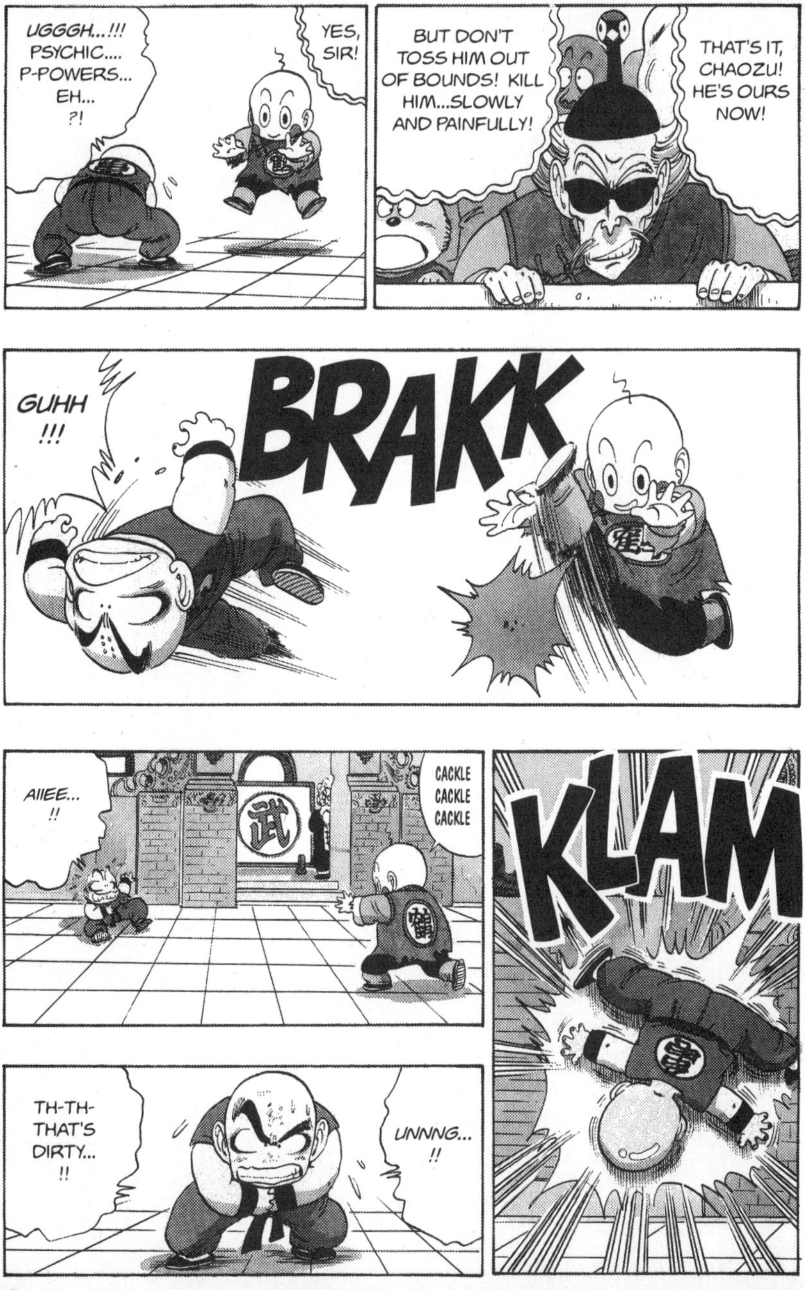
THAT'S IT, CHAOZU! HE'S OURS NOW!
BUT DON'T TOSS HIM OUT OF BOUNDS! KILL HIM...SLOWLY AND PAINFULLY!
YES, SIR!
UGGGH...!!! PSYCHIC.... P-POWERS... EH... ?!
BRAKK
GUHH !!!
KLAM
CACKLE CACKLE CACKLE
AIIEE... !!
UNNNG... !!
TH-TH-THAT'S DIRTY... !!

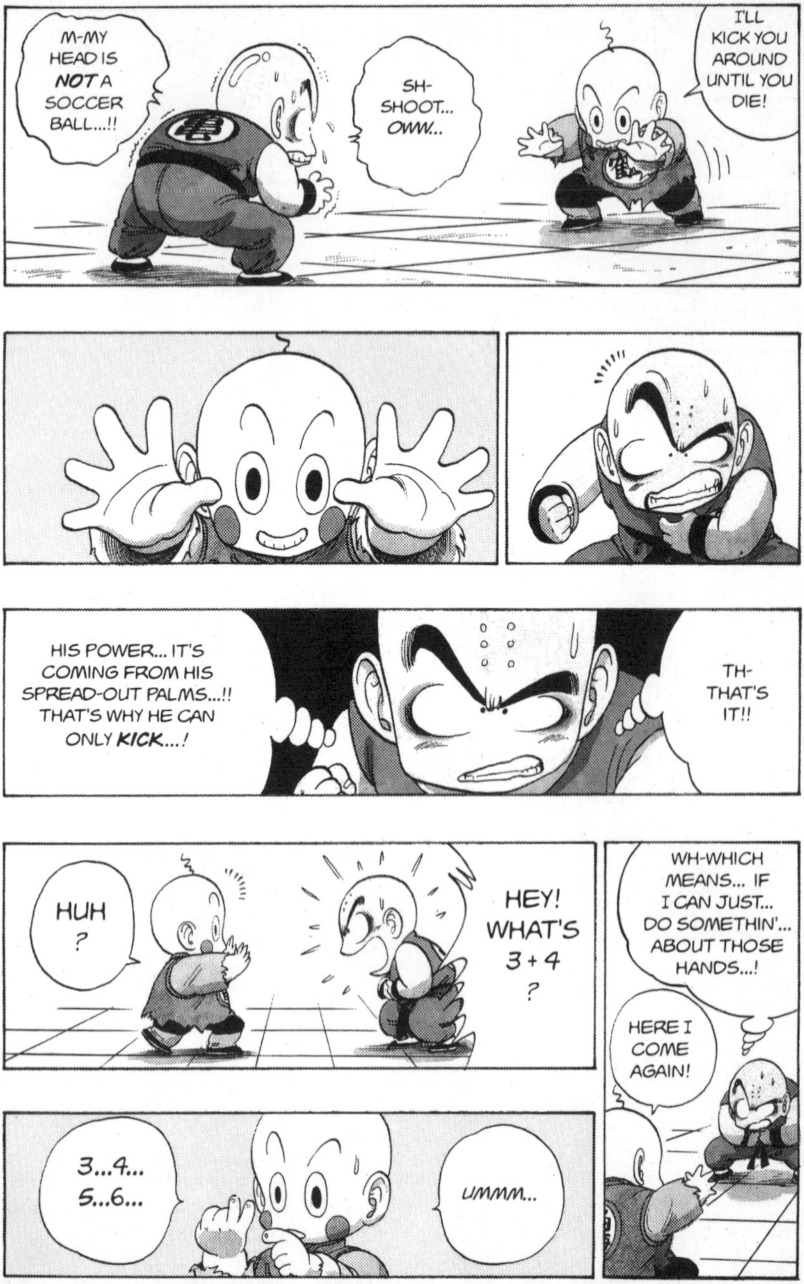

I'LL KICK YOU AROUND UNTIL YOU DIE!
SH-SHOOT... OWW...
M-MY HEAD IS NOT A SOCCER BALL...!!
TH-THAT'S IT!!
HIS POWER... IT'S COMING FROM HIS SPREAD-OUT PALMS...!! THAT'S WHY HE CAN ONLY KICK...!
WH-WHICH MEANS... IF I CAN JUST... DO SOMETHIN'... ABOUT THOSE HANDS...!
HERE I COME AGAIN!
HEY! WHAT'S 3 + 4 ?
HUH ?
UMMM...
3...4... 5...6...

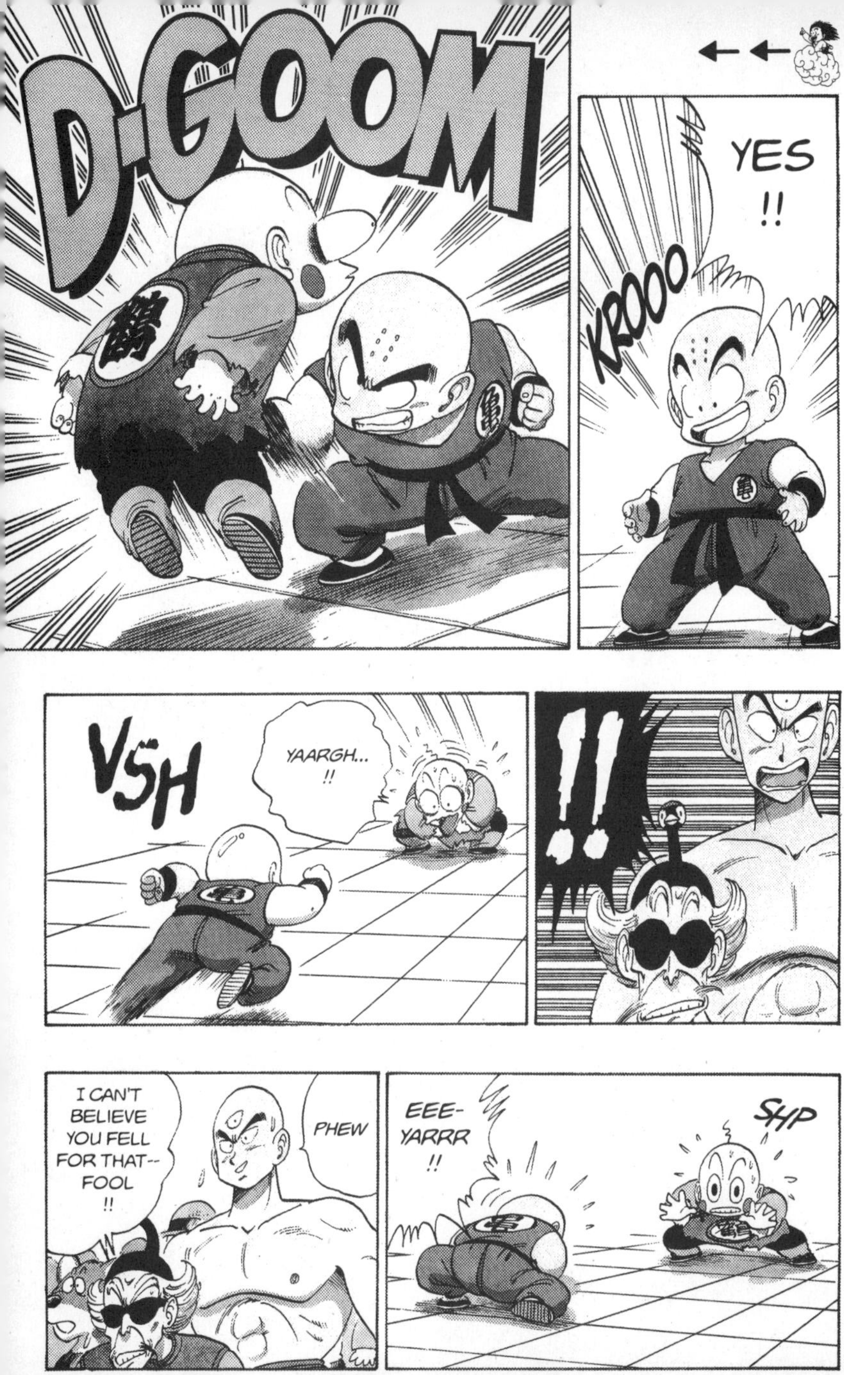

YES !!
KROOO
D-GOOM
!!
YAARGH... !!
VSH
SHP
EEE-YARRR !!
PHEW
I CAN'T BELIEVE YOU FELL FOR THAT-- FOOL !!

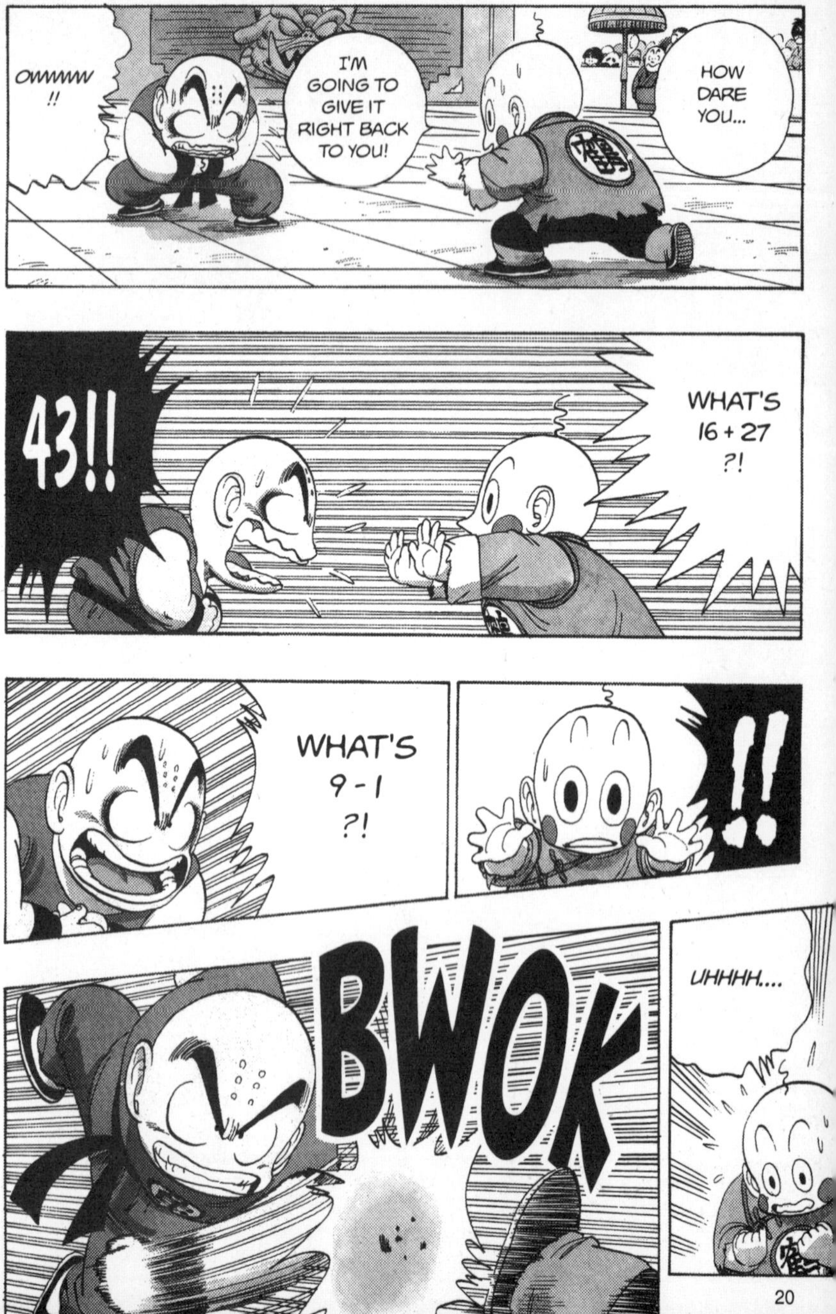
HOW DARE YOU...
I'M GOING TO GIVE IT RIGHT BACK TO YOU!
OWWWW !!
WHAT'S 16 + 27 ?!
43!!
!!
WHAT'S 9 - 1 ?!
UHHHH....
BWOK

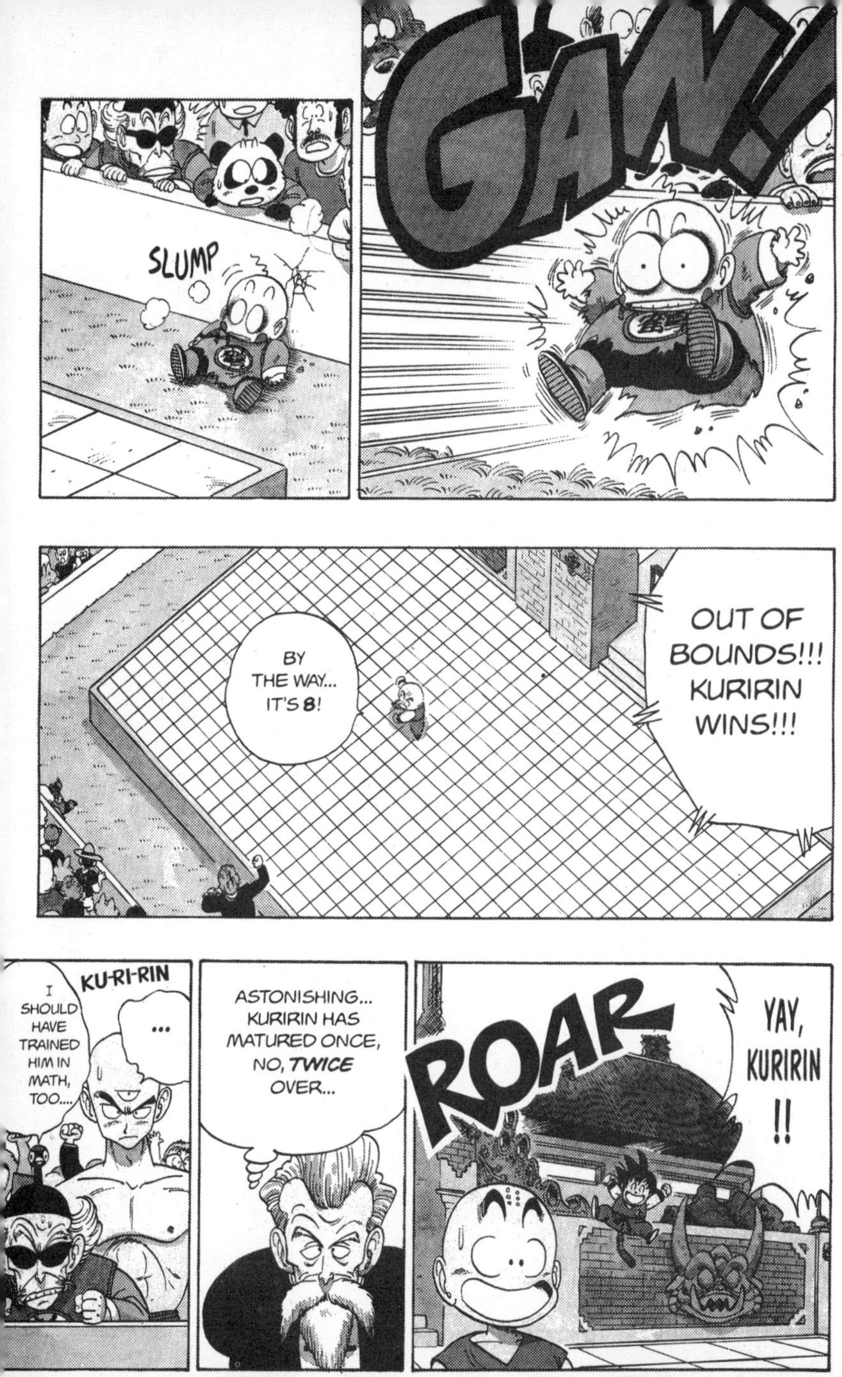
GAN!
SLUMP
OUT OF BOUNDS!!! KURIRIN WINS!!!
BY THE WAY... IT'S **8**!
YAY, KURIRIN !!
ROAR
ASTONISHING... KURIRIN HAS MATURED ONCE, NO, ***TWICE*** OVER...
KU-RI-RIN
...
I SHOULD HAVE TRAINED HIM IN MATH, TOO....

Tale 122 • Goku vs. Panpoot

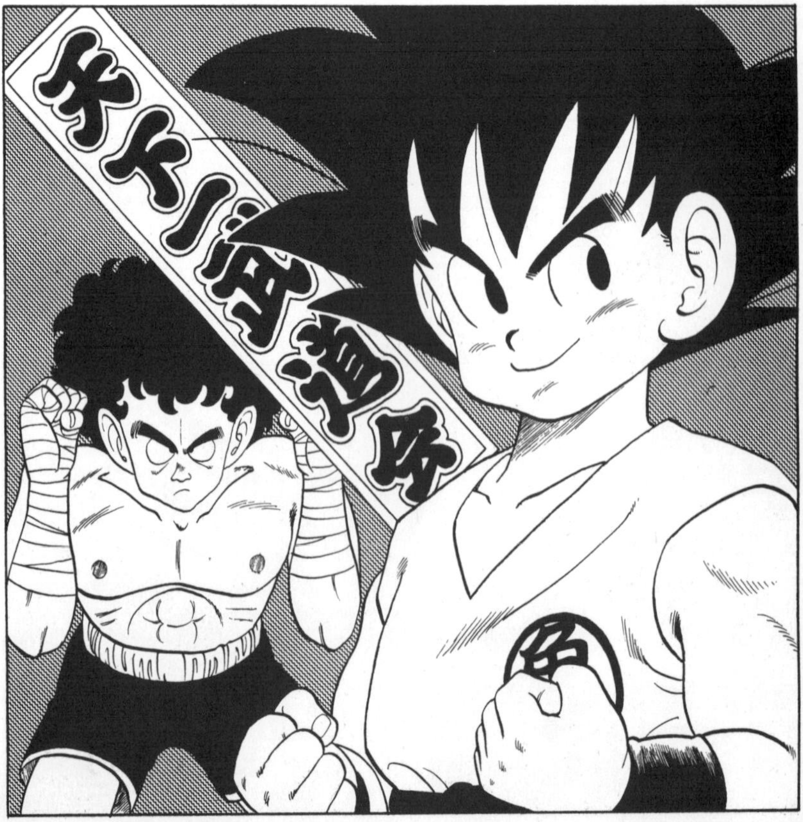

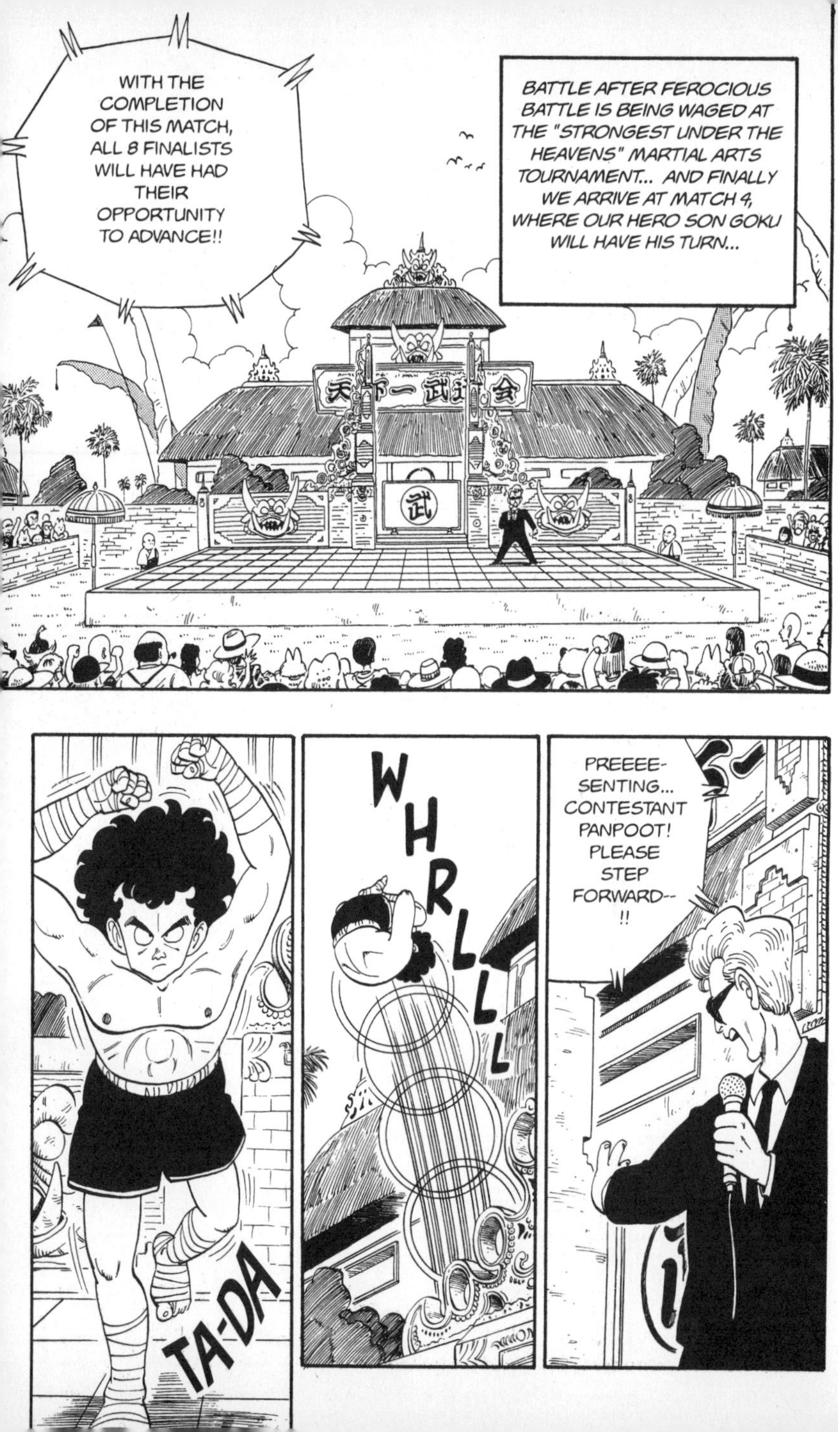
BATTLE AFTER FEROCIOUS BATTLE IS BEING WAGED AT THE "STRONGEST UNDER THE HEAVENS" MARTIAL ARTS TOURNAMENT... AND FINALLY WE ARRIVE AT MATCH 4, WHERE OUR HERO SON GOKU WILL HAVE HIS TURN...
WITH THE COMPLETION OF THIS MATCH, ALL 8 FINALISTS WILL HAVE HAD THEIR OPPORTUNITY TO ADVANCE!!
PREEEE-SENTING... CONTESTANT PANPOOT! PLEASE STEP FORWARD-- !!
WHRLLL
TA-DA

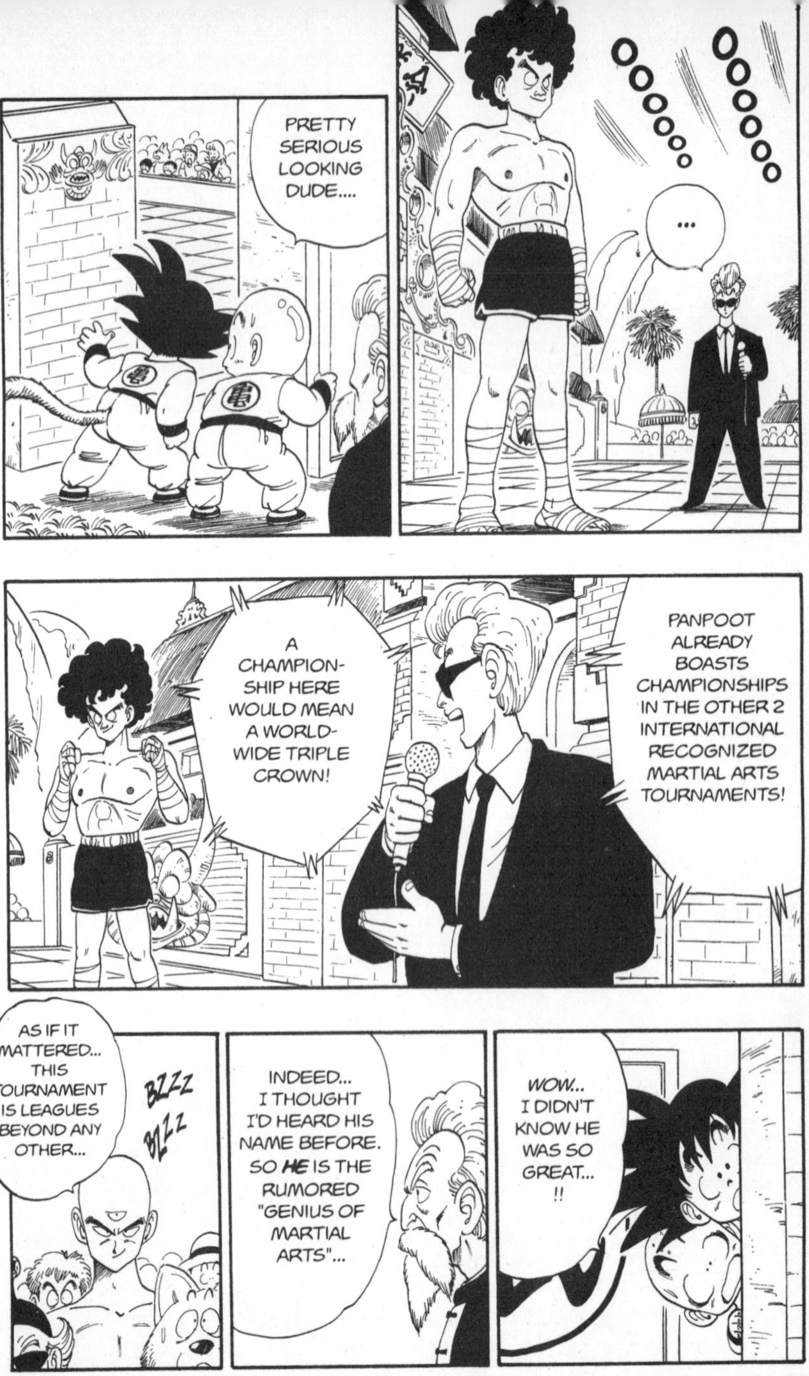
OOOOOOO
OOOOOOO
...
PRETTY SERIOUS LOOKING DUDE....
PANPOOT ALREADY BOASTS CHAMPIONSHIPS IN THE OTHER 2 INTERNATIONAL RECOGNIZED MARTIAL ARTS TOURNAMENTS!
A CHAMPIONSHIP HERE WOULD MEAN A WORLD-WIDE TRIPLE CROWN!
WOW... I DIDN'T KNOW HE WAS SO GREAT... !!
INDEED... I THOUGHT I'D HEARD HIS NAME BEFORE. SO HE IS THE RUMORED "GENIUS OF MARTIAL ARTS"...
AS IF IT MATTERED... THIS TOURNAMENT IS LEAGUES BEYOND ANY OTHER...
BZZZ
BZZZ

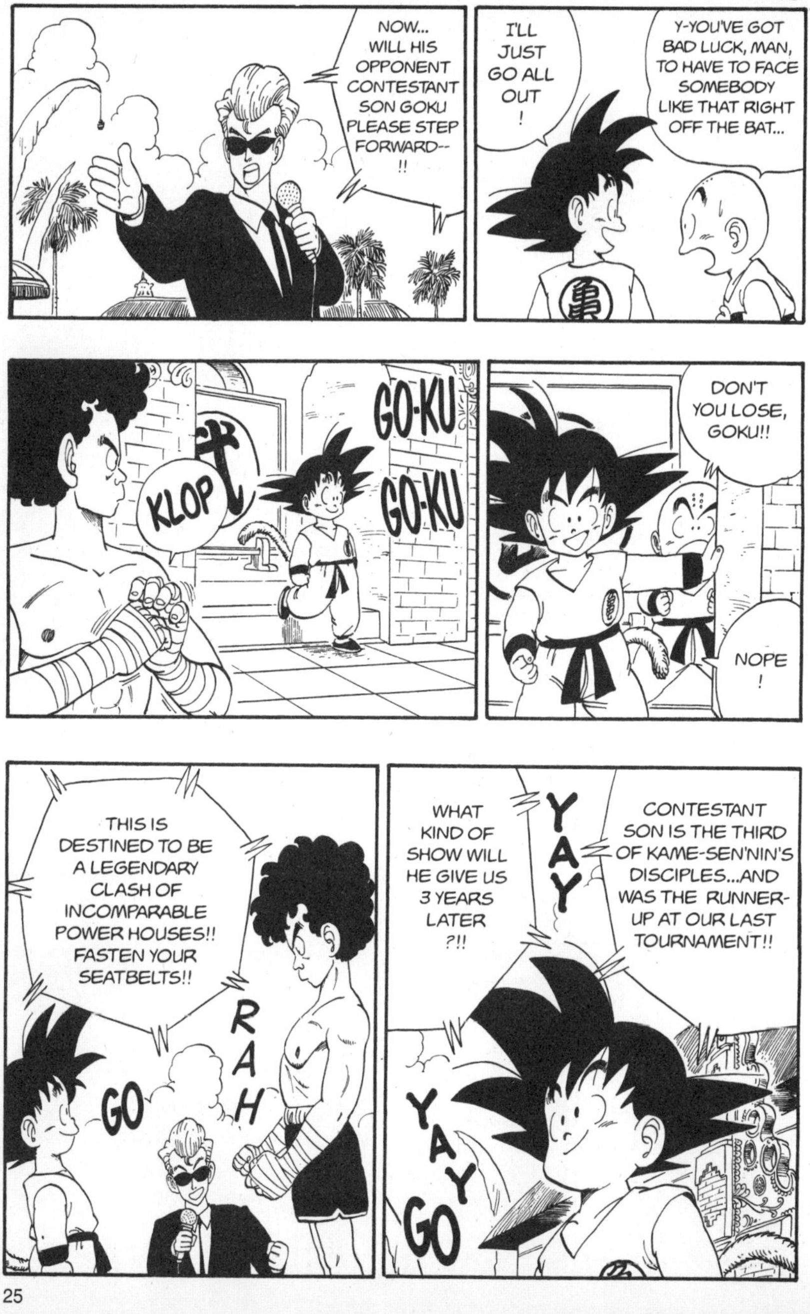
Y-YOU'VE GOT BAD LUCK, MAN, TO HAVE TO FACE SOMEBODY LIKE THAT RIGHT OFF THE BAT...
I'LL JUST GO ALL OUT !
NOW... WILL HIS OPPONENT CONTESTANT SON GOKU PLEASE STEP FORWARD-- !!
DON'T YOU LOSE, GOKU!!
NOPE !
GO-KU
GO-KU
KLOP
CONTESTANT SON IS THE THIRD OF KAME-SEN'NIN'S DISCIPLES...AND WAS THE RUNNER-UP AT OUR LAST TOURNAMENT!!
YAY
WHAT KIND OF SHOW WILL HE GIVE US 3 YEARS LATER ?!!
YAY YAY
GO
THIS IS DESTINED TO BE A LEGENDARY CLASH OF INCOMPARABLE POWER HOUSES!! FASTEN YOUR SEATBELTS!!
RAH
GO

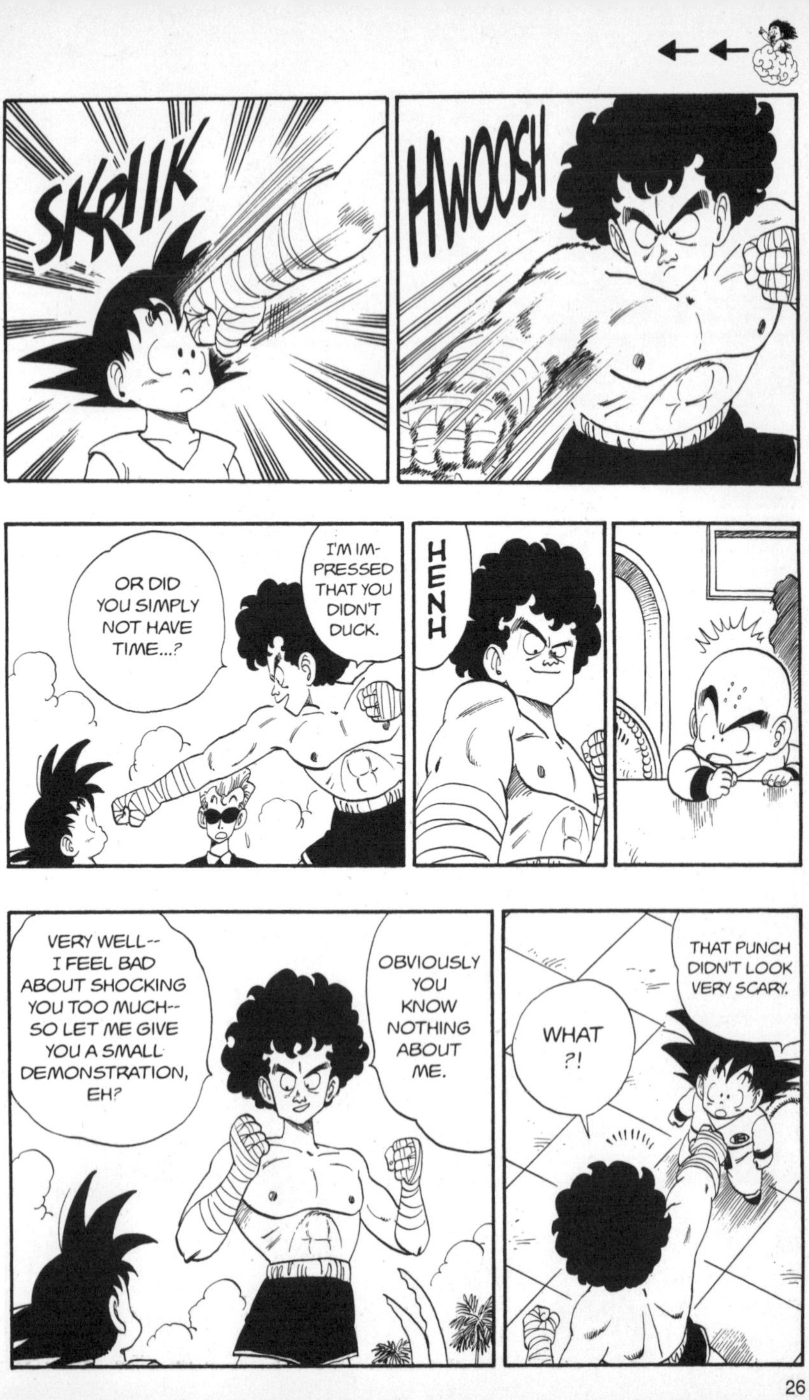
HWOOSH
SKRIIK
HENH
I'M IM-PRESSED THAT YOU DIDN'T DUCK.
OR DID YOU SIMPLY NOT HAVE TIME...?
THAT PUNCH DIDN'T LOOK VERY SCARY.
WHAT ?!
OBVIOUSLY YOU KNOW NOTHING ABOUT ME.
VERY WELL-- I FEEL BAD ABOUT SHOCKING YOU TOO MUCH-- SO LET ME GIVE YOU A SMALL DEMONSTRATION, EH?

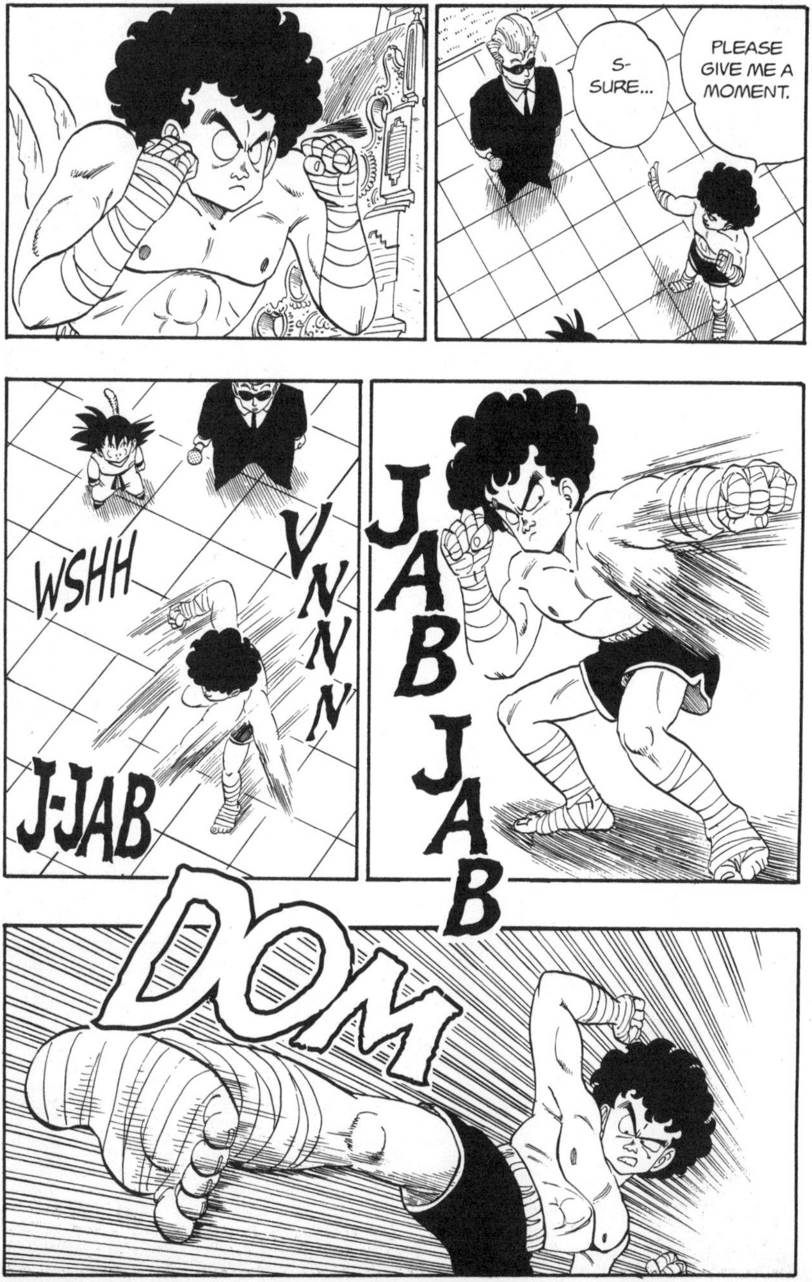
PLEASE GIVE ME A MOMENT.
S- SURE...
JAB JAB
VNNN
WSHH
J-JAB
DOM

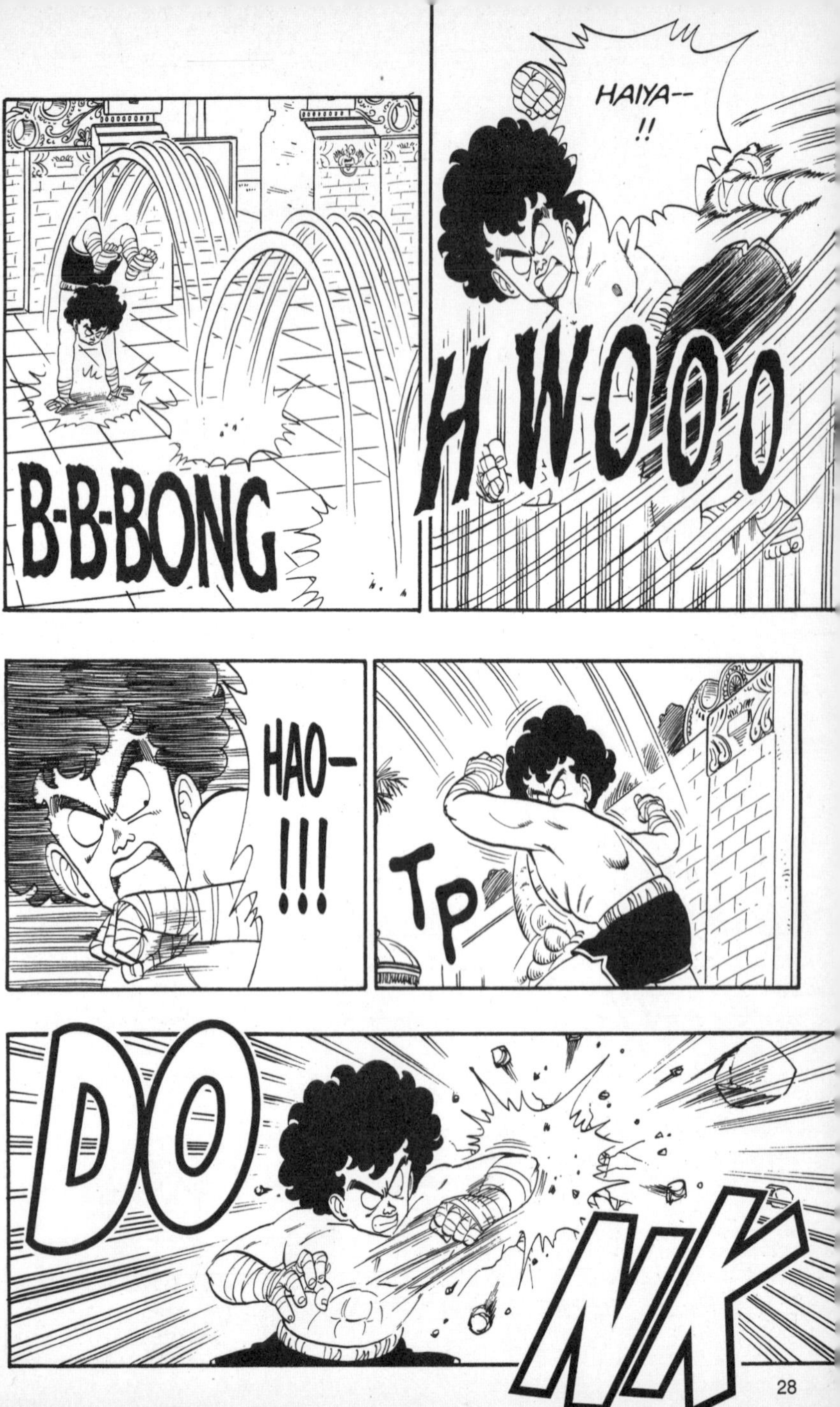
HAIYA-- !!
HWOOO
B-B-BONG
TP
HAO-!!!
DONK

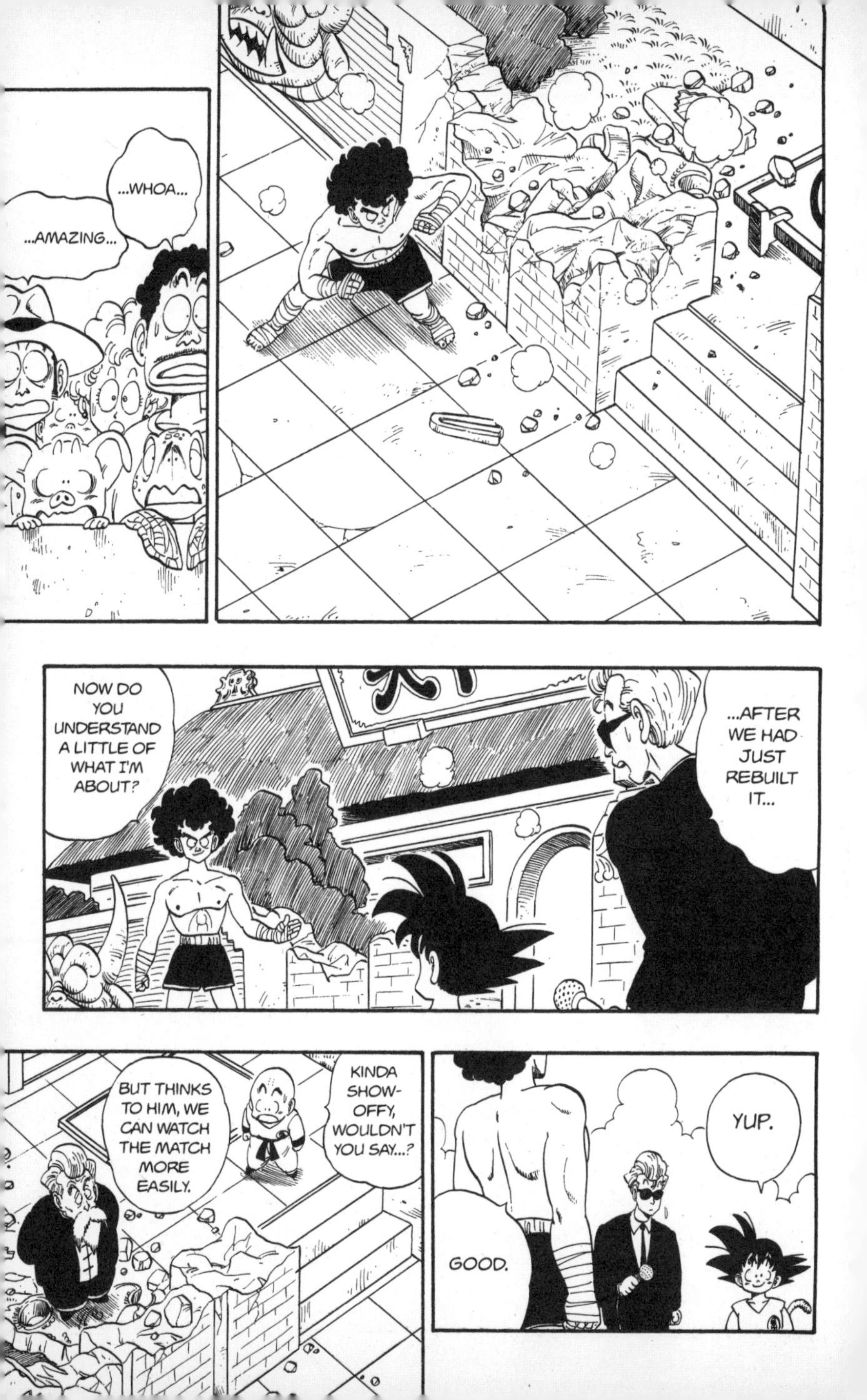
...WHOA...
...AMAZING...
...AFTER WE HAD JUST REBUILT IT...
NOW DO YOU UNDERSTAND A LITTLE OF WHAT I'M ABOUT?
YUP.
GOOD.
KINDA SHOW-OFFY, WOULDN'T YOU SAY...?
BUT THINKS TO HIM, WE CAN WATCH THE MATCH MORE EASILY.

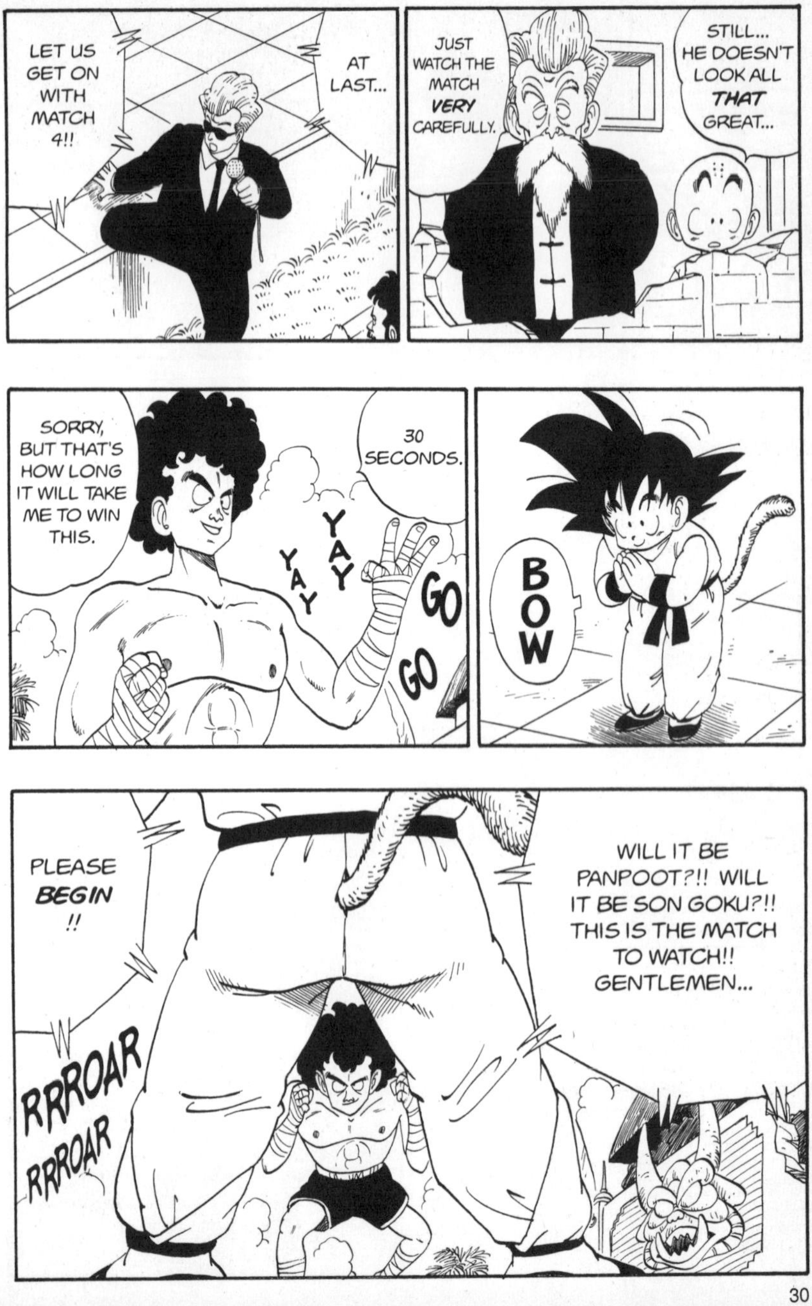
STILL... HE DOESN'T LOOK ALL **THAT** GREAT...
JUST WATCH THE MATCH **VERY** CAREFULLY.
AT LAST...
LET US GET ON WITH MATCH 4!!
BOW
30 SECONDS.
SORRY, BUT THAT'S HOW LONG IT WILL TAKE ME TO WIN THIS.
YAY
YAY
GO
GO
WILL IT BE PANPOOT?!! WILL IT BE SON GOKU?!! THIS IS THE MATCH TO WATCH!! GENTLEMEN...
PLEASE **BEGIN** !!
RRROAR
RRROAR

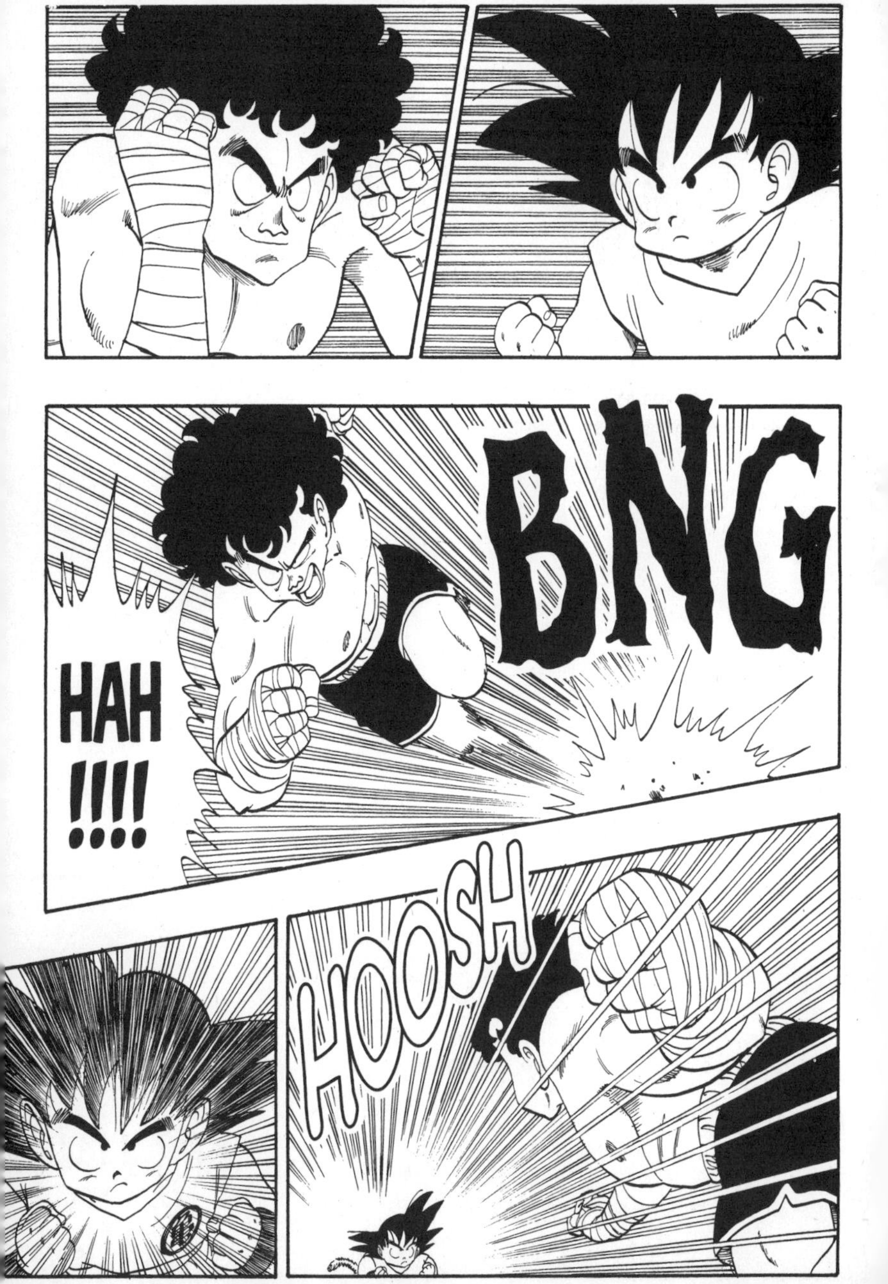
BNG
HAH!!!!
HOOSH

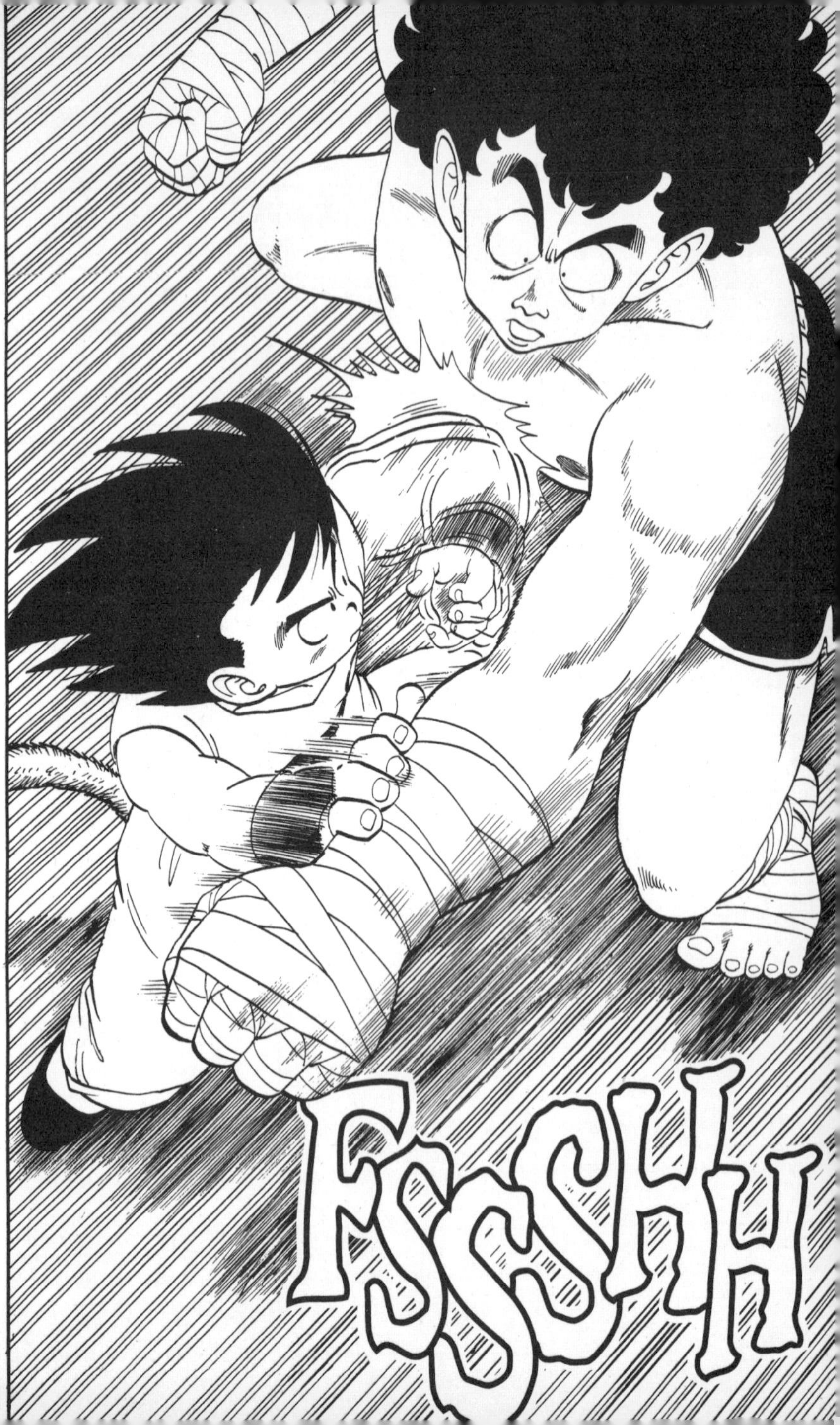
FSSSH

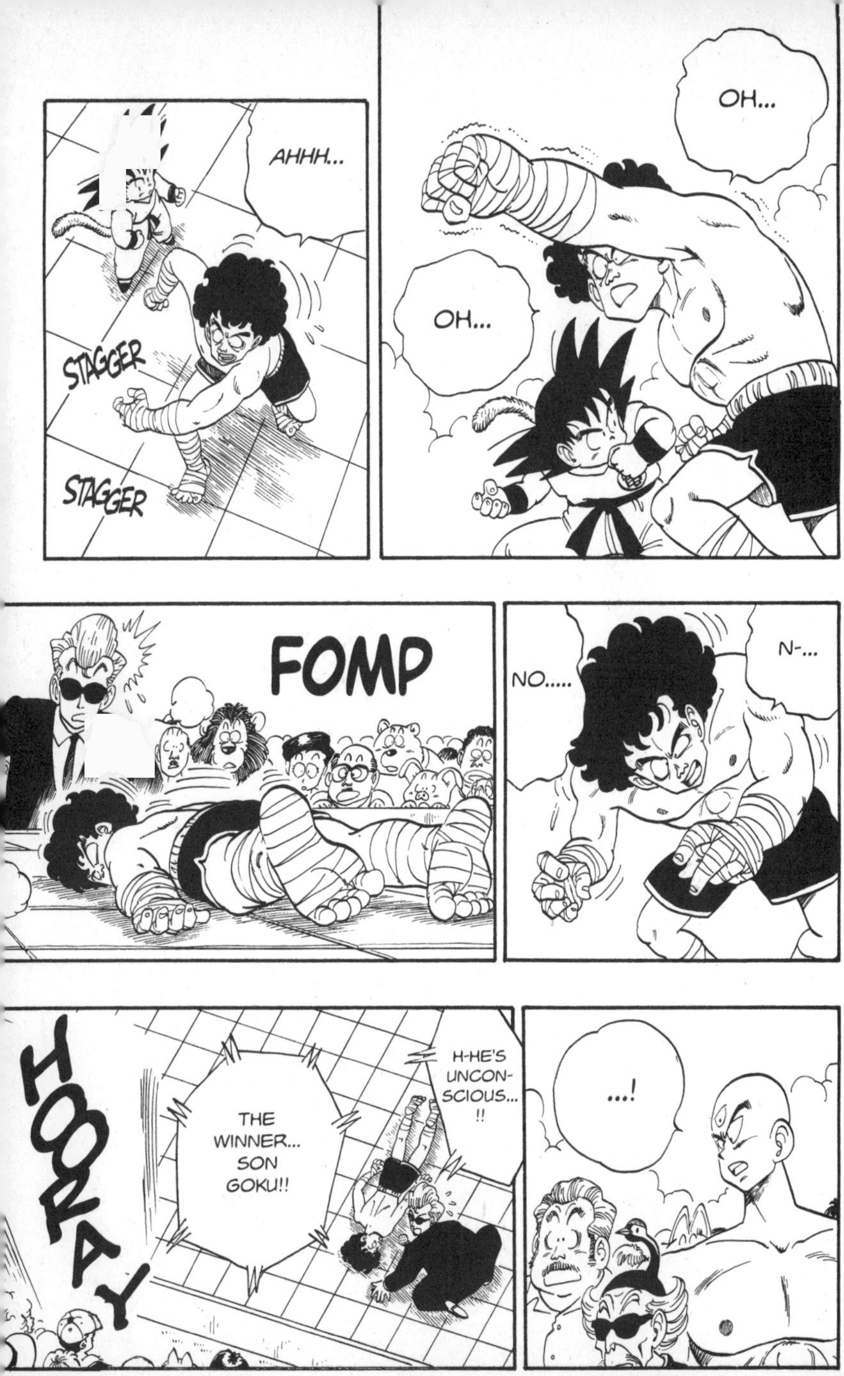

OH...
OH...
AHHH...
STAGGER
STAGGER
N-...
NO.....
FOMP
...!
H-HE'S UNCON-SCIOUS... !!
THE WINNER... SON GOKU!!
HOORAY

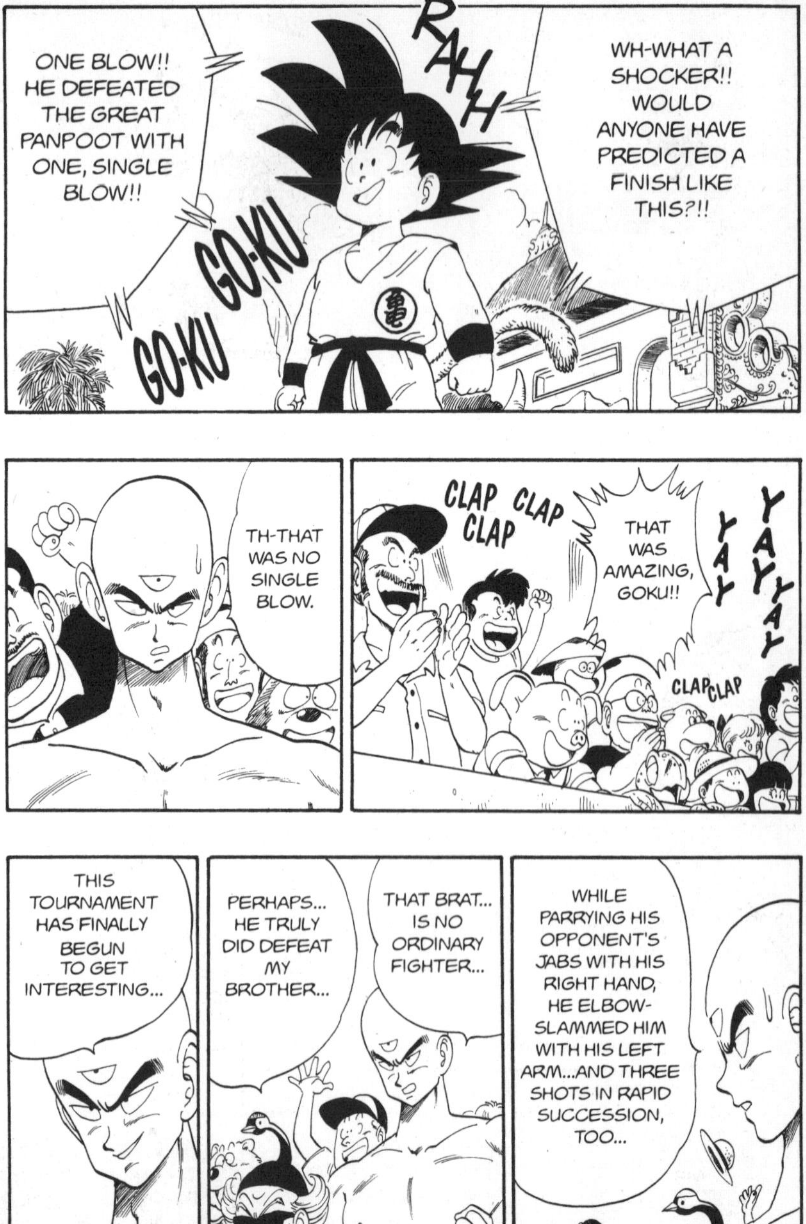

WH-WHAT A SHOCKER!! WOULD ANYONE HAVE PREDICTED A FINISH LIKE THIS?!!
RAHHH
ONE BLOW!! HE DEFEATED THE GREAT PANPOOT WITH ONE, SINGLE BLOW!!
GO-KU
GO-KU
YAY YAY YAY
THAT WAS AMAZING, GOKU!!
CLAP CLAP CLAP
CLAP CLAP
TH-THAT WAS NO SINGLE BLOW.
WHILE PARRYING HIS OPPONENT'S JABS WITH HIS RIGHT HAND, HE ELBOW-SLAMMED HIM WITH HIS LEFT ARM...AND THREE SHOTS IN RAPID SUCCESSION, TOO...
THAT BRAT... IS NO ORDINARY FIGHTER...
PERHAPS... HE TRULY DID DEFEAT MY BROTHER...
THIS TOURNAMENT HAS FINALLY BEGUN TO GET INTERESTING...

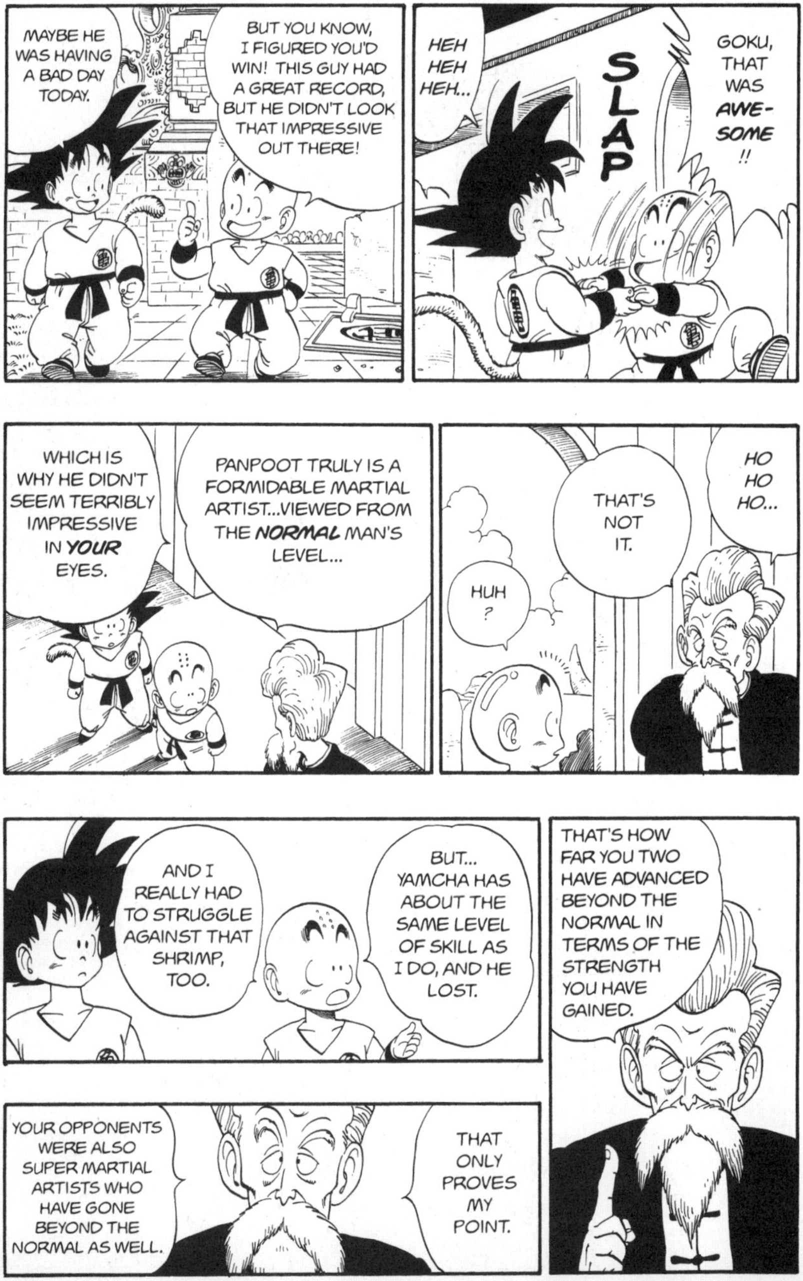
GOKU, THAT WAS AWESOME!!
SLAP
HEH HEH HEH...
BUT YOU KNOW, I FIGURED YOU'D WIN! THIS GUY HAD A GREAT RECORD, BUT HE DIDN'T LOOK THAT IMPRESSIVE OUT THERE!
MAYBE HE WAS HAVING A BAD DAY TODAY.
HO HO HO...
THAT'S NOT IT.
HUH?
PANPOOT TRULY IS A FORMIDABLE MARTIAL ARTIST...VIEWED FROM THE NORMAL MAN'S LEVEL...
WHICH IS WHY HE DIDN'T SEEM TERRIBLY IMPRESSIVE IN YOUR EYES.
THAT'S HOW FAR YOU TWO HAVE ADVANCED BEYOND THE NORMAL IN TERMS OF THE STRENGTH YOU HAVE GAINED.
BUT... YAMCHA HAS ABOUT THE SAME LEVEL OF SKILL AS I DO, AND HE LOST.
AND I REALLY HAD TO STRUGGLE AGAINST THAT SHRIMP, TOO.
THAT ONLY PROVES MY POINT.
YOUR OPPONENTS WERE ALSO SUPER MARTIAL ARTISTS WHO HAVE GONE BEYOND THE NORMAL AS WELL.

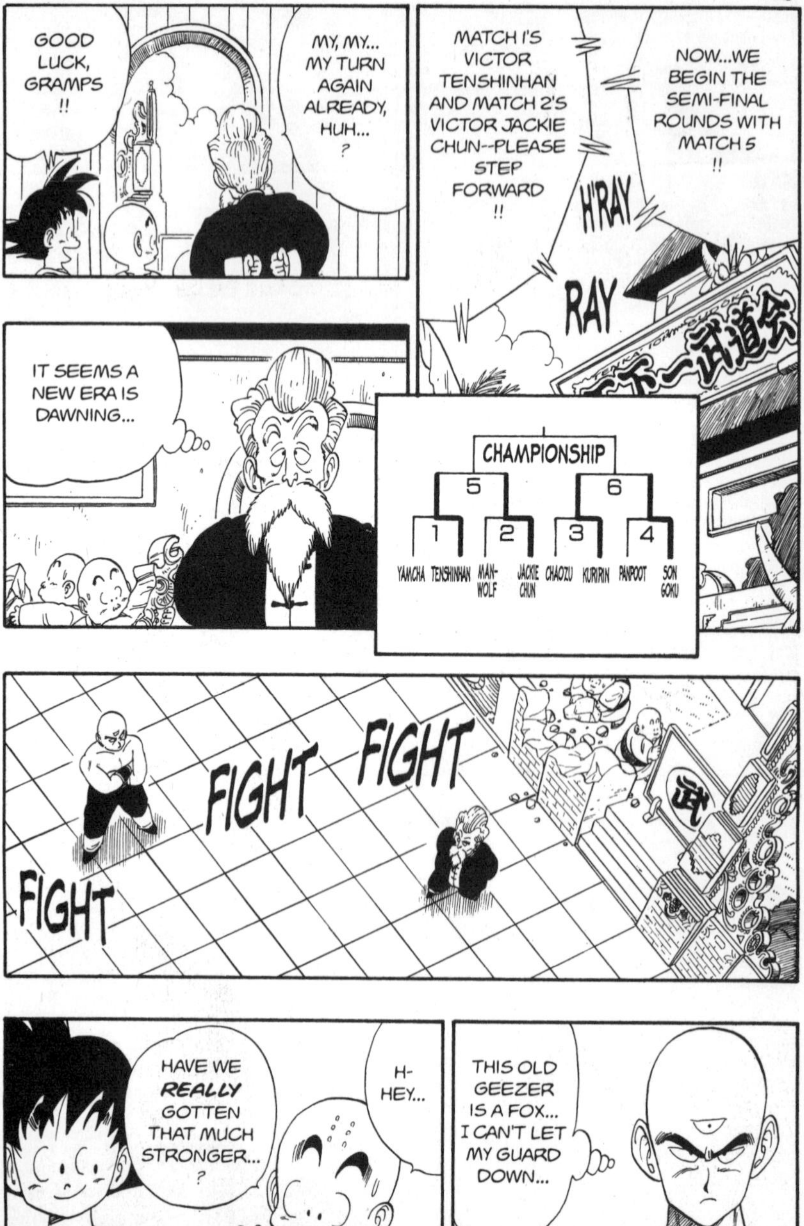
NOW...WE BEGIN THE SEMI-FINAL ROUNDS WITH MATCH 5 !!
MATCH 1'S VICTOR TENSHINHAN AND MATCH 2'S VICTOR JACKIE CHUN--PLEASE STEP FORWARD !!
H'RAY
RAY
CHAMPIONSHIP
5
6
1
2
3
4
YAMCHA
TENSHINHAN
MAN-WOLF
JACKIE CHUN
CHAOZU
KURIRIN
PANPOOT
SON GOKU
MY, MY... MY TURN AGAIN ALREADY, HUH... ?
GOOD LUCK, GRAMPS !!
IT SEEMS A NEW ERA IS DAWNING...
FIGHT
FIGHT
FIGHT
THIS OLD GEEZER IS A FOX... I CAN'T LET MY GUARD DOWN...
H- HEY...
HAVE WE *REALLY* GOTTEN THAT MUCH STRONGER... ?

***NEXT:* The Next Generation of Fighters**

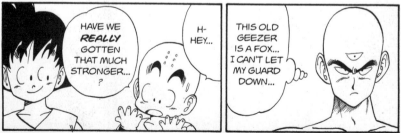

Tale 123

Tenshinhan vs. Jackie Chun

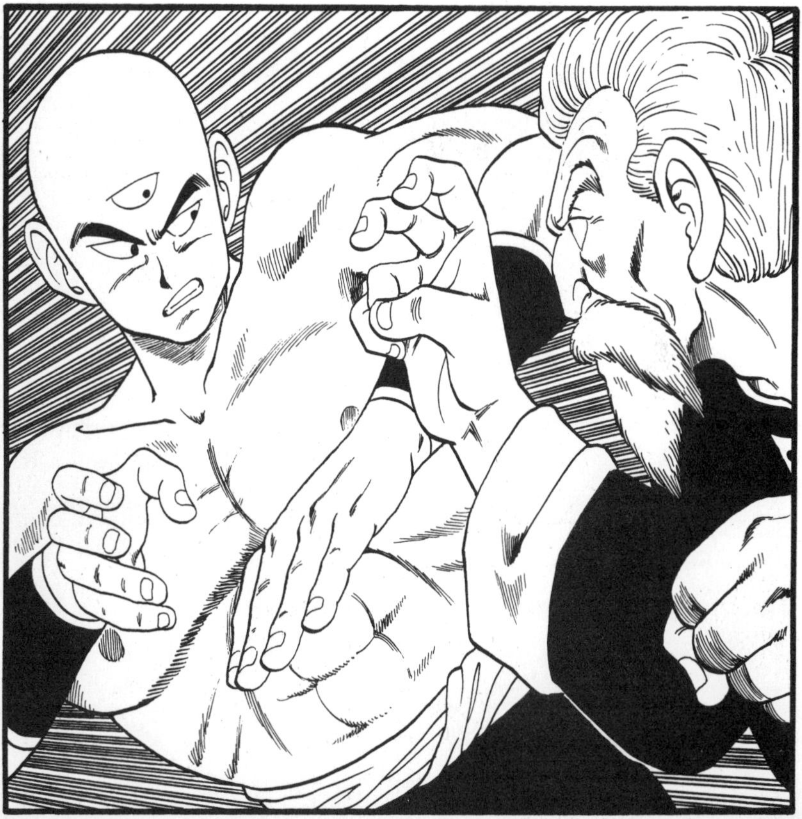

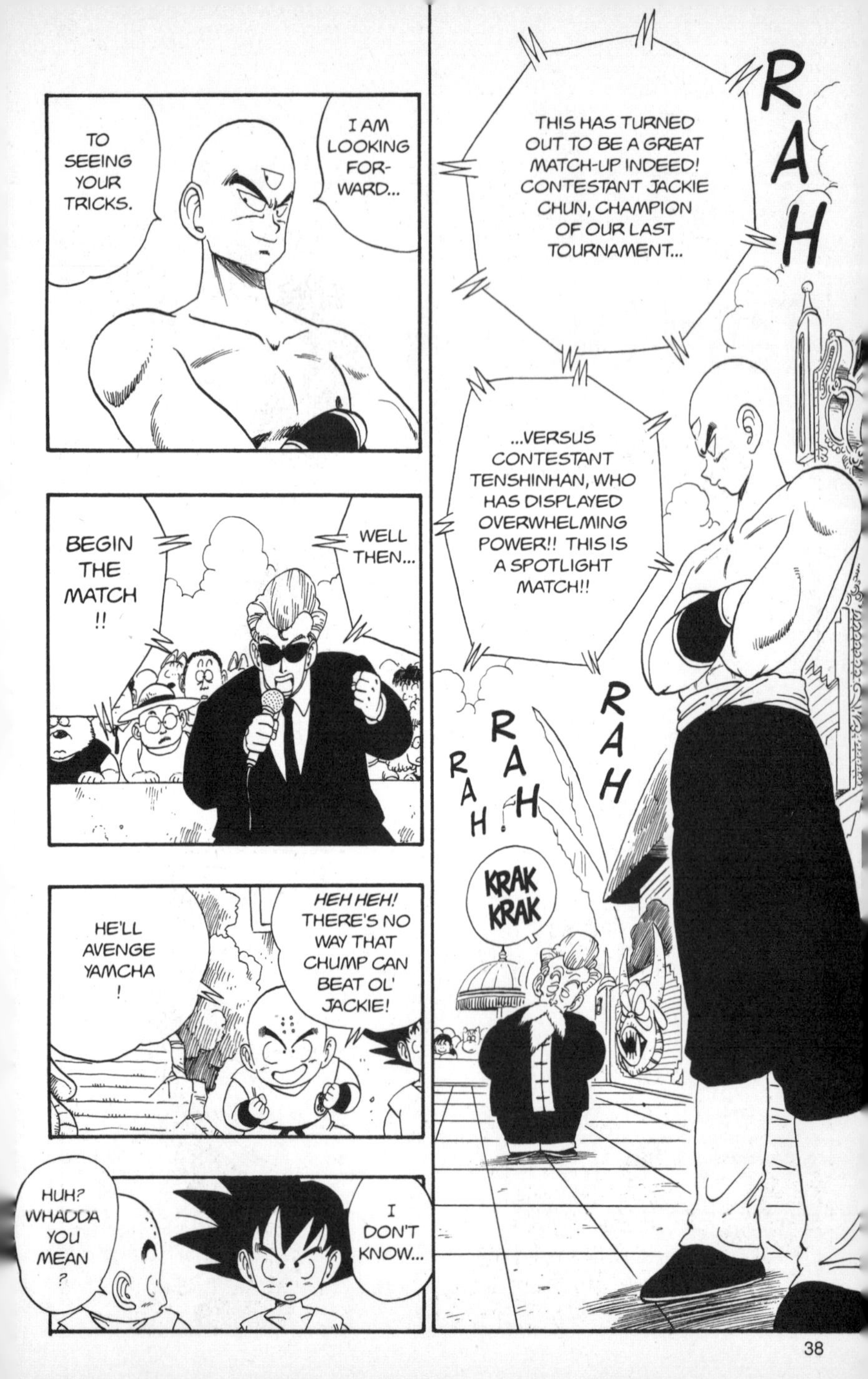
RAH
THIS HAS TURNED OUT TO BE A GREAT MATCH-UP INDEED! CONTESTANT JACKIE CHUN, CHAMPION OF OUR LAST TOURNAMENT...
...VERSUS CONTESTANT TENSHINHAN, WHO HAS DISPLAYED OVERWHELMING POWER!! THIS IS A SPOTLIGHT MATCH!!
RAH
RAH
RAH
KRAK KRAK
I AM LOOKING FOR-WARD...
TO SEEING YOUR TRICKS.
WELL THEN...
BEGIN THE MATCH !!
HEH HEH! THERE'S NO WAY THAT CHUMP CAN BEAT OL' JACKIE!
HE'LL AVENGE YAMCHA !
I DON'T KNOW...
HUH? WHADDA YOU MEAN ?

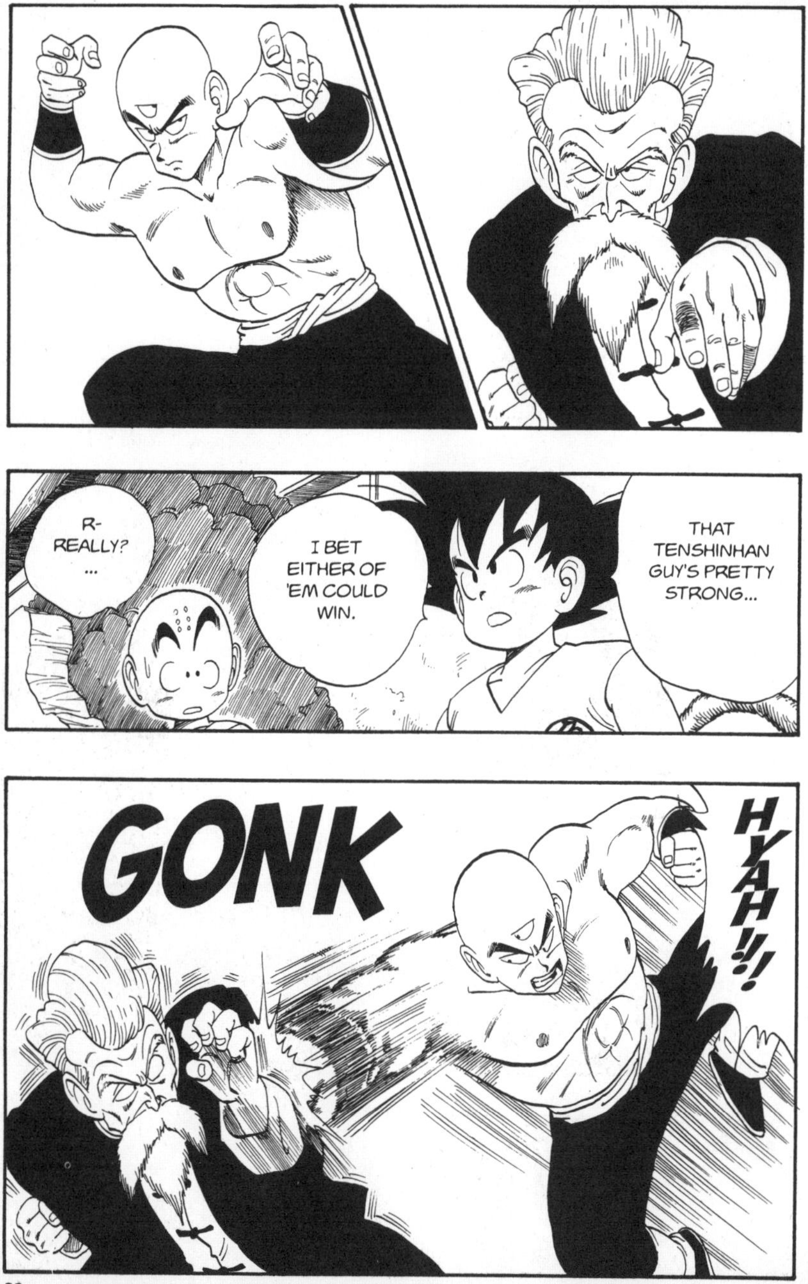
THAT TENSHINHAN GUY'S PRETTY STRONG...
I BET EITHER OF 'EM COULD WIN.
R-REALLY? ...
HYAH!!!
GONK

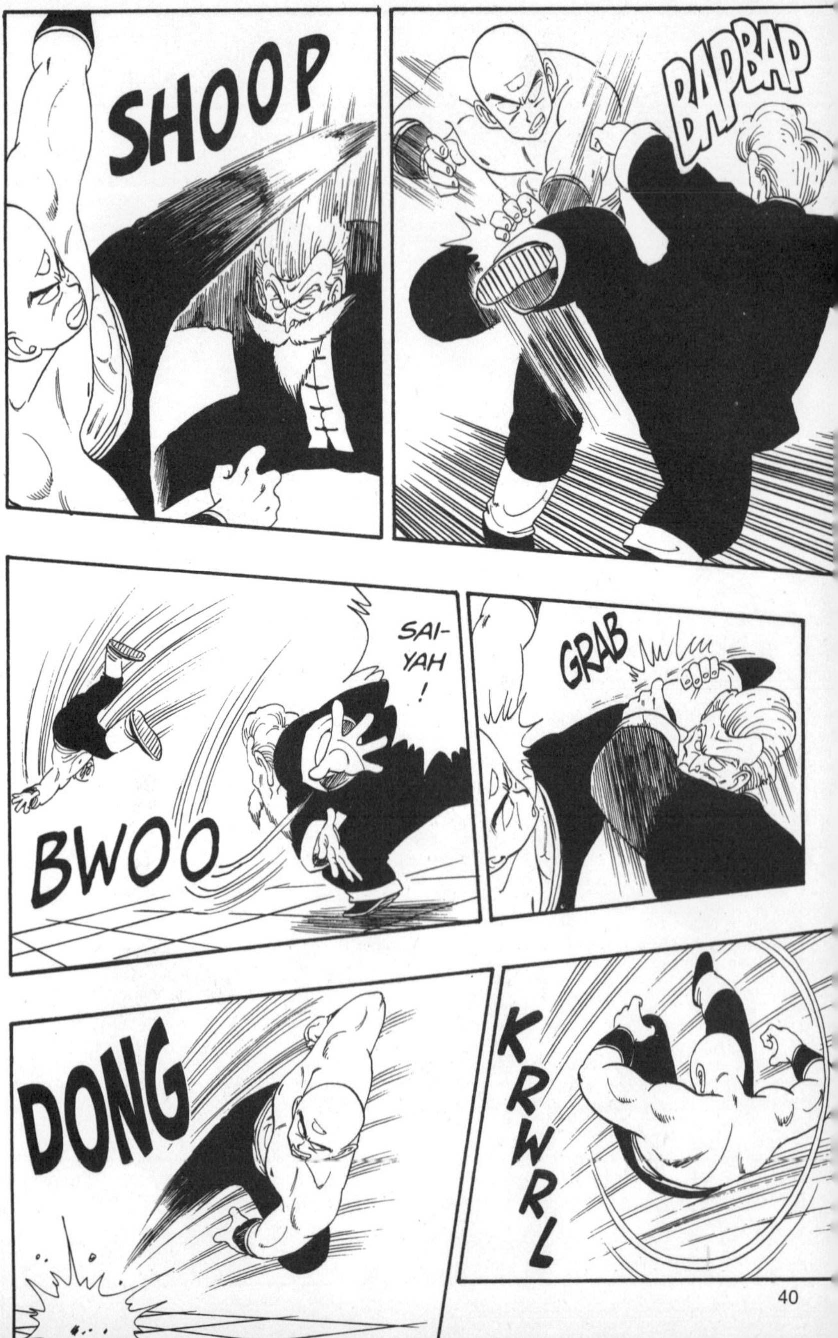
BAPBAP
SHOOP
GRAB
SAI-YAH!
BWOO
KRWRL
DONG

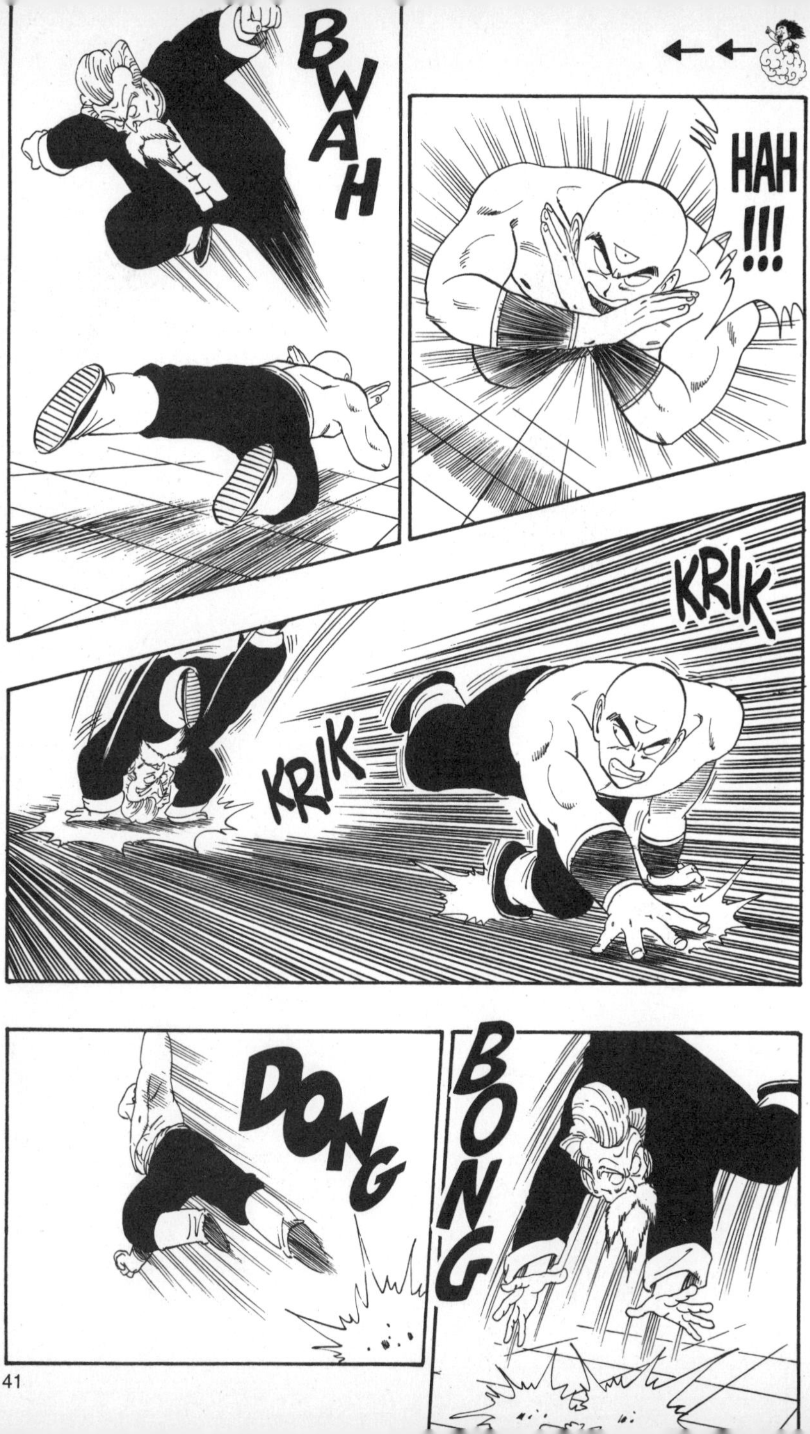
HAH!!!
BWAH
KRIK
KRIK
BONG
DONG

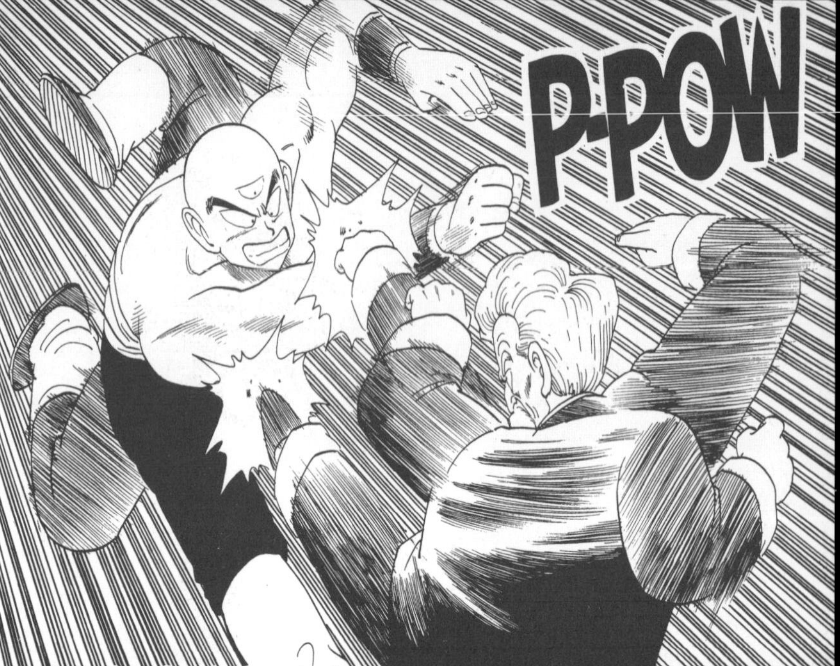
P-POW
G-GONK

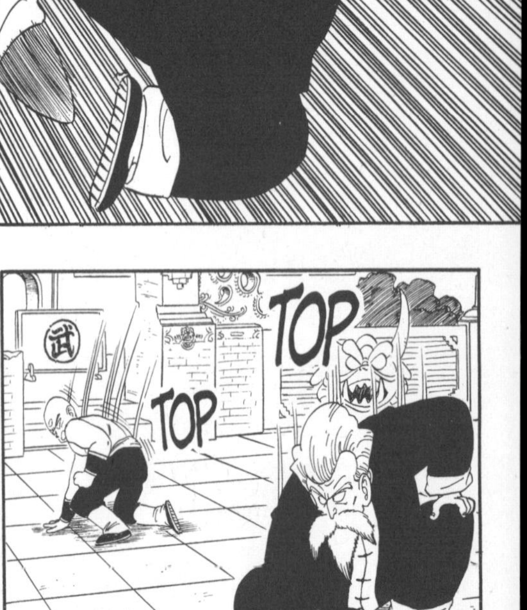
TOP
TOP

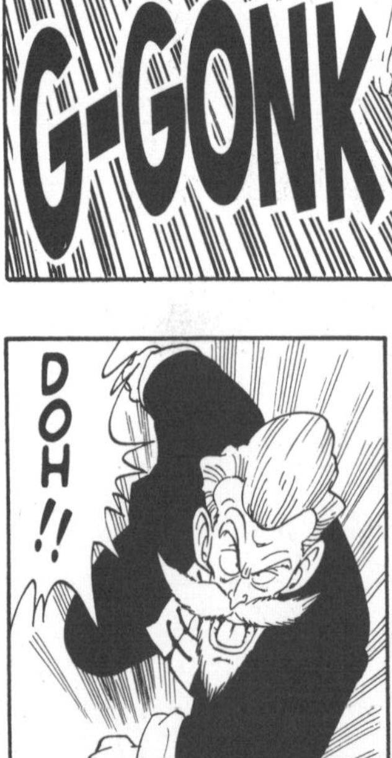
DOH!!

HYOOO   HYOOO

BAP BAP BAP

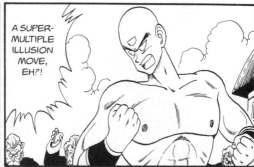

A SUPER-MULTIPLE ILLUSION MOVE, EH?!

43

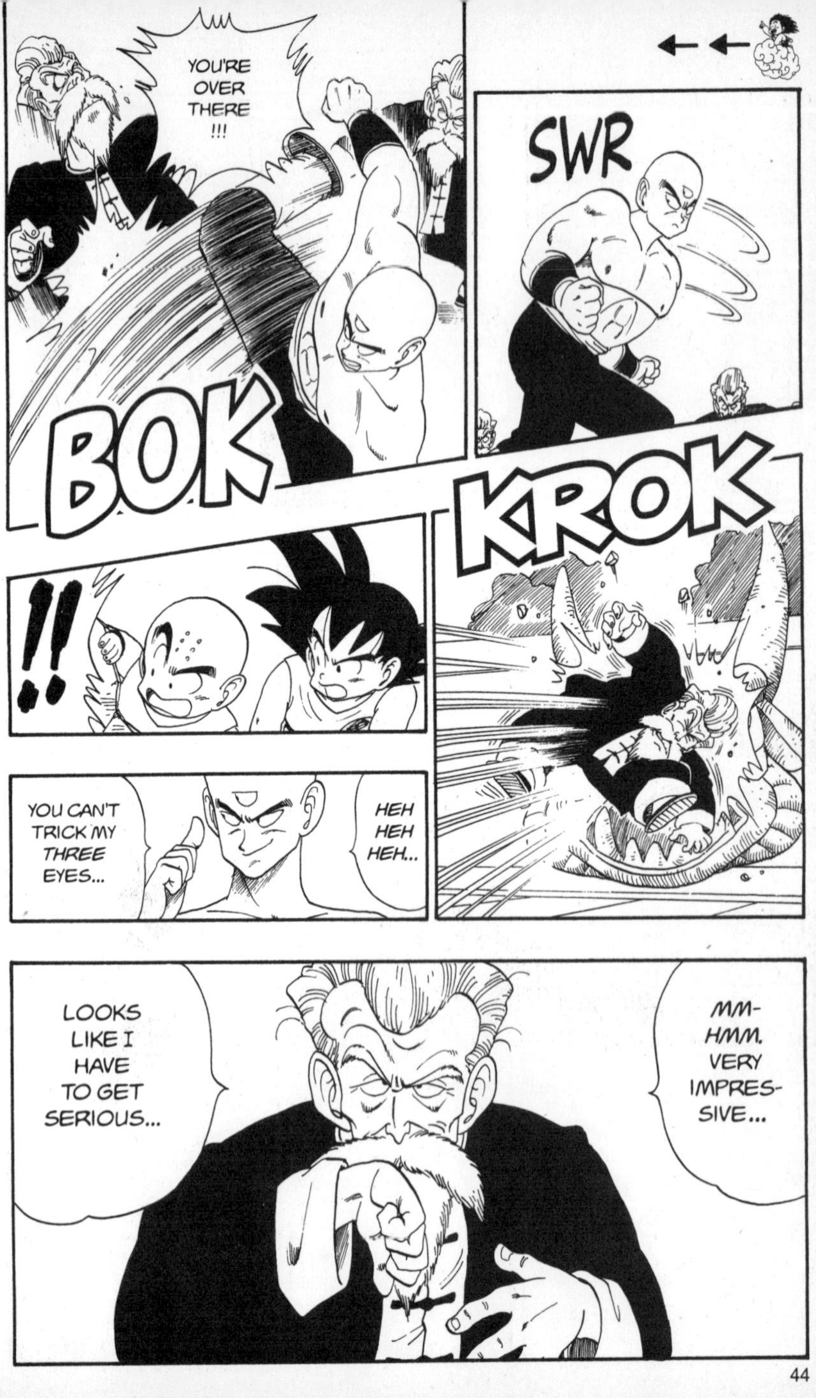

SWR
YOU'RE OVER THERE !!!
BOK
KROK
!!
HEH HEH HEH...
YOU CAN'T TRICK MY THREE EYES...
MM-HMM. VERY IMPRES-SIVE...
LOOKS LIKE I HAVE TO GET SERIOUS...

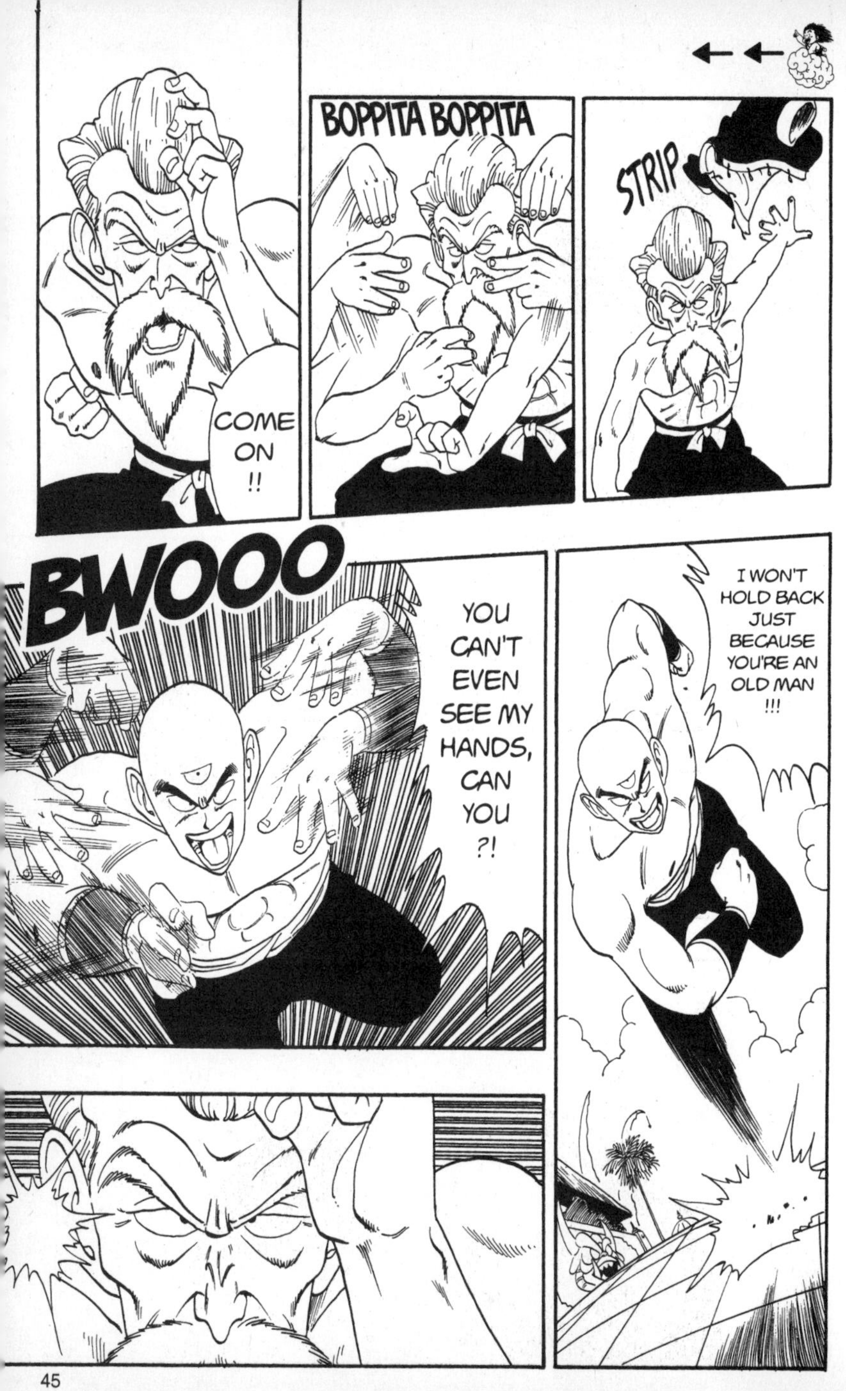
STRIP
BOPPITA BOPPITA
COME ON !!
I WON'T HOLD BACK JUST BECAUSE YOU'RE AN OLD MAN !!!
BWOOO
YOU CAN'T EVEN SEE MY HANDS, CAN YOU ?!

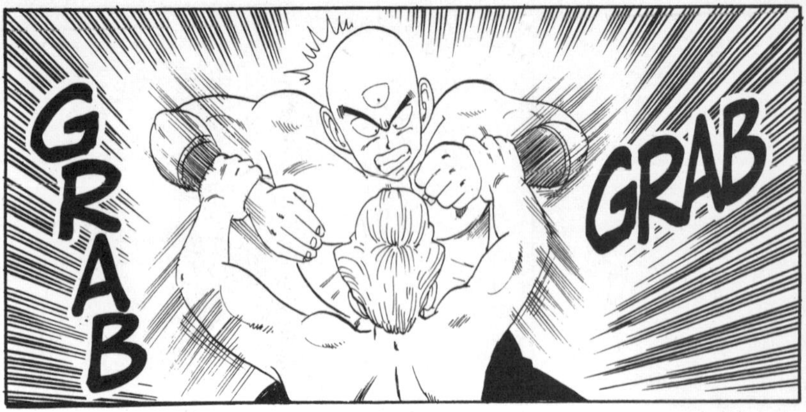
GRAB
GRAB
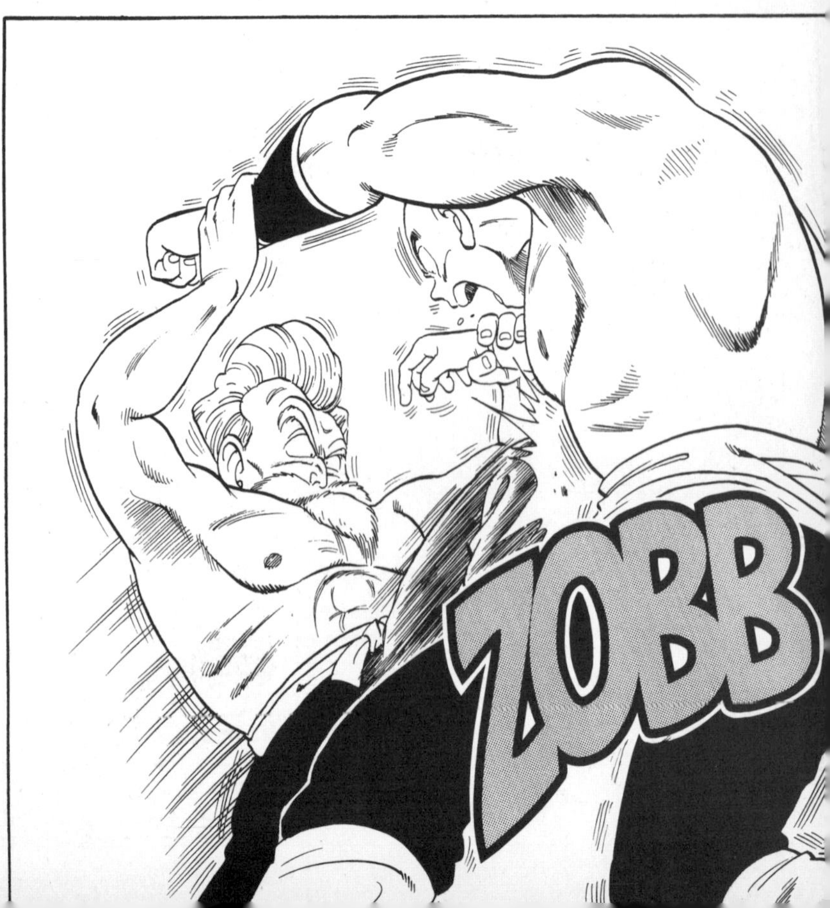
ZOBB

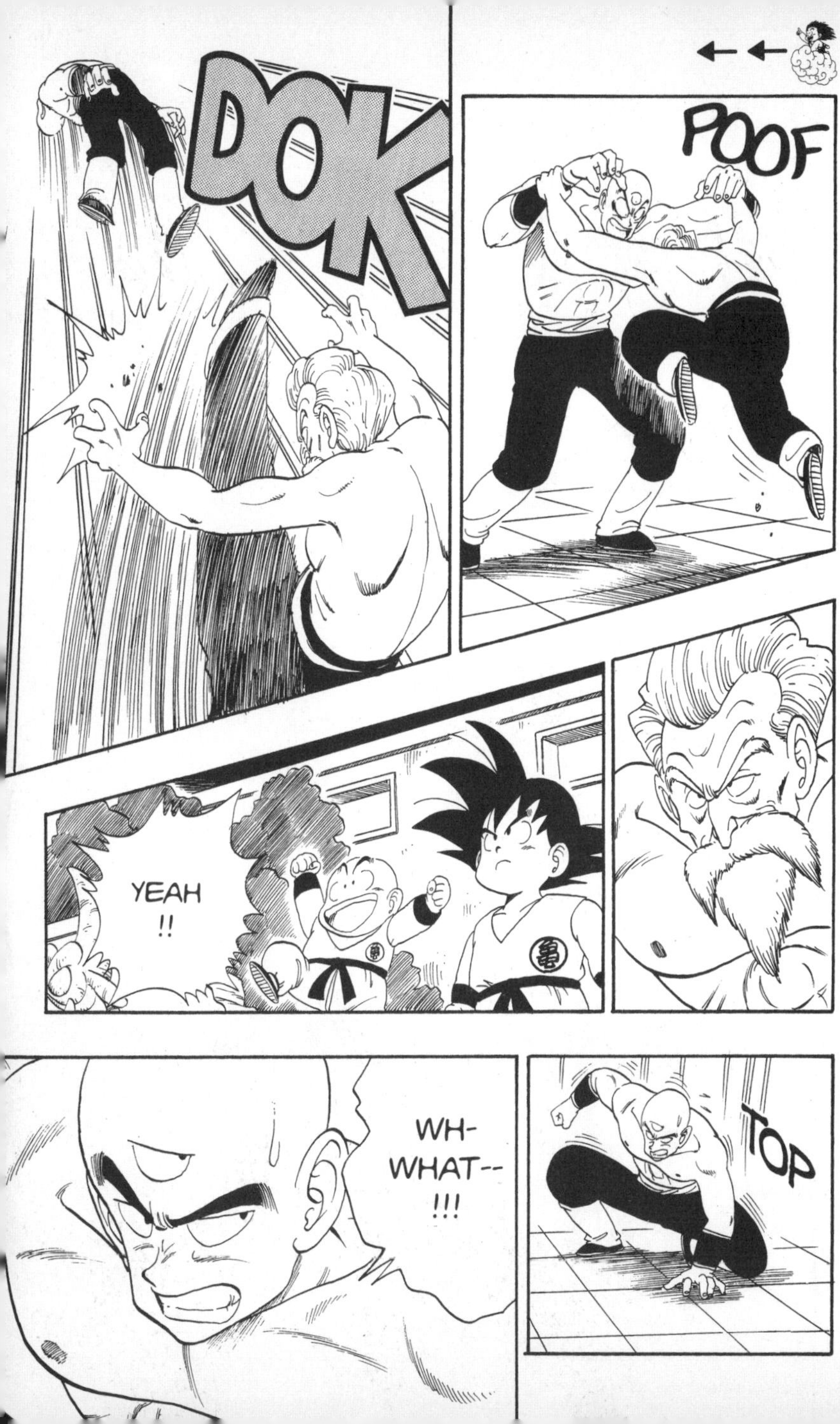
POOF
DOK
YEAH !!
TOP
WH- WHAT-- !!!

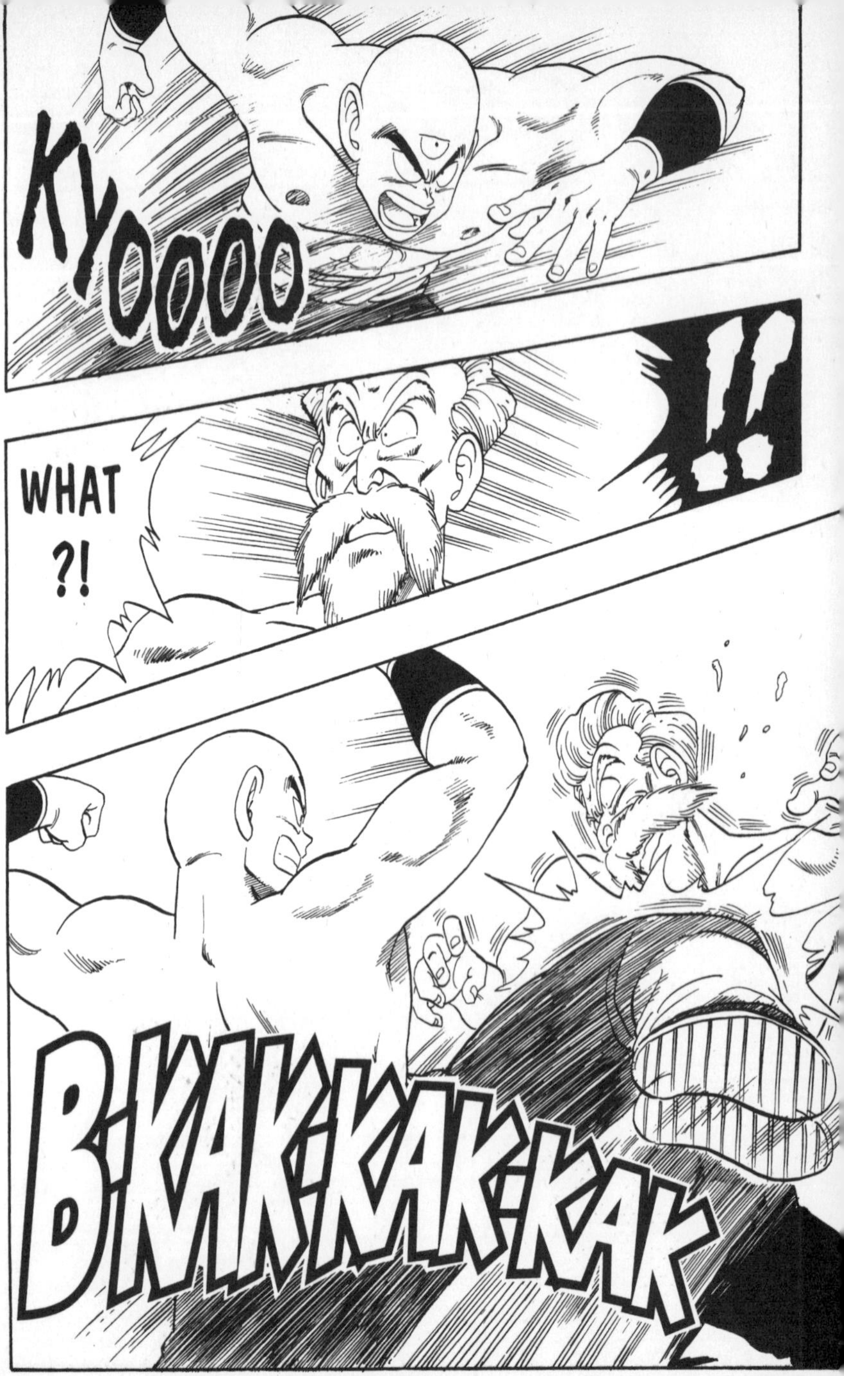
KYOOOO
!!
WHAT ?!
B-KAK-KAK-KAK-KAK

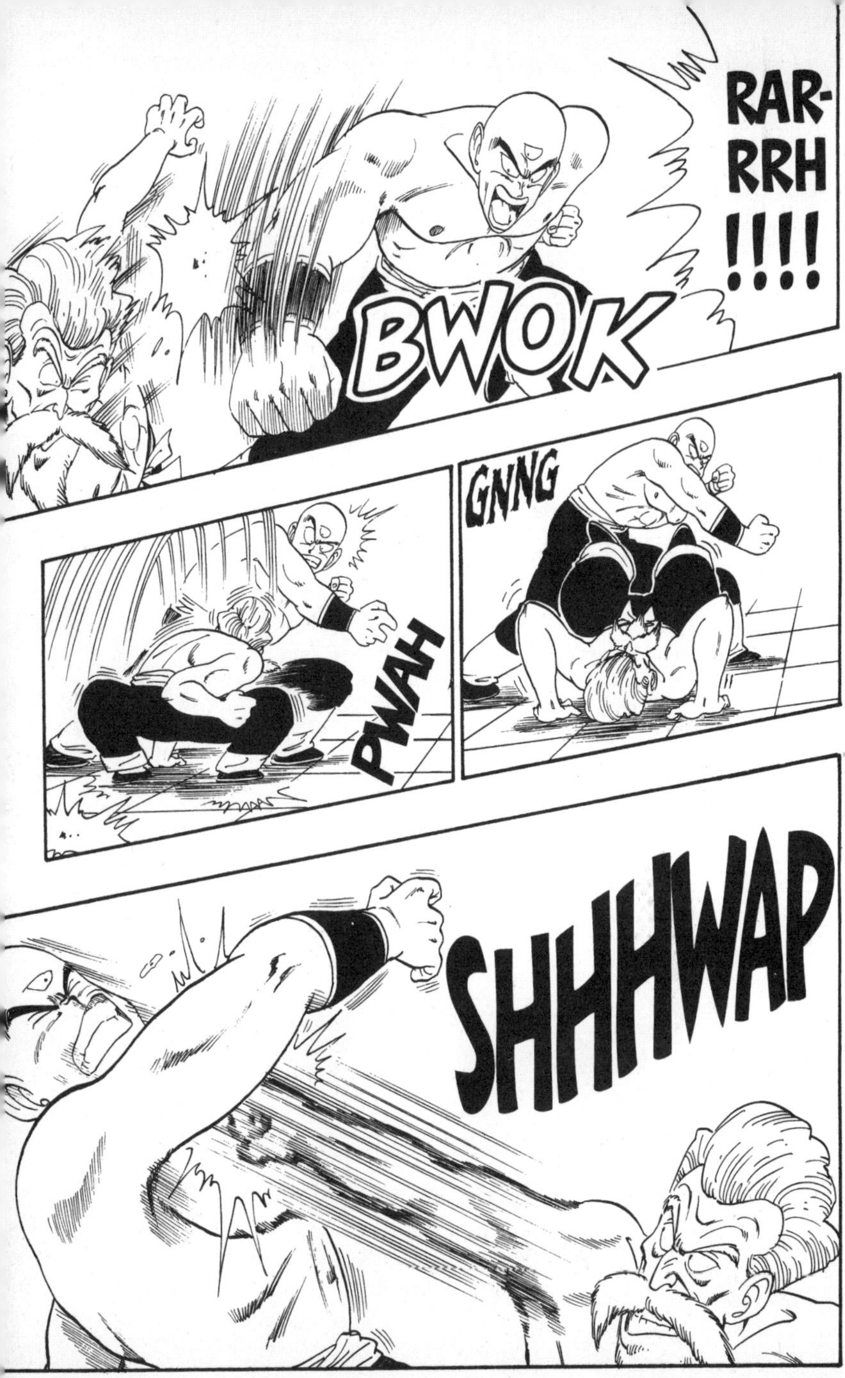
RAR-RRH!!!!
BWOK
GNNG
PWAH
SHHHWAP

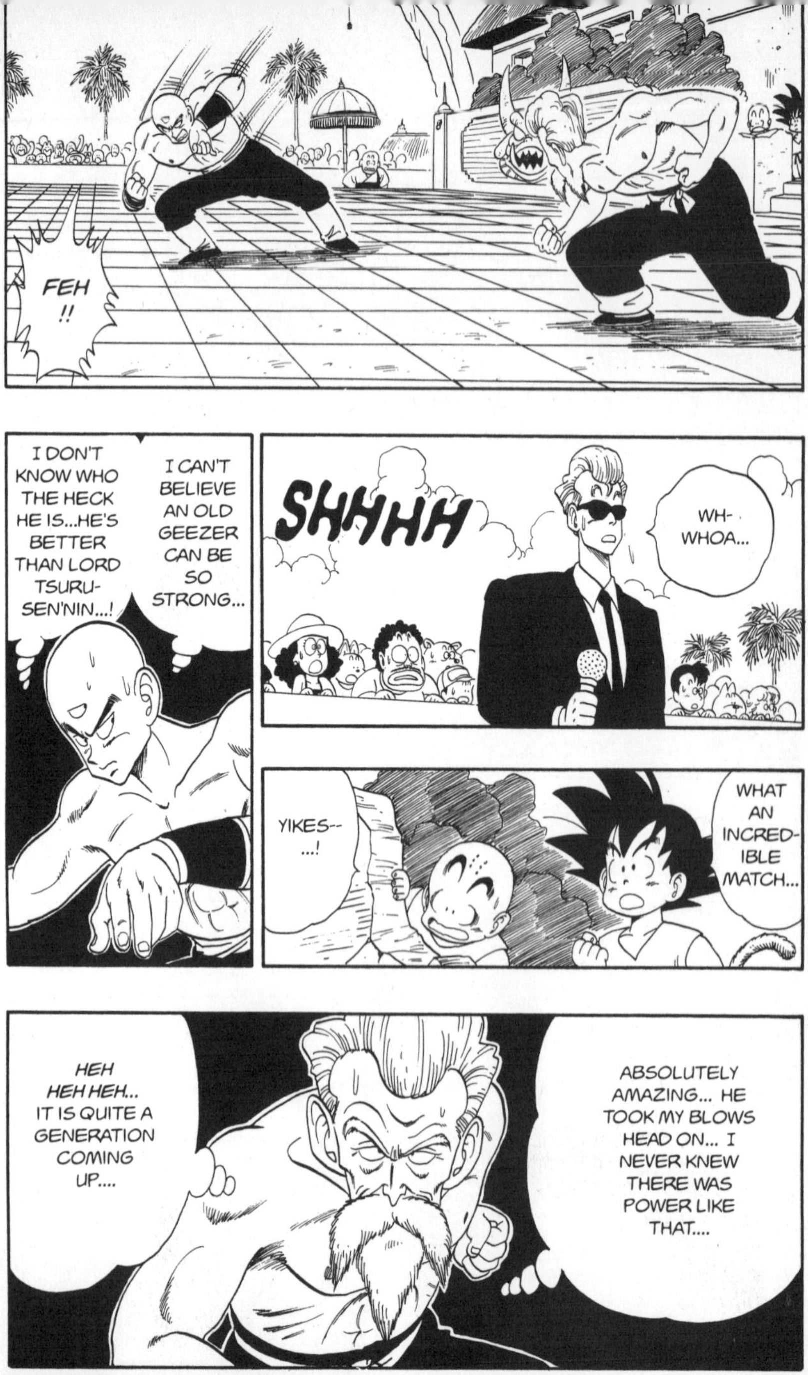
FEH!!
SHHHH
WH-WHOA...
WHAT AN INCREDIBLE MATCH...
YIKES--...!
I CAN'T BELIEVE AN OLD GEEZER CAN BE SO STRONG...
I DON'T KNOW WHO THE HECK HE IS...HE'S BETTER THAN LORD TSURU-SEN'NIN...!
ABSOLUTELY AMAZING... HE TOOK MY BLOWS HEAD ON... I NEVER KNEW THERE WAS POWER LIKE THAT....
HEH HEH HEH... IT IS QUITE A GENERATION COMING UP....

NEXT: Good and Evil

Tale 124
Young Tenshinhan

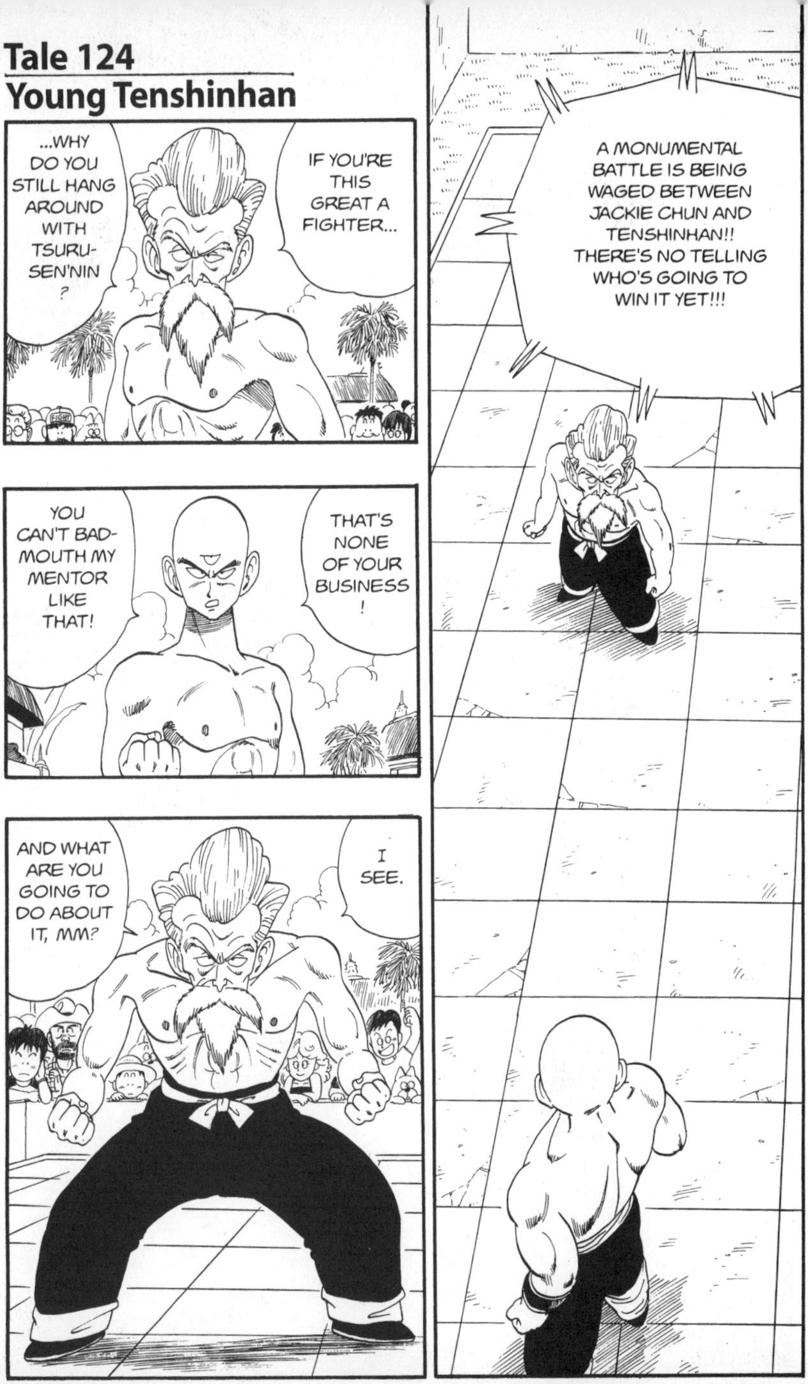
A MONUMENTAL BATTLE IS BEING WAGED BETWEEN JACKIE CHUN AND TENSHINHAN!! THERE'S NO TELLING WHO'S GOING TO WIN IT YET!!!
IF YOU'RE THIS GREAT A FIGHTER...
...WHY DO YOU STILL HANG AROUND WITH TSURU-SEN'NIN?
FIGHT
THAT'S NONE OF YOUR BUSINESS!
YOU CAN'T BAD-MOUTH MY MENTOR LIKE THAT!
I SEE.
AND WHAT ARE YOU GOING TO DO ABOUT IT, MM?

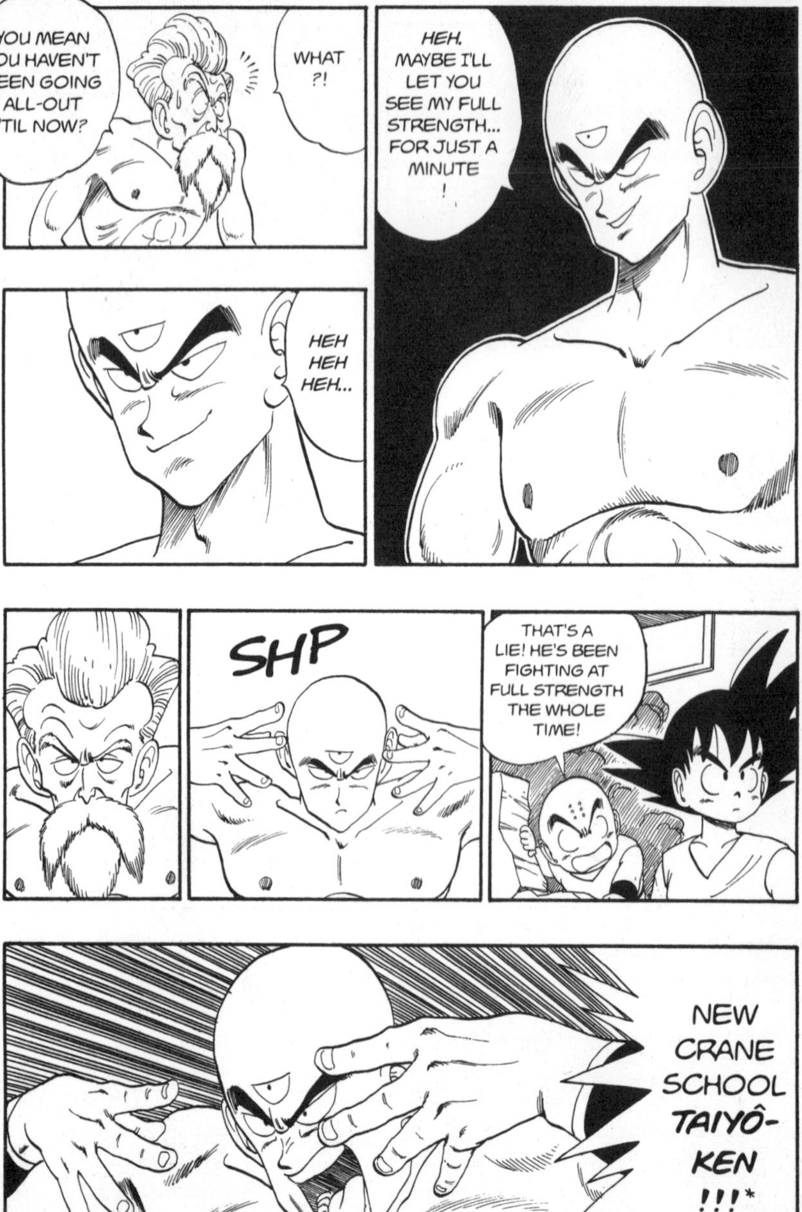
HEH. MAYBE I'LL LET YOU SEE MY FULL STRENGTH... FOR JUST A MINUTE !
WHAT ?!
YOU MEAN YOU HAVEN'T BEEN GOING ALL-OUT 'TIL NOW?
HEH HEH HEH...
THAT'S A LIE! HE'S BEEN FIGHTING AT FULL STRENGTH THE WHOLE TIME!
SHP
NEW CRANE SCHOOL TAIYÔ-KEN !!!*

*A.K.A.... "FIST OF THE SUN"!--ED.

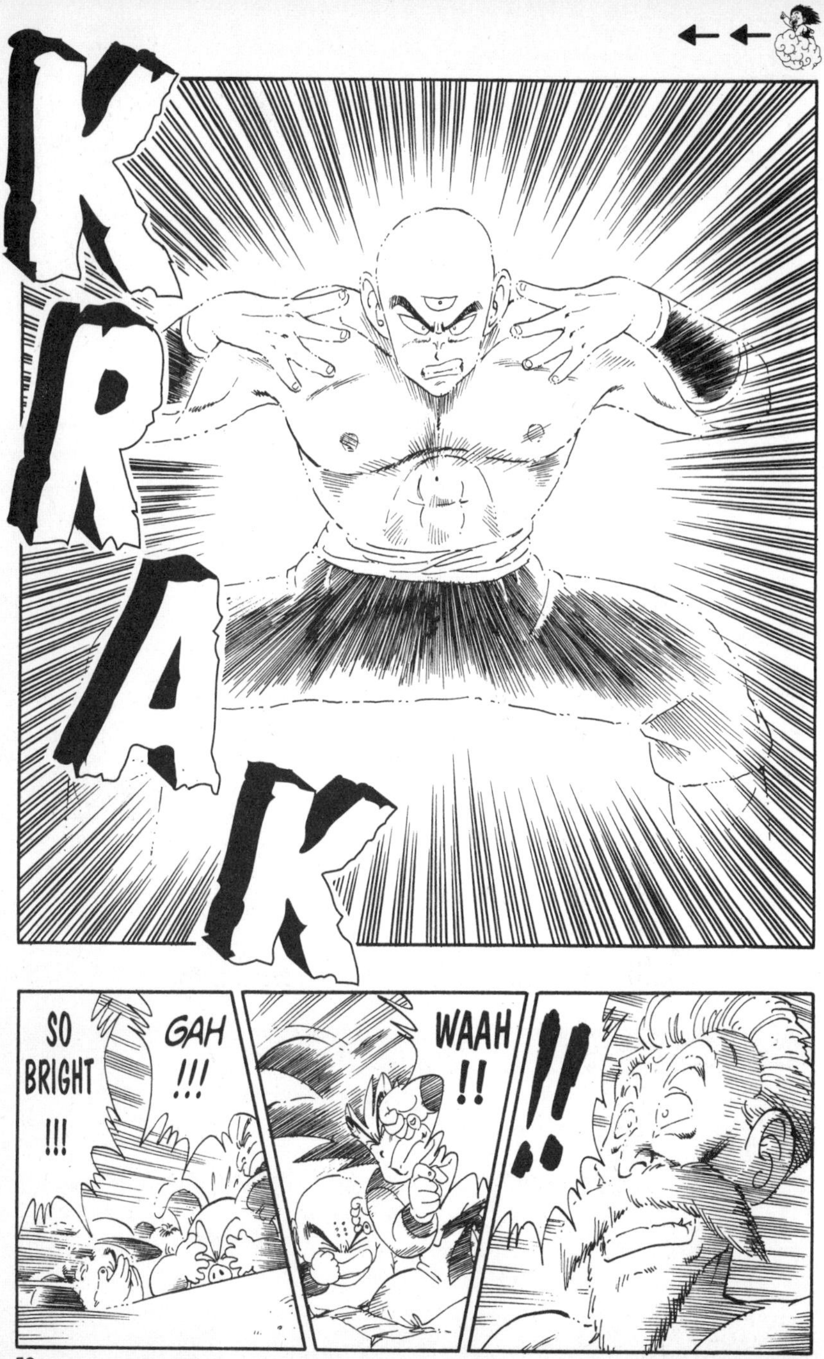
KRAAK
!!
WAAH !!
GAH !!!
SO BRIGHT !!!

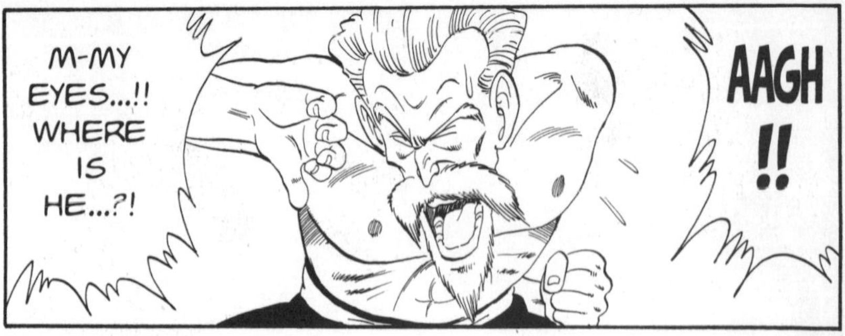
AAGH !!
M-MY EYES...!! WHERE IS HE...?!
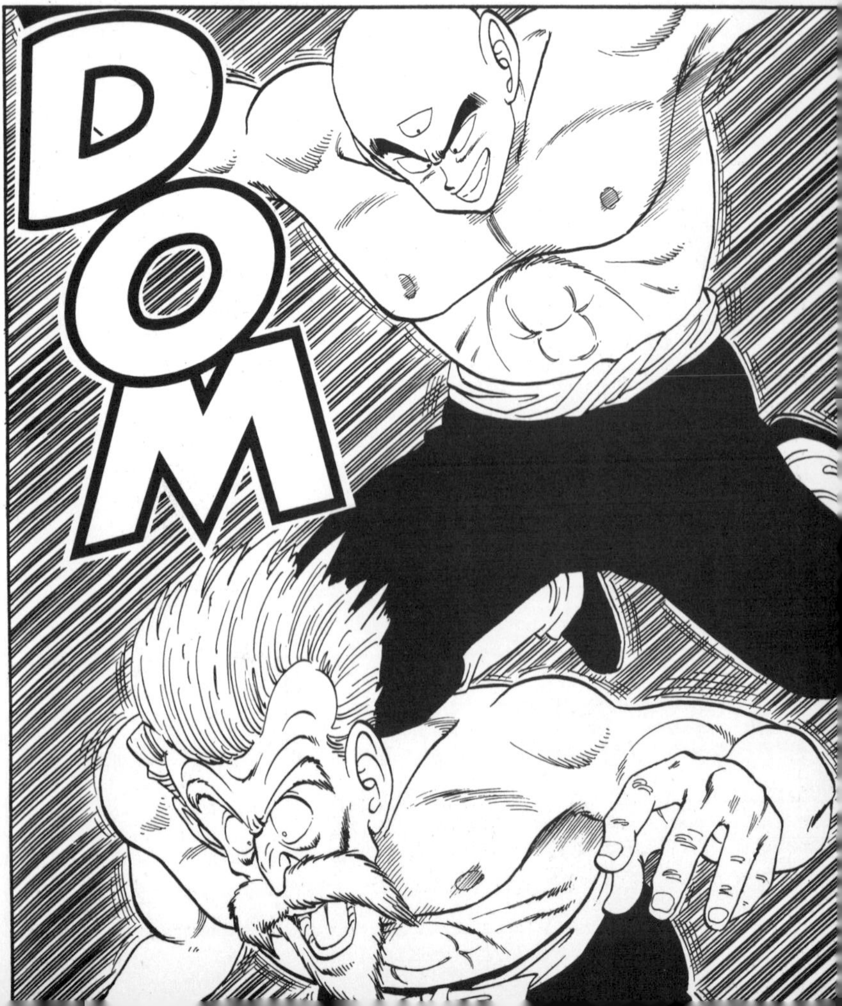
DOM

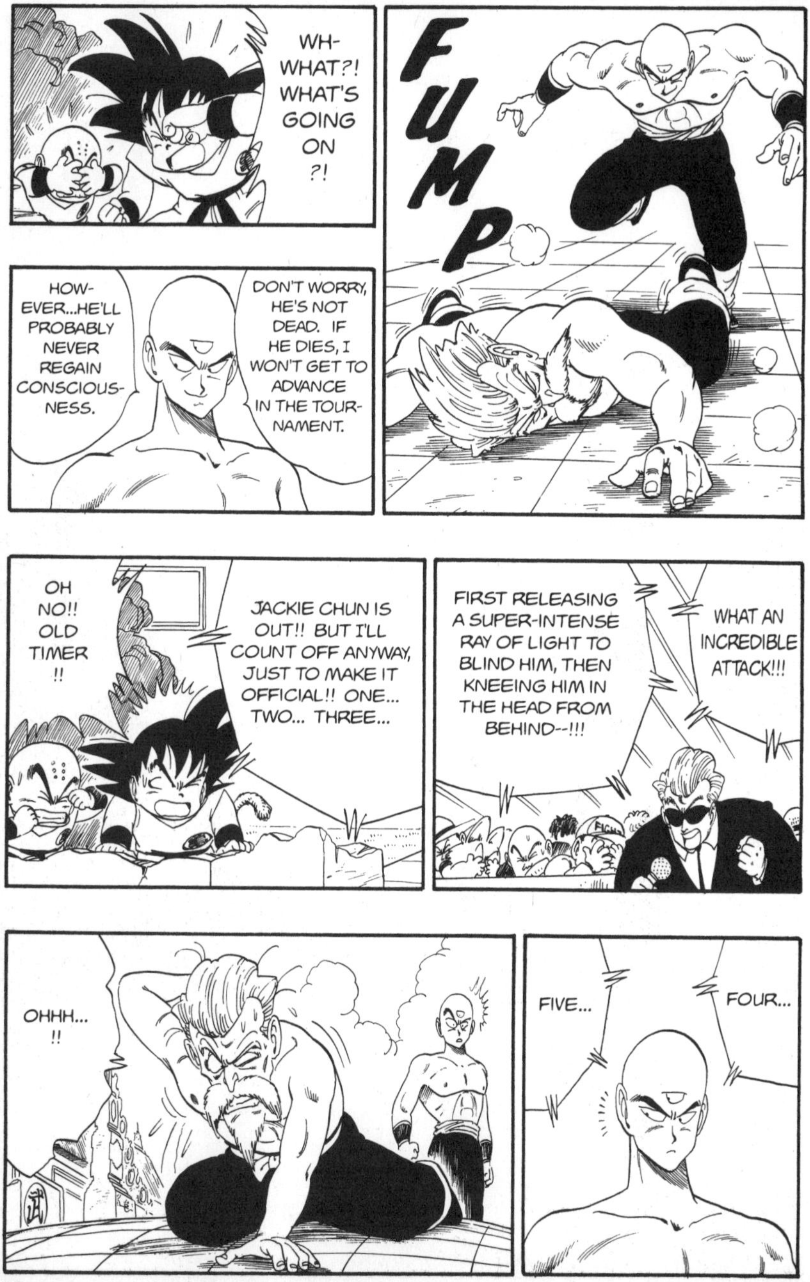
FUMP
WH- WHAT?! WHAT'S GOING ON ?!
DON'T WORRY, HE'S NOT DEAD. IF HE DIES, I WON'T GET TO ADVANCE IN THE TOUR-NAMENT.
HOW-EVER...HE'LL PROBABLY NEVER REGAIN CONSCIOUS-NESS.
WHAT AN INCREDIBLE ATTACK!!!
FIRST RELEASING A SUPER-INTENSE RAY OF LIGHT TO BLIND HIM, THEN KNEEING HIM IN THE HEAD FROM BEHIND--!!!
JACKIE CHUN IS OUT!! BUT I'LL COUNT OFF ANYWAY, JUST TO MAKE IT OFFICIAL!! ONE... TWO... THREE...
OH NO!! OLD TIMER !!
FOUR...
FIVE...
OHHH... !!

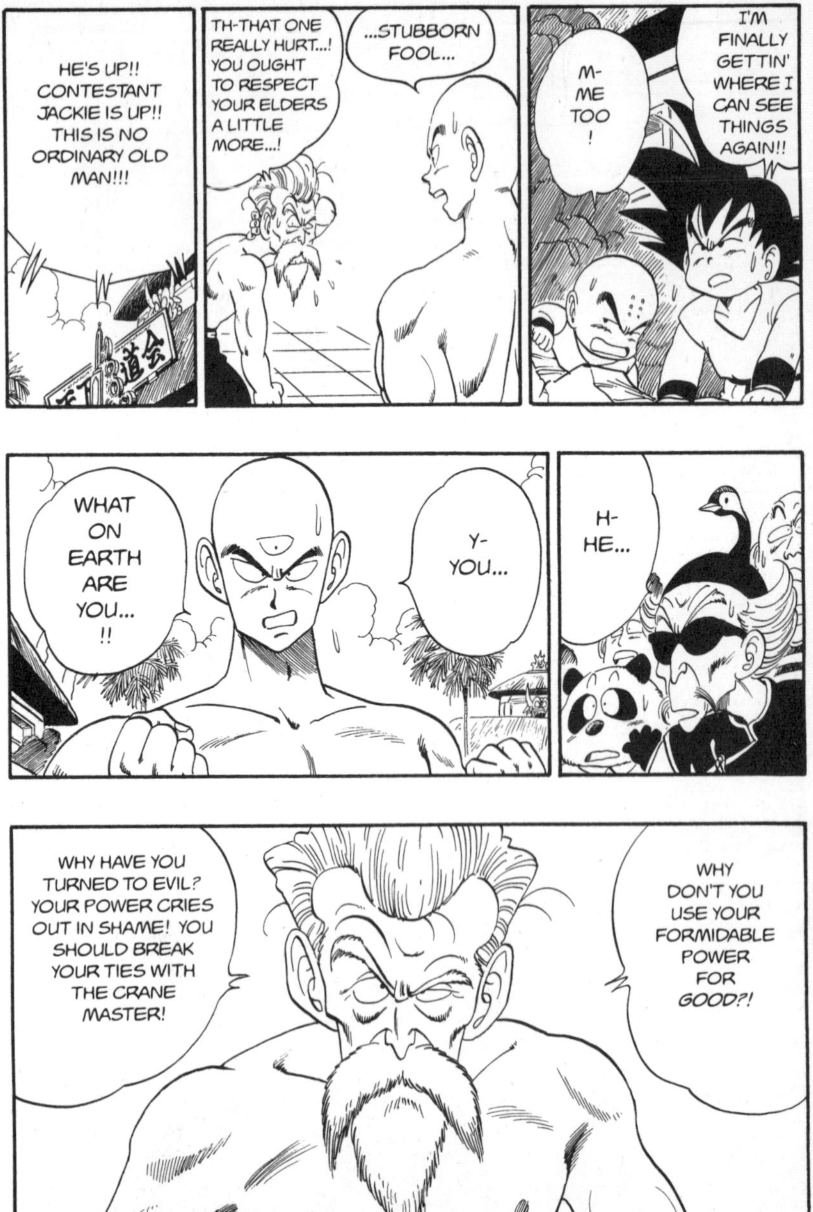
I'M FINALLY GETTIN' WHERE I CAN SEE THINGS AGAIN!!
M-ME TOO!
...STUBBORN FOOL...
TH-THAT ONE REALLY HURT...! YOU OUGHT TO RESPECT YOUR ELDERS A LITTLE MORE...!
HE'S UP!! CONTESTANT JACKIE IS UP!! THIS IS NO ORDINARY OLD MAN!!!
H-HE...
Y-YOU...
WHAT ON EARTH ARE YOU...!!
WHY DON'T YOU USE YOUR FORMIDABLE POWER FOR *GOOD?!*
WHY HAVE YOU TURNED TO EVIL? YOUR POWER CRIES OUT IN SHAME! YOU SHOULD BREAK YOUR TIES WITH THE CRANE MASTER!

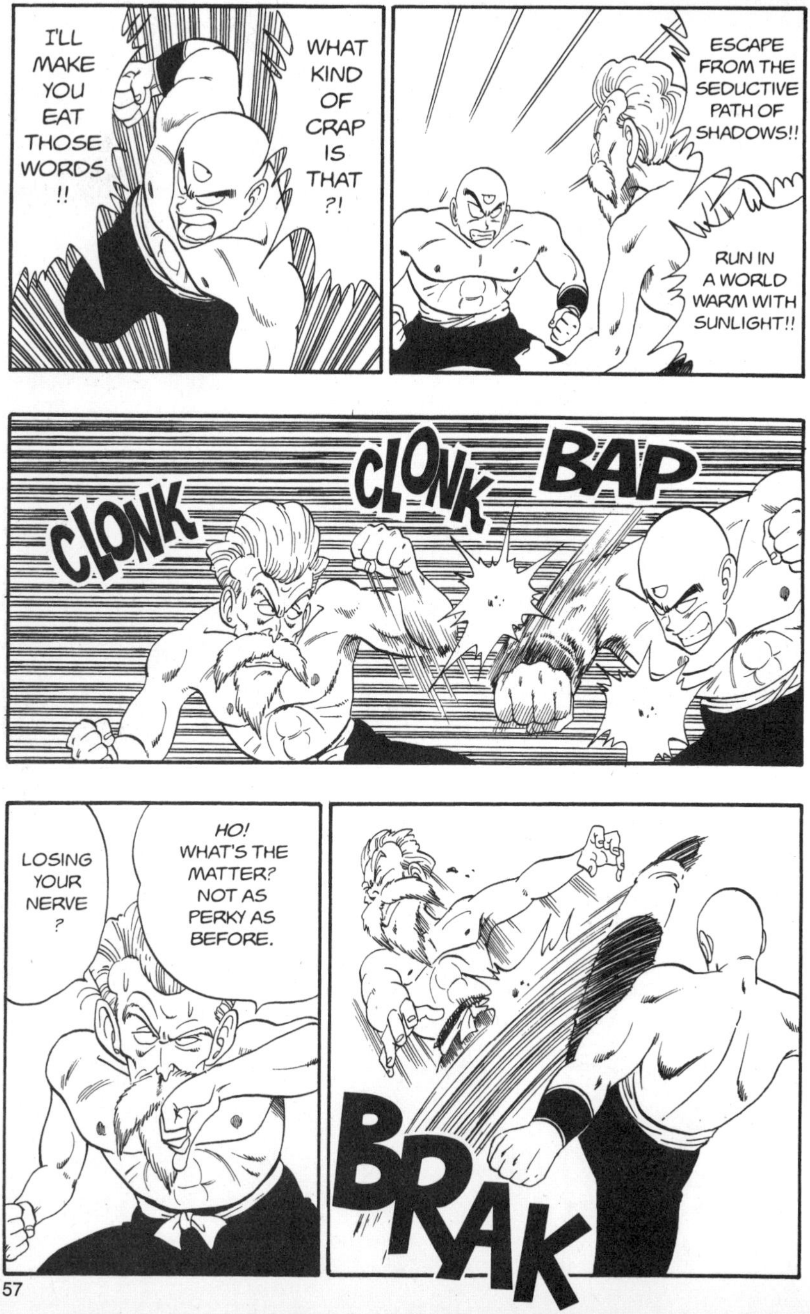
ESCAPE FROM THE SEDUCTIVE PATH OF SHADOWS!!
RUN IN A WORLD WARM WITH SUNLIGHT!!
WHAT KIND OF CRAP IS THAT?!
I'LL MAKE YOU EAT THOSE WORDS!!
BAP
CLONK
CLONK
BRAK
HO! WHAT'S THE MATTER? NOT AS PERKY AS BEFORE.
LOSING YOUR NERVE?

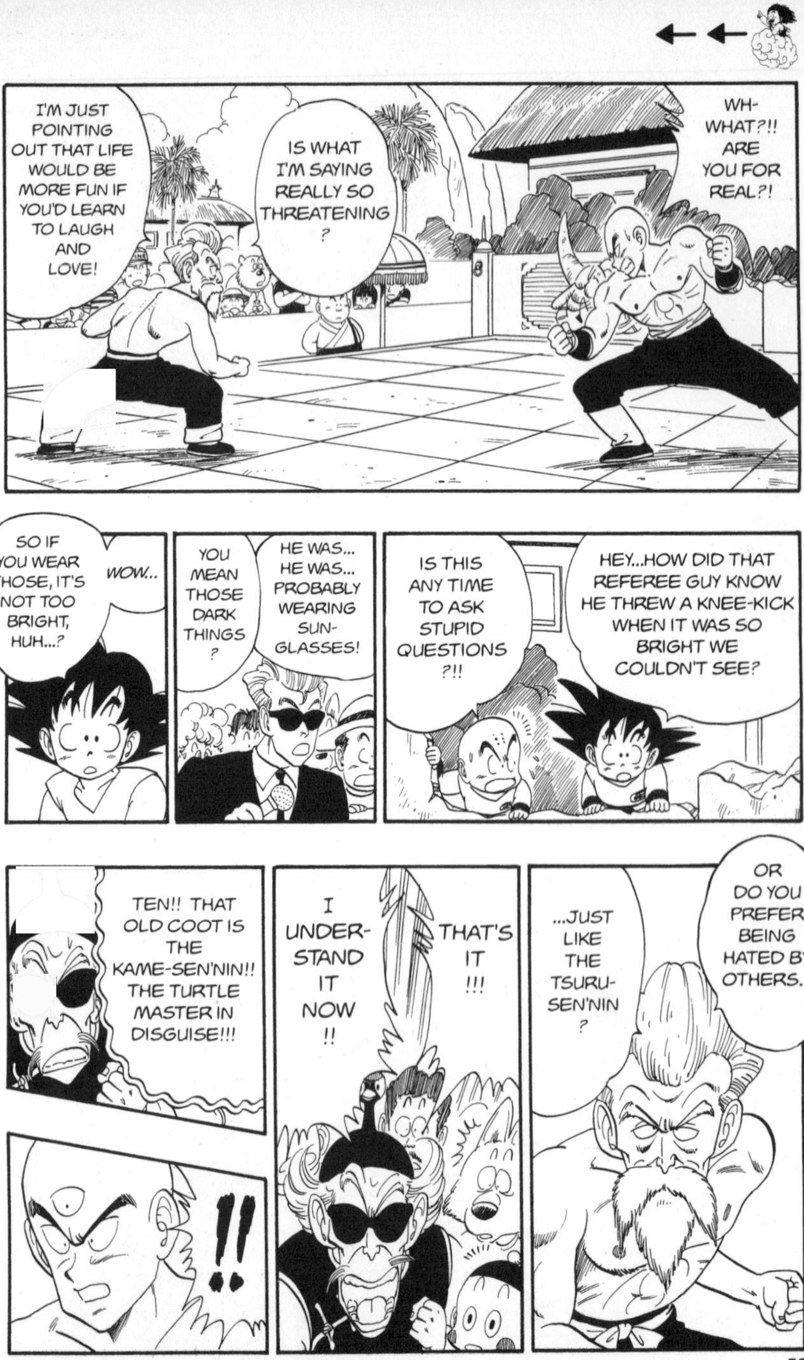
WH-WHAT?!! ARE YOU FOR REAL?!
IS WHAT I'M SAYING REALLY SO THREATENING?
I'M JUST POINTING OUT THAT LIFE WOULD BE MORE FUN IF YOU'D LEARN TO LAUGH AND LOVE!
HEY...HOW DID THAT REFEREE GUY KNOW HE THREW A KNEE-KICK WHEN IT WAS SO BRIGHT WE COULDN'T SEE?
IS THIS ANY TIME TO ASK STUPID QUESTIONS?!!
HE WAS... HE WAS... PROBABLY WEARING SUN-GLASSES!
YOU MEAN THOSE DARK THINGS?
WOW...
SO IF YOU WEAR THOSE, IT'S NOT TOO BRIGHT, HUH...?
OR DO YOU PREFER BEING HATED BY OTHERS...
...JUST LIKE THE TSURU-SEN'NIN?
THAT'S IT!!!
I UNDER-STAND IT NOW!!
TEN!! THAT OLD COOT IS THE KAME-SEN'NIN!! THE TURTLE MASTER IN DISGUISE!!!
!!

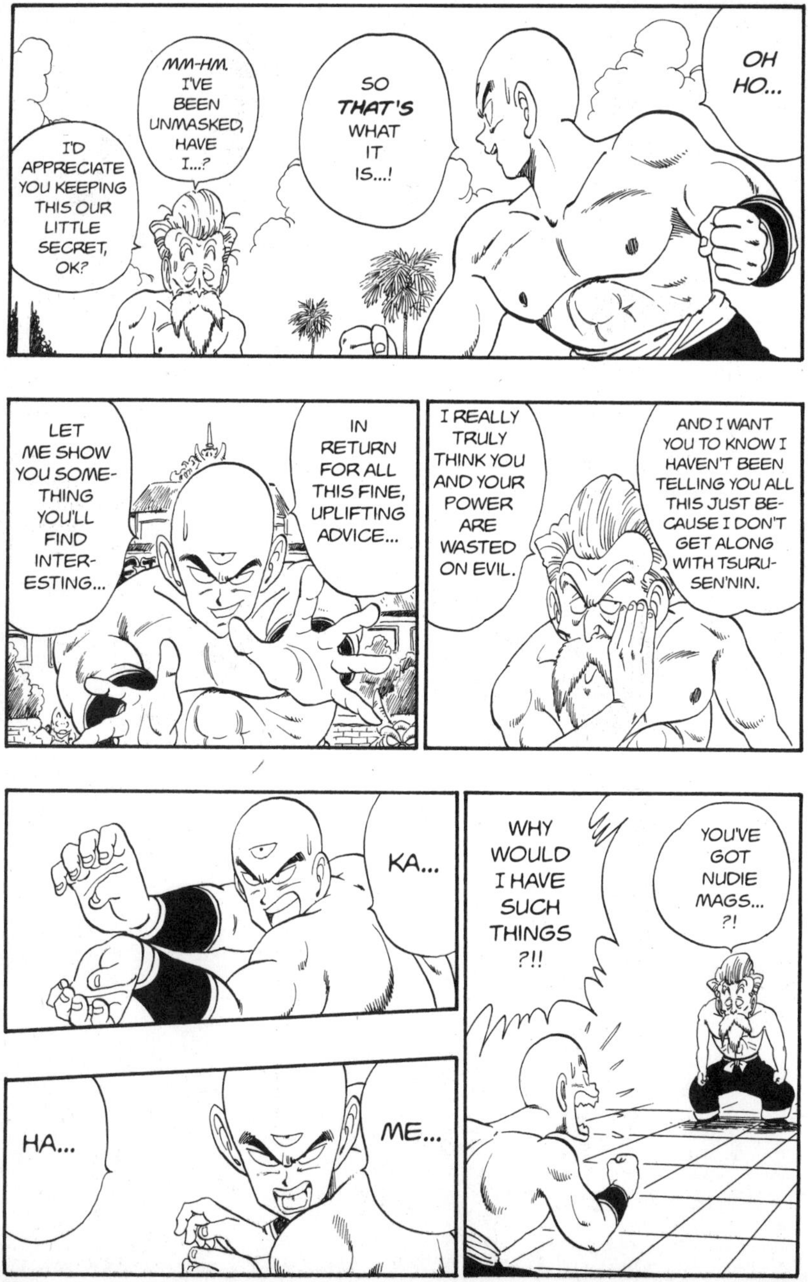
OH HO...
SO THAT'S WHAT IT IS...!
MM-HM. I'VE BEEN UNMASKED, HAVE I...?
I'D APPRECIATE YOU KEEPING THIS OUR LITTLE SECRET, OK?
AND I WANT YOU TO KNOW I HAVEN'T BEEN TELLING YOU ALL THIS JUST BE-CAUSE I DON'T GET ALONG WITH TSURU-SEN'NIN.
I REALLY TRULY THINK YOU AND YOUR POWER ARE WASTED ON EVIL.
IN RETURN FOR ALL THIS FINE, UPLIFTING ADVICE...
LET ME SHOW YOU SOME-THING YOU'LL FIND INTER-ESTING...
YOU'VE GOT NUDIE MAGS...?!
WHY WOULD I HAVE SUCH THINGS?!!
KA...
ME...
HA...

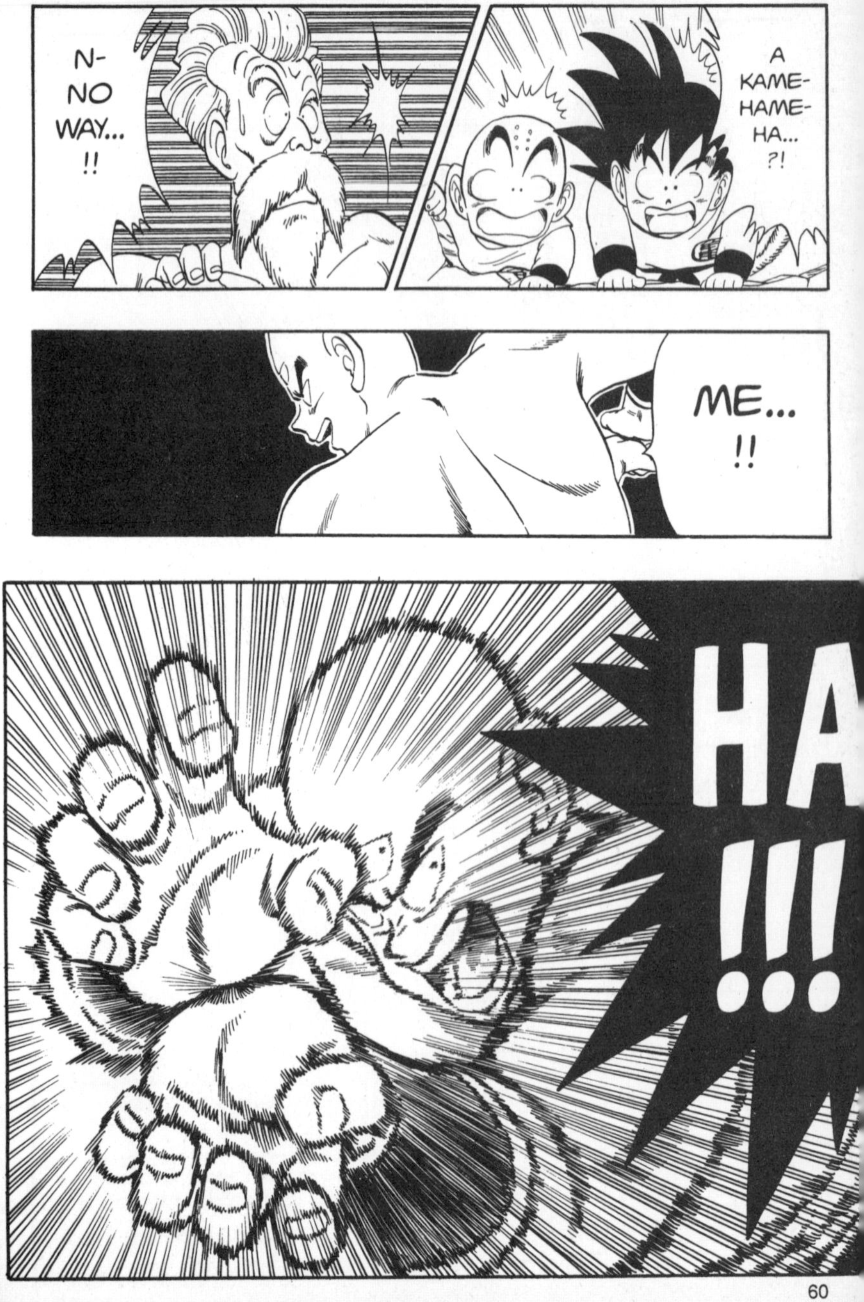
A KAME-HAME-HA...?!
N-NO WAY...!!
ME...!!
HA!!!

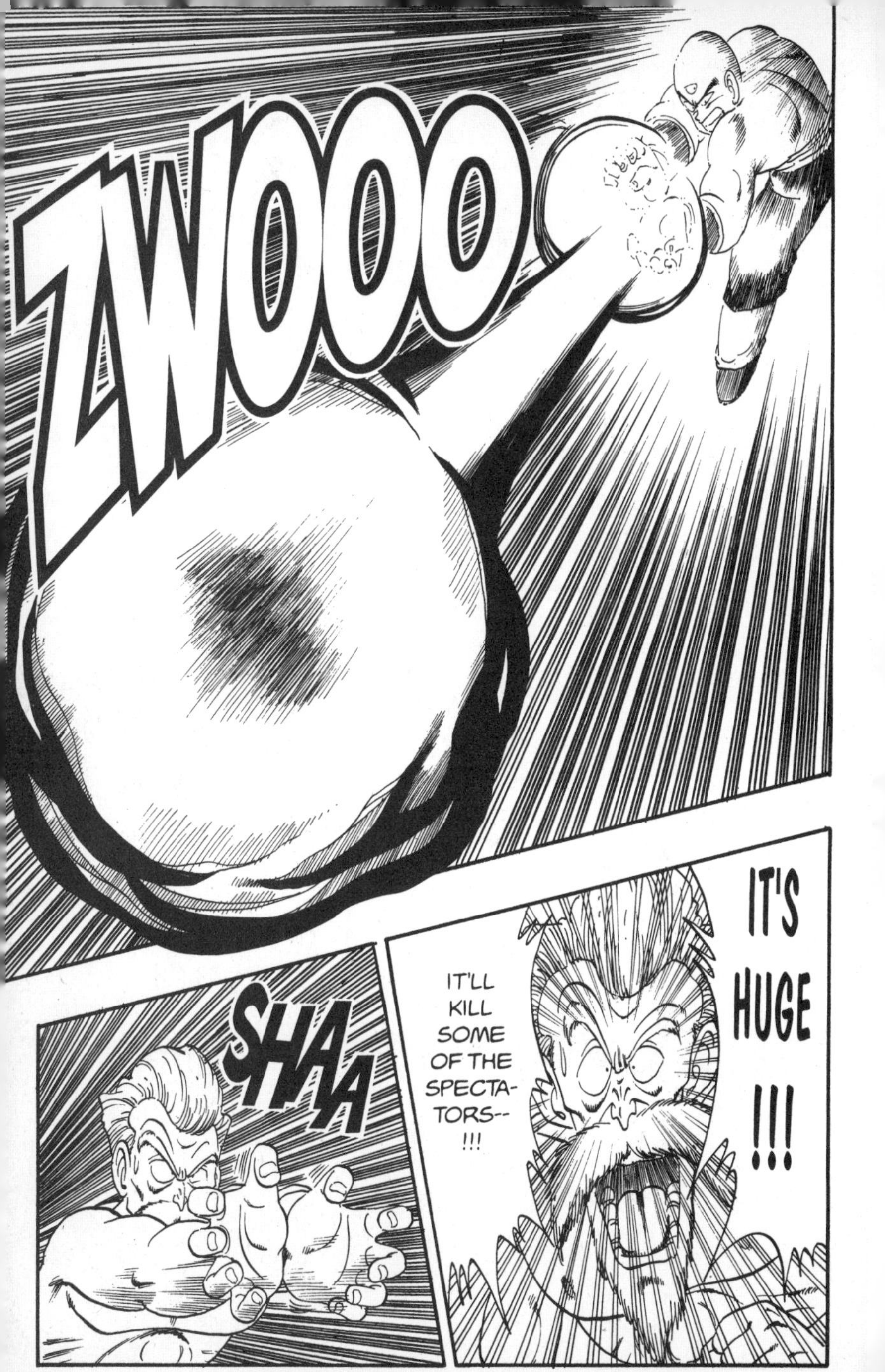
ZWOOO
IT'S HUGE!!!
IT'LL KILL SOME OF THE SPECTATORS--!!!
SHAA

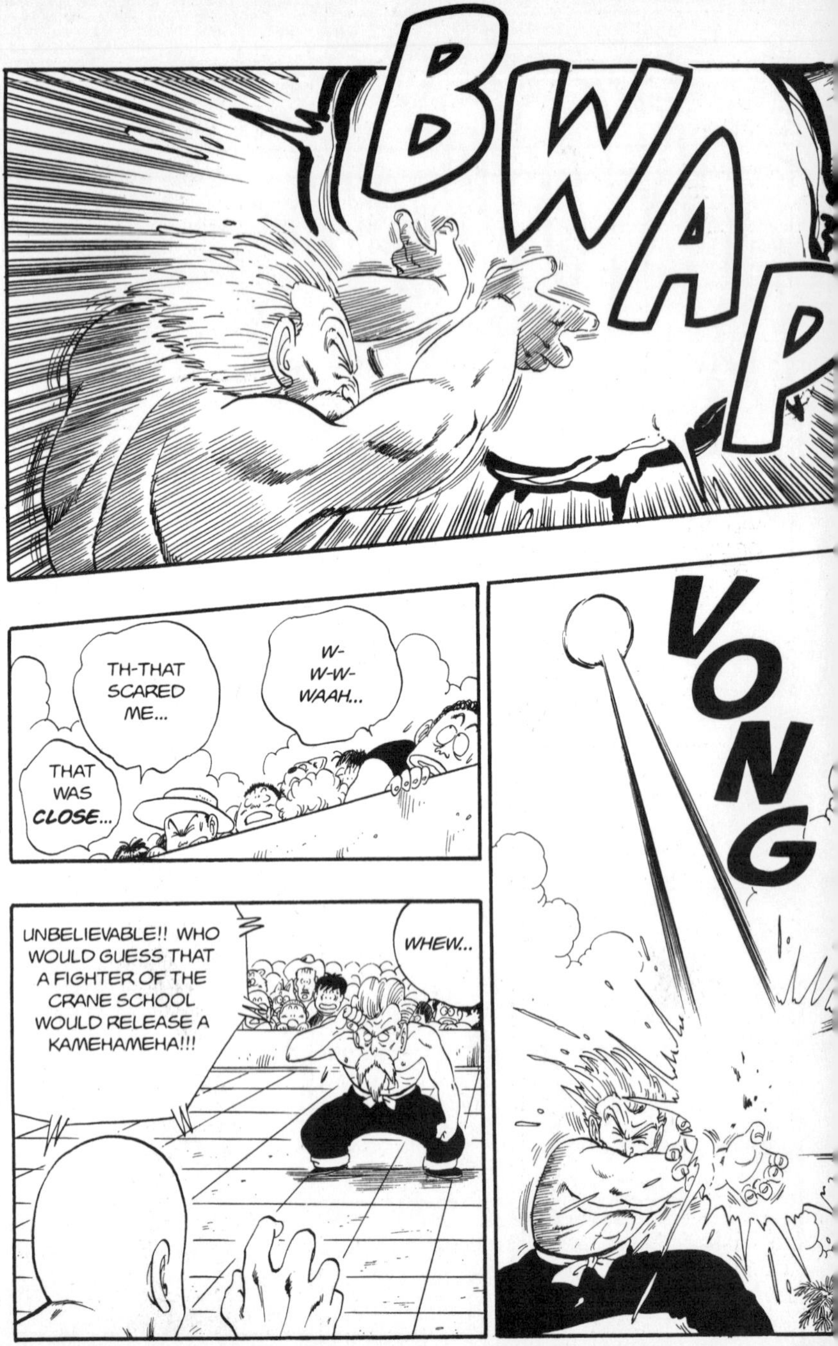
BWAP
VONG
W-W-W-WAAH...
TH-THAT SCARED ME...
THAT WAS ***CLOSE***...
WHEW...
UNBELIEVABLE!! WHO WOULD GUESS THAT A FIGHTER OF THE CRANE SCHOOL WOULD RELEASE A KAMEHAMEHA!!!

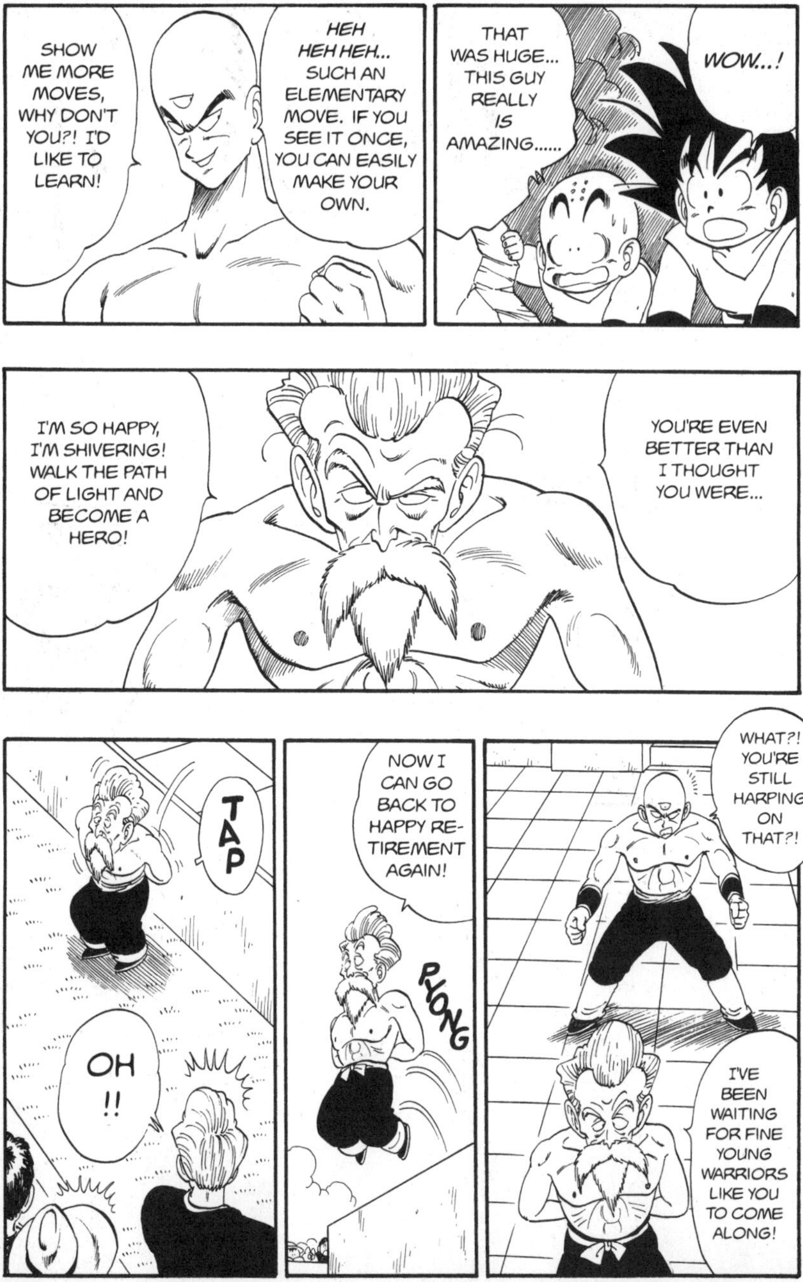
WOW...!
THAT WAS HUGE... THIS GUY REALLY IS AMAZING......
HEH HEH HEH... SUCH AN ELEMENTARY MOVE. IF YOU SEE IT ONCE, YOU CAN EASILY MAKE YOUR OWN.
SHOW ME MORE MOVES, WHY DON'T YOU?! I'D LIKE TO LEARN!
YOU'RE EVEN BETTER THAN I THOUGHT YOU WERE...
I'M SO HAPPY, I'M SHIVERING! WALK THE PATH OF LIGHT AND BECOME A HERO!
WHAT?! YOU'RE STILL HARPING ON THAT?!
I'VE BEEN WAITING FOR FINE YOUNG WARRIORS LIKE YOU TO COME ALONG!
NOW I CAN GO BACK TO HAPPY RE-TIREMENT AGAIN!
PYONG
TAP
OH !!

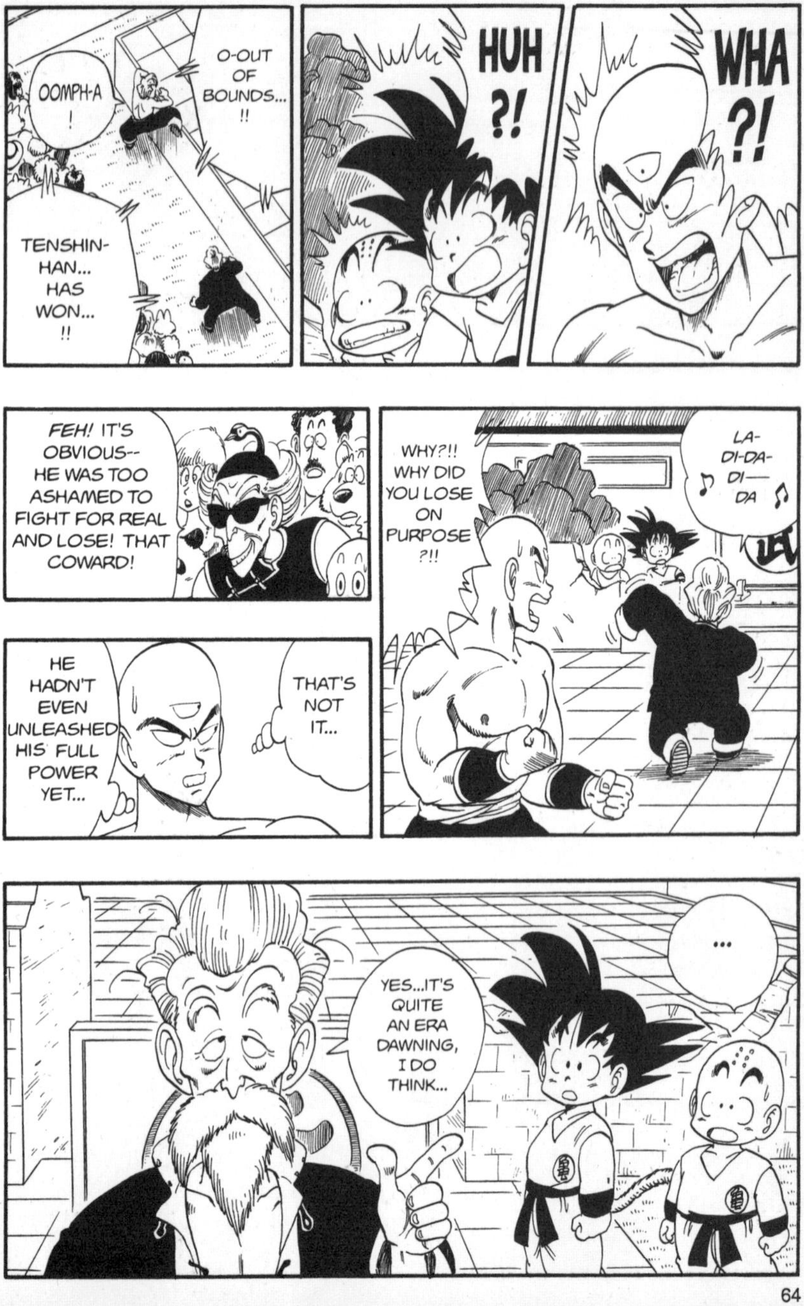
WHA ?!
HUH ?!
O-OUT OF BOUNDS... !!
OOMPH-A !
TENSHIN-HAN... HAS WON... !!
LA-DI-DA-DI—DA ♪ ♫
WHY?!! WHY DID YOU LOSE ON PURPOSE ?!!
FEH! IT'S OBVIOUS-- HE WAS TOO ASHAMED TO FIGHT FOR REAL AND LOSE! THAT COWARD!
THAT'S NOT IT...
HE HADN'T EVEN UNLEASHED HIS FULL POWER YET...
...
YES...IT'S QUITE AN ERA DAWNING, I DO THINK...

Tale 125

Goku vs. Kuririn

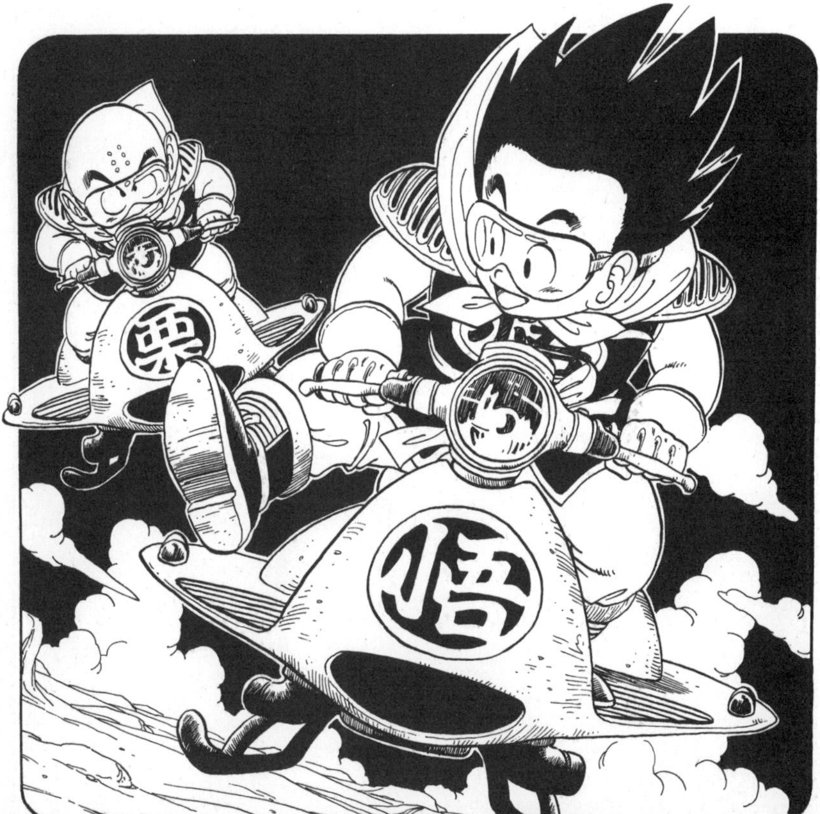
栗
悟

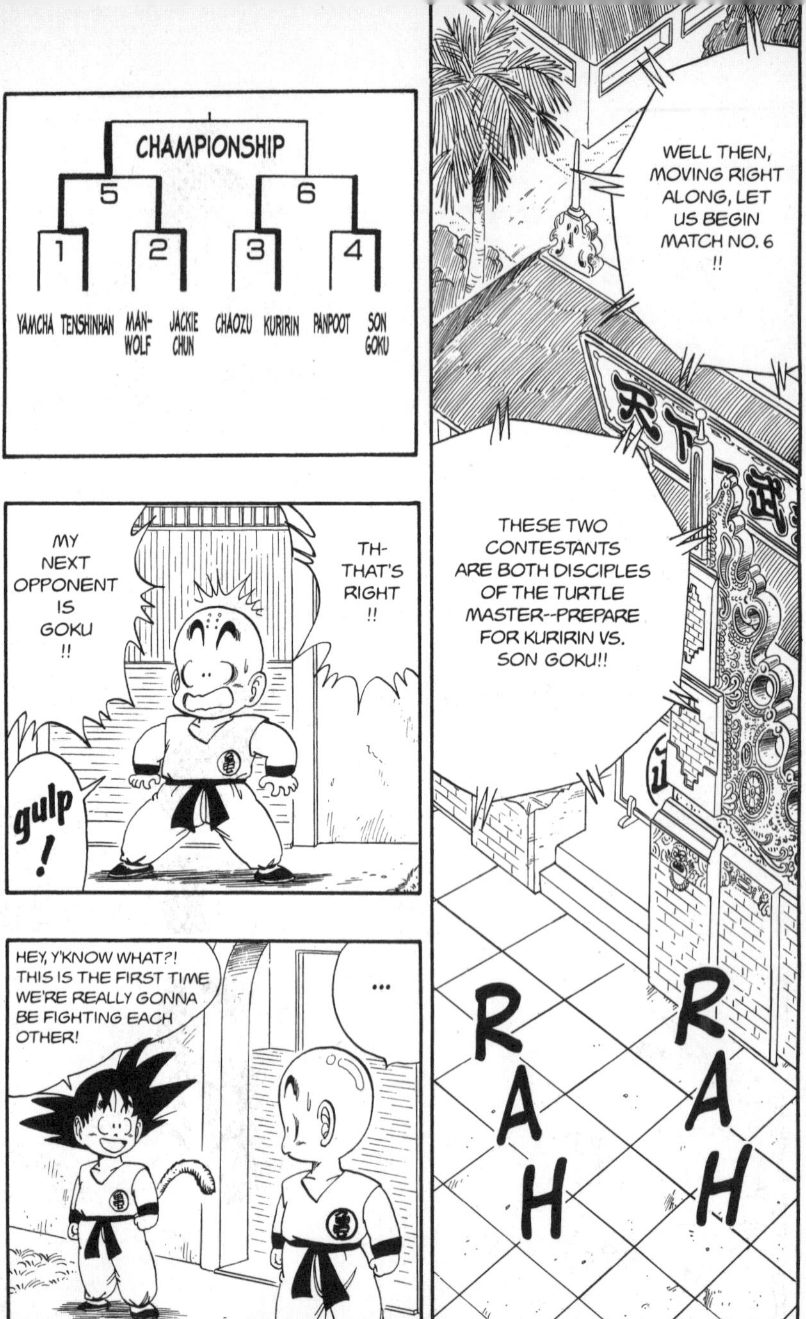
WELL THEN, MOVING RIGHT ALONG, LET US BEGIN MATCH NO. 6 !!
THESE TWO CONTESTANTS ARE BOTH DISCIPLES OF THE TURTLE MASTER--PREPARE FOR KURIRIN VS. SON GOKU!!
RAH
RAH
CHAMPIONSHIP
5
6
1
2
3
4
YAMCHA
TENSHINHAN
MAN-WOLF
JACKIE CHUN
CHAOZU
KURIRIN
PANPOOT
SON GOKU
TH- THAT'S RIGHT !!
MY NEXT OPPONENT IS GOKU !!
gulp !
...
HEY, Y'KNOW WHAT?! THIS IS THE FIRST TIME WE'RE REALLY GONNA BE FIGHTING EACH OTHER!

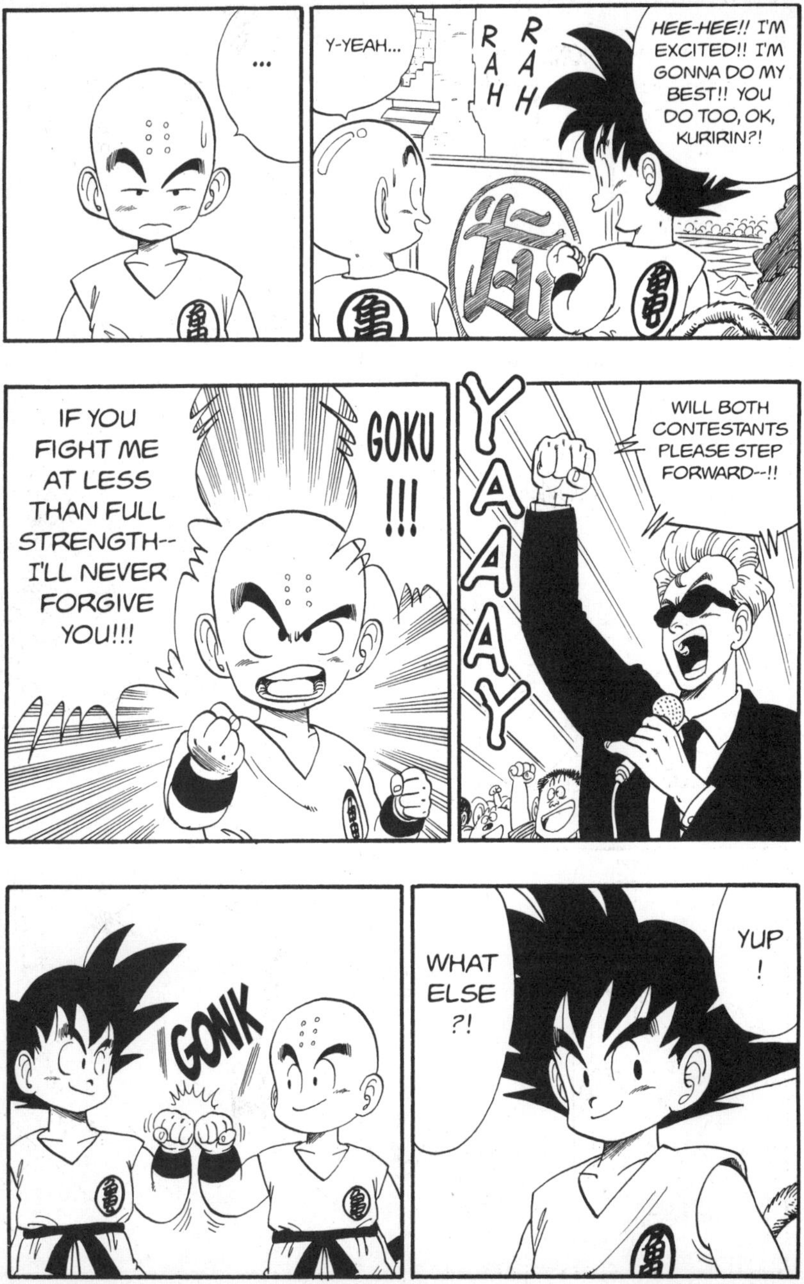

HEE-HEE!! I'M EXCITED!! I'M GONNA DO MY BEST!! YOU DO TOO, OK, KURIRIN?!
RAH RAH
Y-YEAH...
...
WILL BOTH CONTESTANTS PLEASE STEP FORWARD--!!
YAAAAY
GOKU !!!
IF YOU FIGHT ME AT LESS THAN FULL STRENGTH-- I'LL NEVER FORGIVE YOU!!!
YUP !
WHAT ELSE ?!
GONK

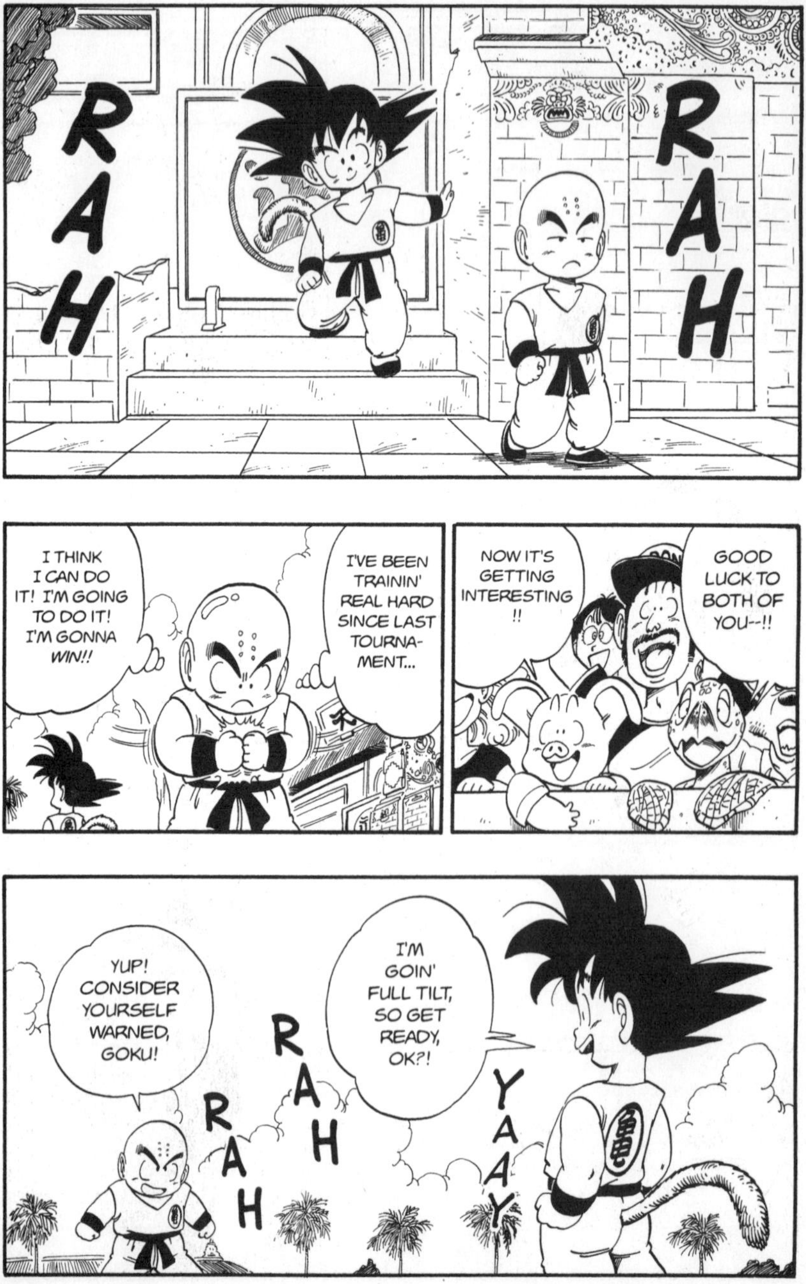
RAH
RAH
GOOD LUCK TO BOTH OF YOU--!!
NOW IT'S GETTING INTERESTING !!
I'VE BEEN TRAININ' REAL HARD SINCE LAST TOURNAMENT...
I THINK I CAN DO IT! I'M GOING TO DO IT! I'M GONNA WIN!!
I'M GOIN' FULL TILT, SO GET READY, OK?!
YAAY
RAH
RAH
YUP! CONSIDER YOURSELF WARNED, GOKU!

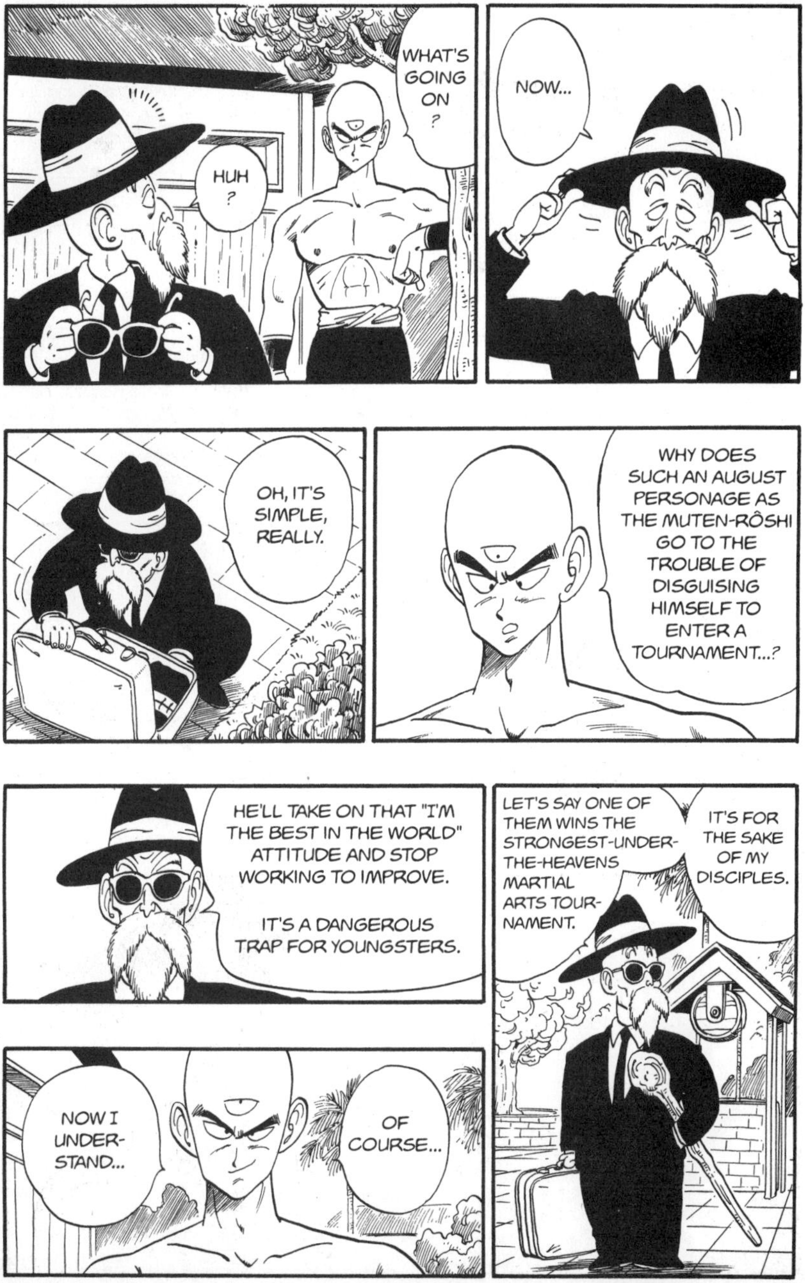
NOW...
WHAT'S GOING ON ?
HUH ?
WHY DOES SUCH AN AUGUST PERSONAGE AS THE MUTEN-RÔSHI GO TO THE TROUBLE OF DISGUISING HIMSELF TO ENTER A TOURNAMENT...?
OH, IT'S SIMPLE, REALLY.
IT'S FOR THE SAKE OF MY DISCIPLES.
LET'S SAY ONE OF THEM WINS THE STRONGEST-UNDER-THE-HEAVENS MARTIAL ARTS TOURNAMENT.
HE'LL TAKE ON THAT "I'M THE BEST IN THE WORLD" ATTITUDE AND STOP WORKING TO IMPROVE.
IT'S A DANGEROUS TRAP FOR YOUNGSTERS.
OF COURSE...
NOW I UNDERSTAND...

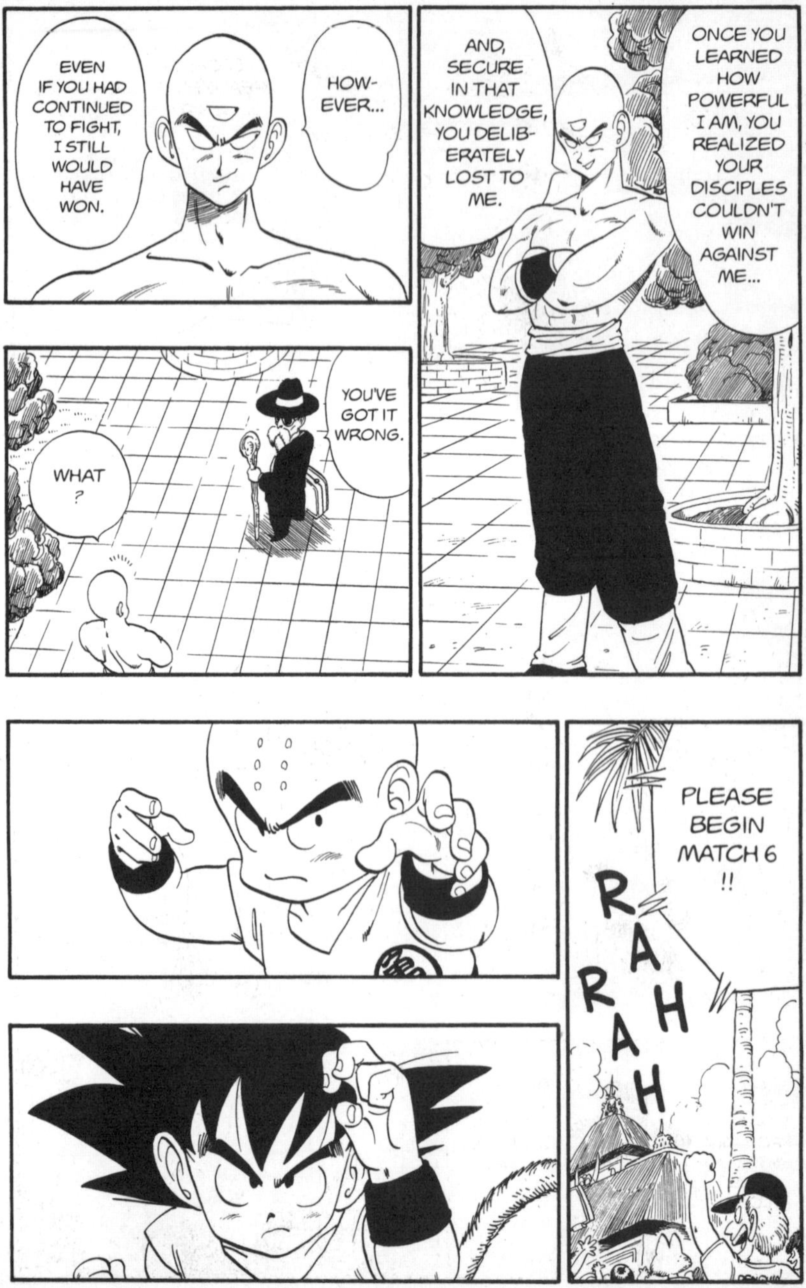
ONCE YOU LEARNED HOW POWERFUL I AM, YOU REALIZED YOUR DISCIPLES COULDN'T WIN AGAINST ME...
AND, SECURE IN THAT KNOWLEDGE, YOU DELIB-ERATELY LOST TO ME.
HOW-EVER...
EVEN IF YOU HAD CONTINUED TO FIGHT, I STILL WOULD HAVE WON.
YOU'VE GOT IT WRONG.
WHAT ?
PLEASE BEGIN MATCH 6 !!
RAH RAH

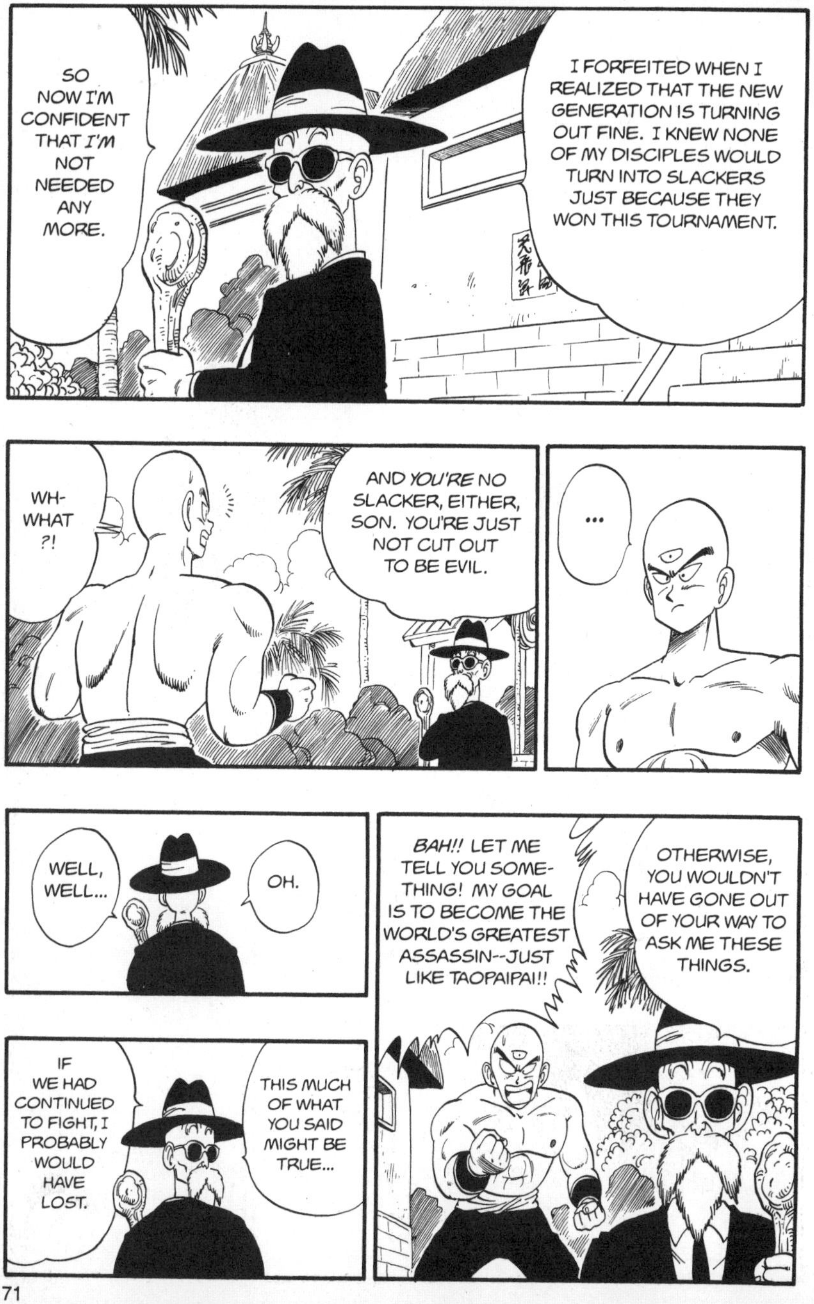

I FORFEITED WHEN I REALIZED THAT THE NEW GENERATION IS TURNING OUT FINE. I KNEW NONE OF MY DISCIPLES WOULD TURN INTO SLACKERS JUST BECAUSE THEY WON THIS TOURNAMENT.
SO NOW I'M CONFIDENT THAT *I'M* NOT NEEDED ANY MORE.
...
AND *YOU'RE* NO SLACKER, EITHER, SON. YOU'RE JUST NOT CUT OUT TO BE EVIL.
WH-WHAT?!
OTHERWISE, YOU WOULDN'T HAVE GONE OUT OF YOUR WAY TO ASK ME THESE THINGS.
BAH!! LET ME TELL YOU SOME-THING! MY GOAL IS TO BECOME THE WORLD'S GREATEST ASSASSIN--JUST LIKE TAOPAIPAI!!
OH.
WELL, WELL...
THIS MUCH OF WHAT YOU SAID MIGHT BE TRUE...
IF WE HAD CONTINUED TO FIGHT, I PROBABLY WOULD HAVE LOST.

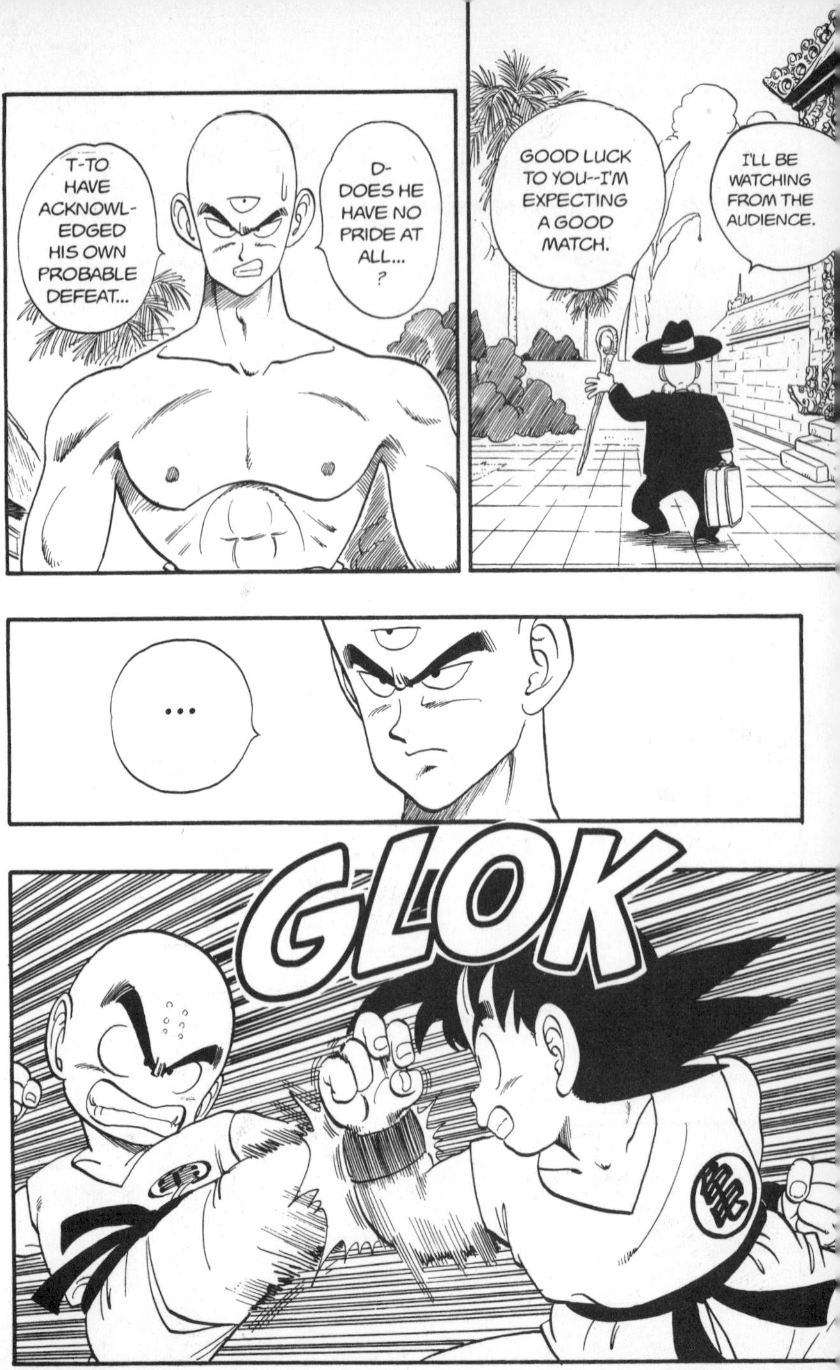
I'LL BE WATCHING FROM THE AUDIENCE.
GOOD LUCK TO YOU--I'M EXPECTING A GOOD MATCH.
D- DOES HE HAVE NO PRIDE AT ALL...?
T-TO HAVE ACKNOWL-EDGED HIS OWN PROBABLE DEFEAT...
...
GLOK

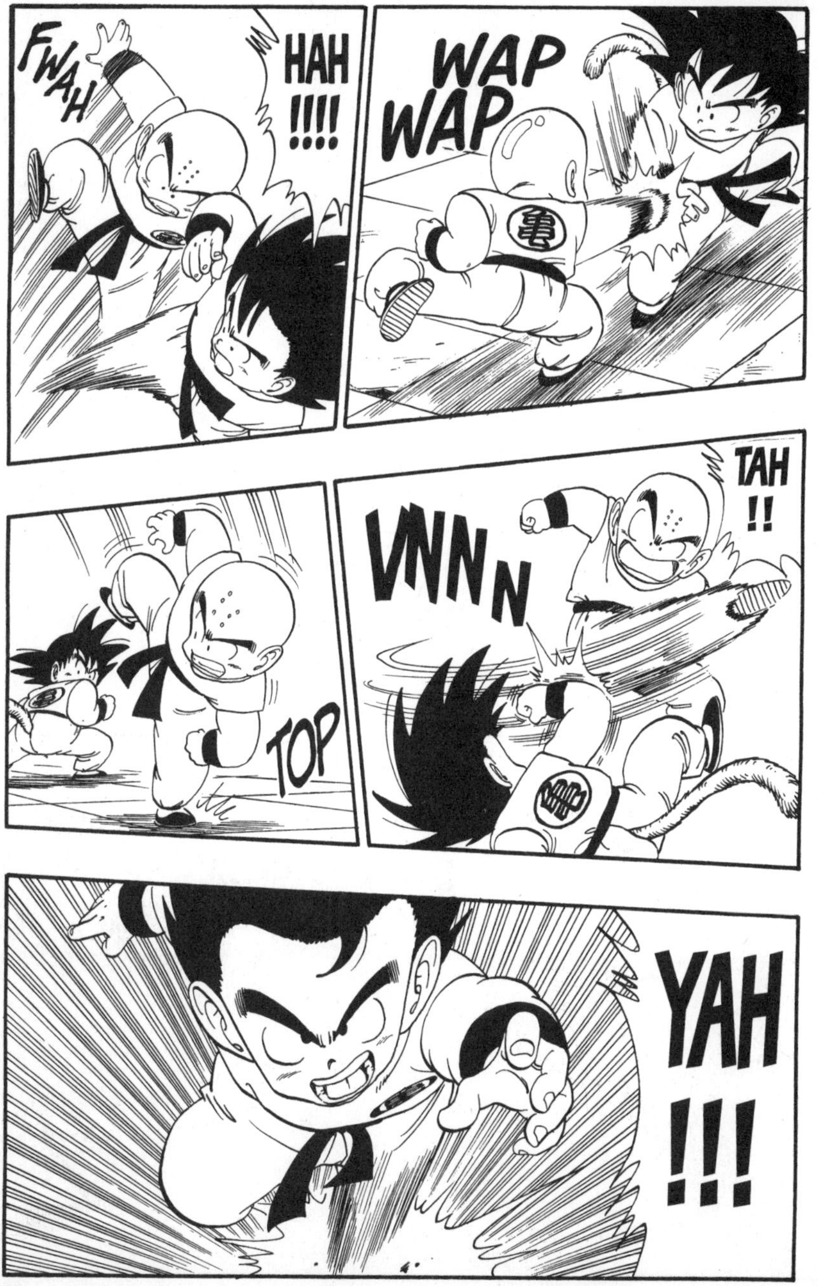
WAP WAP
HAH!!!!
FWAH
TAH!!
VNNN
TOP
YAH!!!

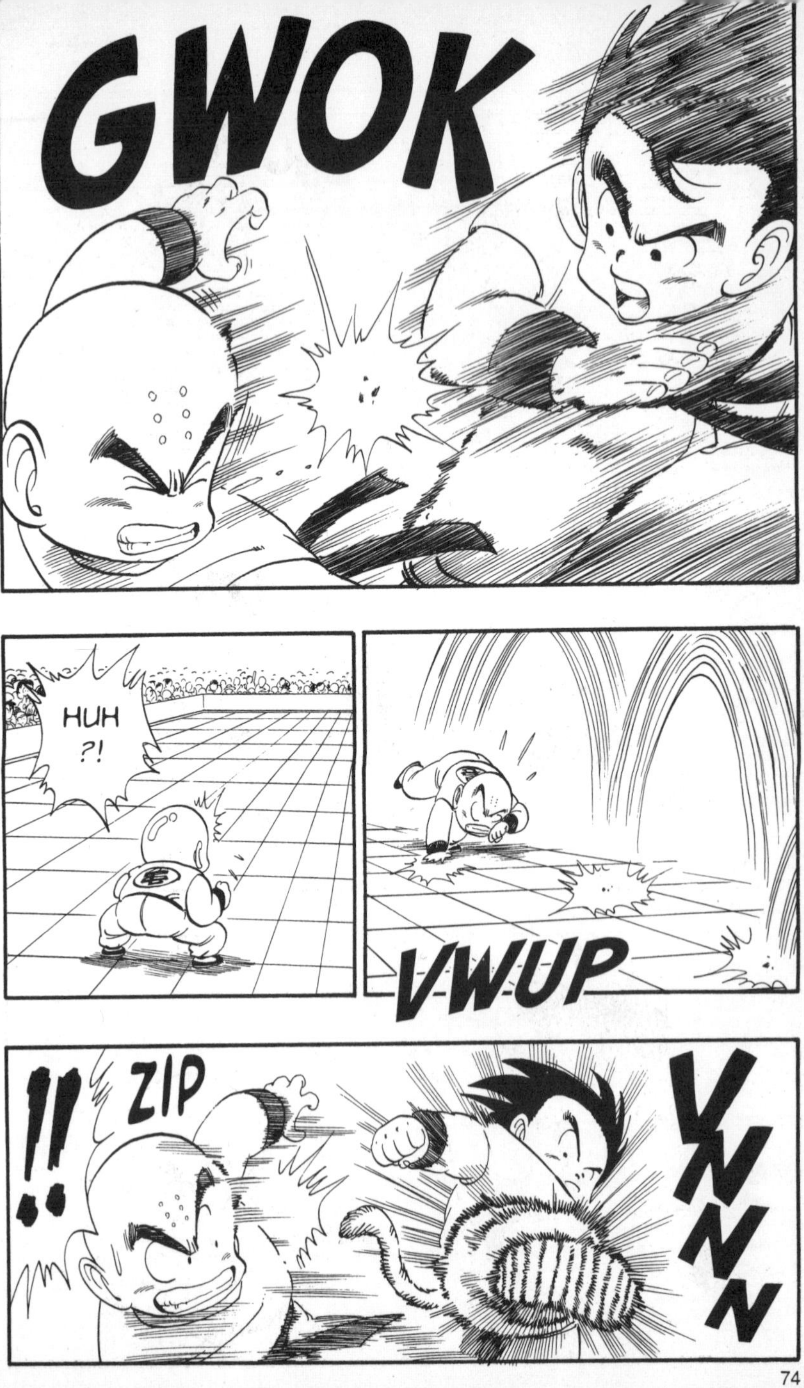
GWOK
VWUP
HUH ?!
VNNN
ZIP
!!

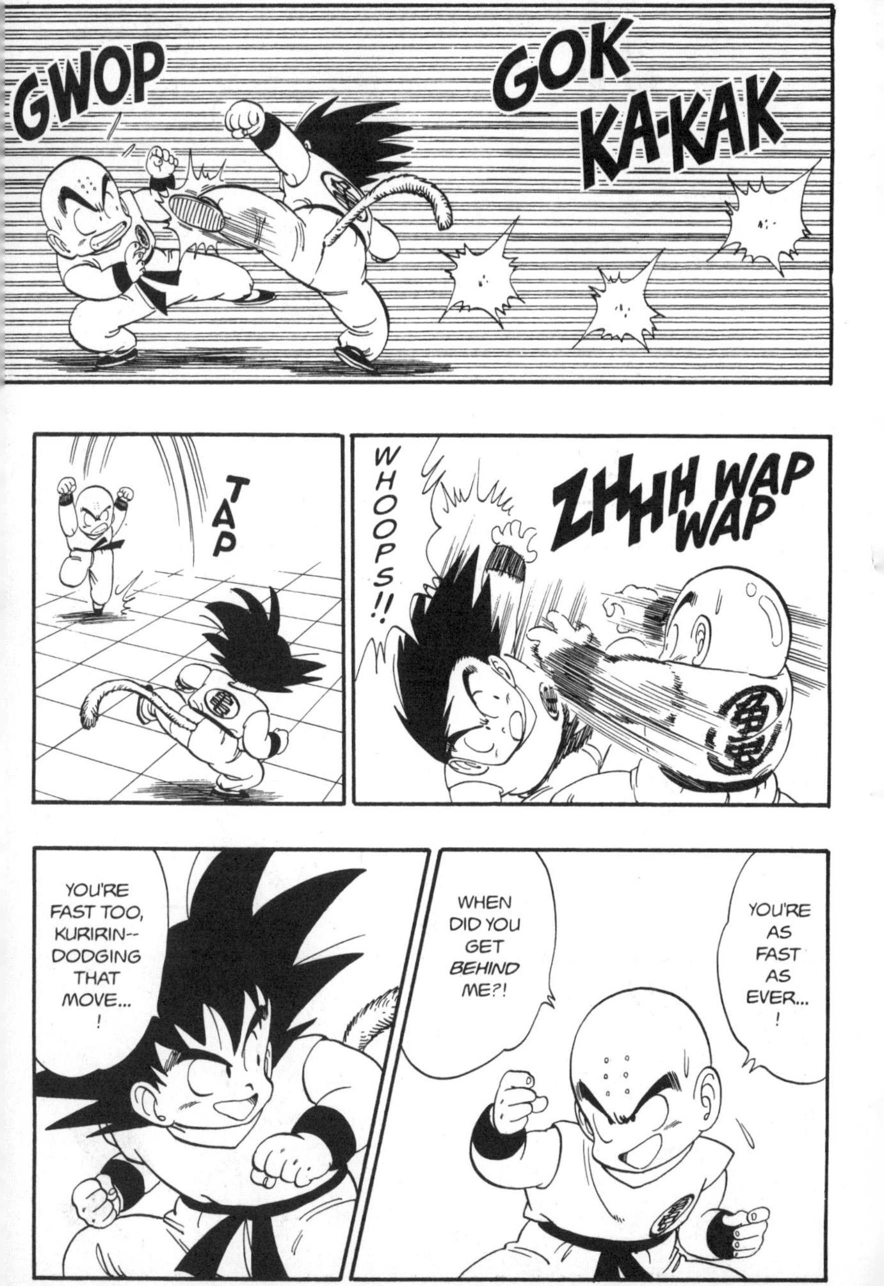
GOK
KA-KAK
GWOP
ZHHH WAP WAP
WHOOPS!!
TAP
YOU'RE AS FAST AS EVER...!
WHEN DID YOU GET BEHIND ME?!
YOU'RE FAST TOO, KURIRIN-- DODGING THAT MOVE...!

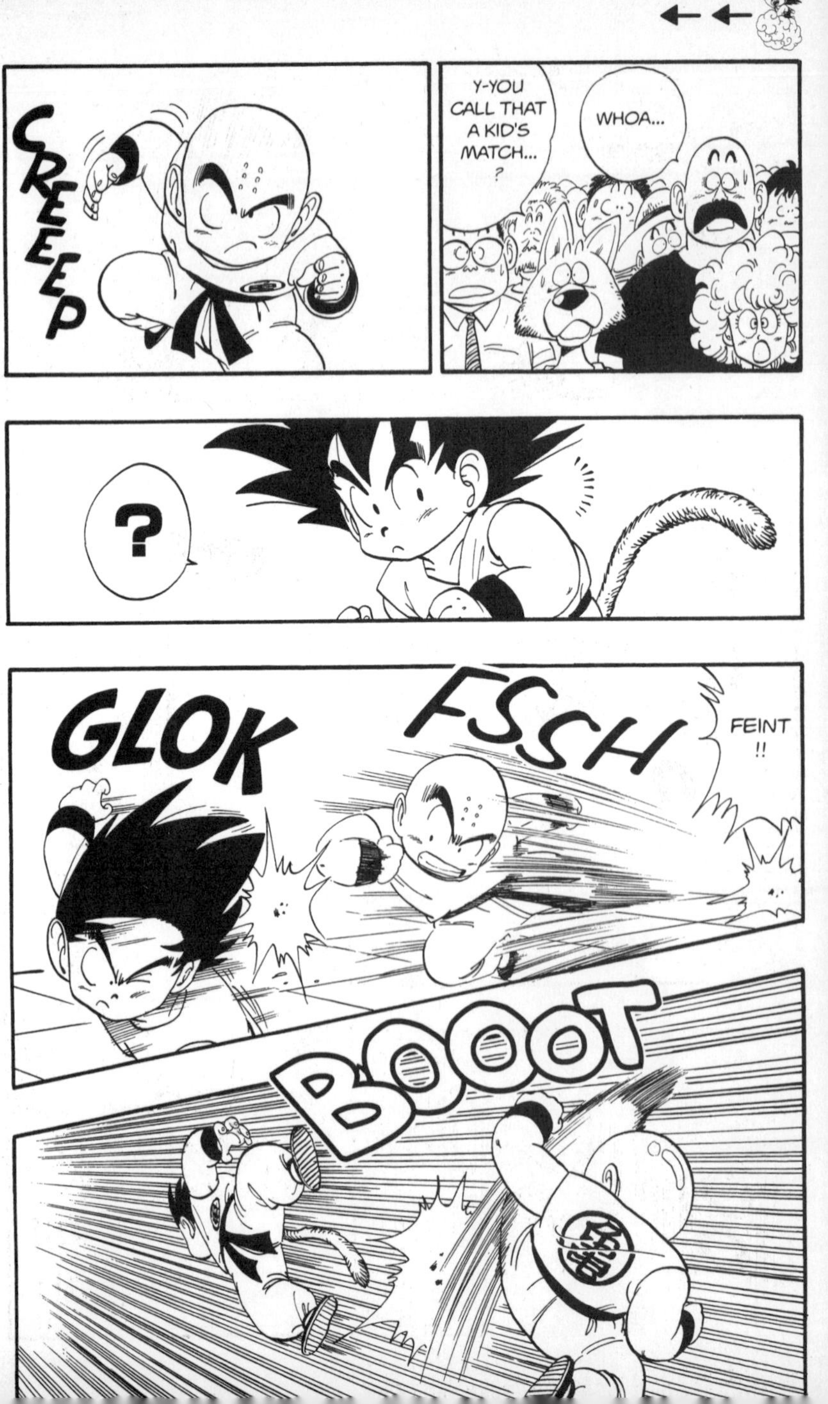
WHOA...
Y-YOU CALL THAT A KID'S MATCH...?
CREEEP
?
FEINT !!
FSSH
GLOK
BOOOT

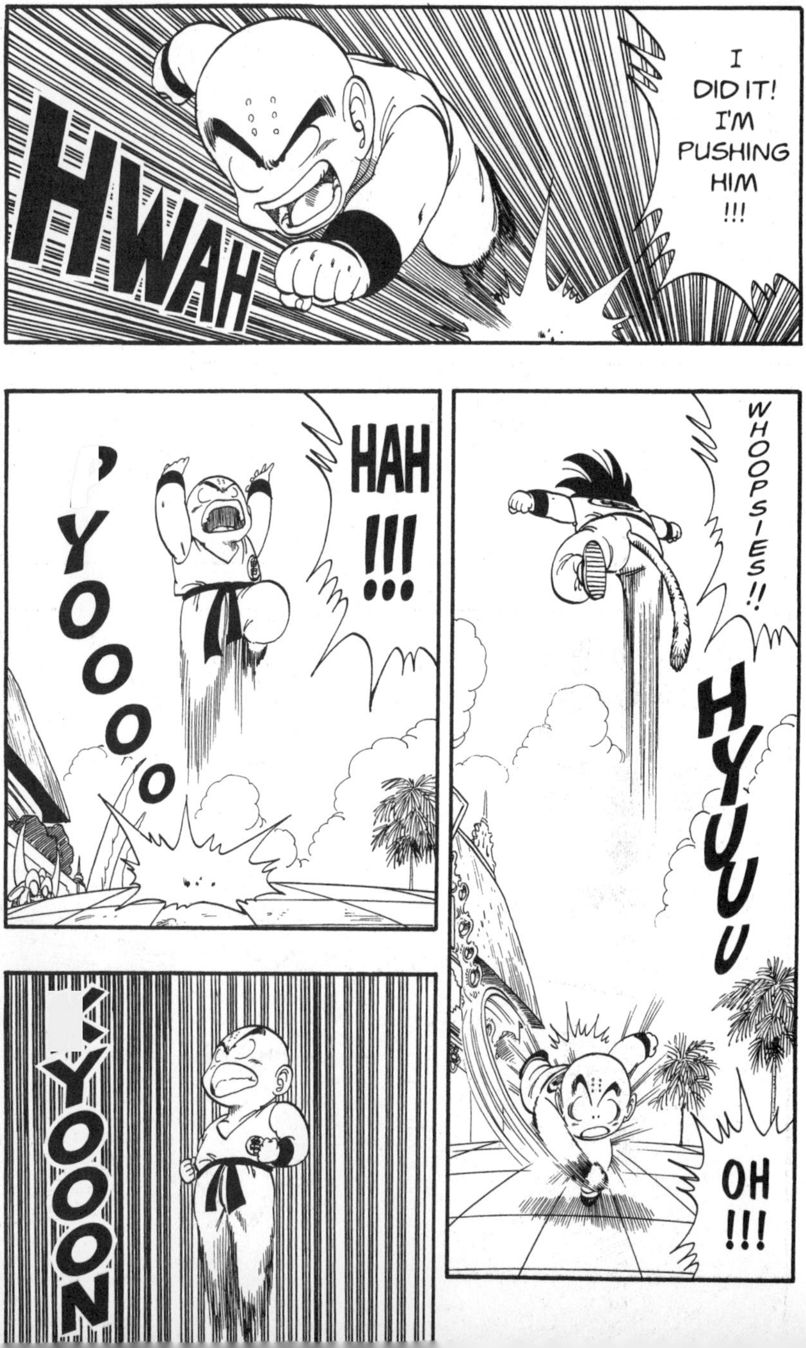
HWAH
I DID IT! I'M PUSHING HIM!!!
WHOOPSIES!!
HYUUUU
OH!!!
HAH!!!
PYOOOOO
KYOOON

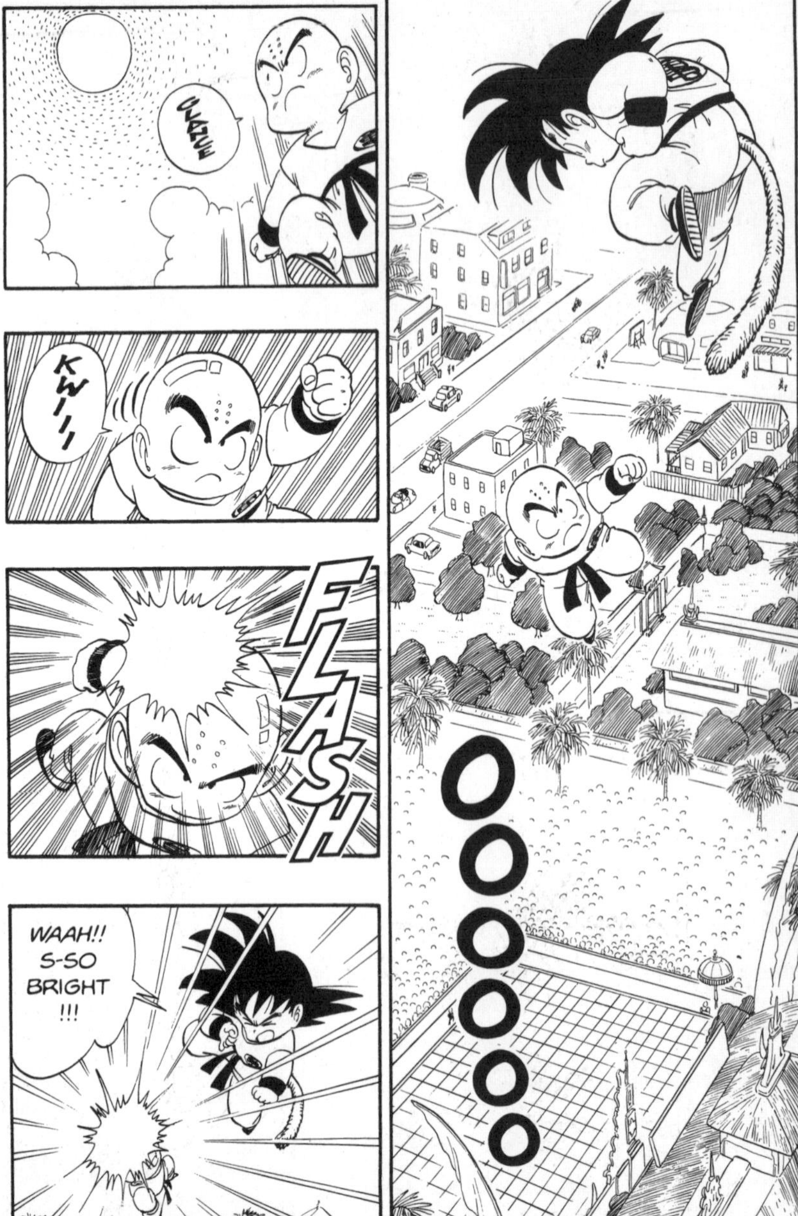
OOOOOOOO
GLANCE
KWIII
FLASH
WAAH!! S-SO BRIGHT !!!

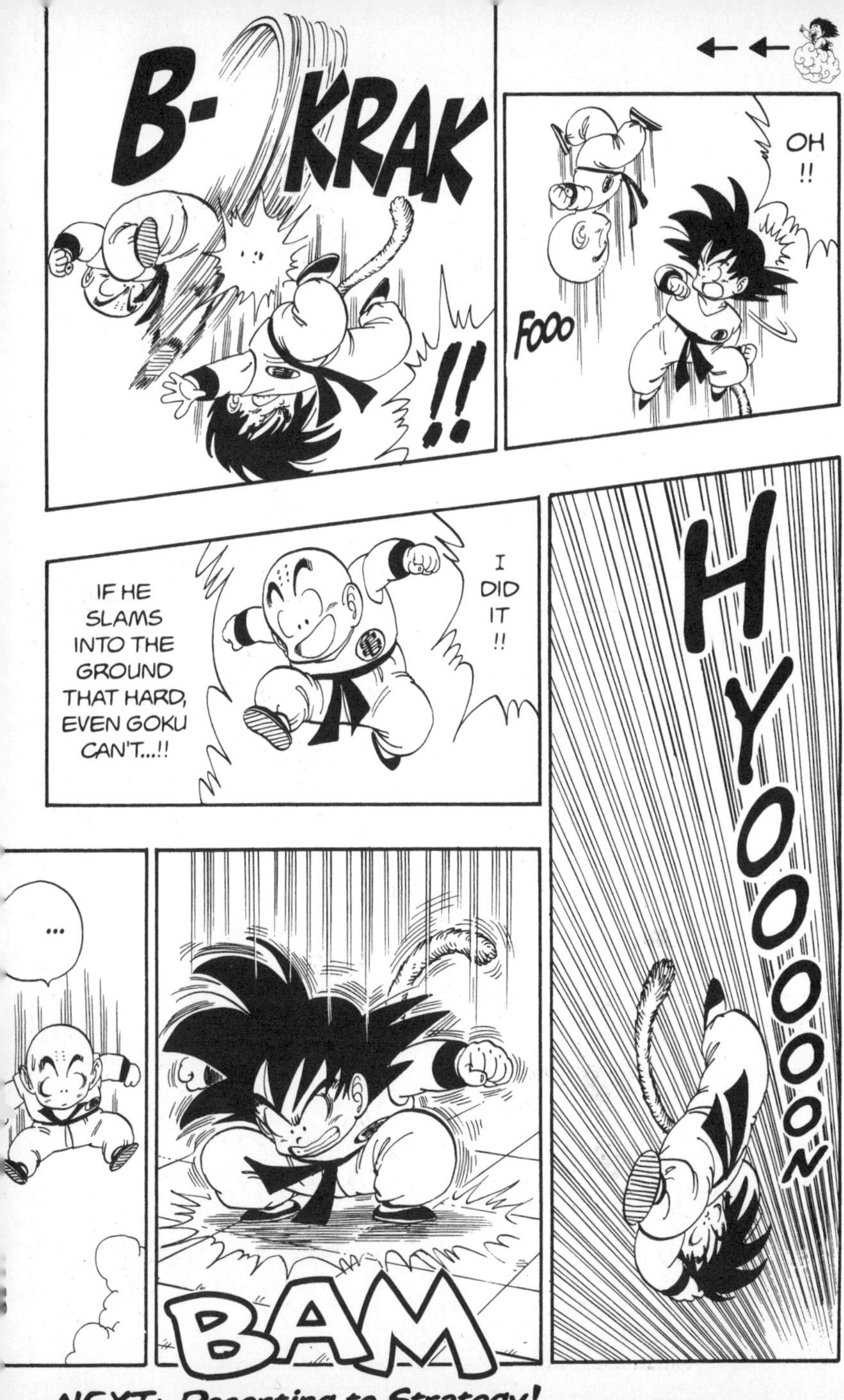
OH !!
FOOO
B- KRAK !!
HYOOOOOOON
I DID IT !!
IF HE SLAMS INTO THE GROUND THAT HARD, EVEN GOKU CAN'T...!!
BAM
...

NEXT: Resorting to Strategy!

Tale 126
Goku vs. Kuririn, Part 2

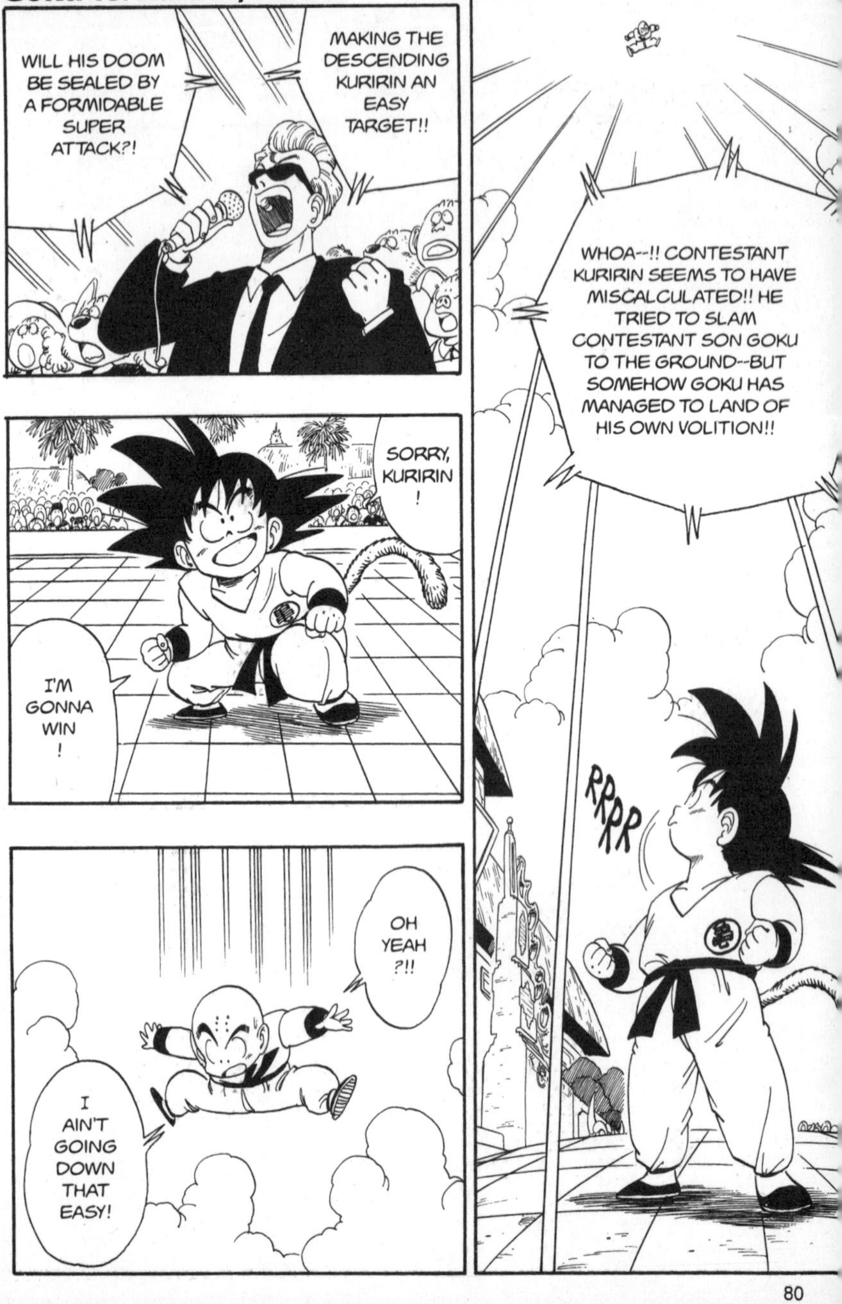

WILL HIS DOOM BE SEALED BY A FORMIDABLE SUPER ATTACK?!
MAKING THE DESCENDING KURIRIN AN EASY TARGET!!
I'M GONNA WIN!
SORRY, KURIRIN!
I AIN'T GOING DOWN THAT EASY!
OH YEAH?!!
WHOA--!! CONTESTANT KURIRIN SEEMS TO HAVE MISCALCULATED!! HE TRIED TO SLAM CONTESTANT SON GOKU TO THE GROUND--BUT SOMEHOW GOKU HAS MANAGED TO LAND OF HIS OWN VOLITION!!
RRRR

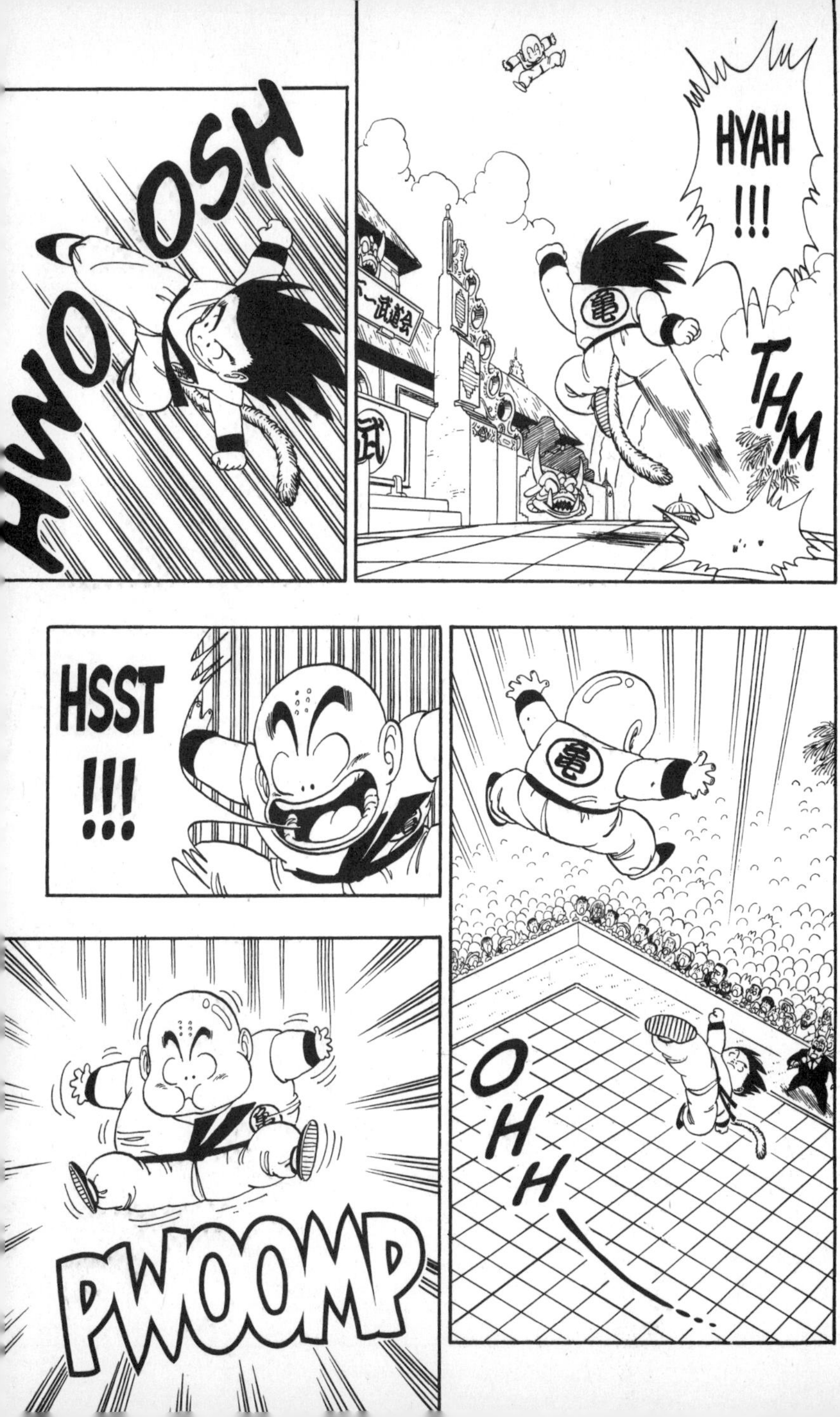
HYAH !!!
THM
WHOOSH
OHH
HSST !!!
PWOOMP

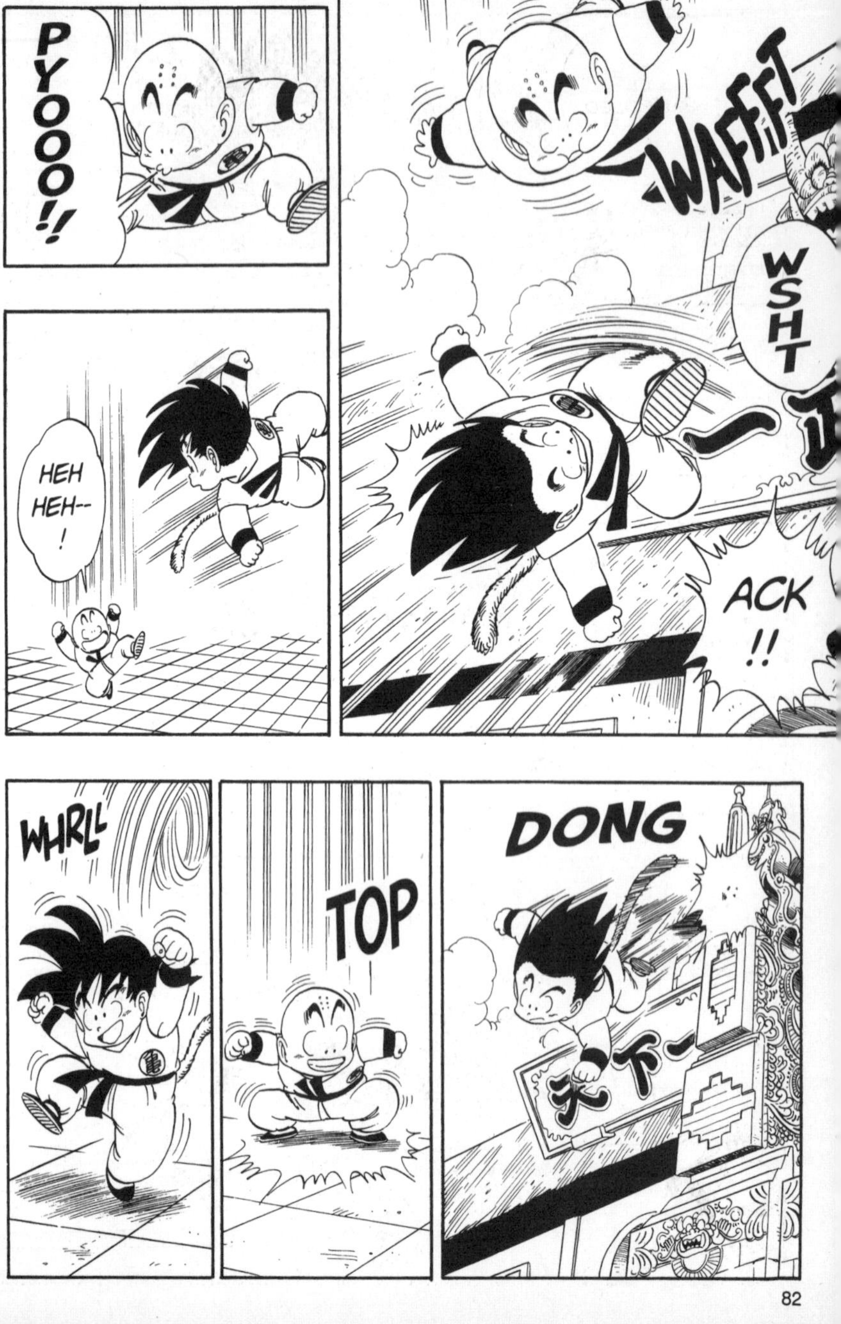
WAFFFT
WSHT
ACK!!
PYOOO!!
HEH HEH--!
DONG
TOP
WHRLL

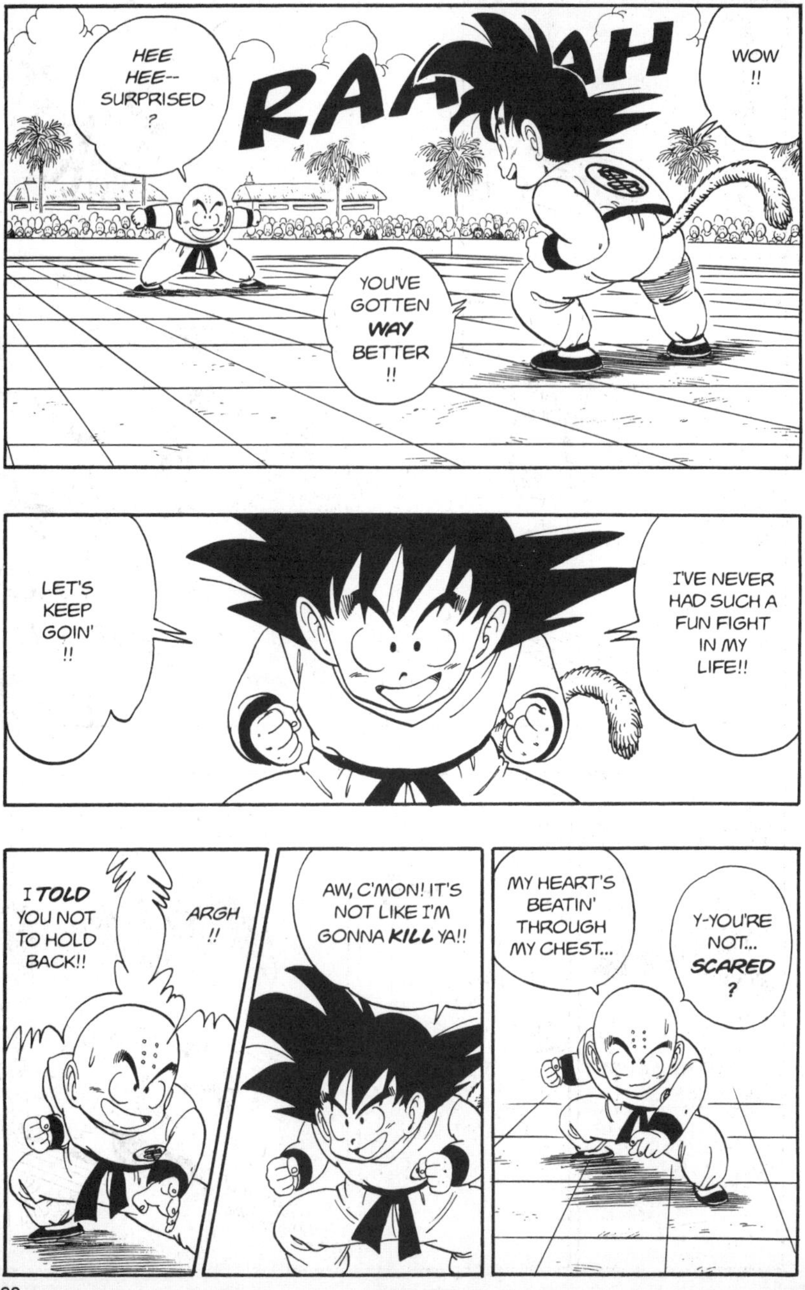
WOW !!
RAAAAH
HEE HEE-- SURPRISED ?
YOU'VE GOTTEN **WAY** BETTER !!
I'VE NEVER HAD SUCH A FUN FIGHT IN MY LIFE!!
LET'S KEEP GOIN' !!
Y-YOU'RE NOT... **SCARED** ?
MY HEART'S BEATIN' THROUGH MY CHEST...
AW, C'MON! IT'S NOT LIKE I'M GONNA **KILL** YA!!
ARGH !!
I **TOLD** YOU NOT TO HOLD BACK!!

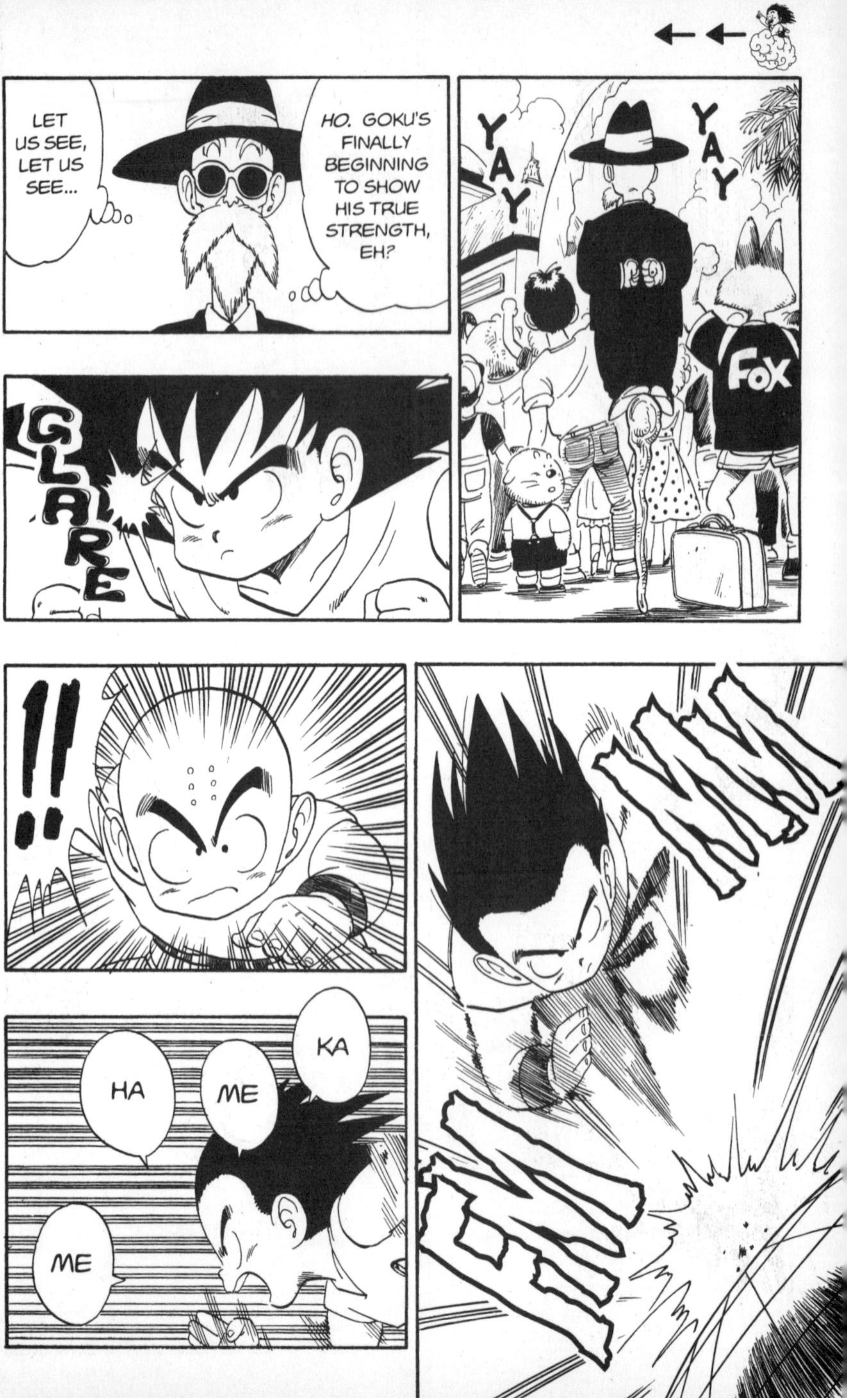
YAY
YAY
HO. GOKU'S FINALLY BEGINNING TO SHOW HIS TRUE STRENGTH, EH?
LET US SEE, LET US SEE...
GLARE
!!
KA
ME
HA
ME

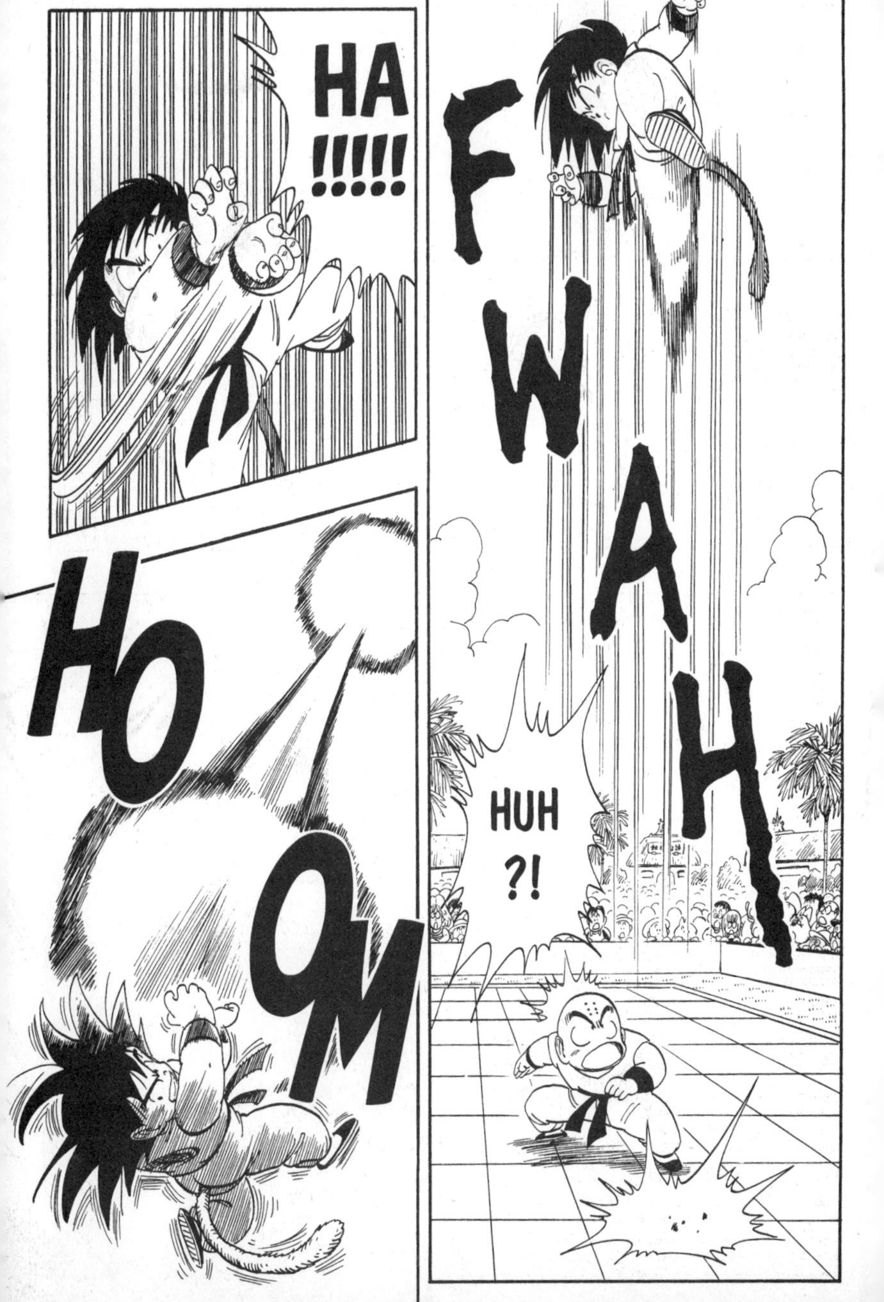
FWAH
HUH ?!
HA !!!!!
HOOM

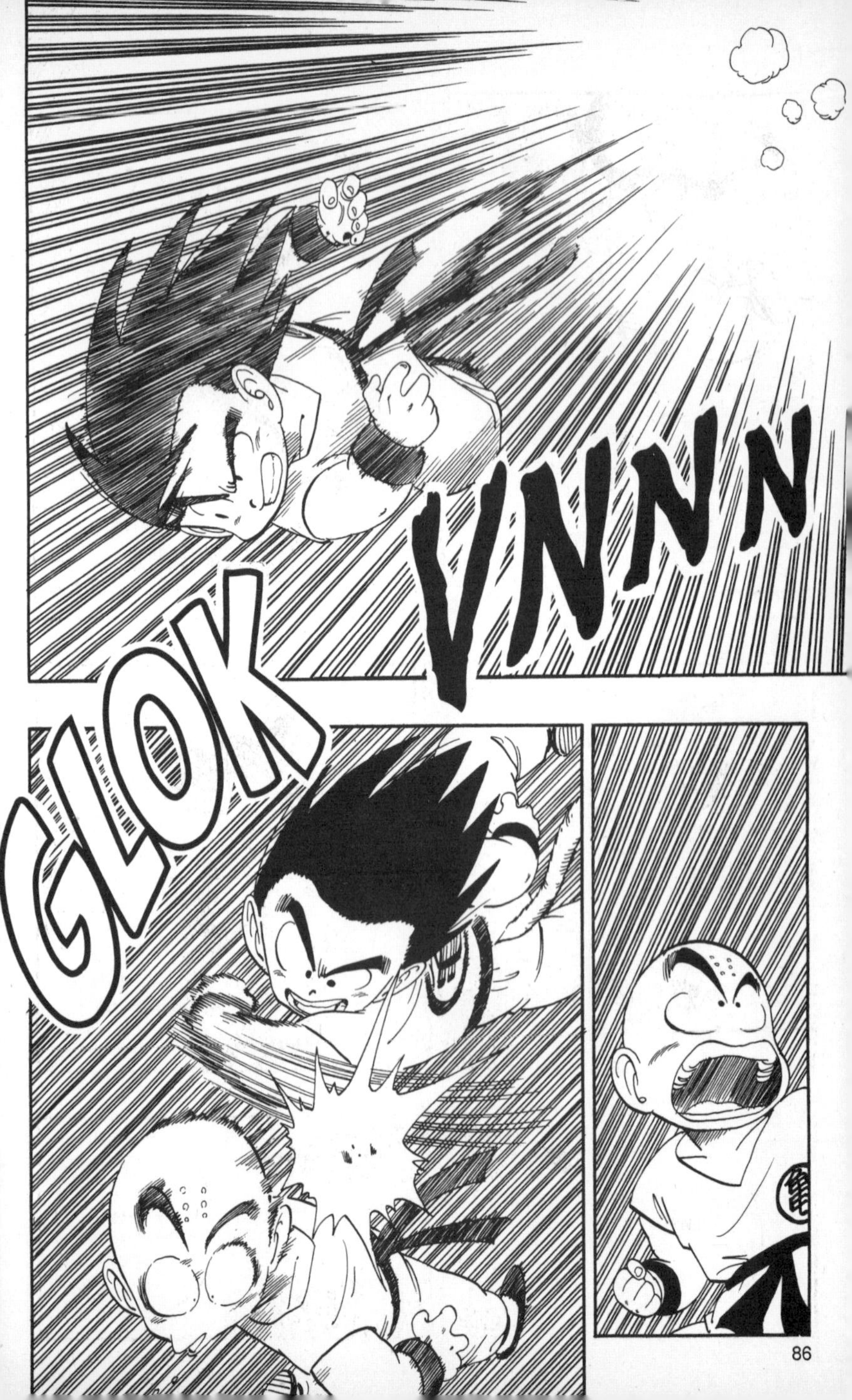
VNNN
GLOK

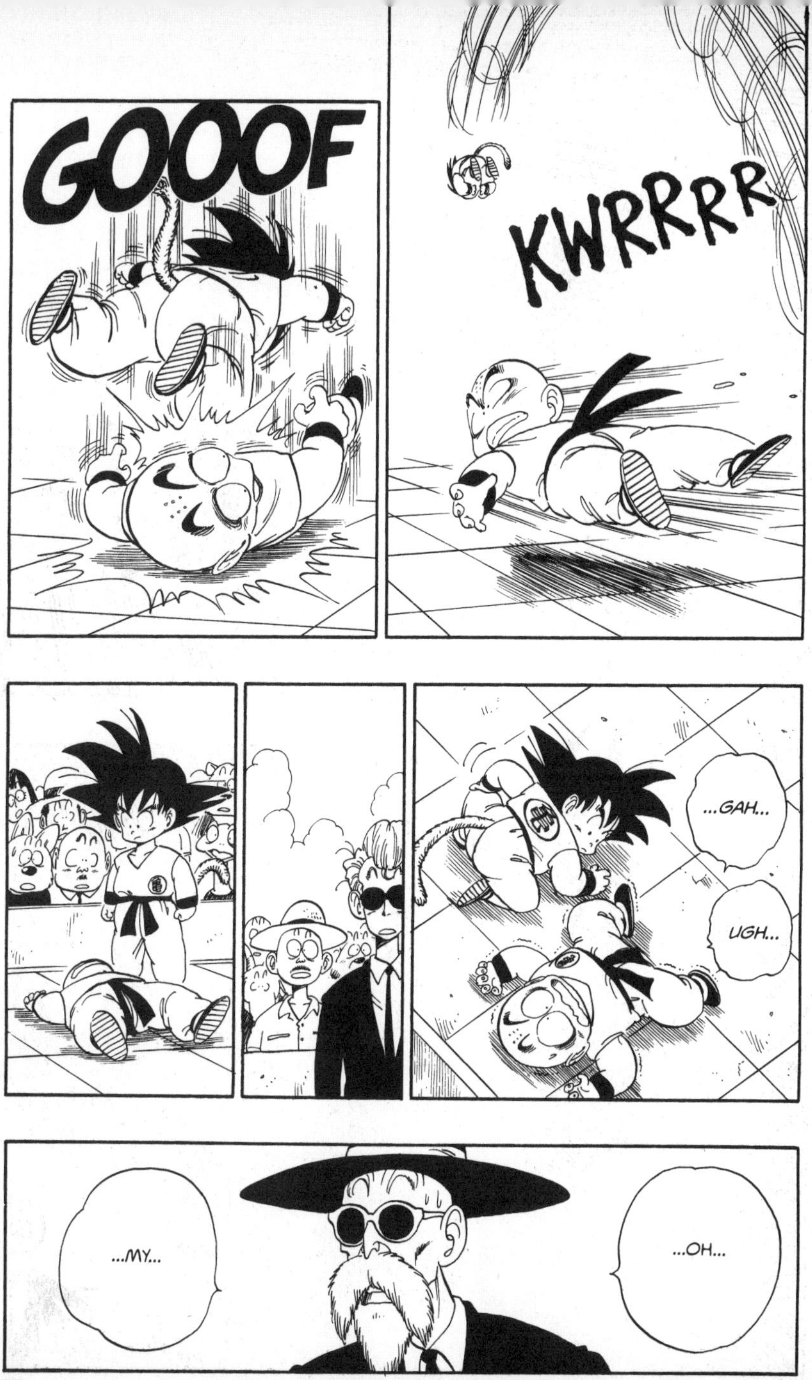
KWRRRR
GOOOF
...GAH...
UGH...
...OH...
...MY...

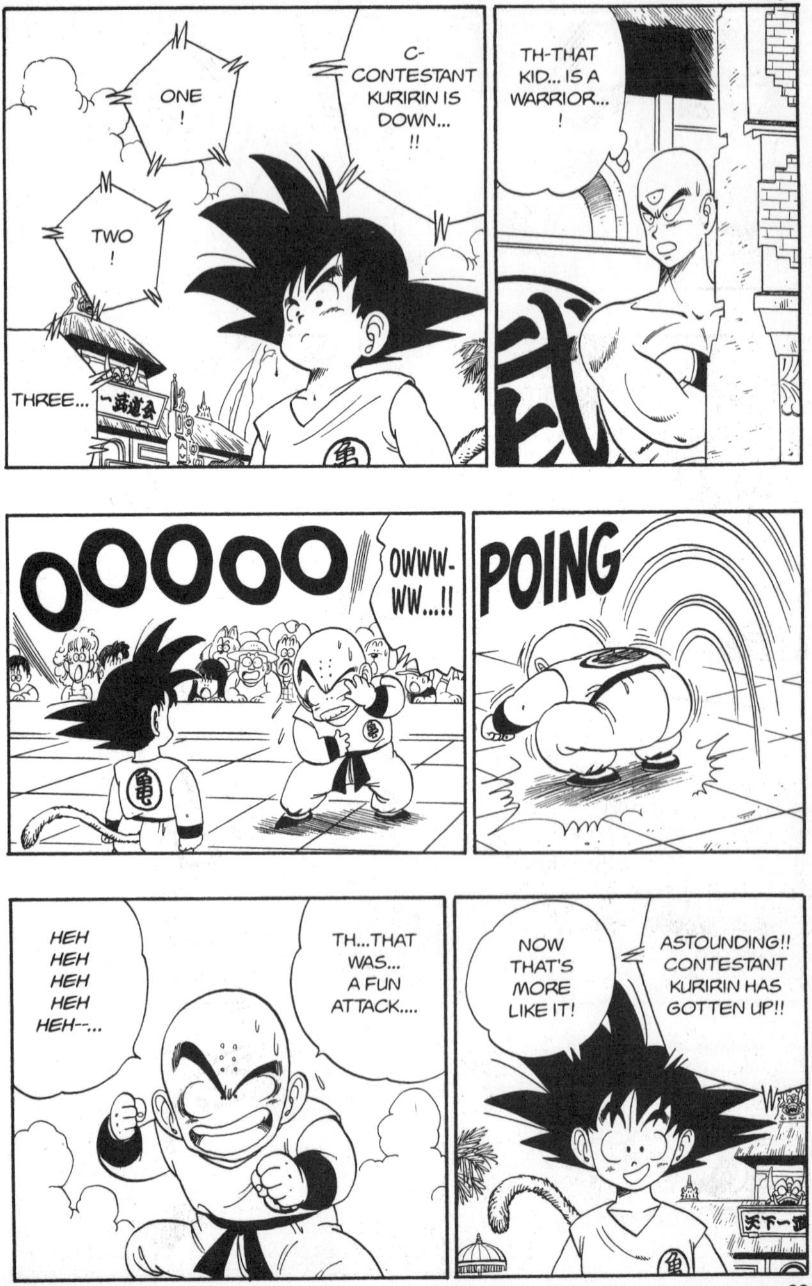
TH-THAT KID... IS A WARRIOR...!
C- CONTESTANT KURIRIN IS DOWN...!!
ONE!
TWO!
THREE...
POING
OWWW-WW...!!
OOOOO
ASTOUNDING!! CONTESTANT KURIRIN HAS GOTTEN UP!!
NOW THAT'S MORE LIKE IT!
TH...THAT WAS... A FUN ATTACK....
HEH HEH HEH HEH HEH--...

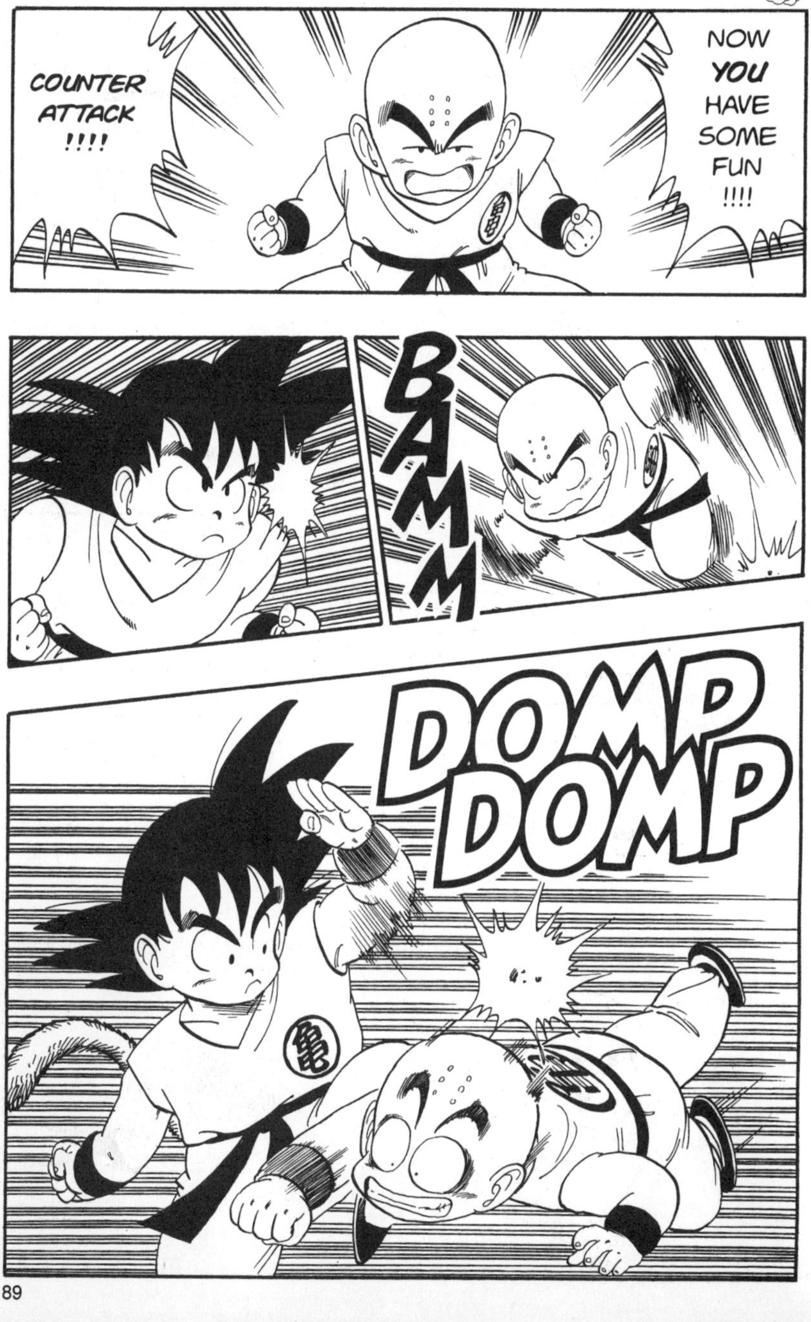
NOW YOU HAVE SOME FUN !!!!
COUNTER ATTACK !!!!
BAMM
DOMP DOMP

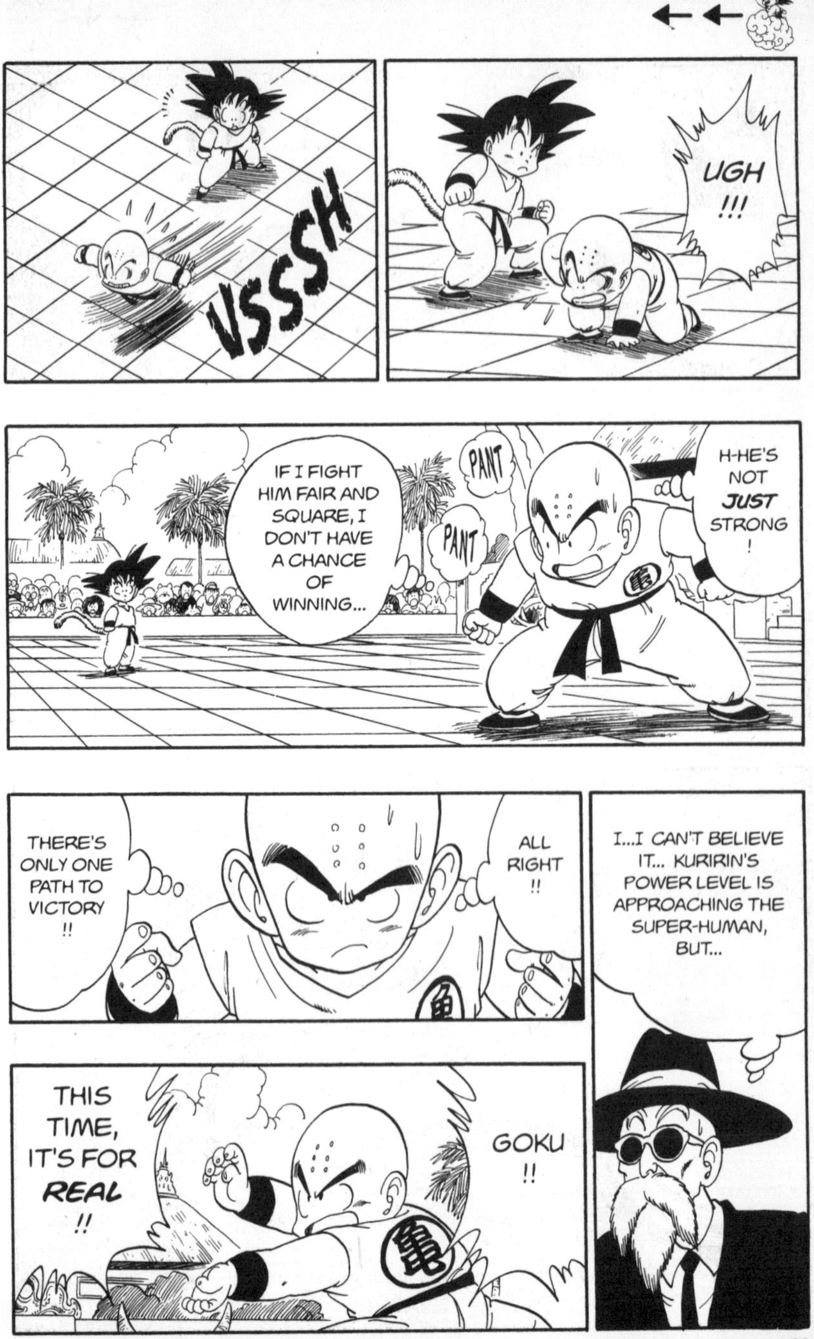
UGH !!!
VSSSH
H-HE'S NOT JUST STRONG !
PANT
PANT
IF I FIGHT HIM FAIR AND SQUARE, I DON'T HAVE A CHANCE OF WINNING...
I...I CAN'T BELIEVE IT... KURIRIN'S POWER LEVEL IS APPROACHING THE SUPER-HUMAN, BUT...
ALL RIGHT !!
THERE'S ONLY ONE PATH TO VICTORY !!
GOKU !!
THIS TIME, IT'S FOR REAL !!

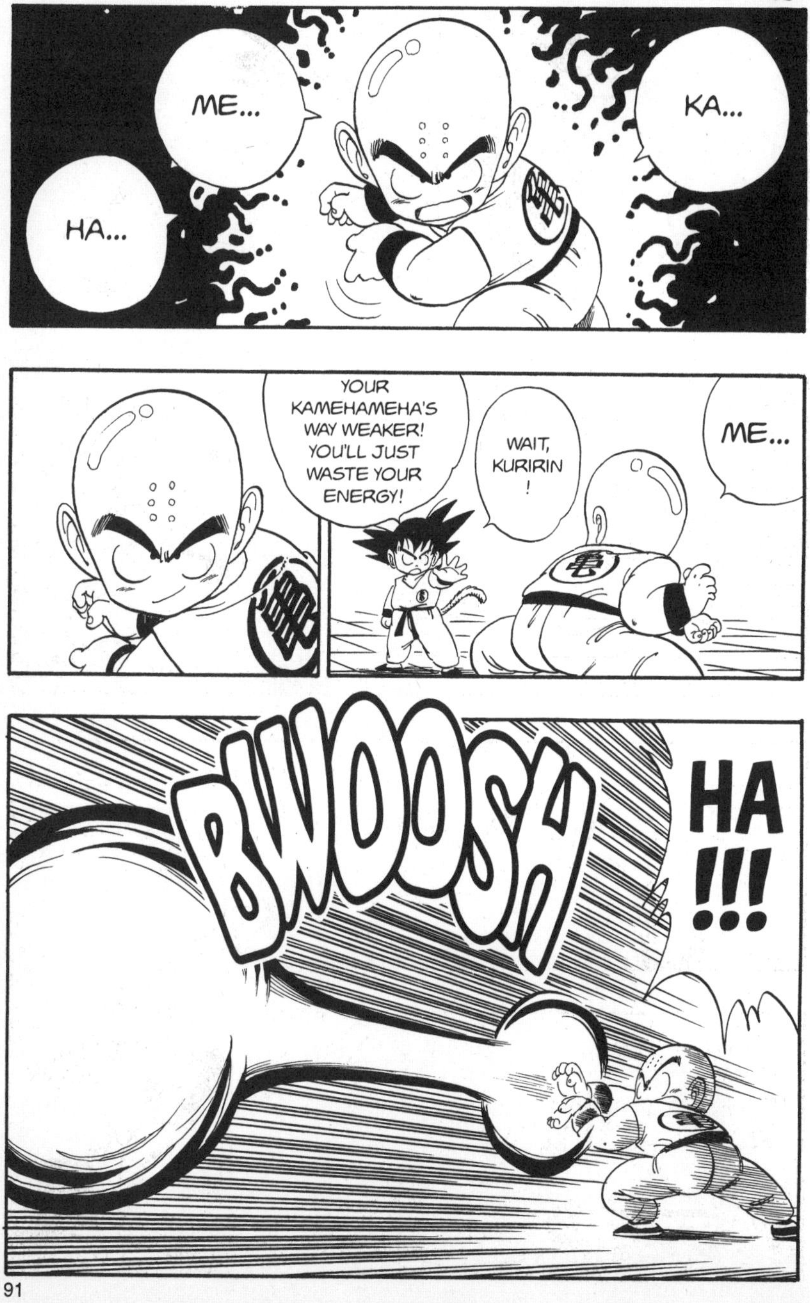
KA...
ME...
HA...
ME...
WAIT, KURIRIN!
YOUR KAMEHAMEHA'S WAY WEAKER! YOU'LL JUST WASTE YOUR ENERGY!
HA!!!
BWOOSH

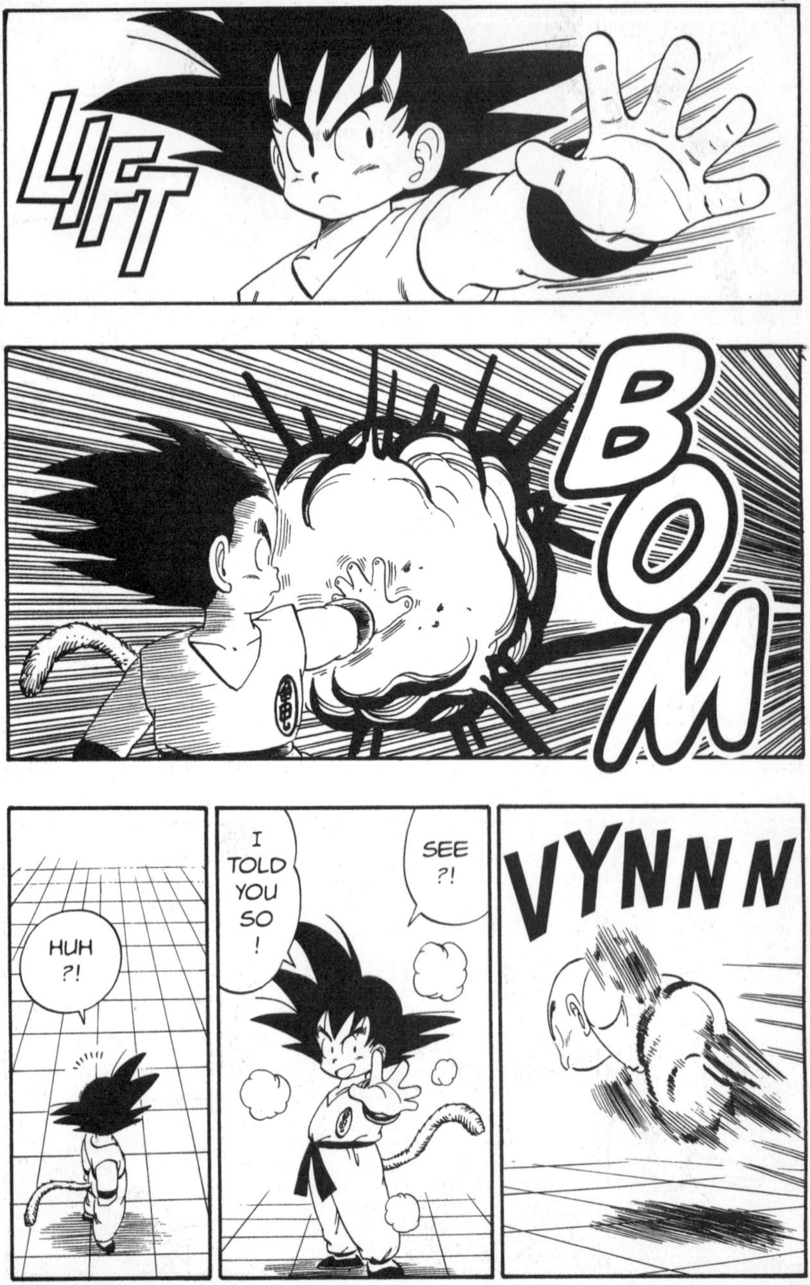
LIFT
BOOM
VYNNN
SEE ?!
I TOLD YOU SO !
HUH ?!

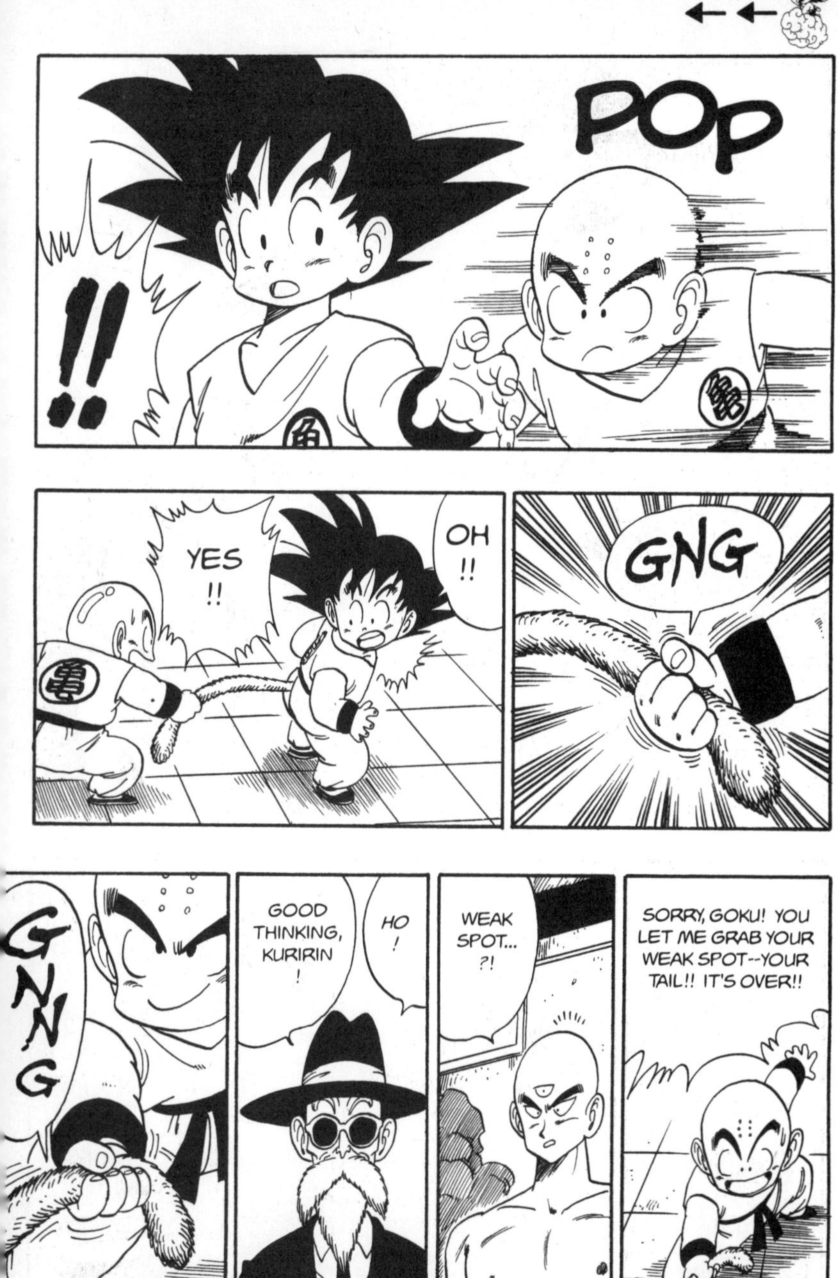
POP
!!
GNG
OH !!
YES !!
SORRY, GOKU! YOU LET ME GRAB YOUR WEAK SPOT--YOUR TAIL!! IT'S OVER!!
WEAK SPOT... ?!
HO !
GOOD THINKING, KURIRIN !
GNNG

NEXT: Kuririn 1, Tail 0

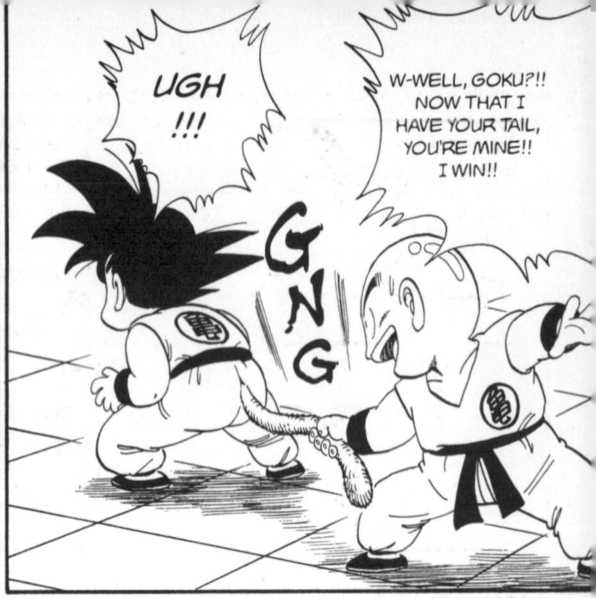
W-WELL, GOKU?!! NOW THAT I HAVE YOUR TAIL, YOU'RE MINE!! I WIN!!
UGH !!!
GNG

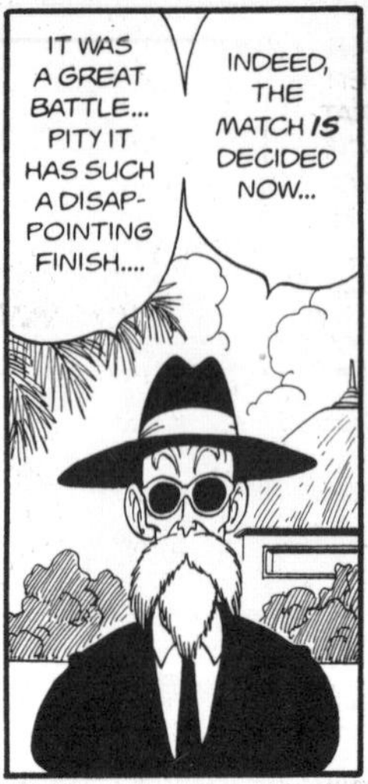
INDEED, THE MATCH IS DECIDED NOW...
IT WAS A GREAT BATTLE... PITY IT HAS SUCH A DISAPPOINTING FINISH....

Tale 127 • Goku vs. Kuririn, Part 3

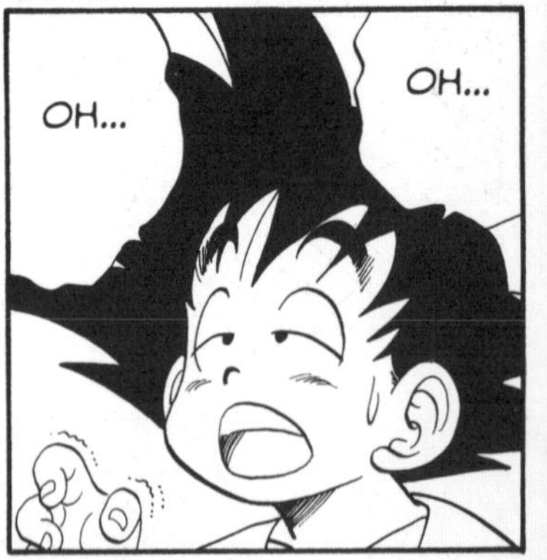
OH...
OH...

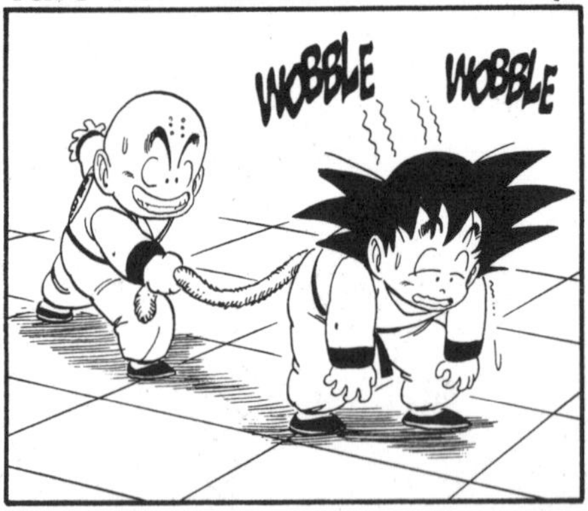
WOBBLE
WOBBLE

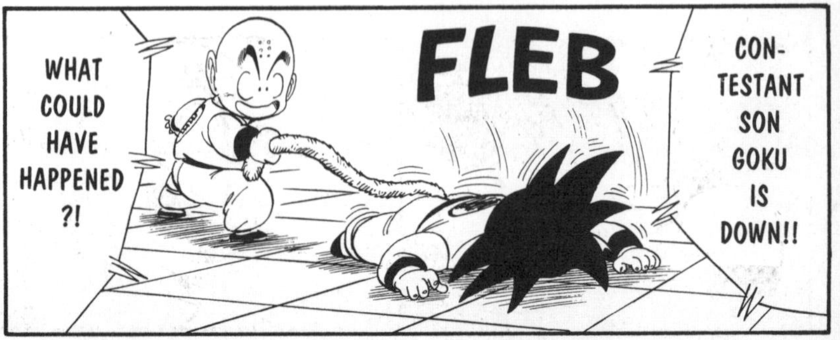
CONTESTANT SON GOKU IS DOWN!!
FLEB
WHAT COULD HAVE HAPPENED ?!

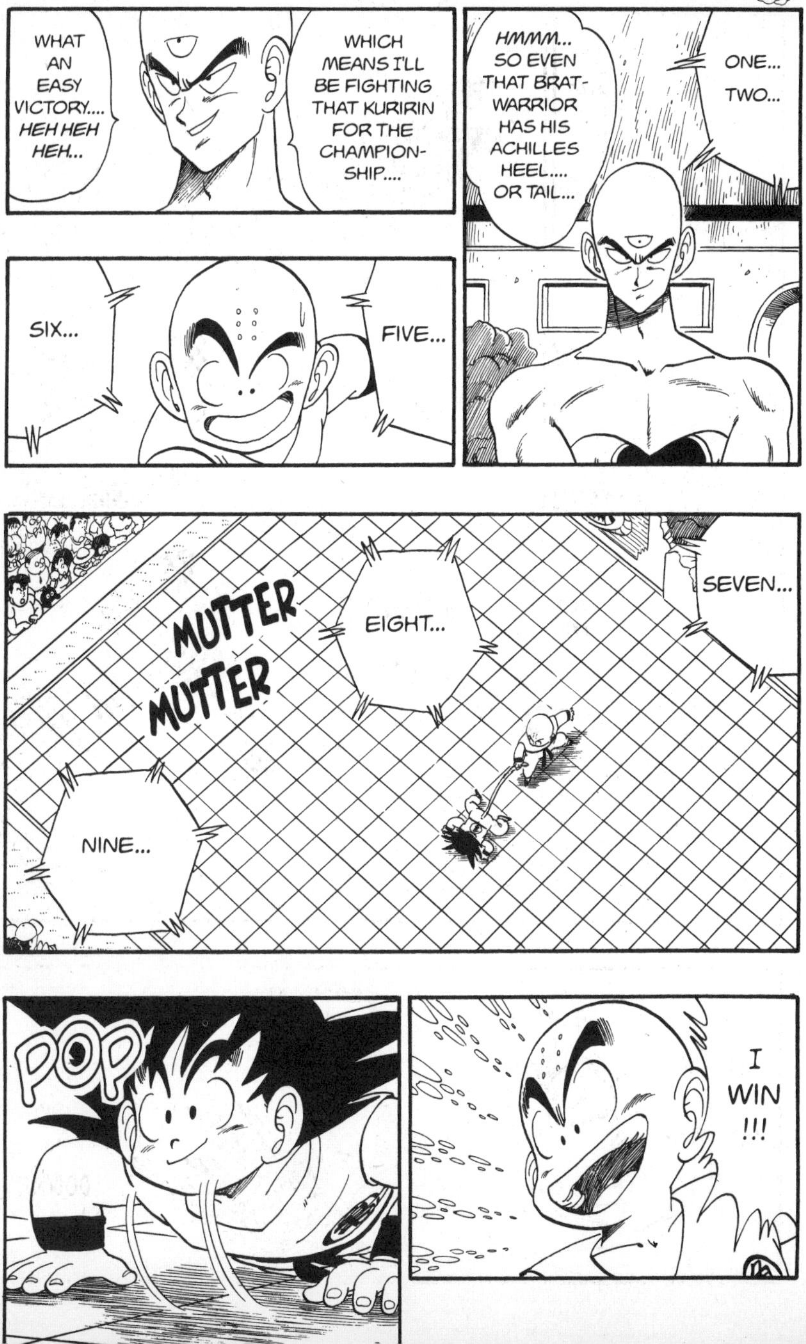
ONE... TWO...
HMMM... SO EVEN THAT BRAT-WARRIOR HAS HIS ACHILLES HEEL.... OR TAIL...
WHICH MEANS I'LL BE FIGHTING THAT KURIRIN FOR THE CHAMPIONSHIP....
WHAT AN EASY VICTORY.... HEH HEH HEH...
FIVE...
SIX...
SEVEN...
EIGHT...
MUTTER MUTTER
NINE...
I WIN !!!
POP

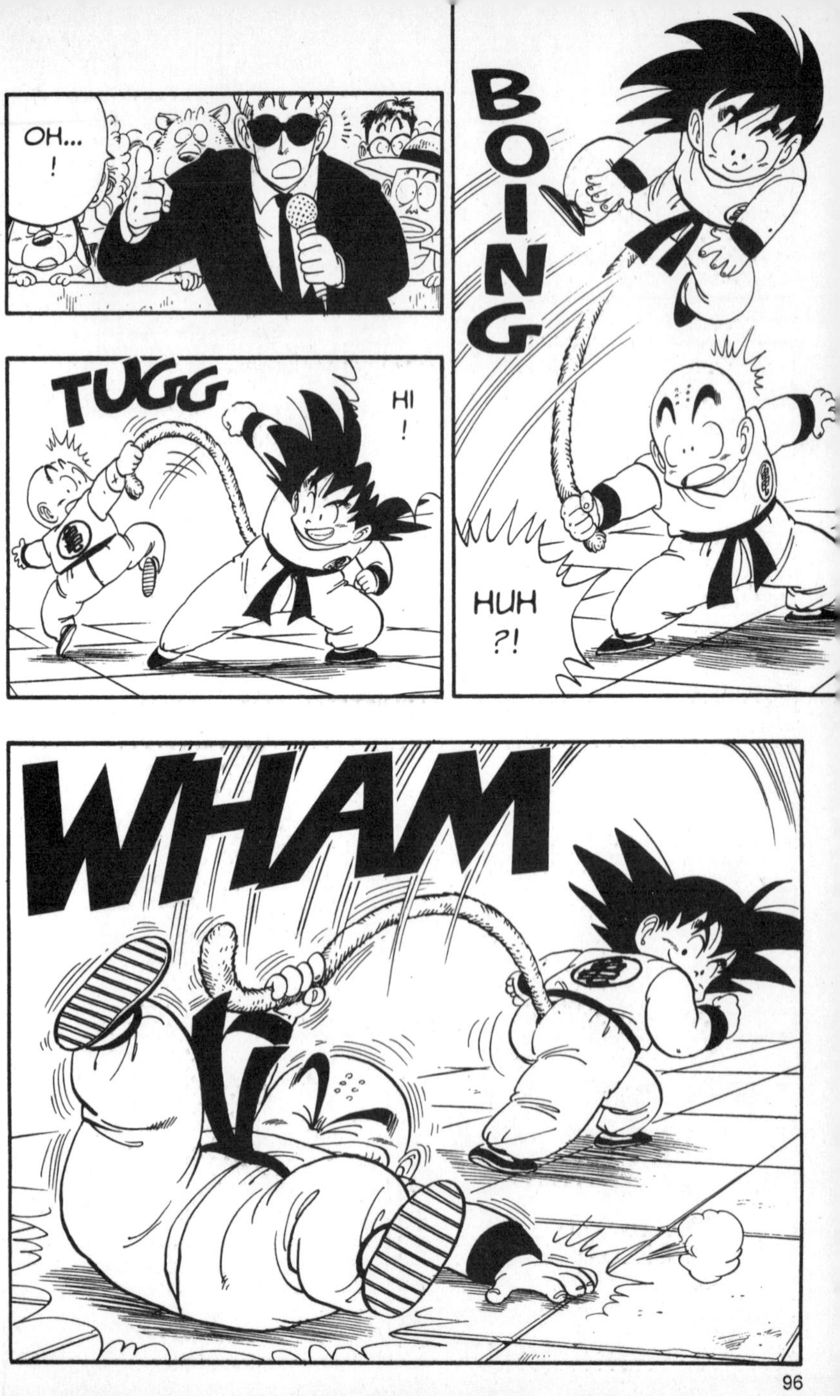
BOING
HUH ?!
OH... !
TUGG
HI !
WHAM

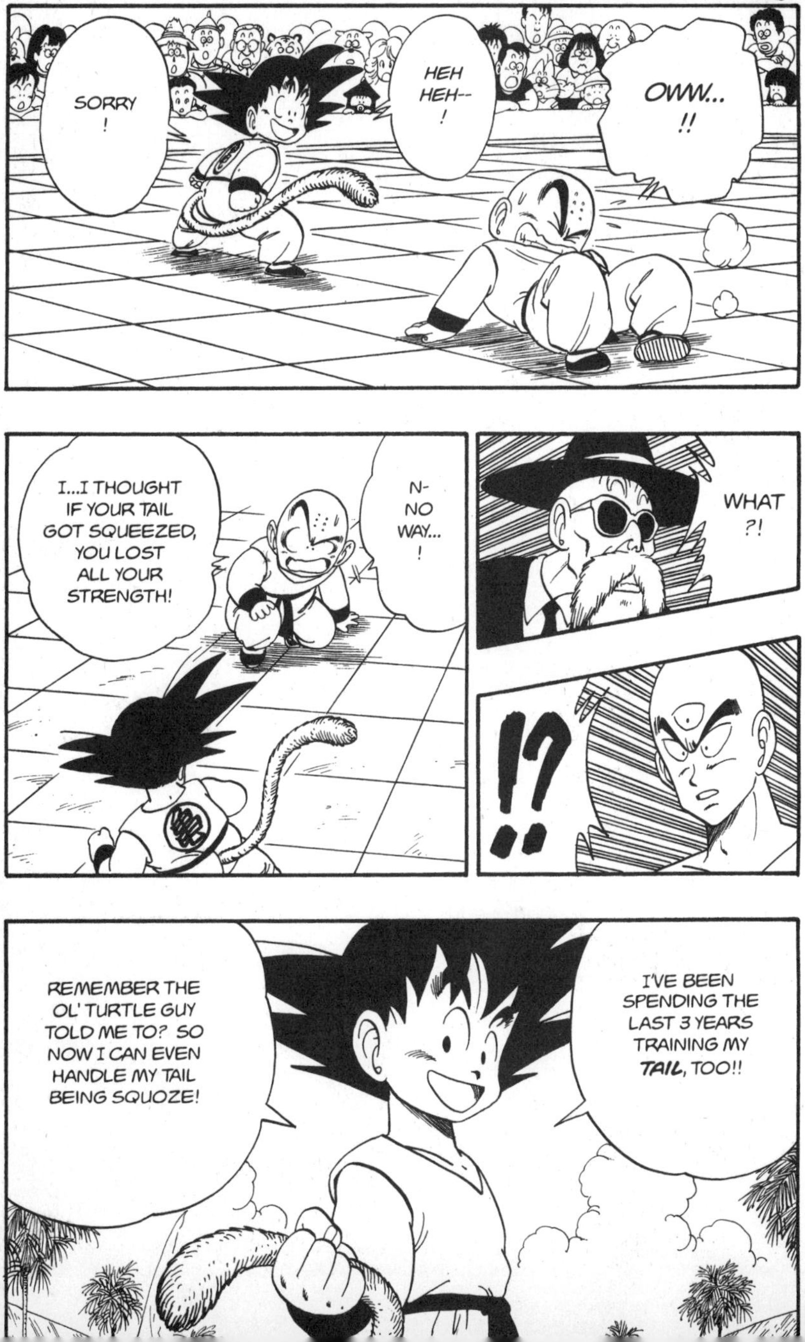
OWW...!!
HEH HEH--!
SORRY!
WHAT?!
!?!!
N-NO WAY...!
I...I THOUGHT IF YOUR TAIL GOT SQUEEZED, YOU LOST ALL YOUR STRENGTH!
I'VE BEEN SPENDING THE LAST 3 YEARS TRAINING MY **TAIL**, TOO!!
REMEMBER THE OL' TURTLE GUY TOLD ME TO? SO NOW I CAN EVEN HANDLE MY TAIL BEING SQUOZE!

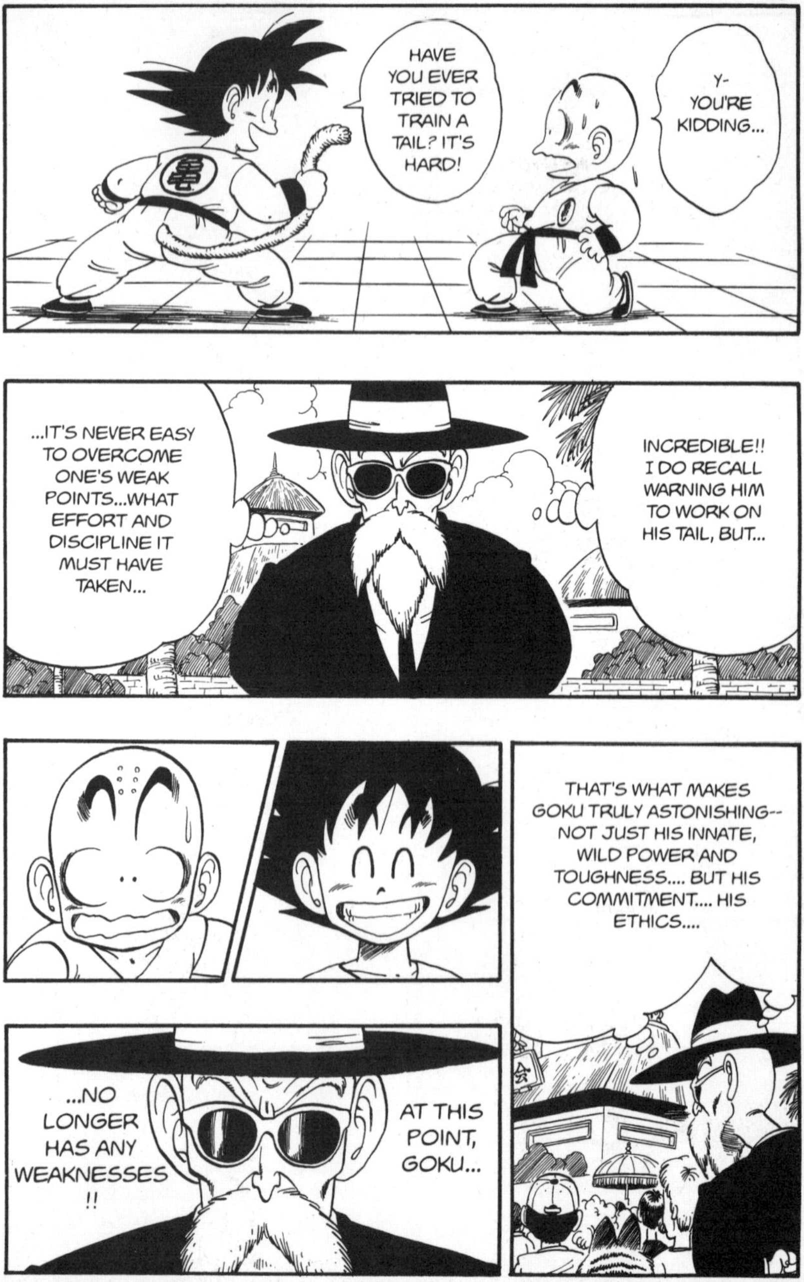
Y- YOU'RE KIDDING...
HAVE YOU EVER TRIED TO TRAIN A TAIL? IT'S HARD!
INCREDIBLE!! I DO RECALL WARNING HIM TO WORK ON HIS TAIL, BUT...
...IT'S NEVER EASY TO OVERCOME ONE'S WEAK POINTS...WHAT EFFORT AND DISCIPLINE IT MUST HAVE TAKEN...
THAT'S WHAT MAKES GOKU TRULY ASTONISHING-- NOT JUST HIS INNATE, WILD POWER AND TOUGHNESS.... BUT HIS COMMITMENT.... HIS ETHICS....
AT THIS POINT, GOKU...
...NO LONGER HAS ANY WEAKNESSES !!

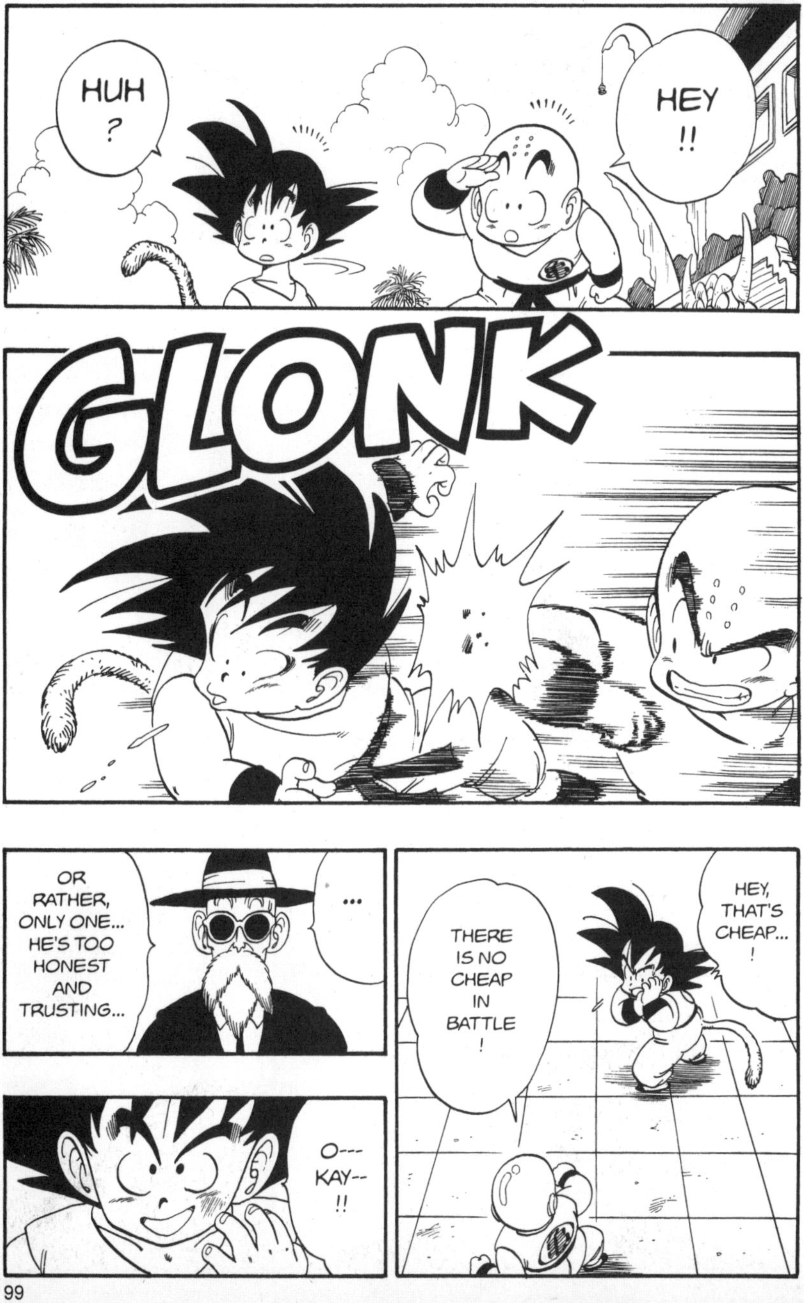
HEY !!
HUH ?
GLONK
HEY, THAT'S CHEAP... !
THERE IS NO CHEAP IN BATTLE !
...
OR RATHER, ONLY ONE... HE'S TOO HONEST AND TRUSTING...
O--- KAY-- !!

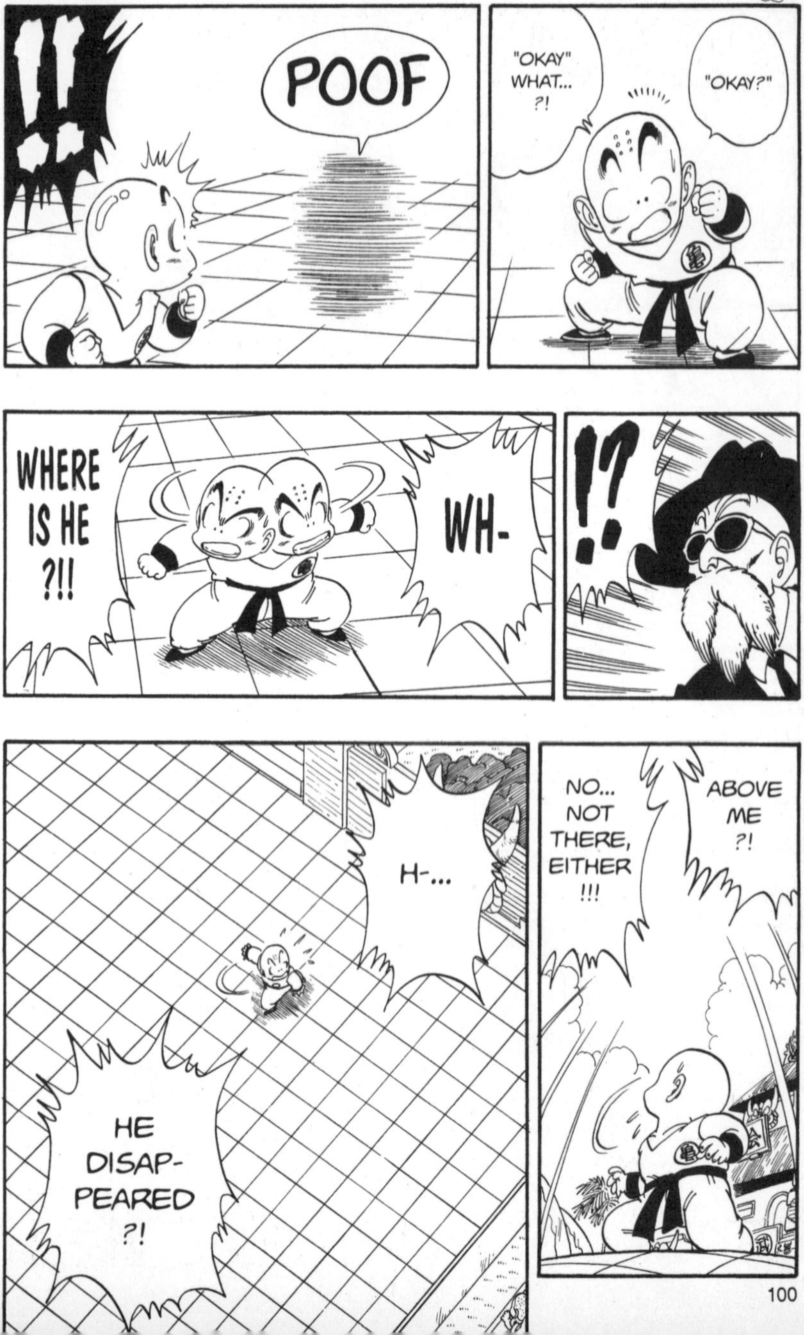
"OKAY?"
"OKAY" WHAT... ?!
POOF
!!
!?
WH-
WHERE IS HE ?!!
ABOVE ME ?!
NO... NOT THERE, EITHER !!!
H-...
HE DISAP-PEARED ?!

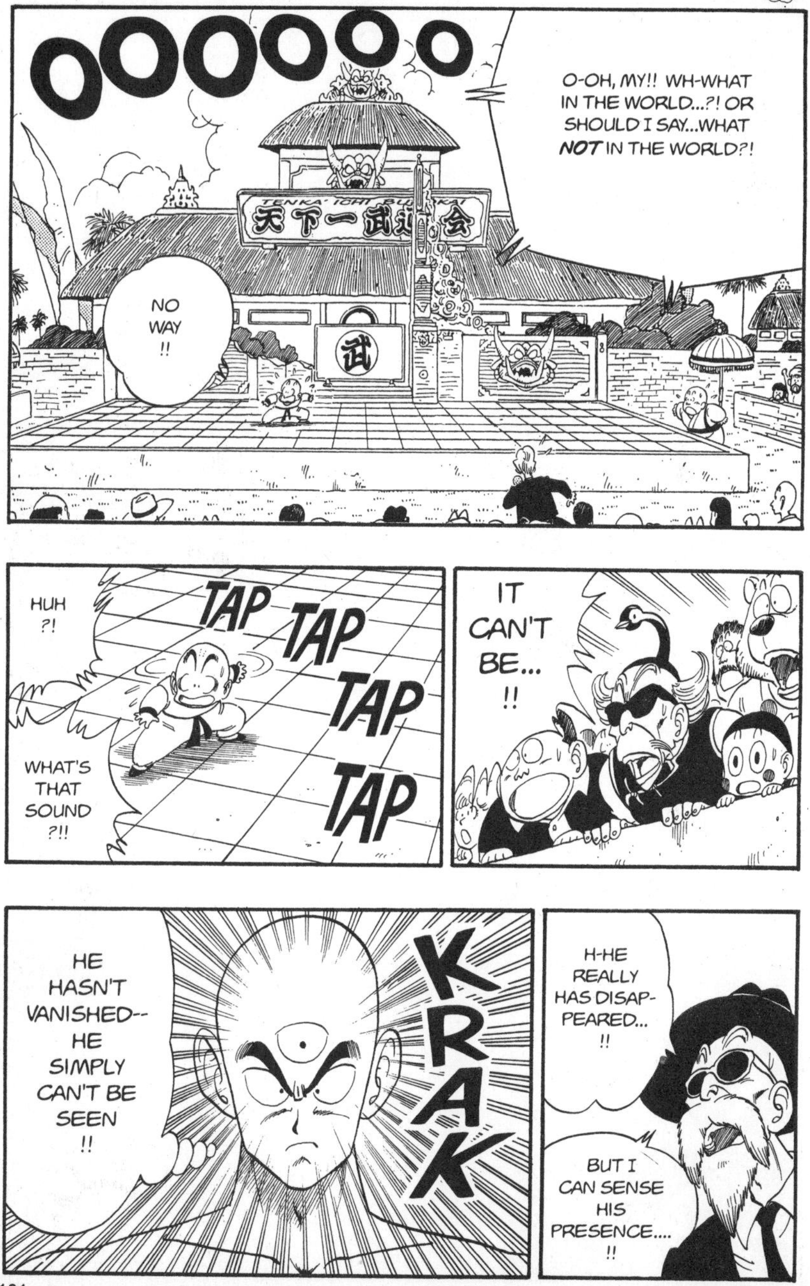
O-OH, MY!! WH-WHAT IN THE WORLD...?! OR SHOULD I SAY...WHAT *NOT* IN THE WORLD?!
OOOOOO
NO WAY !!
IT CAN'T BE... !!
HUH ?!
TAP TAP TAP TAP
WHAT'S THAT SOUND ?!!
H-HE REALLY HAS DISAP-PEARED... !!
BUT I CAN SENSE HIS PRESENCE.... !!
KRAK
HE HASN'T VANISHED-- HE SIMPLY CAN'T BE SEEN !!

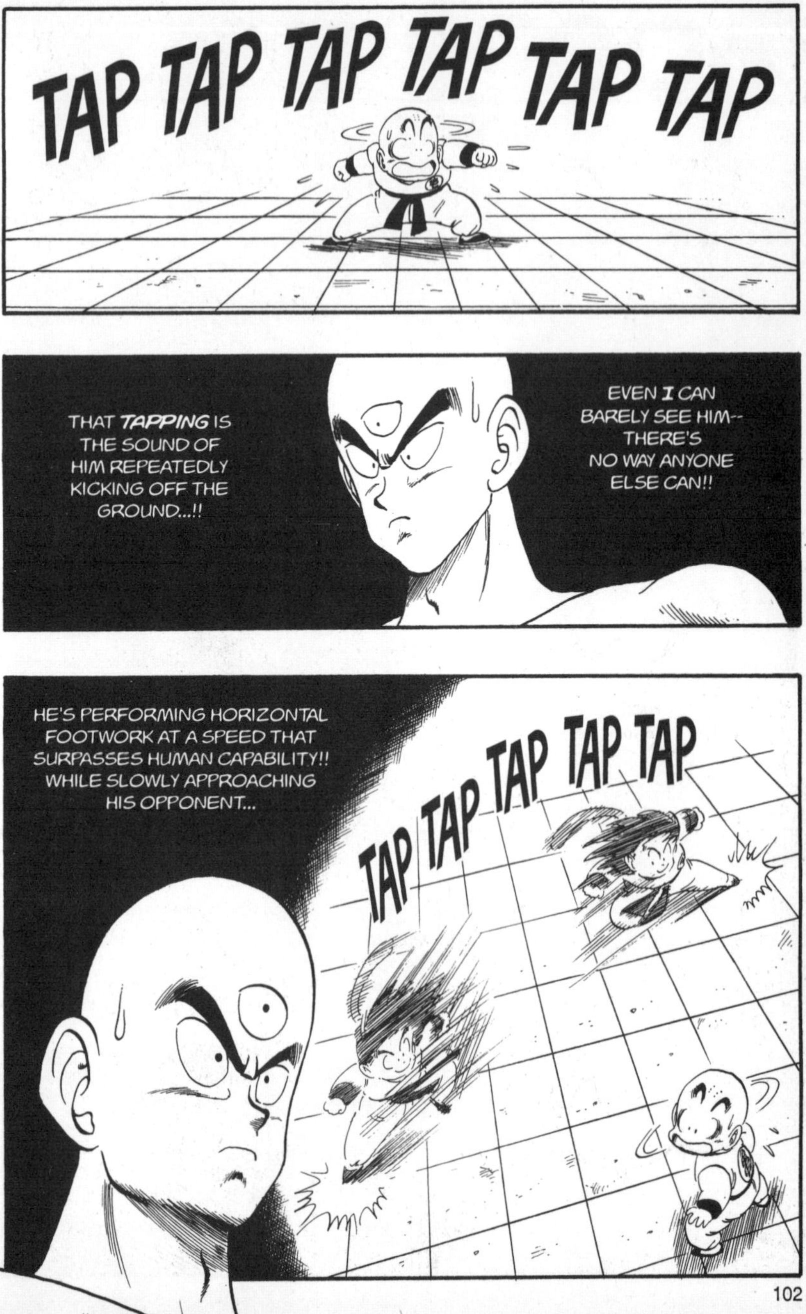
TAP TAP TAP TAP TAP TAP
EVEN I CAN BARELY SEE HIM-- THERE'S NO WAY ANYONE ELSE CAN!!
THAT TAPPING IS THE SOUND OF HIM REPEATEDLY KICKING OFF THE GROUND...!!
HE'S PERFORMING HORIZONTAL FOOTWORK AT A SPEED THAT SURPASSES HUMAN CAPABILITY!! WHILE SLOWLY APPROACHING HIS OPPONENT...
TAP TAP TAP TAP TAP

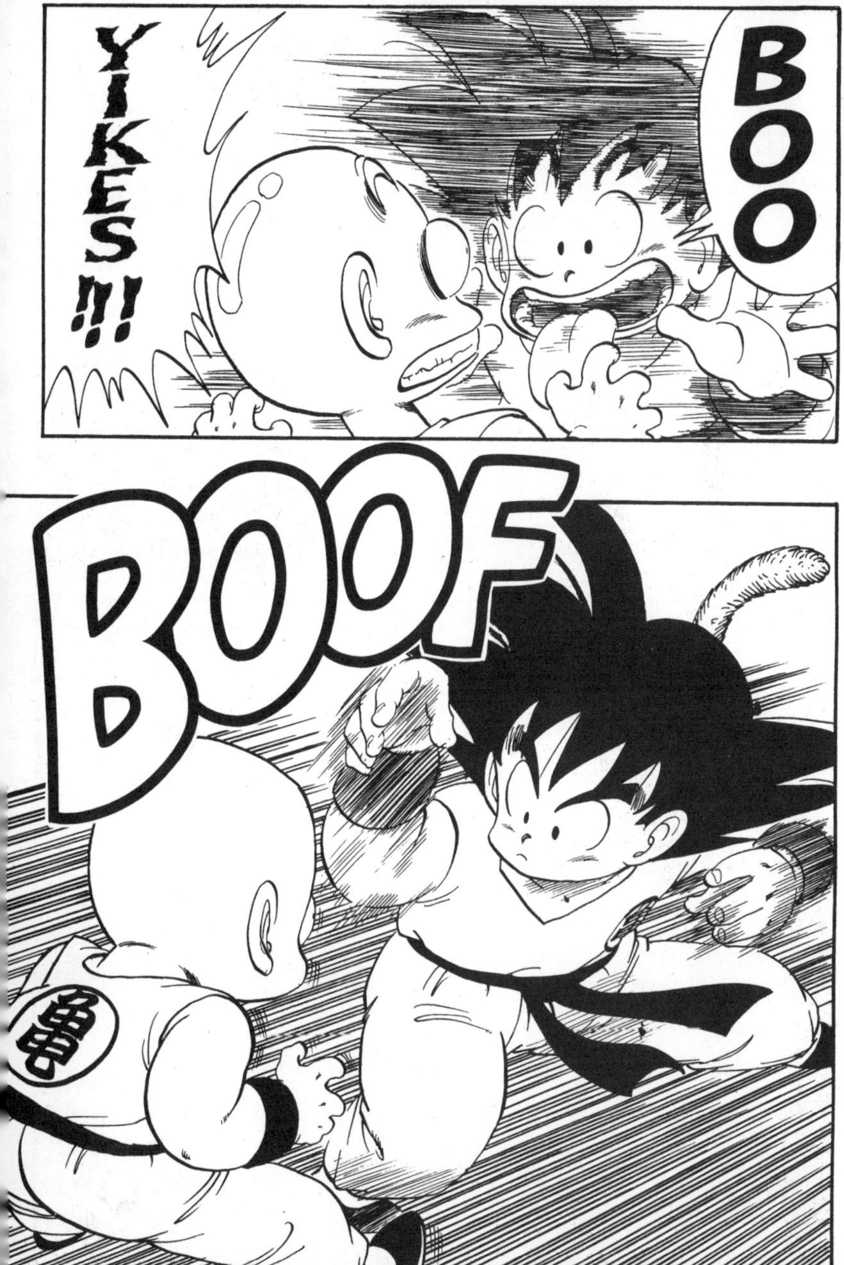
BOO
YIKES!?!
BOOF
亀

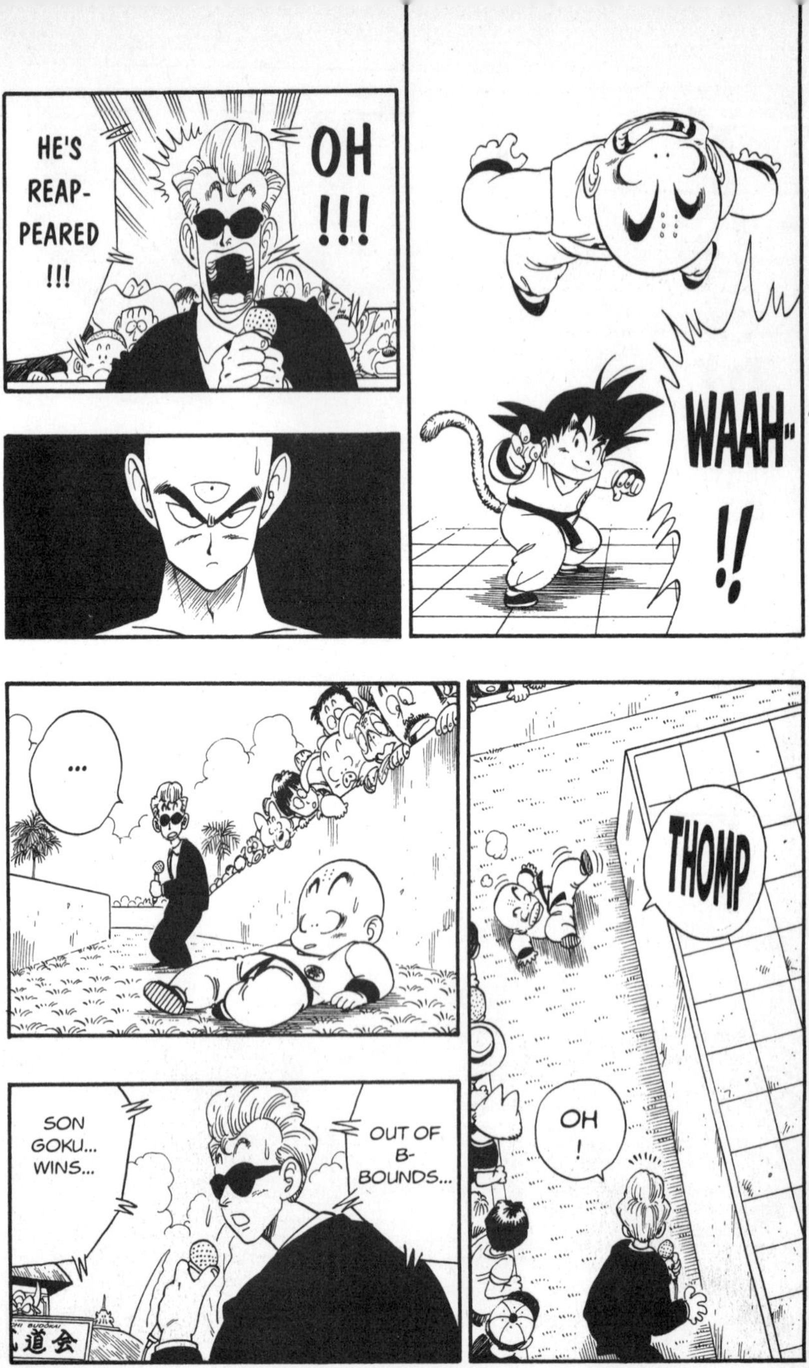
WAAH-!!
OH!!!
HE'S REAP-PEARED!!!
THOMP
OH!
...
OUT OF B-BOUNDS...
SON GOKU... WINS...

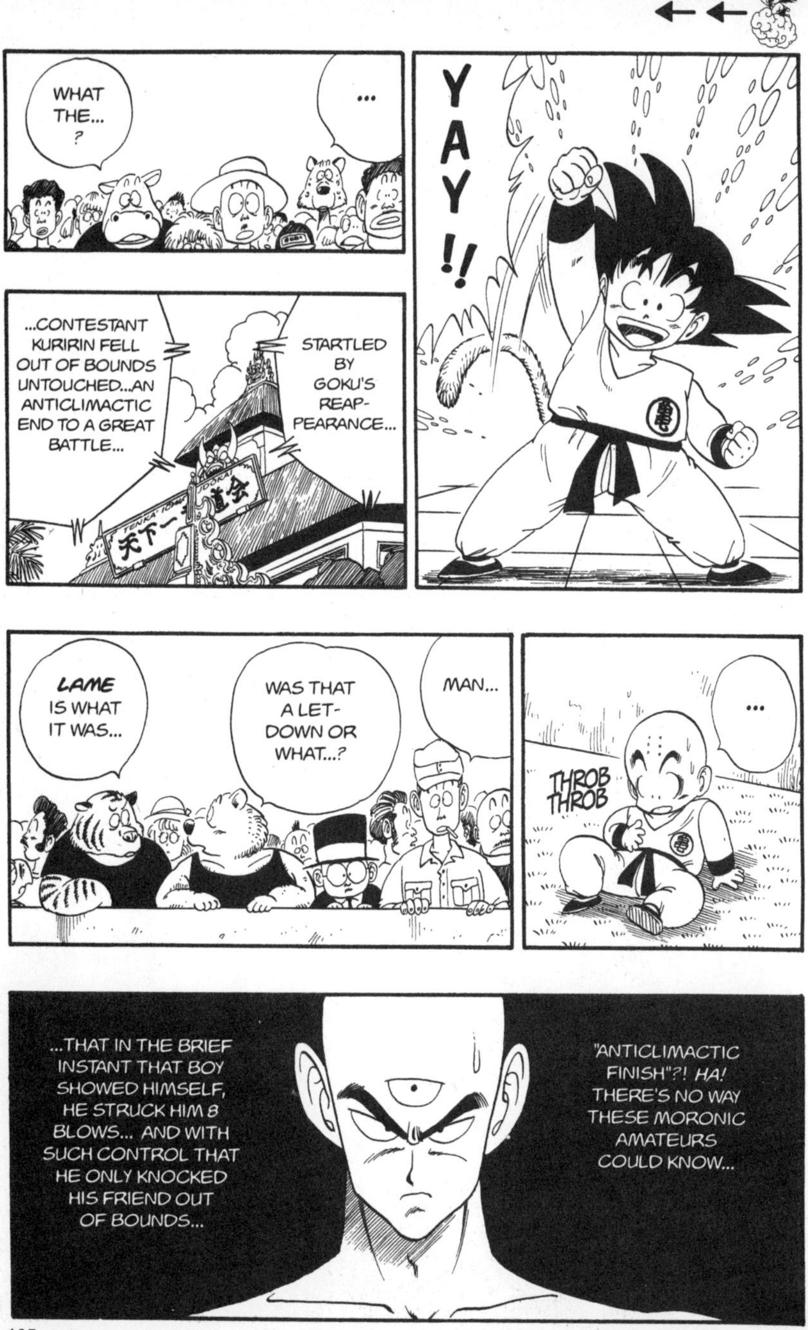
YAY!!
...
WHAT THE... ?
STARTLED BY GOKU'S REAPPEARANCE...
...CONTESTANT KURIRIN FELL OUT OF BOUNDS UNTOUCHED...AN ANTICLIMACTIC END TO A GREAT BATTLE...
...
THROB THROB
MAN...
WAS THAT A LET-DOWN OR WHAT...?
LAME IS WHAT IT WAS...
"ANTICLIMACTIC FINISH"?! HA! THERE'S NO WAY THESE MORONIC AMATEURS COULD KNOW...
...THAT IN THE BRIEF INSTANT THAT BOY SHOWED HIMSELF, HE STRUCK HIM 8 BLOWS... AND WITH SUCH CONTROL THAT HE ONLY KNOCKED HIS FRIEND OUT OF BOUNDS...

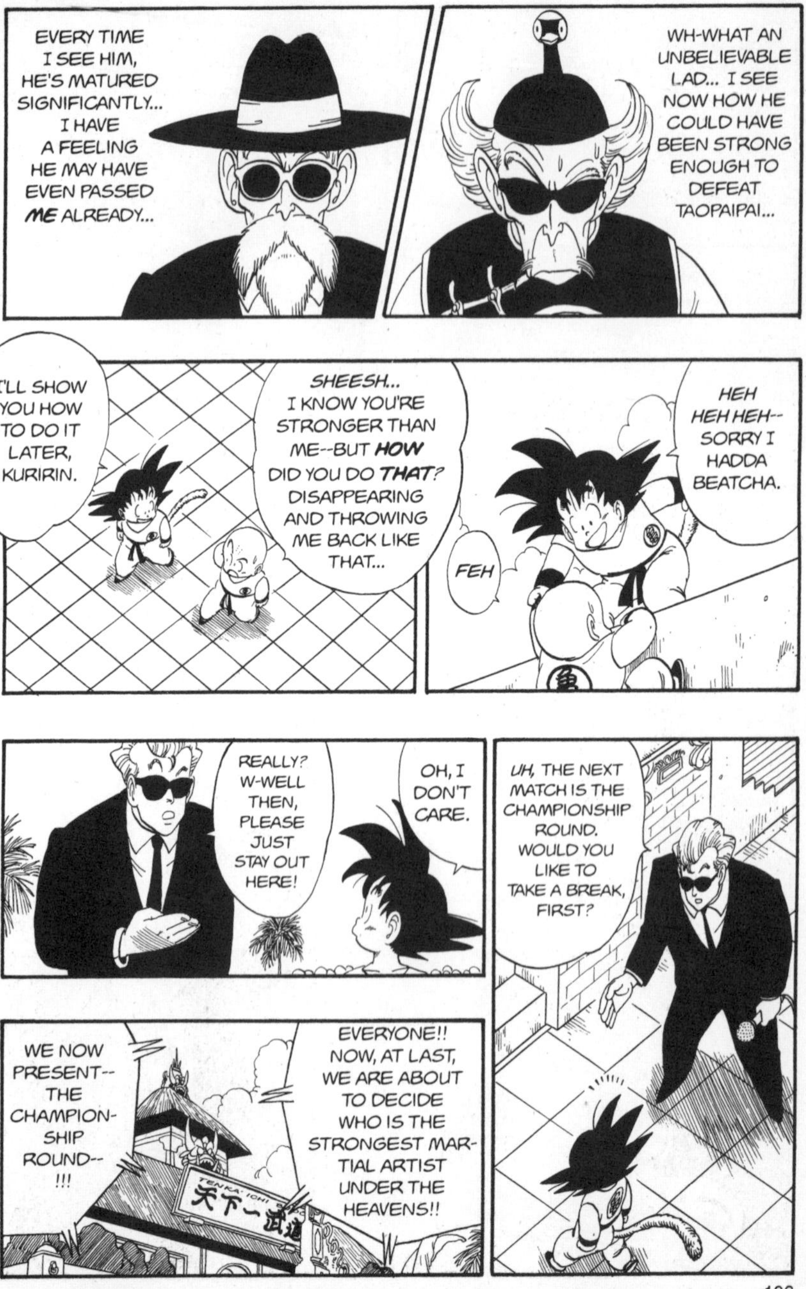
WH-WHAT AN UNBELIEVABLE LAD... I SEE NOW HOW HE COULD HAVE BEEN STRONG ENOUGH TO DEFEAT TAOPAIPAI...
EVERY TIME I SEE HIM, HE'S MATURED SIGNIFICANTLY... I HAVE A FEELING HE MAY HAVE EVEN PASSED ME ALREADY...
HEH HEH HEH-- SORRY I HADDA BEATCHA.
FEH
SHEESH... I KNOW YOU'RE STRONGER THAN ME--BUT HOW DID YOU DO THAT? DISAPPEARING AND THROWING ME BACK LIKE THAT...
I'LL SHOW YOU HOW TO DO IT LATER, KURIRIN.
UH, THE NEXT MATCH IS THE CHAMPIONSHIP ROUND. WOULD YOU LIKE TO TAKE A BREAK, FIRST?
OH, I DON'T CARE.
REALLY? W-WELL THEN, PLEASE JUST STAY OUT HERE!
EVERYONE!! NOW, AT LAST, WE ARE ABOUT TO DECIDE WHO IS THE STRONGEST MAR-TIAL ARTIST UNDER THE HEAVENS!!
WE NOW PRESENT-- THE CHAMPION-SHIP ROUND-- !!!
TENKA'ICHI
天下一武道

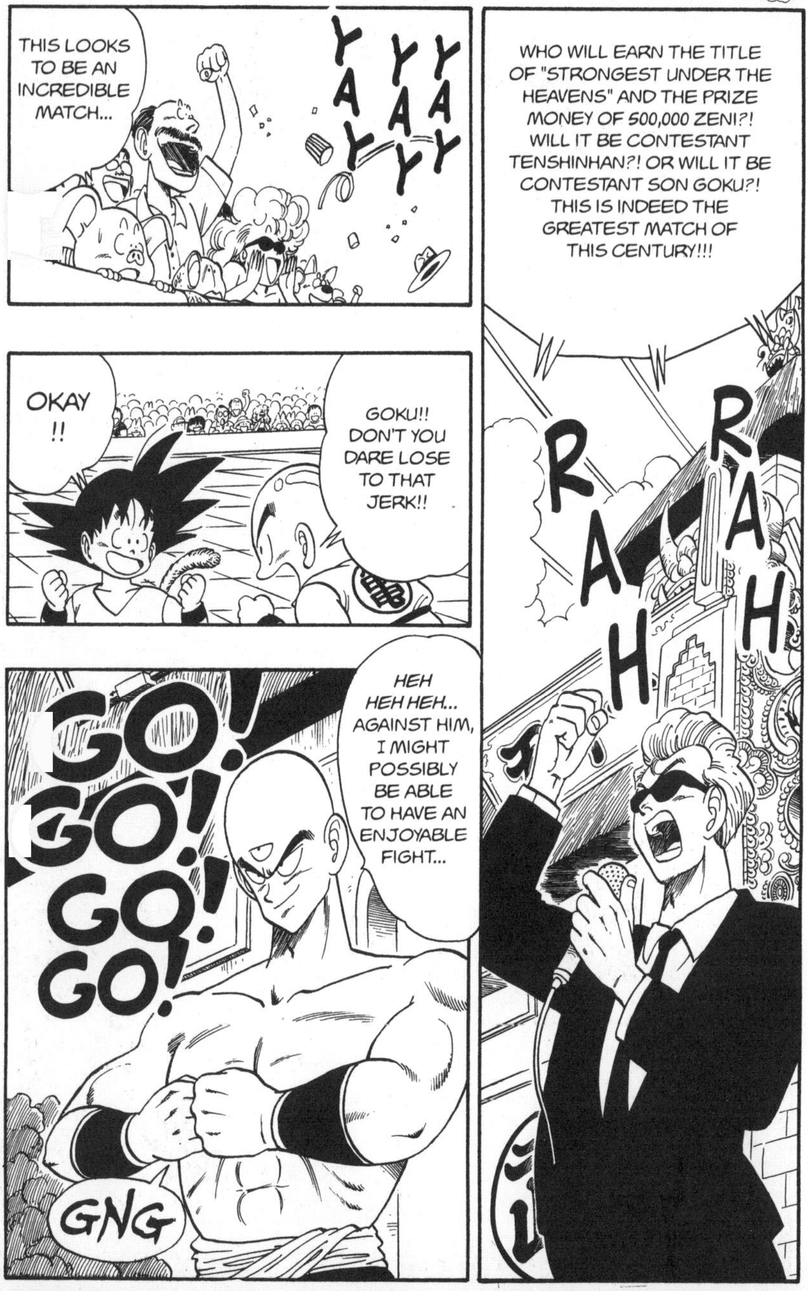
WHO WILL EARN THE TITLE OF "STRONGEST UNDER THE HEAVENS" AND THE PRIZE MONEY OF 500,000 ZENI?! WILL IT BE CONTESTANT TENSHINHAN?! OR WILL IT BE CONTESTANT SON GOKU?! THIS IS INDEED THE GREATEST MATCH OF THIS CENTURY!!!
RAH
RAH
YAY
YAY
YAY
THIS LOOKS TO BE AN INCREDIBLE MATCH...
GOKU!! DON'T YOU DARE LOSE TO THAT JERK!!
OKAY !!
HEH HEH HEH... AGAINST HIM, I MIGHT POSSIBLY BE ABLE TO HAVE AN ENJOYABLE FIGHT...
GO! GO! GO! GO!
GNG

NEXT: The World's Greatest Super Battle!

Tale 128
Goku vs. Tenshinhan

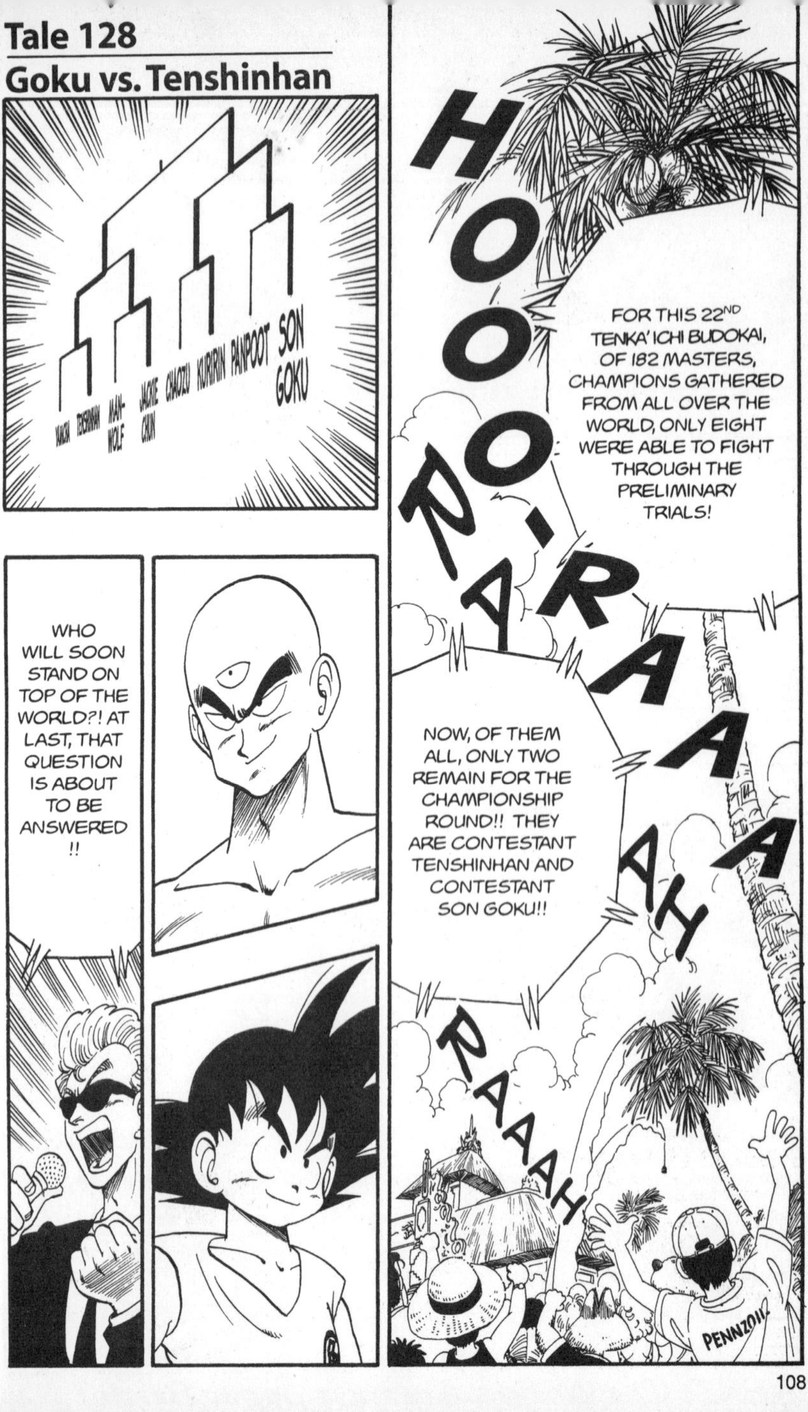

HOOOO-RAAAAH
FOR THIS 22ND TENKA'ICHI BUDOKAI, OF 182 MASTERS, CHAMPIONS GATHERED FROM ALL OVER THE WORLD, ONLY EIGHT WERE ABLE TO FIGHT THROUGH THE PRELIMINARY TRIALS!
RA
NOW, OF THEM ALL, ONLY TWO REMAIN FOR THE CHAMPIONSHIP ROUND!! THEY ARE CONTESTANT TENSHINHAN AND CONTESTANT SON GOKU!!
AH
RAAAH
PENNZOIL
YAMCHA
TENSHINHAN
MAN-WOLF
JACKIE CHUN
CHAOZU
KURIRIN
PANPOOT
SON GOKU
WHO WILL SOON STAND ON TOP OF THE WORLD?! AT LAST, THAT QUESTION IS ABOUT TO BE ANSWERED !!

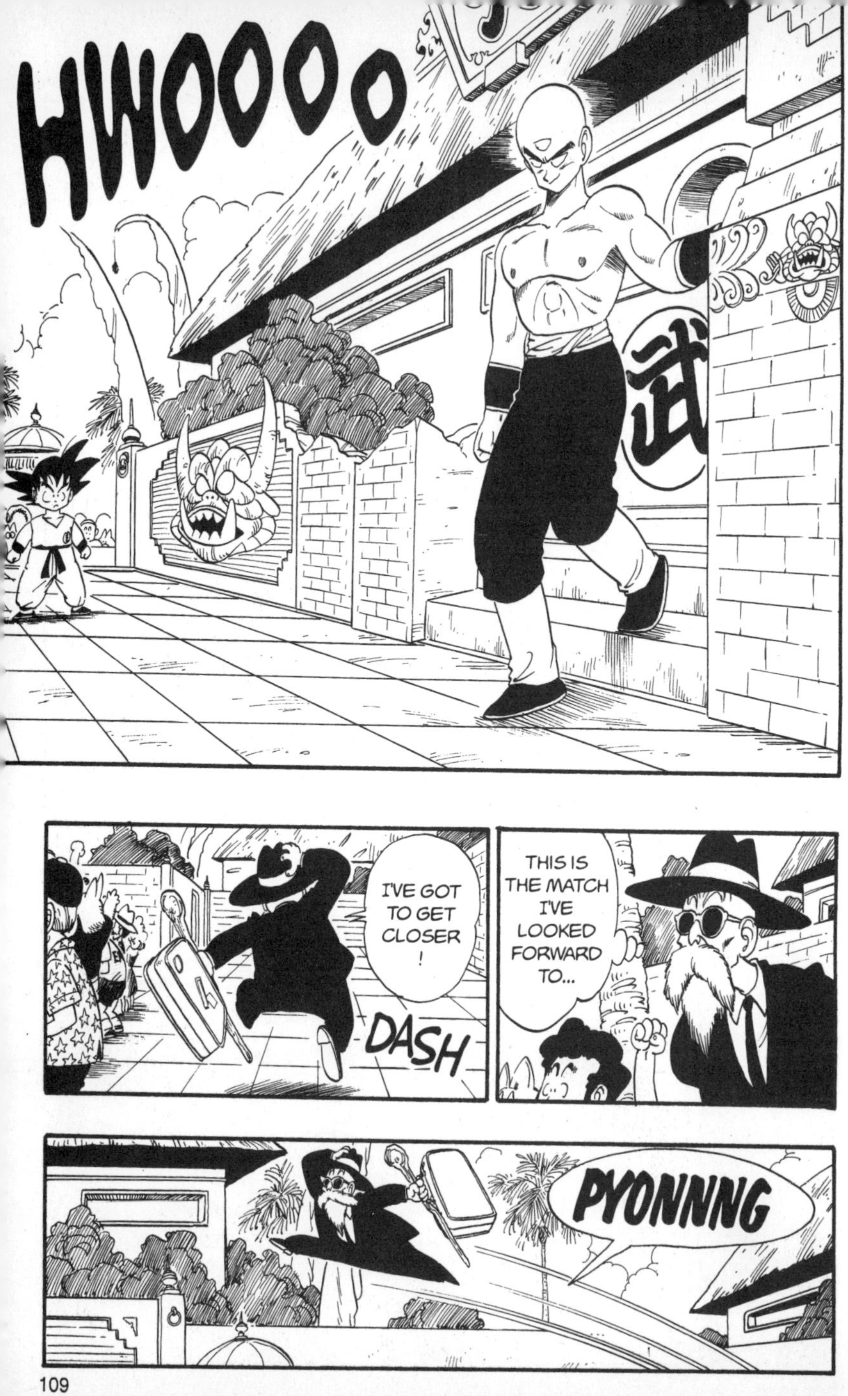
HWOOOO
THIS IS THE MATCH I'VE LOOKED FORWARD TO...
I'VE GOT TO GET CLOSER!
DASH
PYONNNG

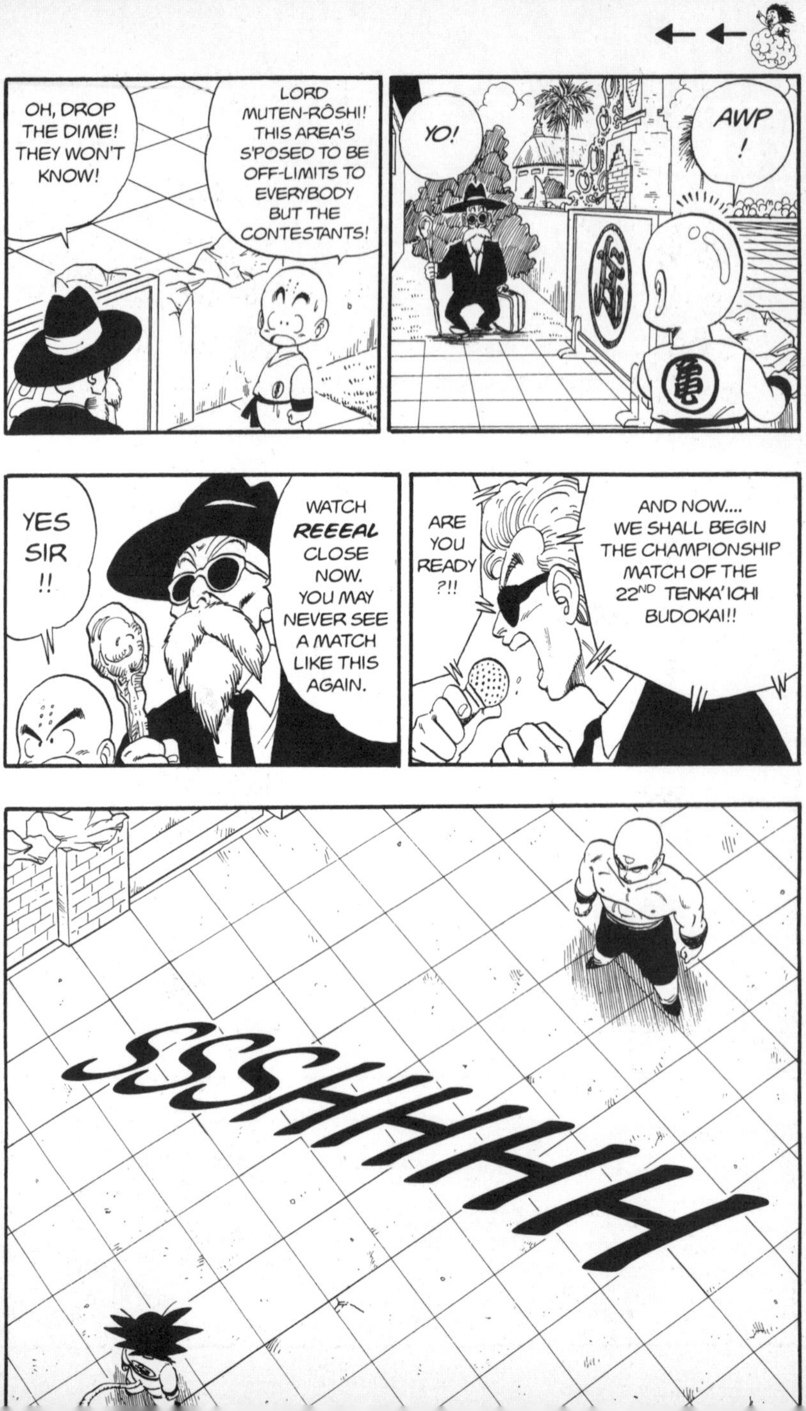
AWP !
YO!
LORD MUTEN-RÔSHI! THIS AREA'S S'POSED TO BE OFF-LIMITS TO EVERYBODY BUT THE CONTESTANTS!
OH, DROP THE DIME! THEY WON'T KNOW!
AND NOW.... WE SHALL BEGIN THE CHAMPIONSHIP MATCH OF THE 22ND TENKA'ICHI BUDOKAI!!
ARE YOU READY ?!!
WATCH REEEAL CLOSE NOW. YOU MAY NEVER SEE A MATCH LIKE THIS AGAIN.
YES SIR !!
SSHHHH

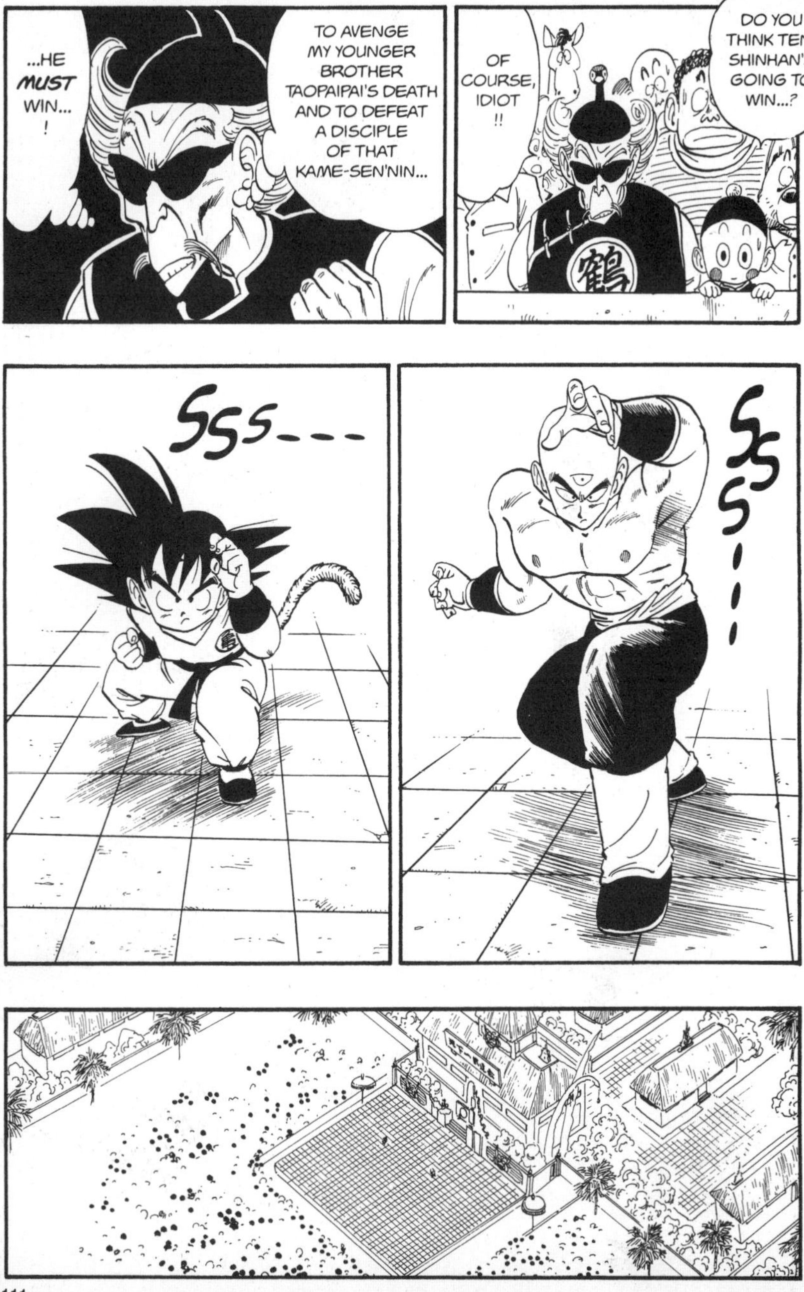

DO YOU THINK TEN-SHINHAN'S GOING TO WIN...?
OF COURSE, IDIOT !!
TO AVENGE MY YOUNGER BROTHER TAOPAIPAI'S DEATH AND TO DEFEAT A DISCIPLE OF THAT KAME-SEN'NIN...
...HE **MUST** WIN... !
SSS
SSS

BEGIN !!!!
DOOMM
GLOK

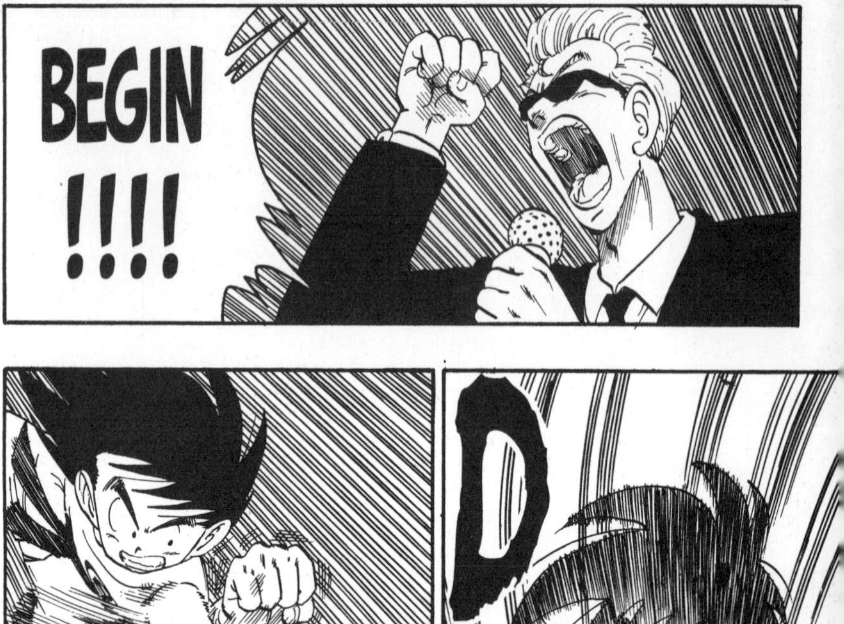

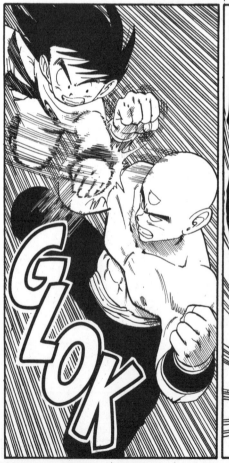

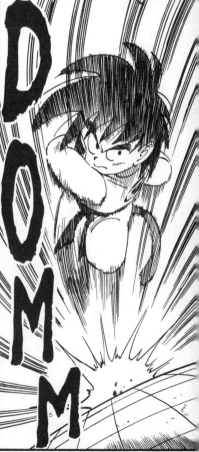

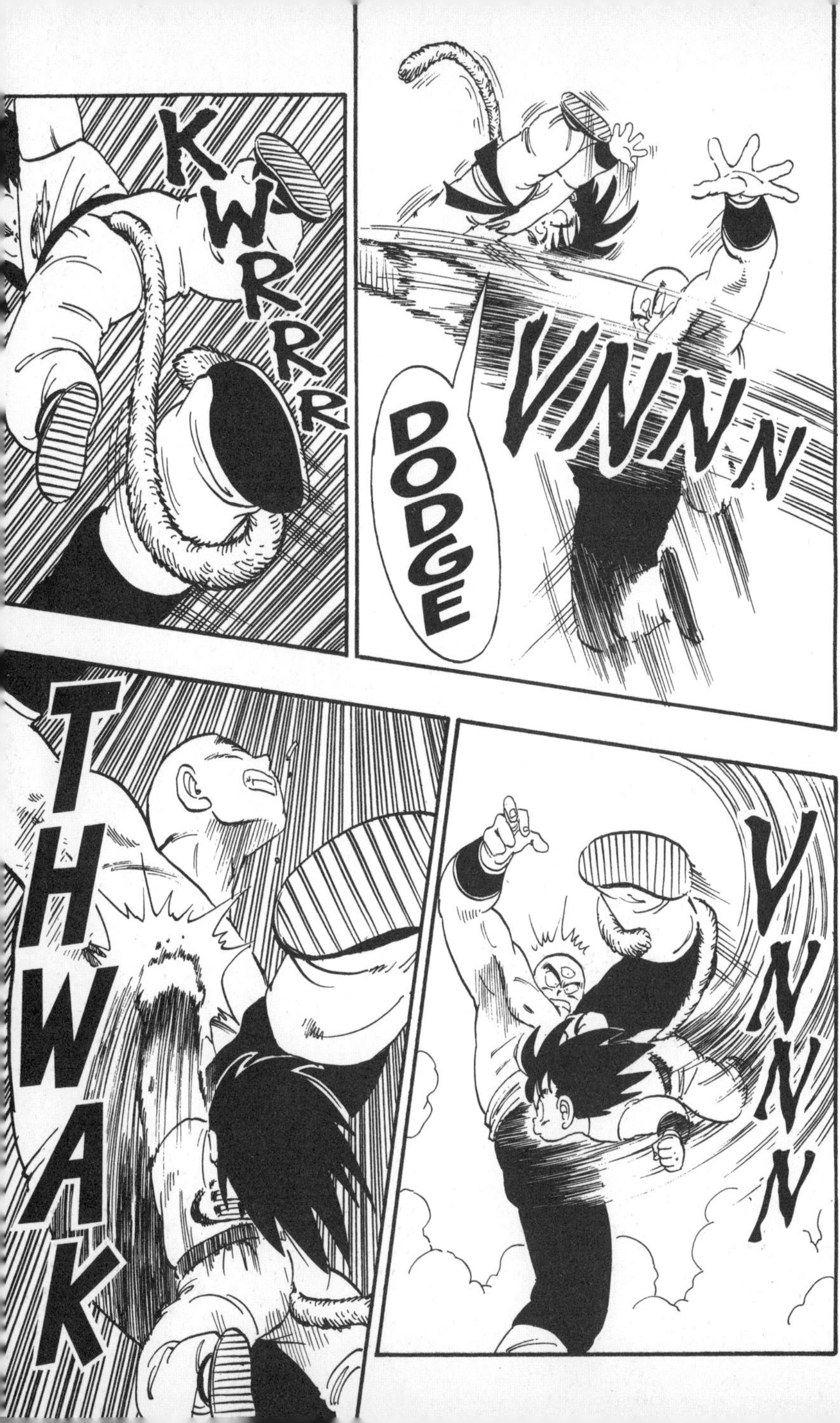
VNNNN
DODGE
KWRRRR
VNNNN
THWAK

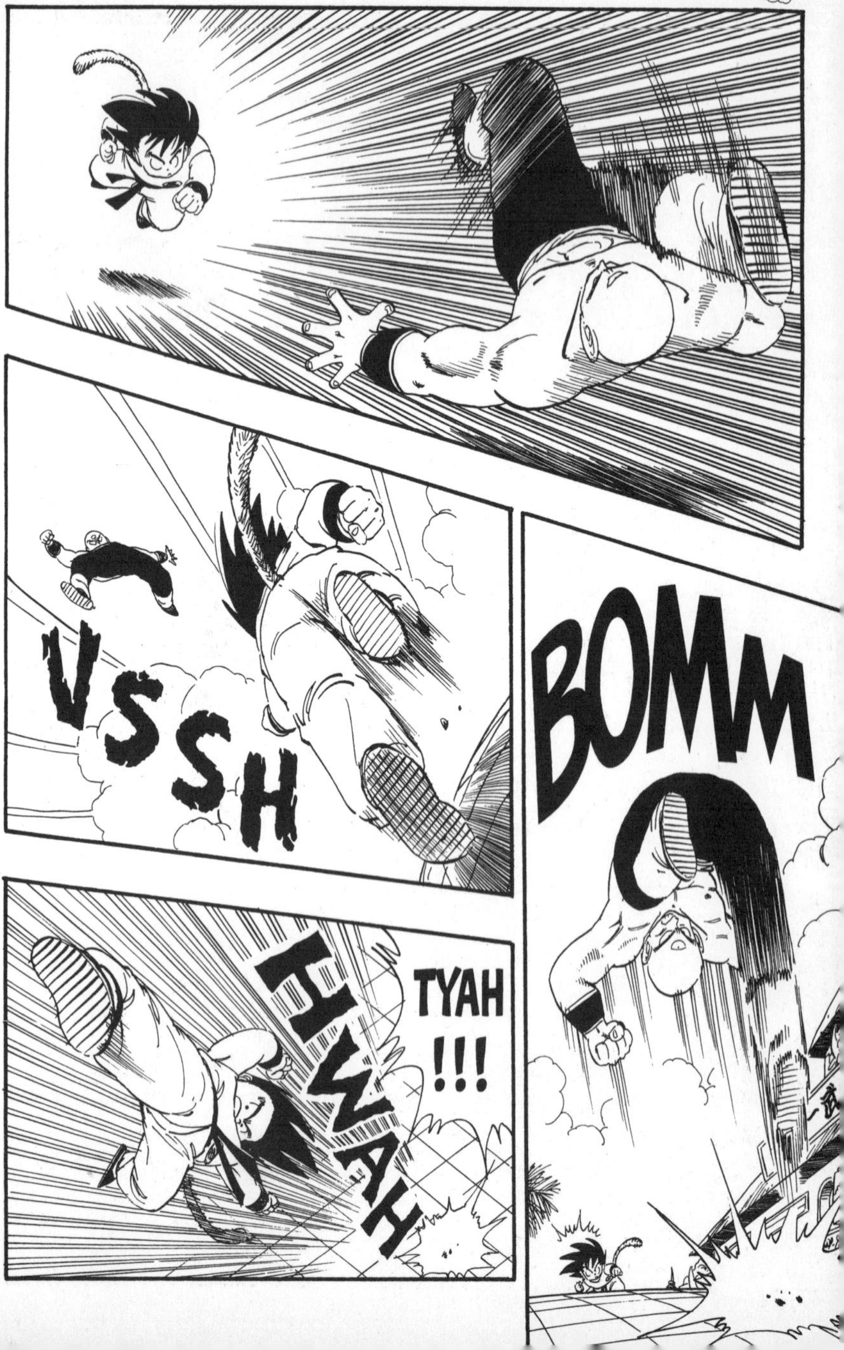
BOMM
VSSH
TYAH!!!
HWAH

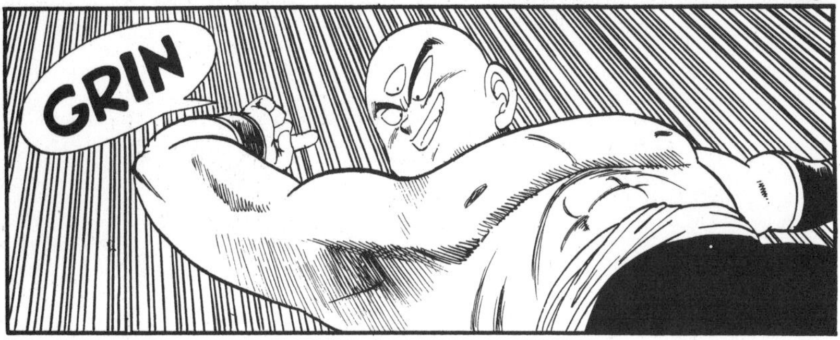
GRIN

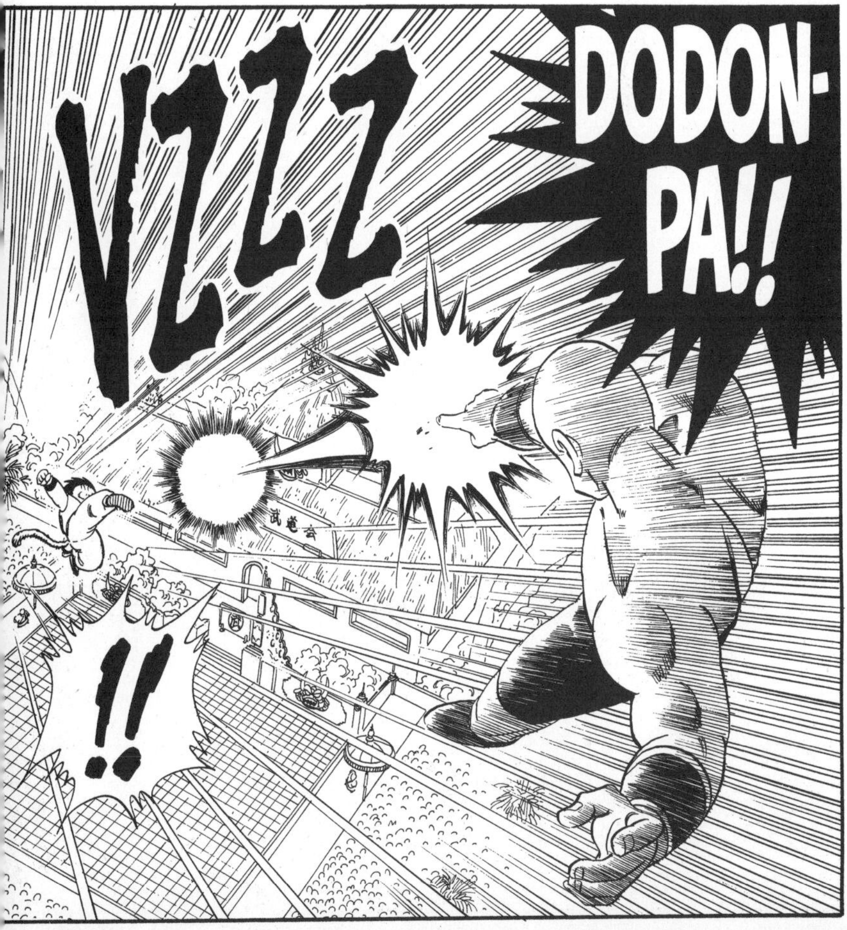
DODON-
PA!!
VZZZ
!!

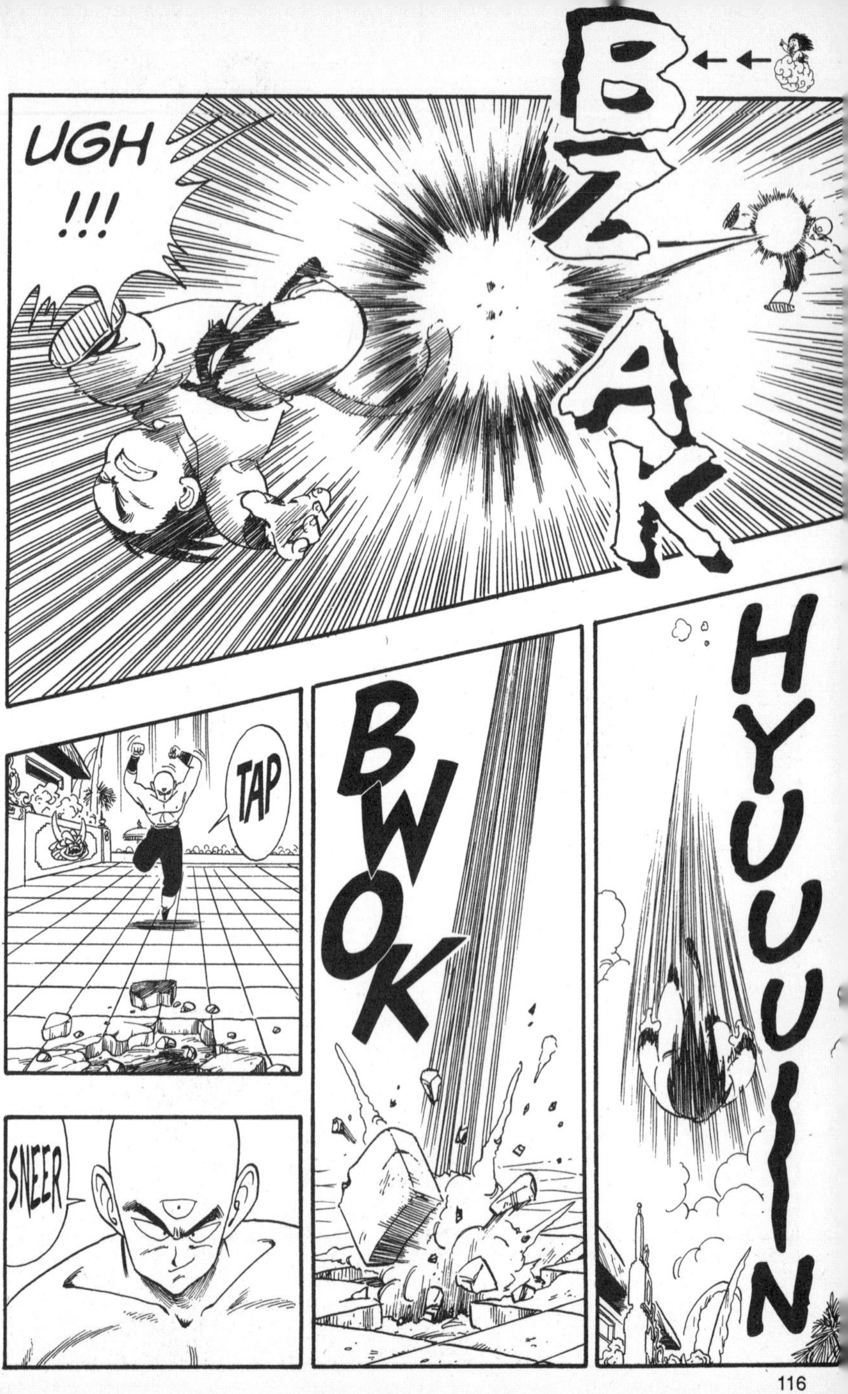
BZAK
UGH !!!
HYUUU—N
BWOK
TAP
SNEER

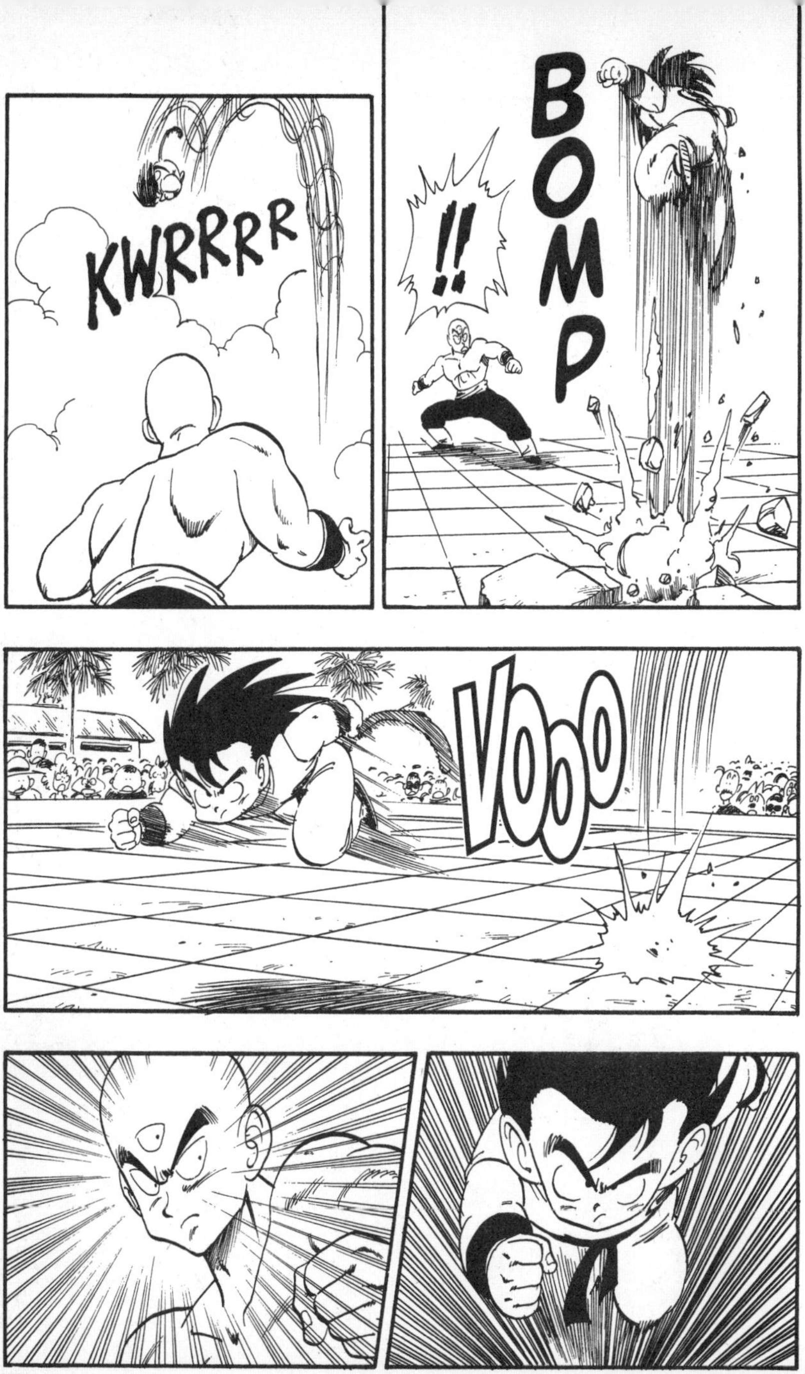
BOMP
!!
KWRRRR
VOOO

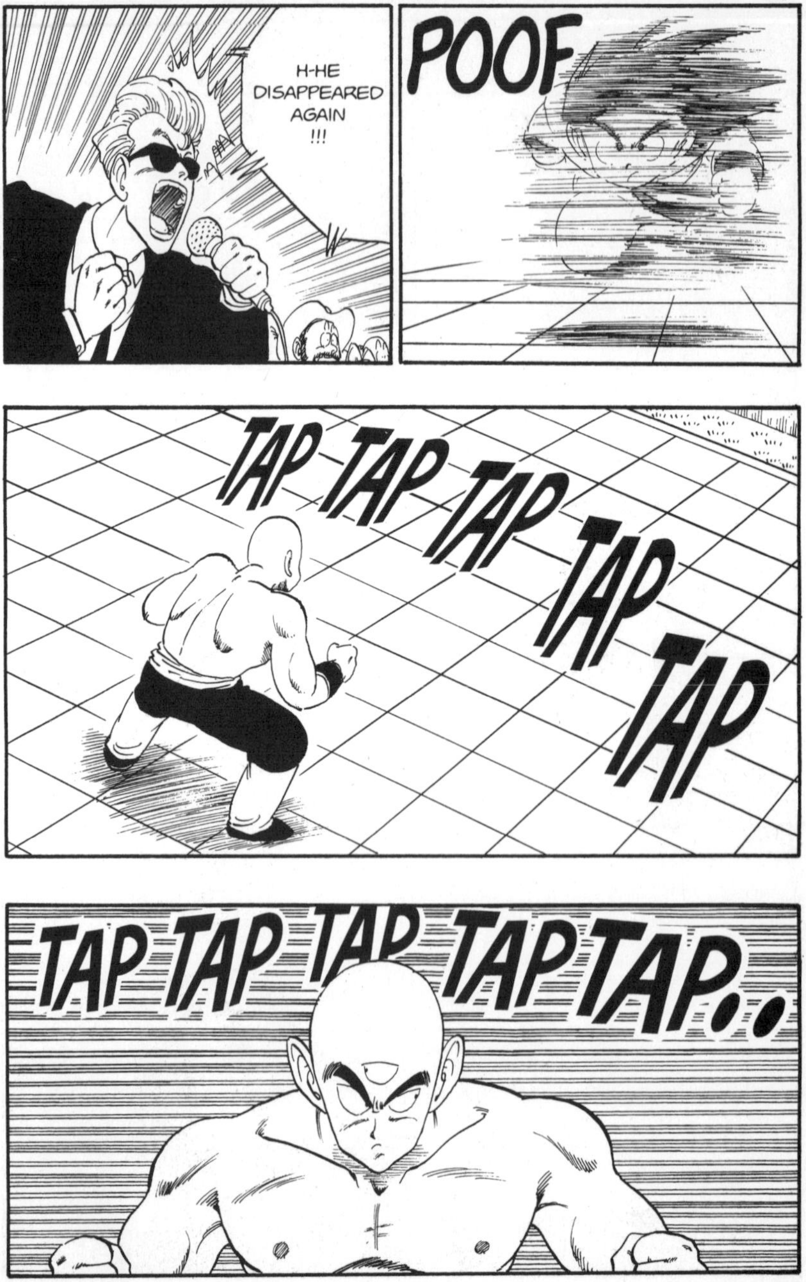
POOF
H-HE DISAPPEARED AGAIN !!!
TAP TAP TAP TAP TAP
TAP TAP TAP TAP TAP..

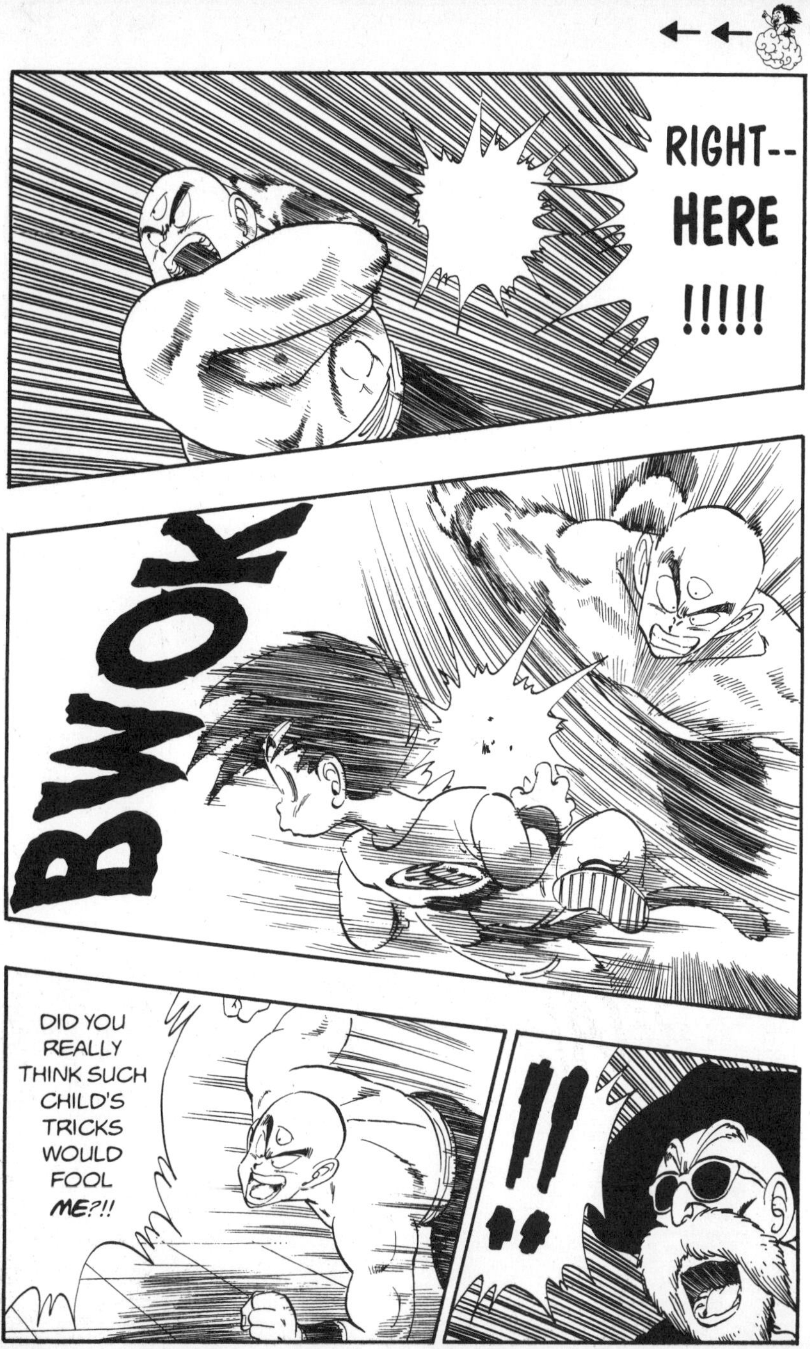
RIGHT-- HERE !!!!!
BWOK
!!
DID YOU REALLY THINK SUCH CHILD'S TRICKS WOULD FOOL ME?!!

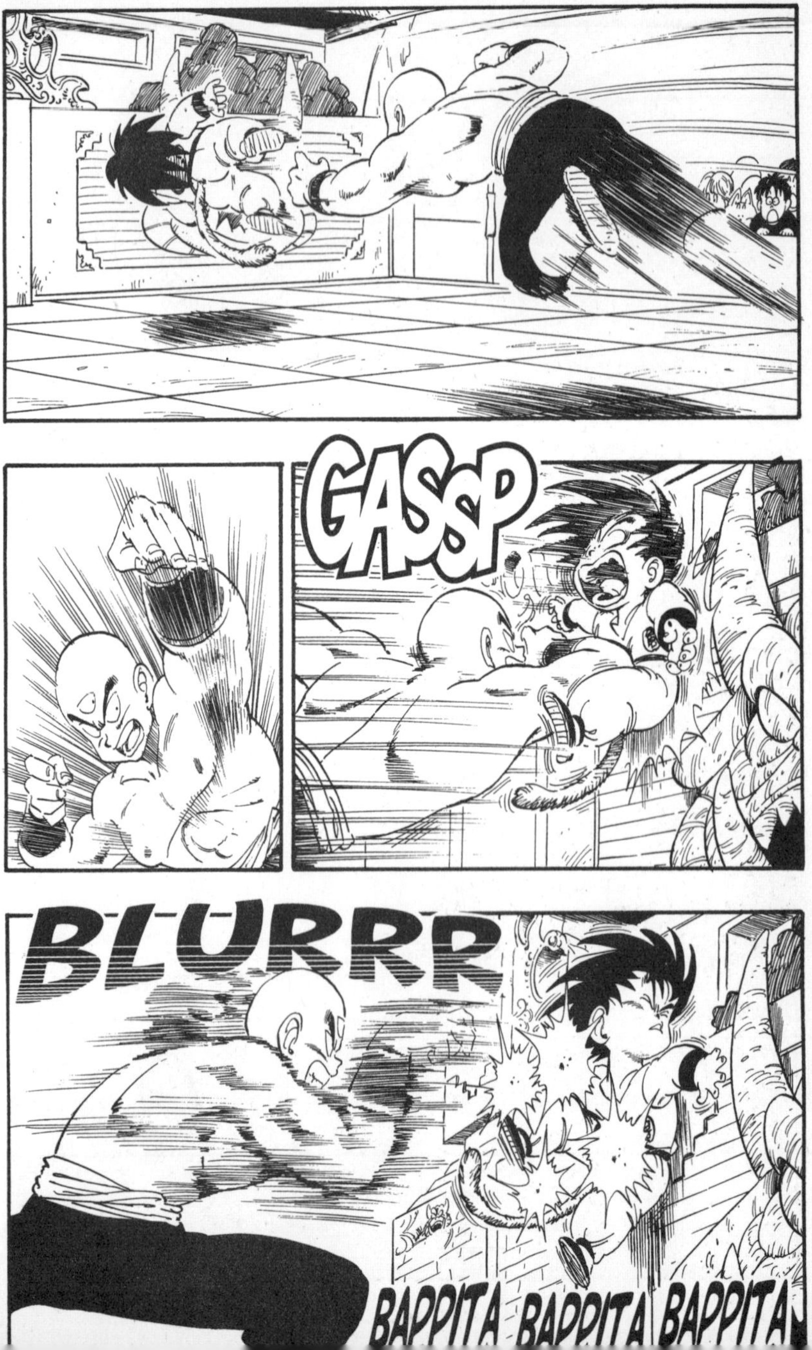
GASSP
BLURRR
BAPPITA BAPPITA BAPPITA

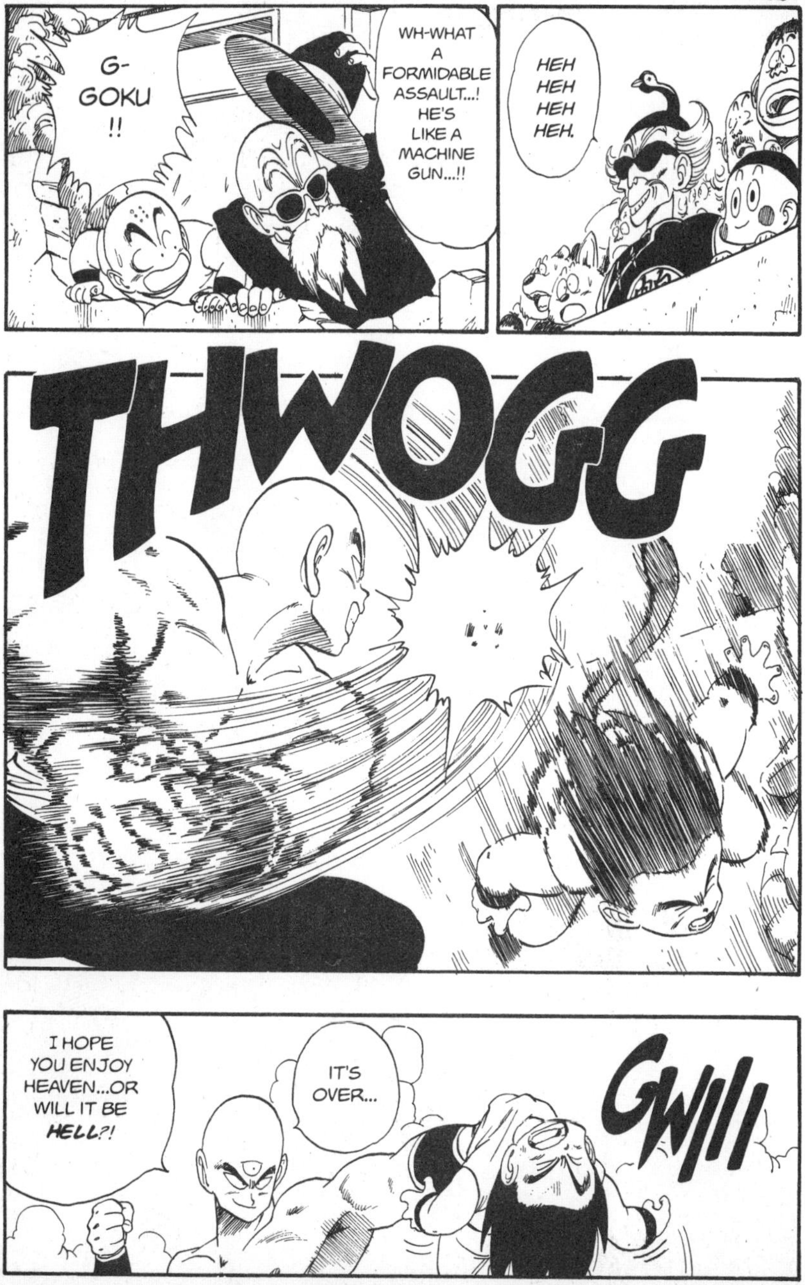
HEH HEH HEH HEH.
WH-WHAT A FORMIDABLE ASSAULT...! HE'S LIKE A MACHINE GUN...!!
G-GOKU!!
THWOGG
GWIII
IT'S OVER...
I HOPE YOU ENJOY HEAVEN...OR WILL IT BE ***HELL***?!

NEXT: The Volleyball Play

Tale 129
The Volleyball Play

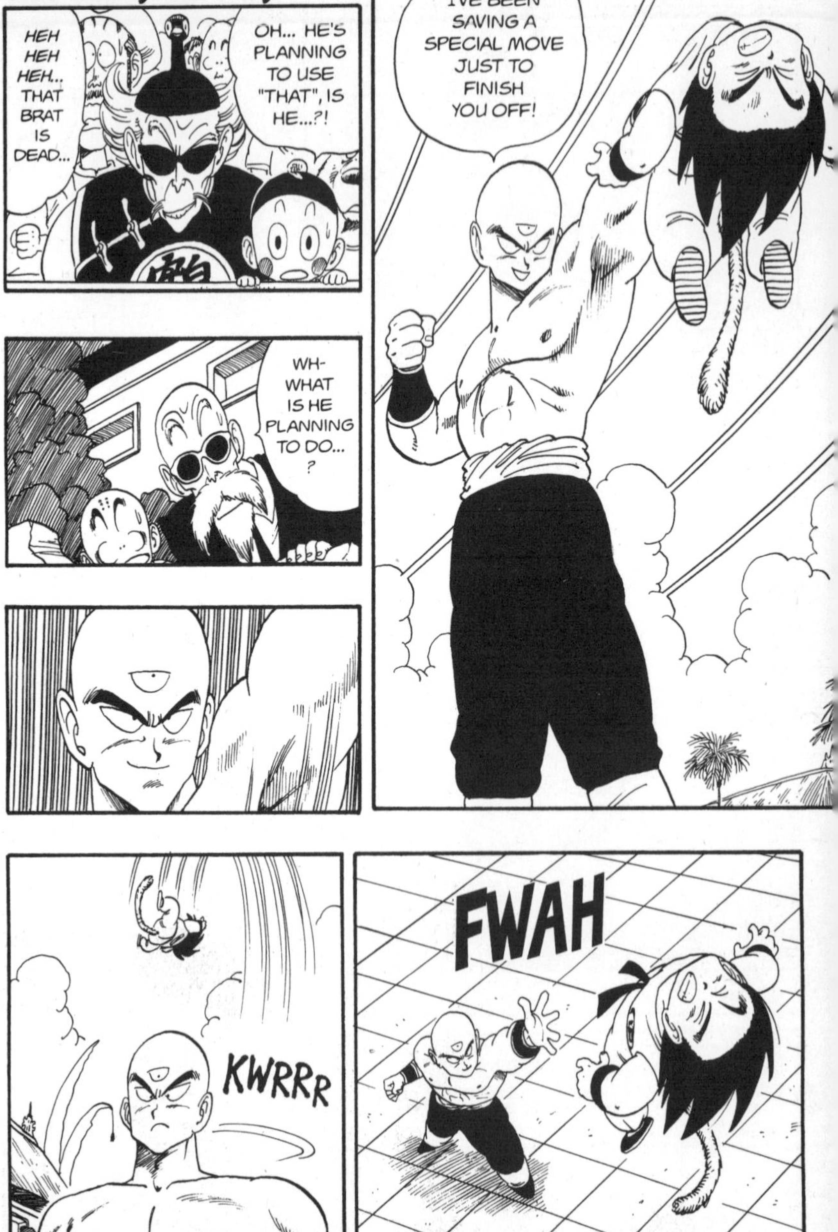
I'VE BEEN SAVING A SPECIAL MOVE JUST TO FINISH YOU OFF!
OH... HE'S PLANNING TO USE "THAT", IS HE...?!
HEH HEH HEH... THAT BRAT IS DEAD...
WH-WHAT IS HE PLANNING TO DO...?
FWAH
KWRRR

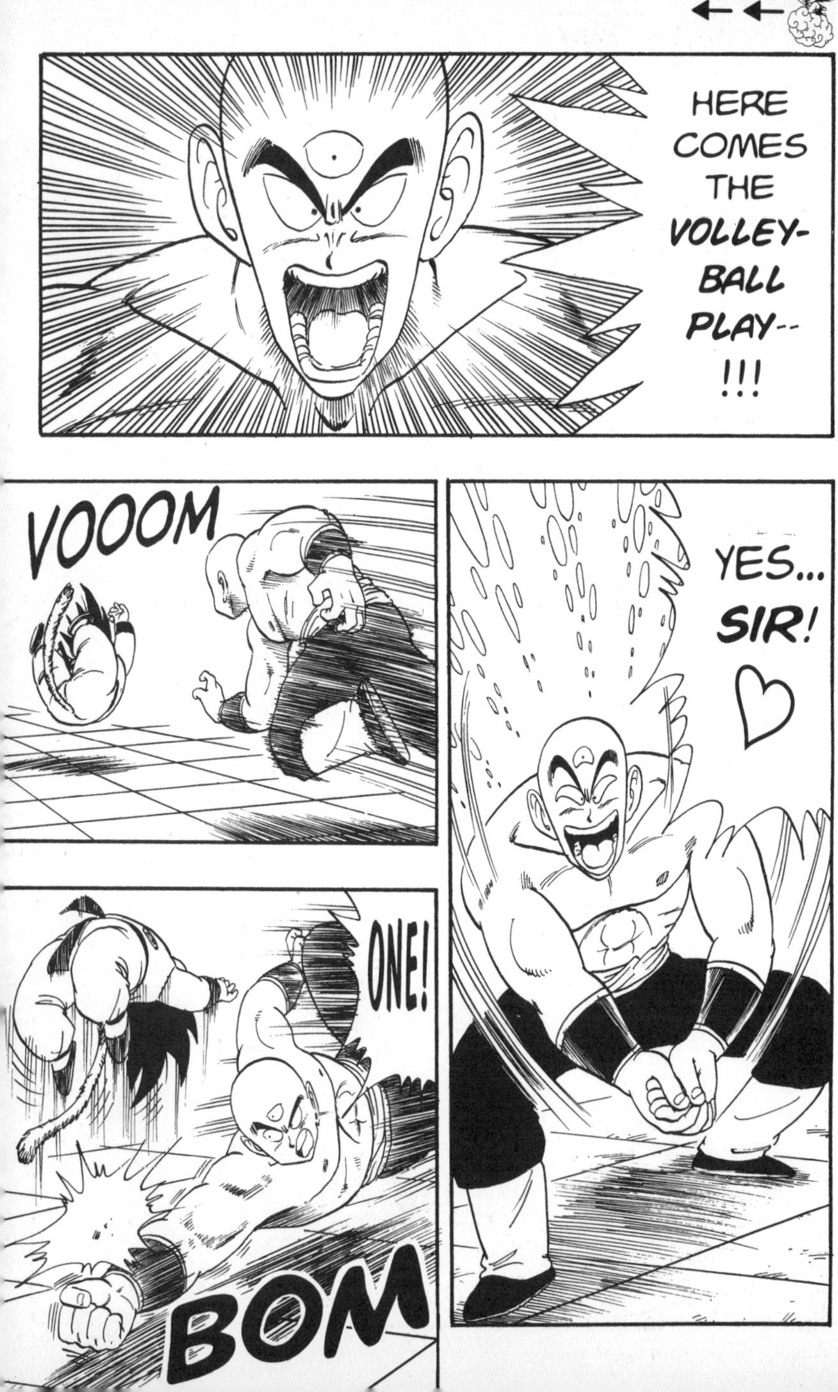
HERE COMES THE VOLLEY-BALL PLAY--!!!
YES... SIR! ♡
VOOOM
ONE!
BOM

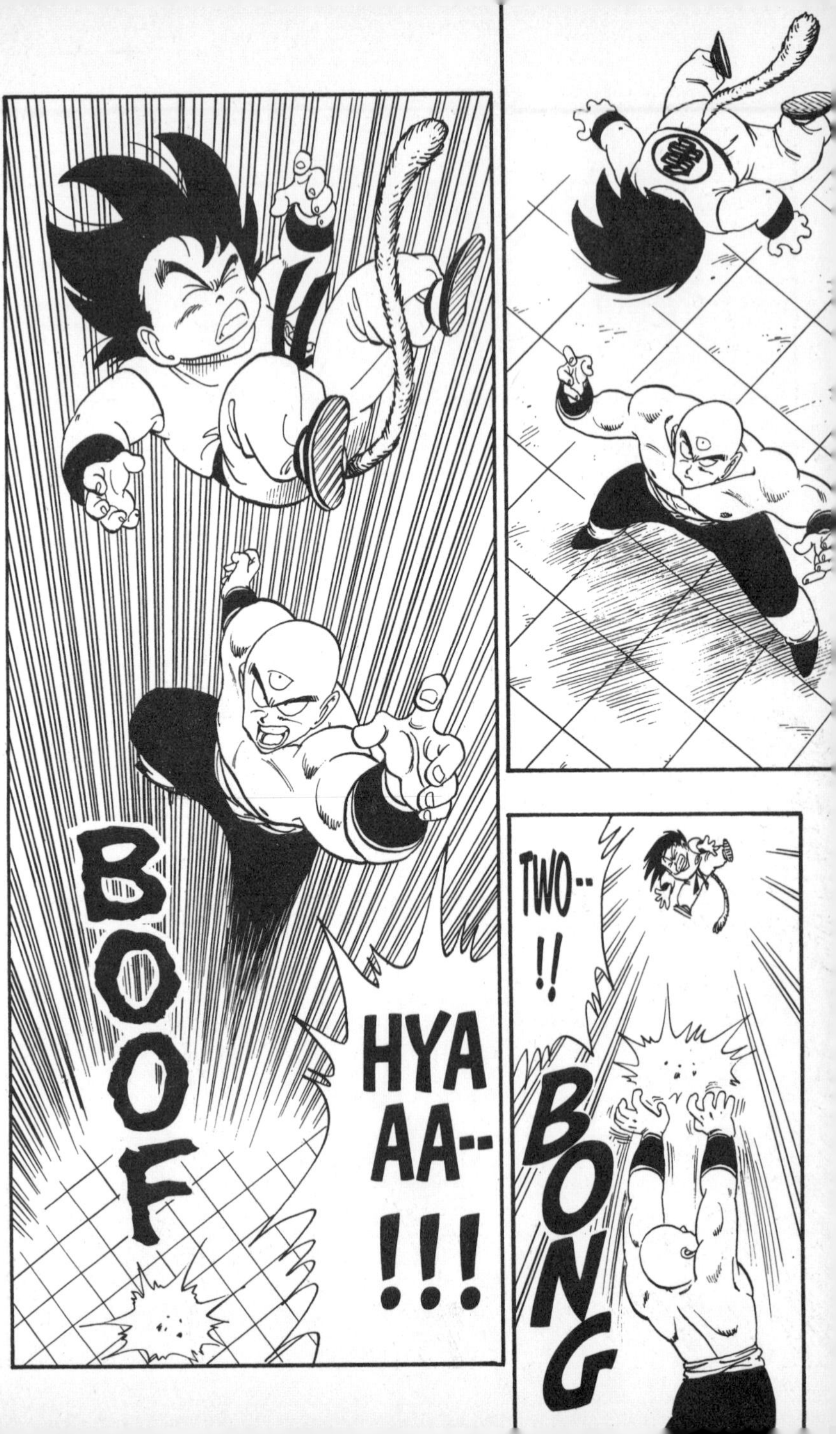
TWO--
!!
BONG
HYA
AA--
!!!
BOOF

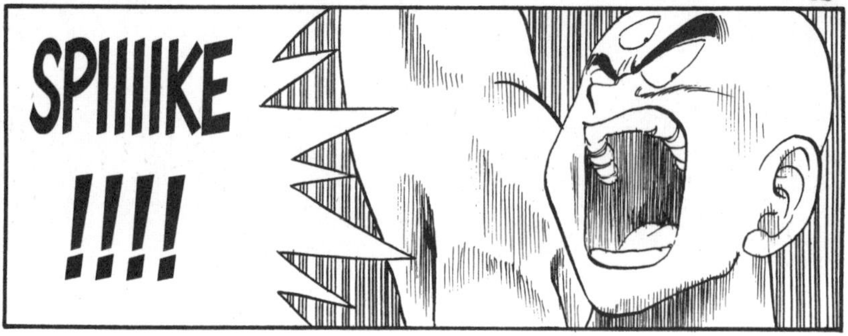
SPIIIKE
!!!!
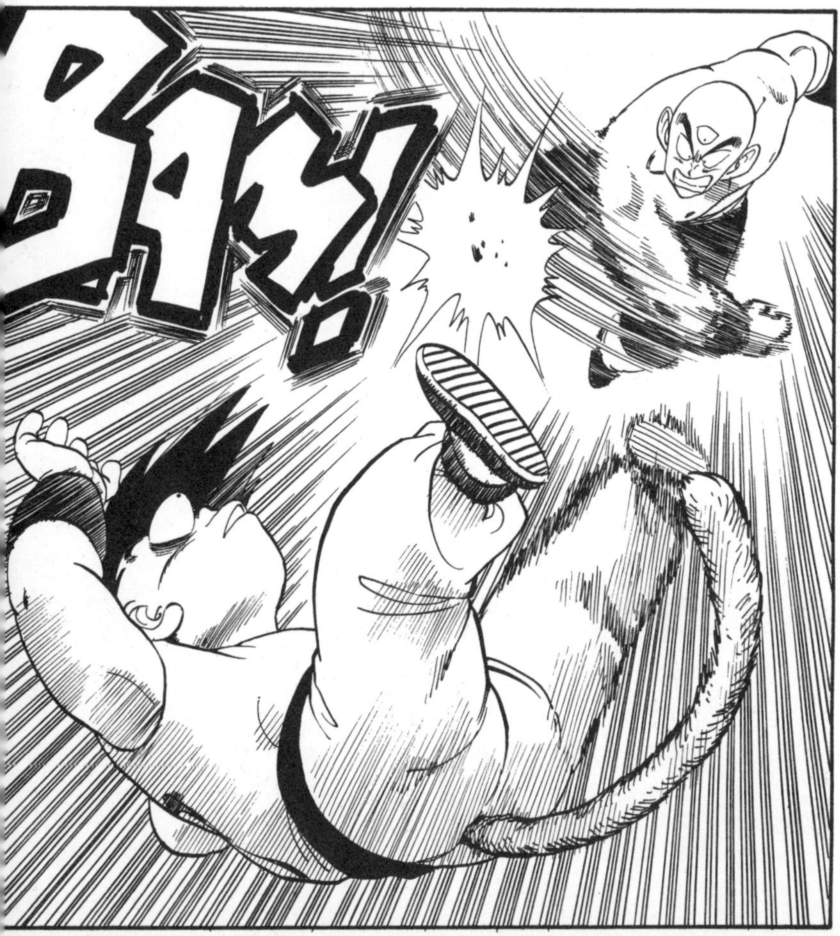

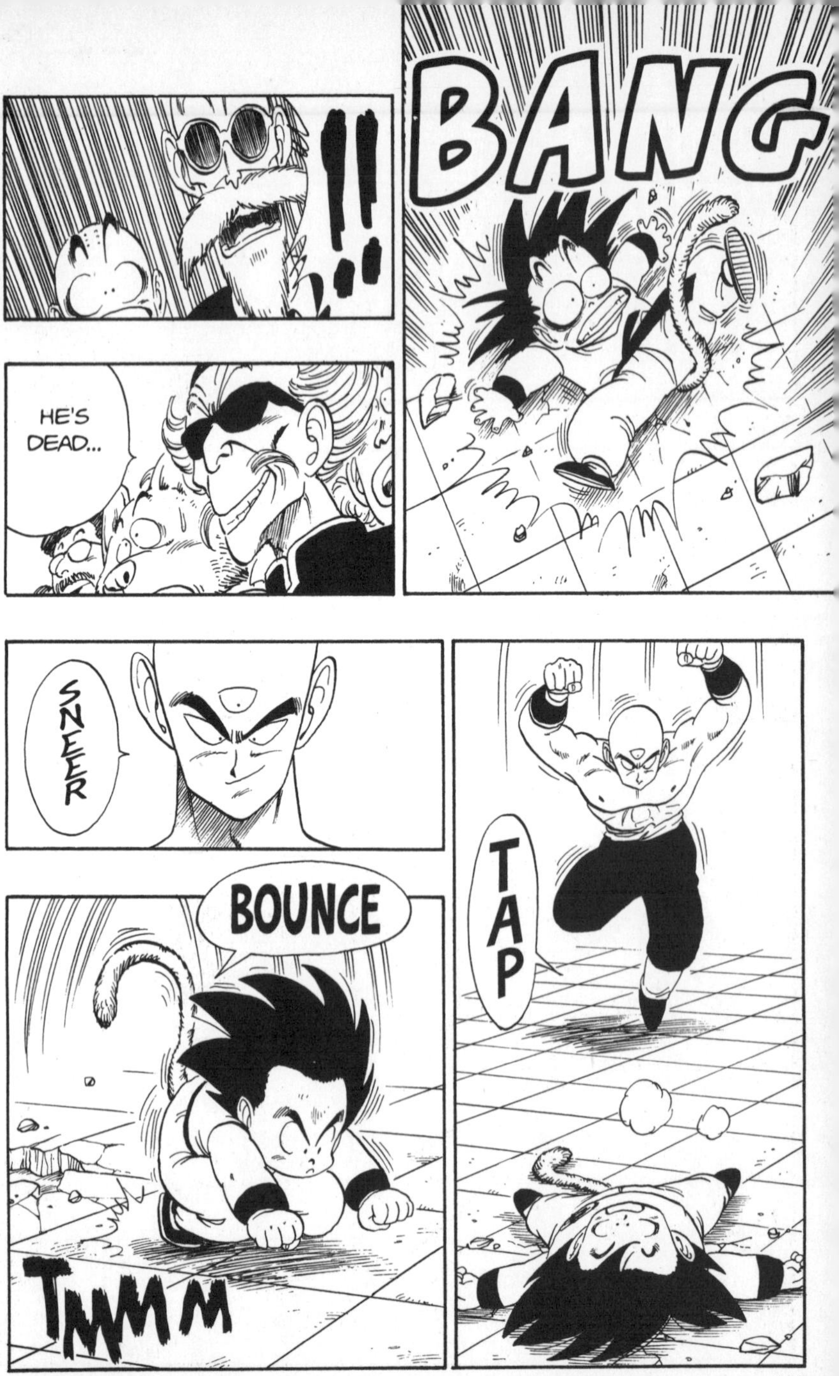
BANG
!!
HE'S DEAD...
TAP
SNEER
BOUNCE
TMMM

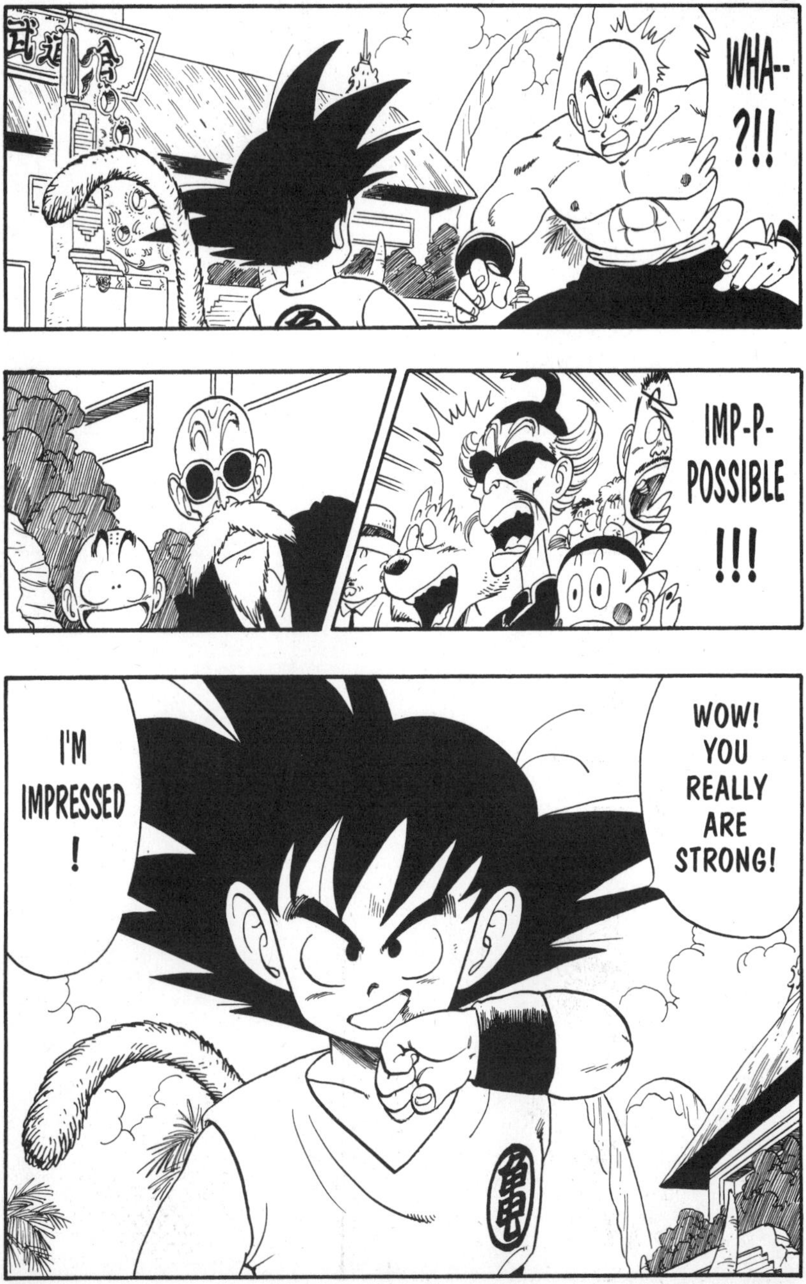
WHA-- ?!!
IMP-P-POSSIBLE !!!
WOW! YOU REALLY ARE STRONG!
I'M IMPRESSED !

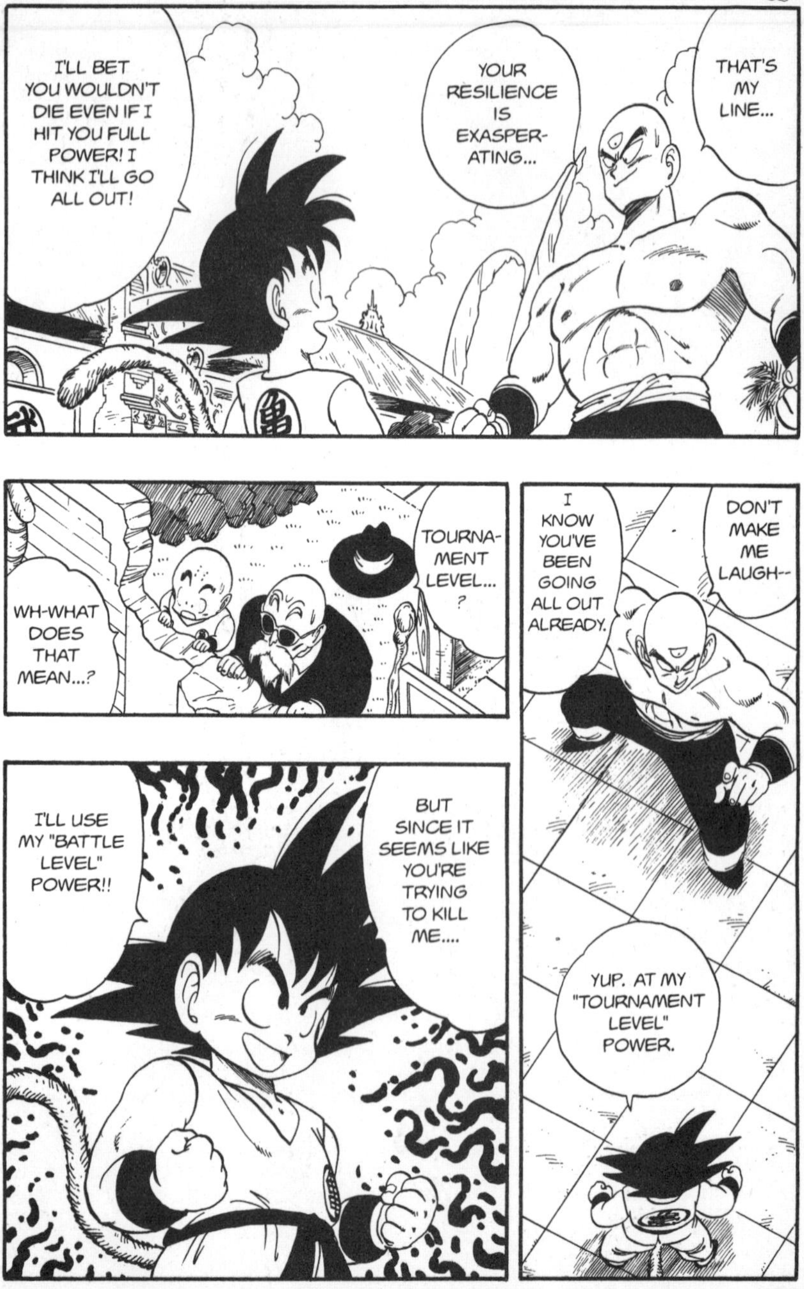
THAT'S MY LINE...
YOUR RESILIENCE IS EXASPER-ATING...
I'LL BET YOU WOULDN'T DIE EVEN IF I HIT YOU FULL POWER! I THINK I'LL GO ALL OUT!
DON'T MAKE ME LAUGH--
I KNOW YOU'VE BEEN GOING ALL OUT ALREADY.
YUP. AT MY "TOURNAMENT LEVEL" POWER.
TOURNA-MENT LEVEL...?
WH-WHAT DOES THAT MEAN...?
BUT SINCE IT SEEMS LIKE YOU'RE TRYING TO KILL ME....
I'LL USE MY "BATTLE LEVEL" POWER!!

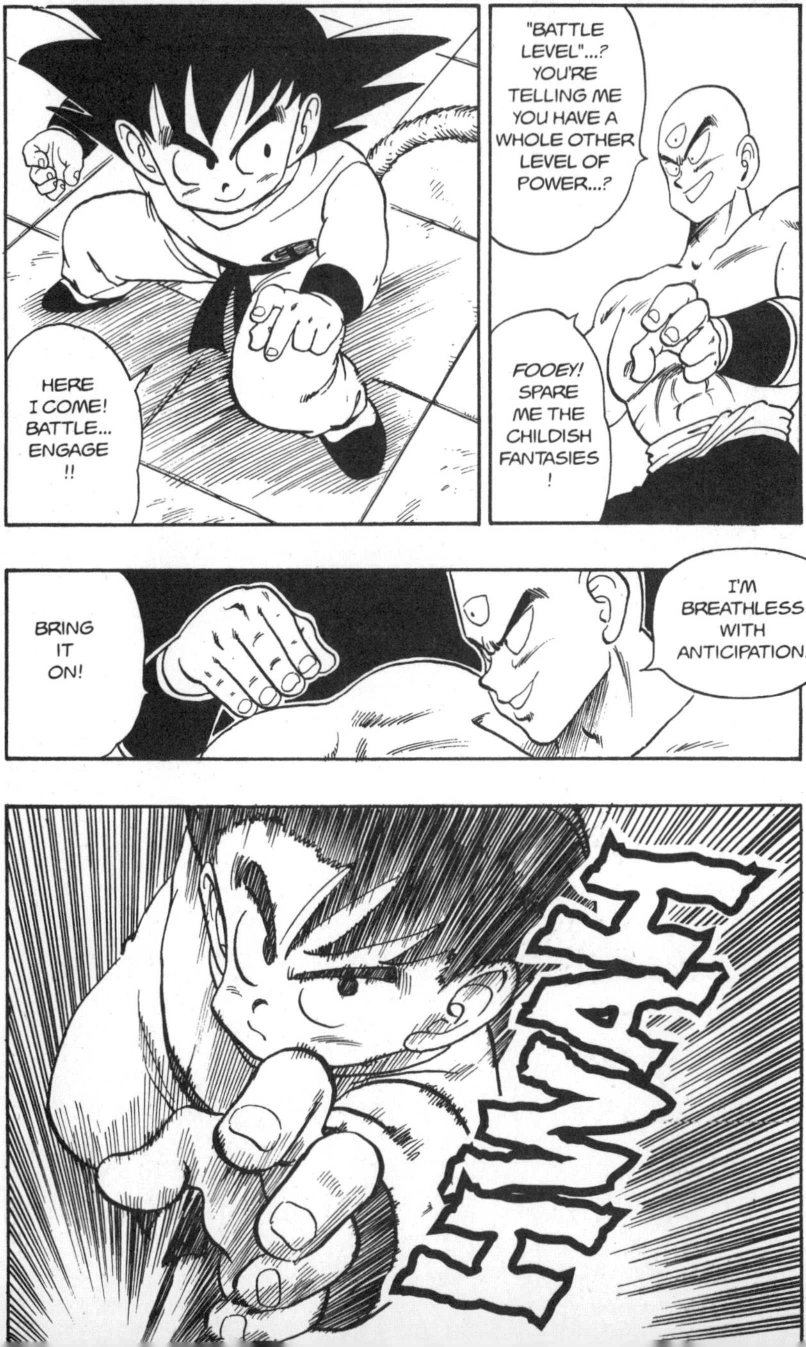
"BATTLE LEVEL"...? YOU'RE TELLING ME YOU HAVE A WHOLE OTHER LEVEL OF POWER...?
FOOEY! SPARE ME THE CHILDISH FANTASIES!
HERE I COME! BATTLE... ENGAGE!!
I'M BREATHLESS WITH ANTICIPATION.
BRING IT ON!

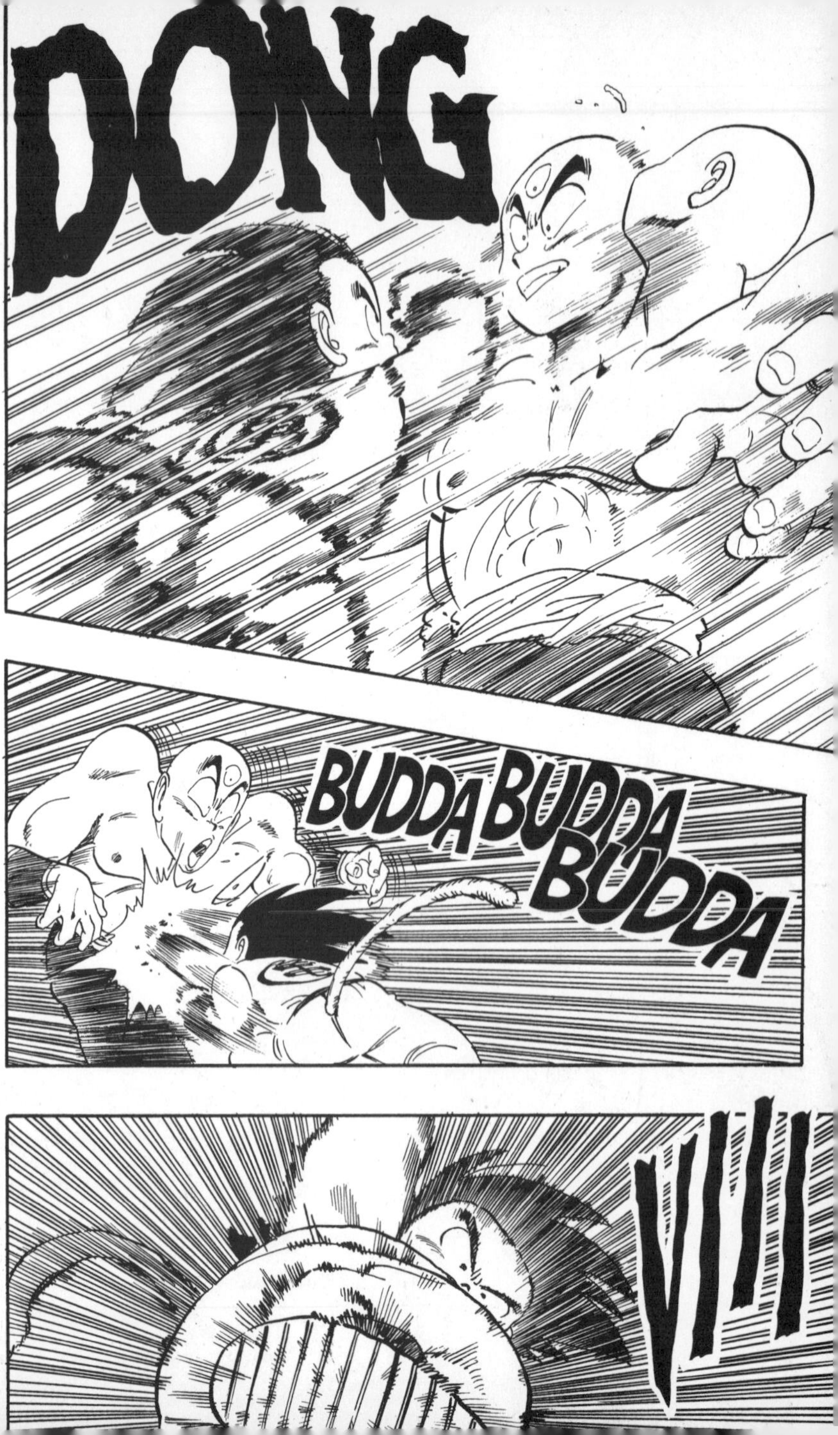
DONG
BUDDA BUDDA BUDDA
VIIII

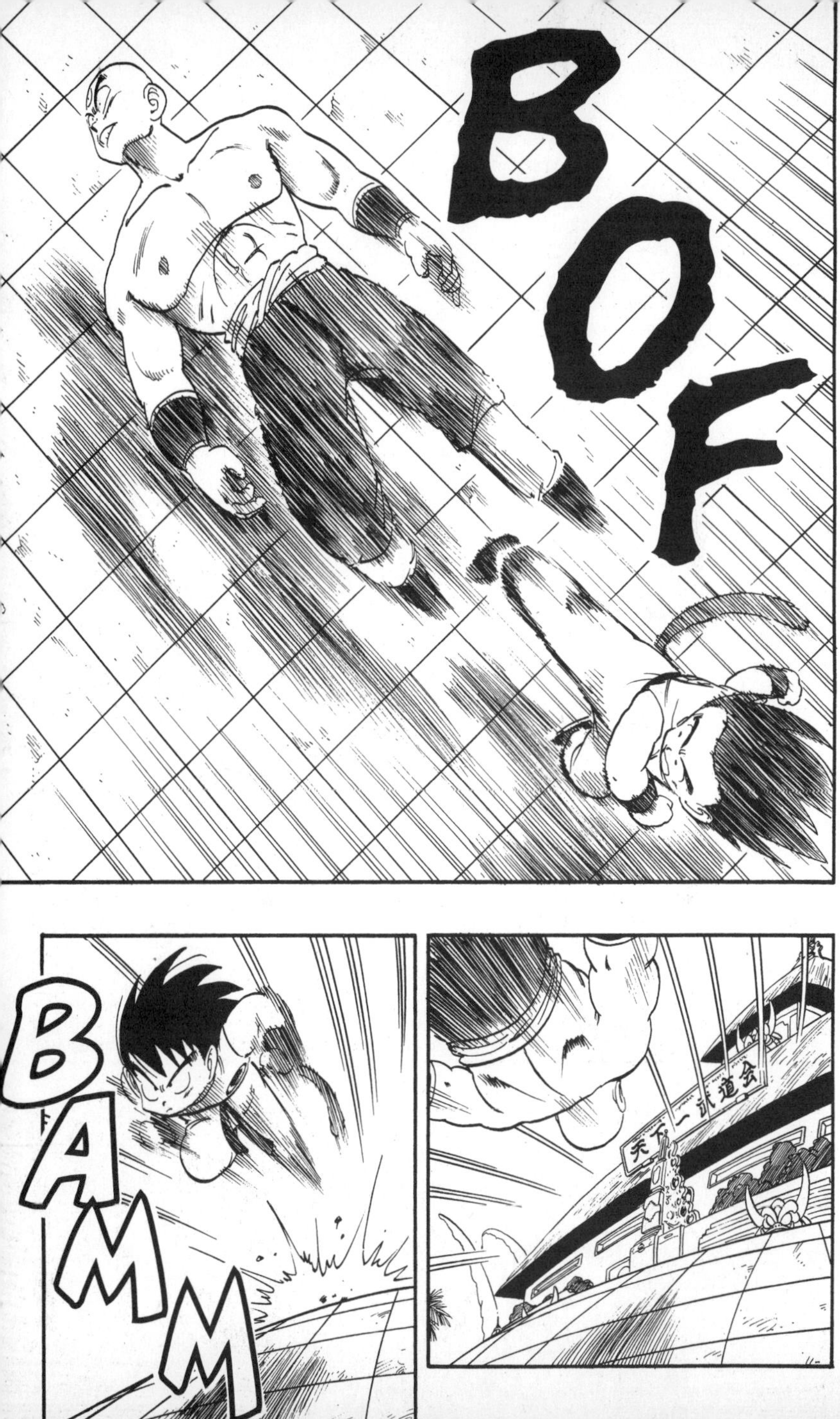
BOF
天下一武道会
BAMMM

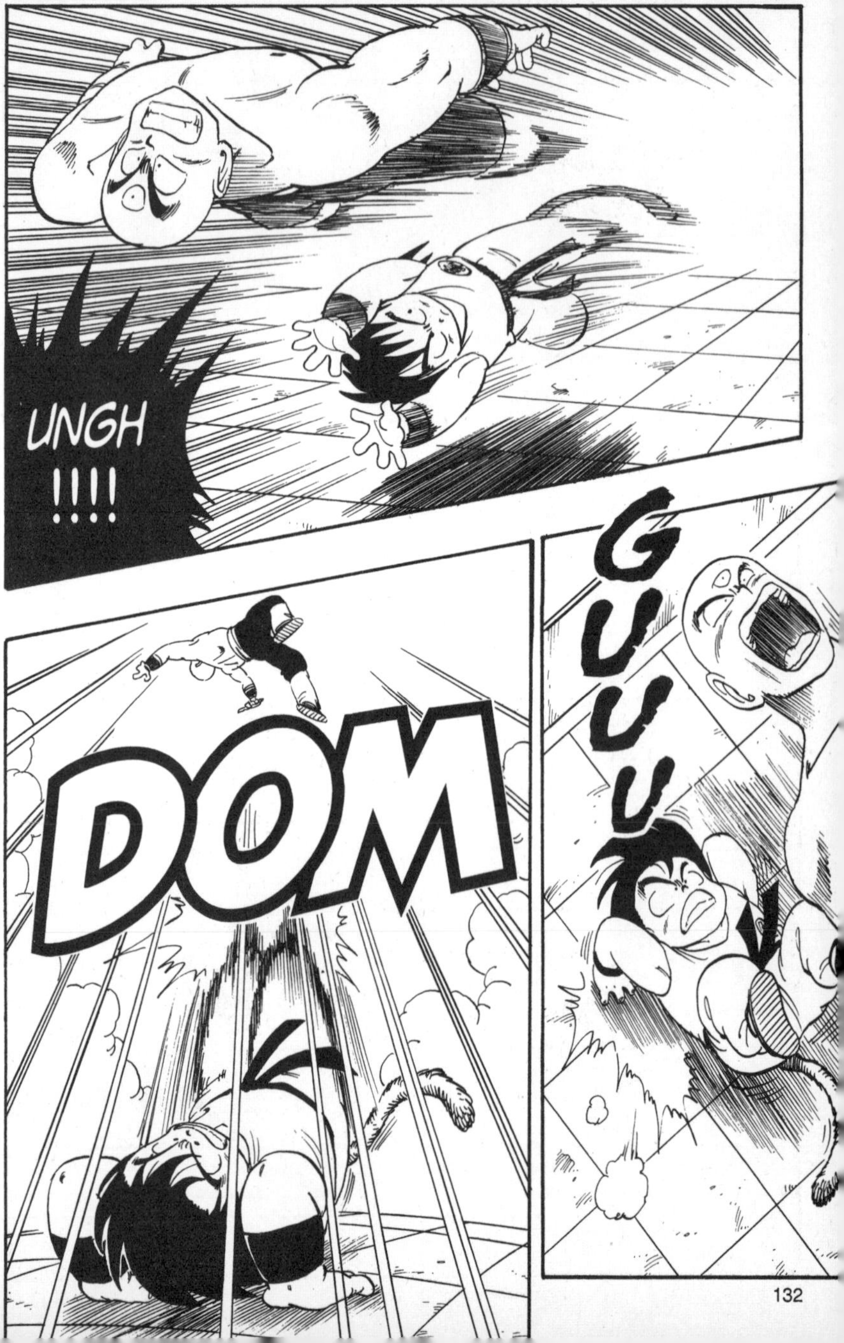
UNGH !!!!
GUUUU
DOM

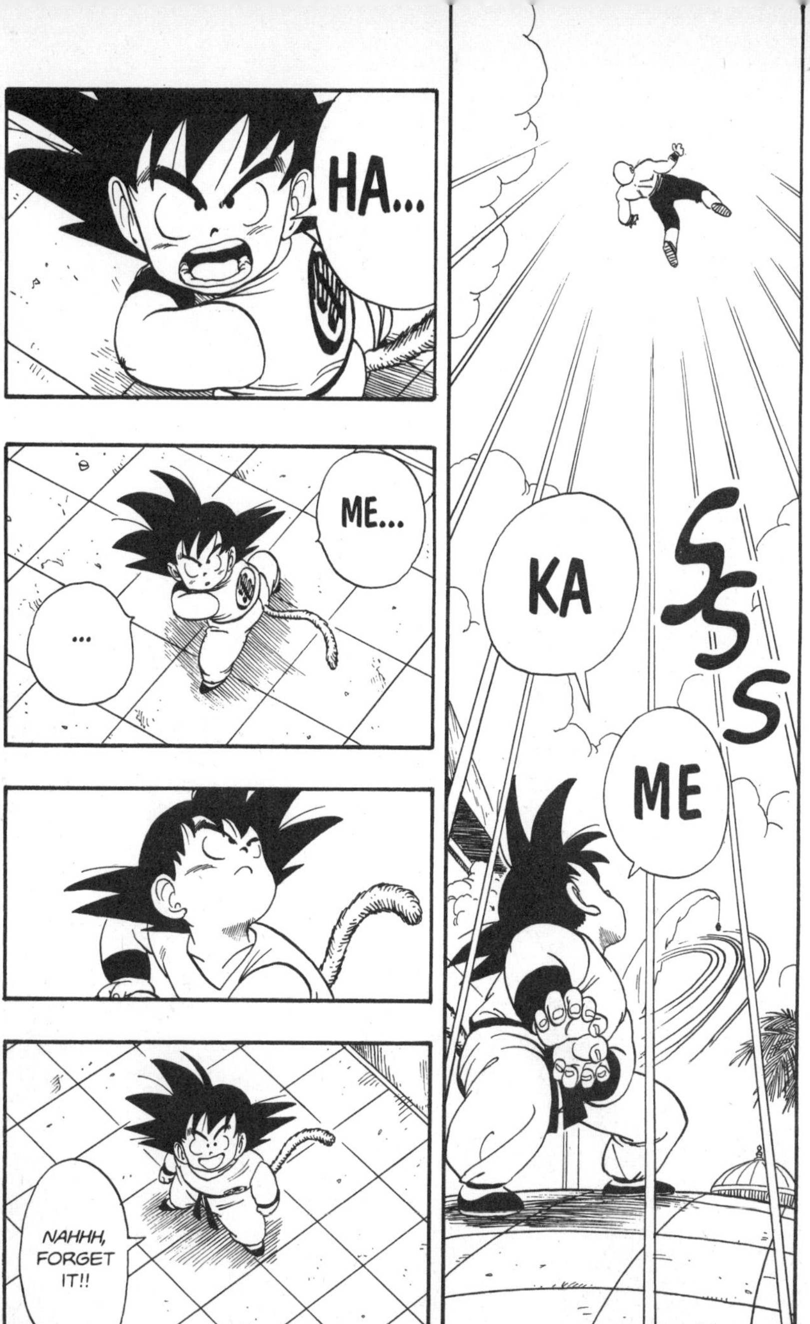
KA
SSS
ME
HA...
ME...
...
NAHHH, FORGET IT!!

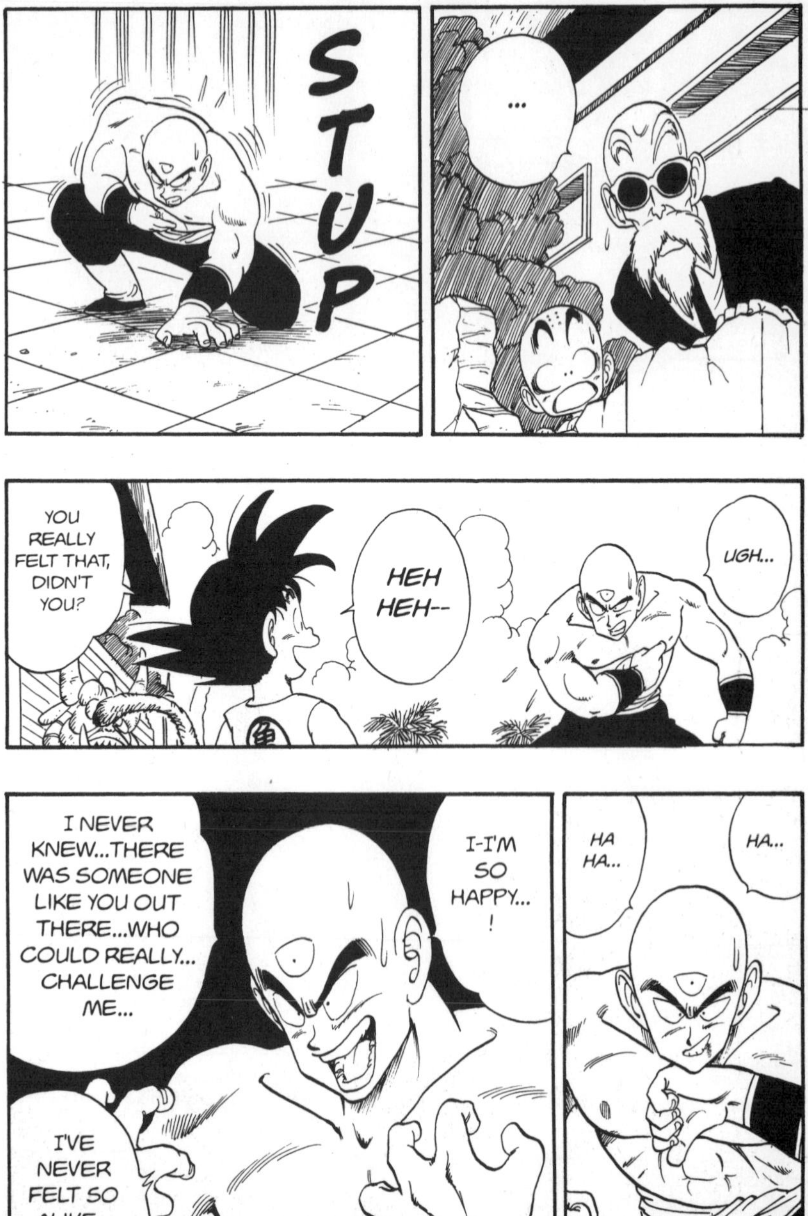
...
STUP
UGH...
HEH HEH--
YOU REALLY FELT THAT, DIDN'T YOU?
HA...
HA HA...
I-I'M SO HAPPY... !
I NEVER KNEW...THERE WAS SOMEONE LIKE YOU OUT THERE...WHO COULD REALLY... CHALLENGE ME...
I'VE NEVER FELT SO ALIVE... !!

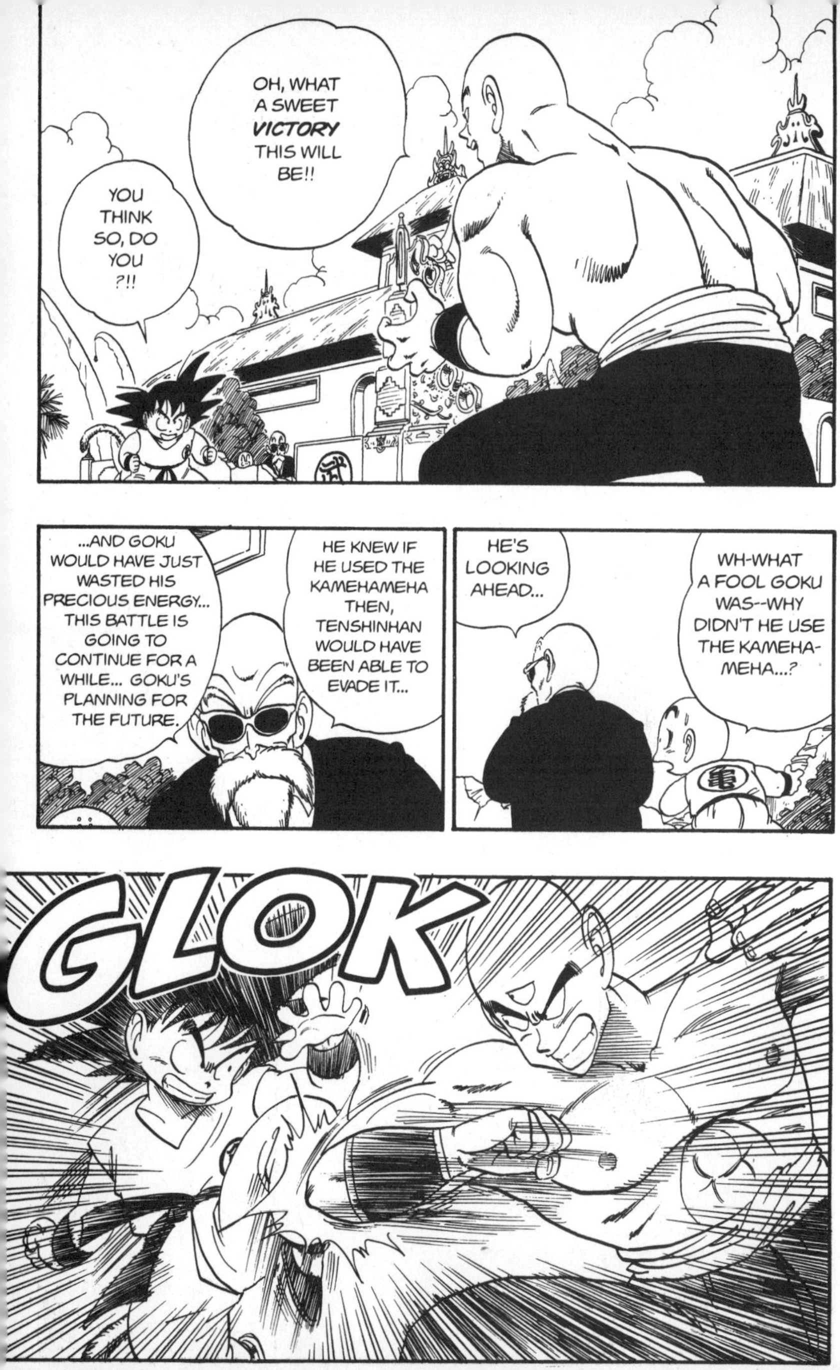
OH, WHAT A SWEET VICTORY THIS WILL BE!!
YOU THINK SO, DO YOU?!!
WH-WHAT A FOOL GOKU WAS--WHY DIDN'T HE USE THE KAMEHA-MEHA...?
HE'S LOOKING AHEAD...
HE KNEW IF HE USED THE KAMEHAMEHA THEN, TENSHINHAN WOULD HAVE BEEN ABLE TO EVADE IT...
...AND GOKU WOULD HAVE JUST WASTED HIS PRECIOUS ENERGY... THIS BATTLE IS GOING TO CONTINUE FOR A WHILE... GOKU'S PLANNING FOR THE FUTURE.
GLOK

NEXT: Tenshinhan in a Pinch!

Tale 130
The Fist of the Sun

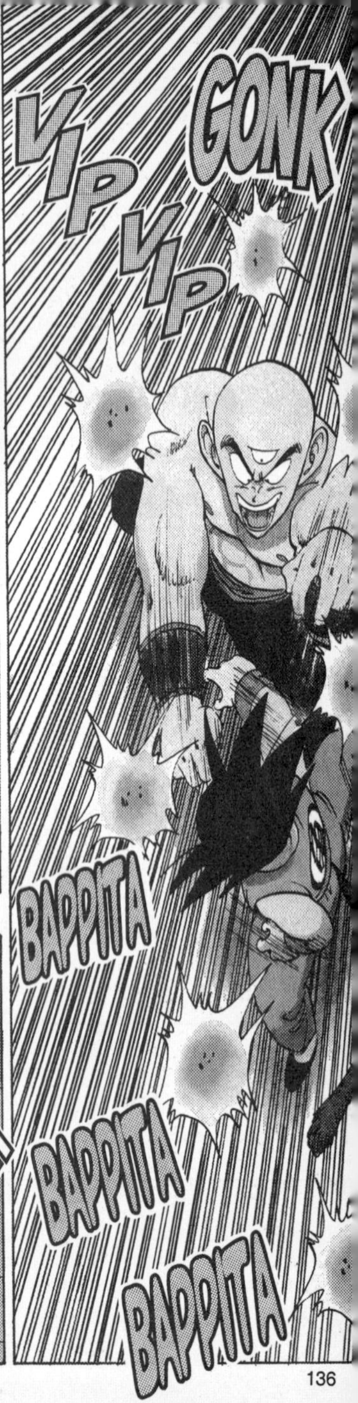
GONK
VIP
VIP
BAPPITA
BAPPITA
BAPPITA

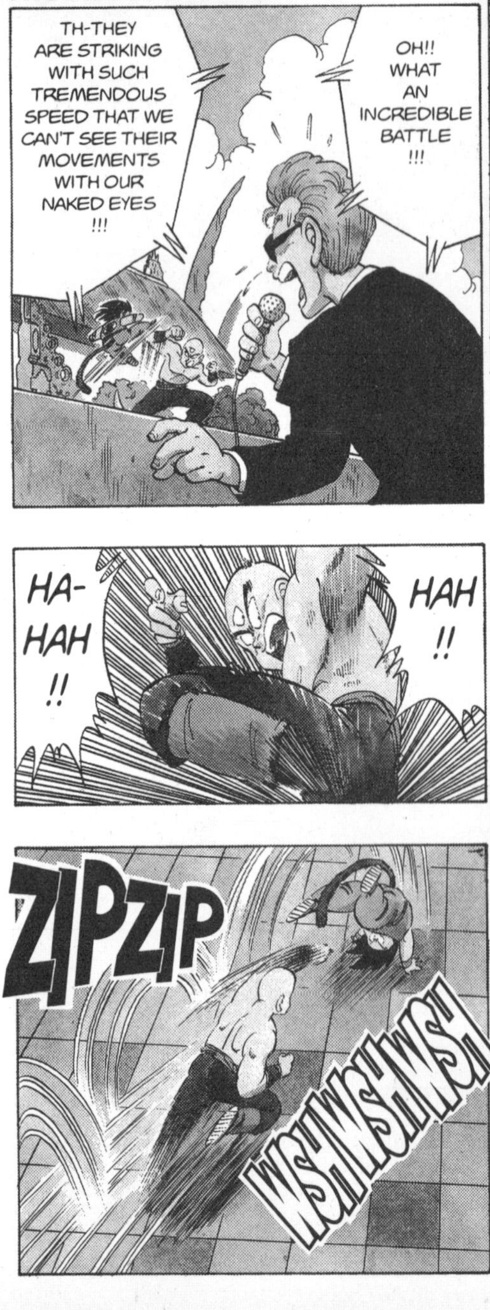
OH!! WHAT AN INCREDIBLE BATTLE !!!
TH-THEY ARE STRIKING WITH SUCH TREMENDOUS SPEED THAT WE CAN'T SEE THEIR MOVEMENTS WITH OUR NAKED EYES !!!
HAH !!
HA-HAH !!
ZIPZIP
WSH! WSH! WSH! WSH!

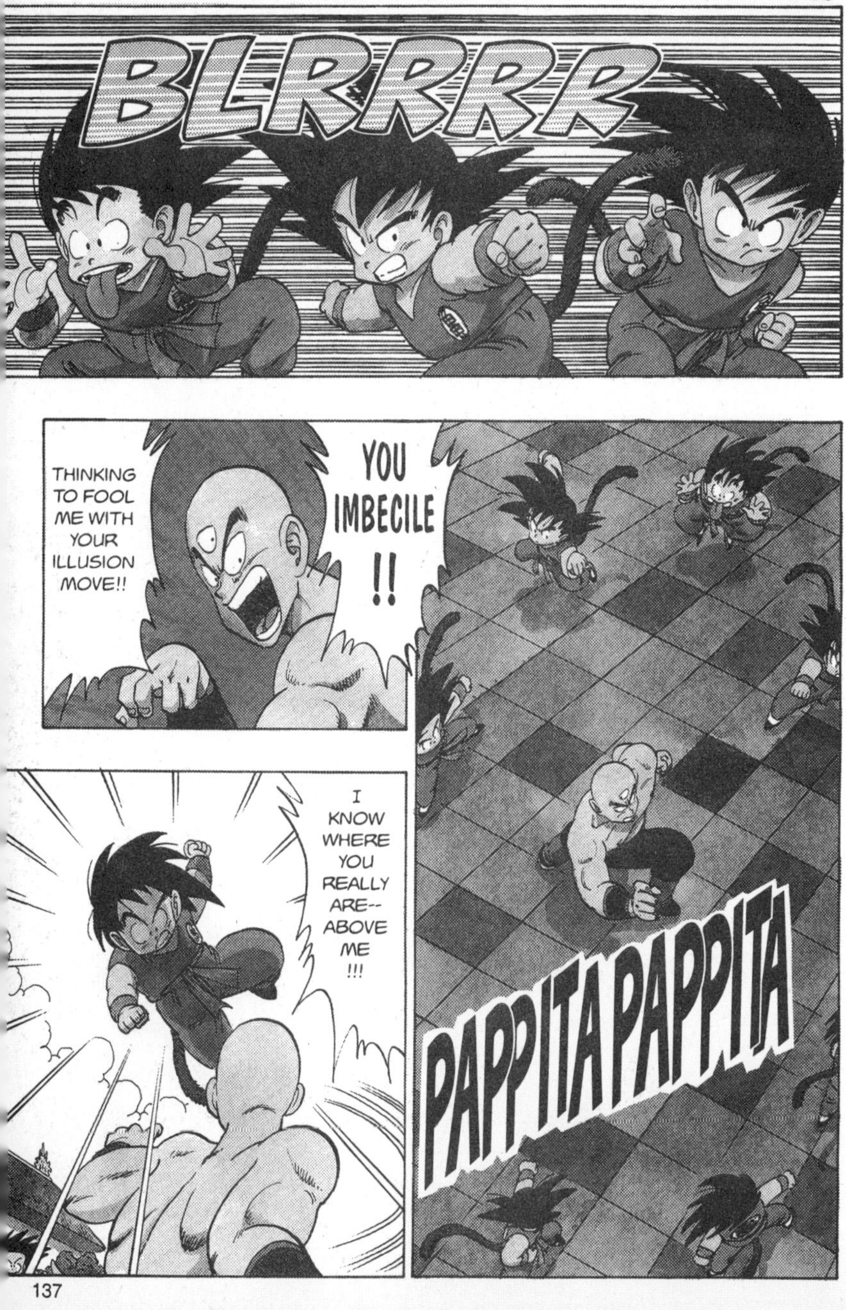
BLRRRR
PAPPITA PAPPITA
YOU IMBECILE!!
THINKING TO FOOL ME WITH YOUR ILLUSION MOVE!!
I KNOW WHERE YOU REALLY ARE-- ABOVE ME!!!

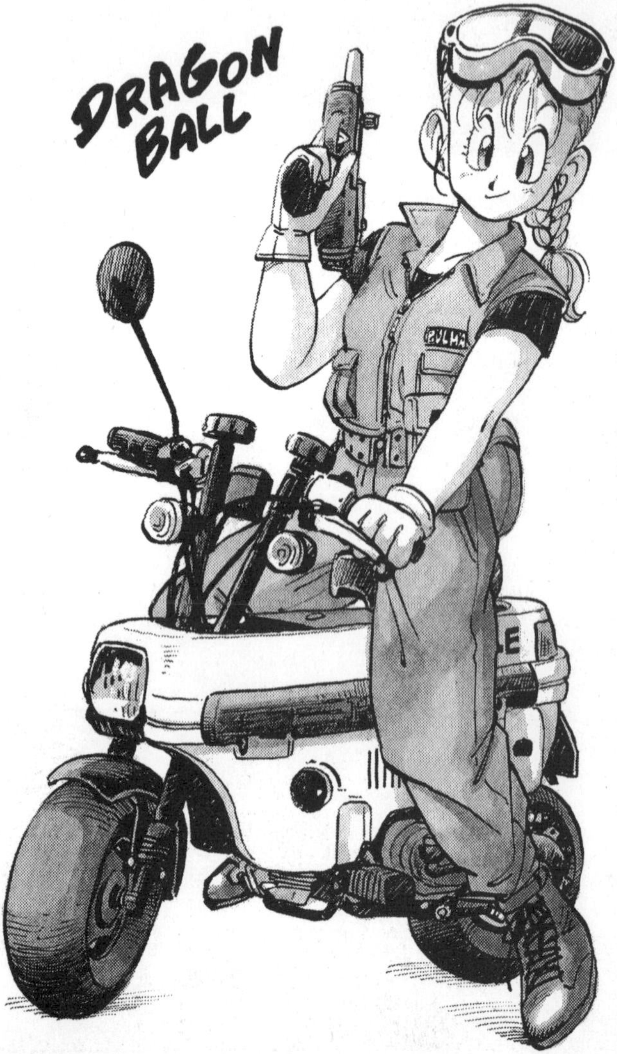
DRAGON BALL

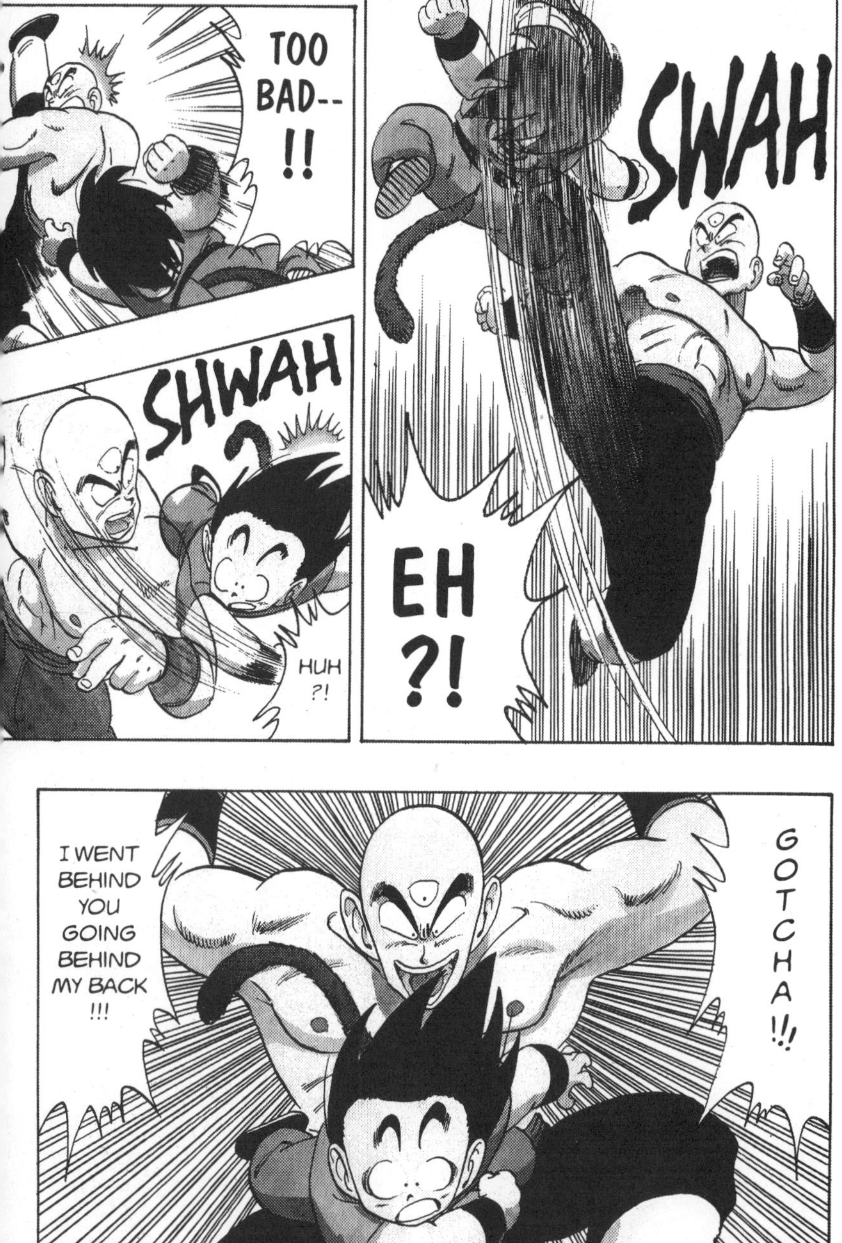
SWAH
EH ?!
TOO BAD-- !!
SHWAH
HUH ?!
GOTCHA!!!
I WENT BEHIND YOU GOING BEHIND MY BACK !!!

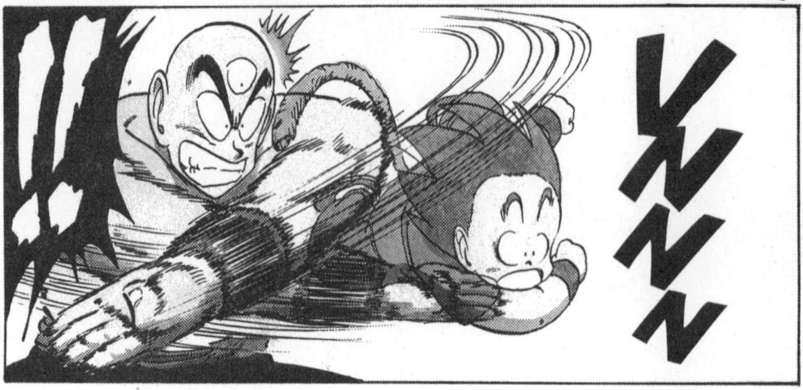
VNNN
!!

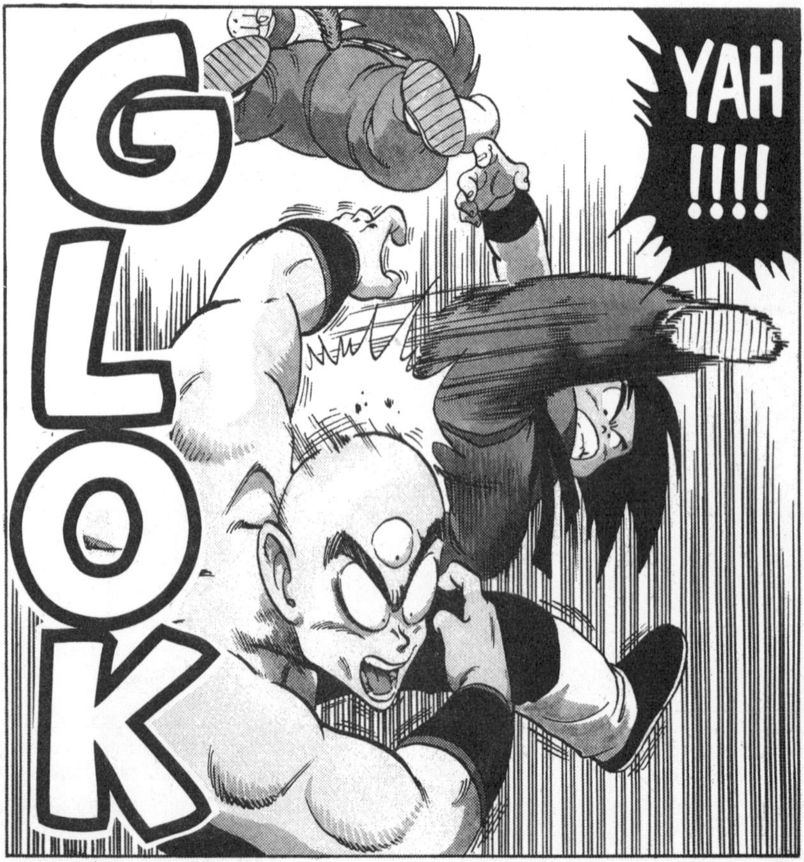
YAH !!!!
GLOK

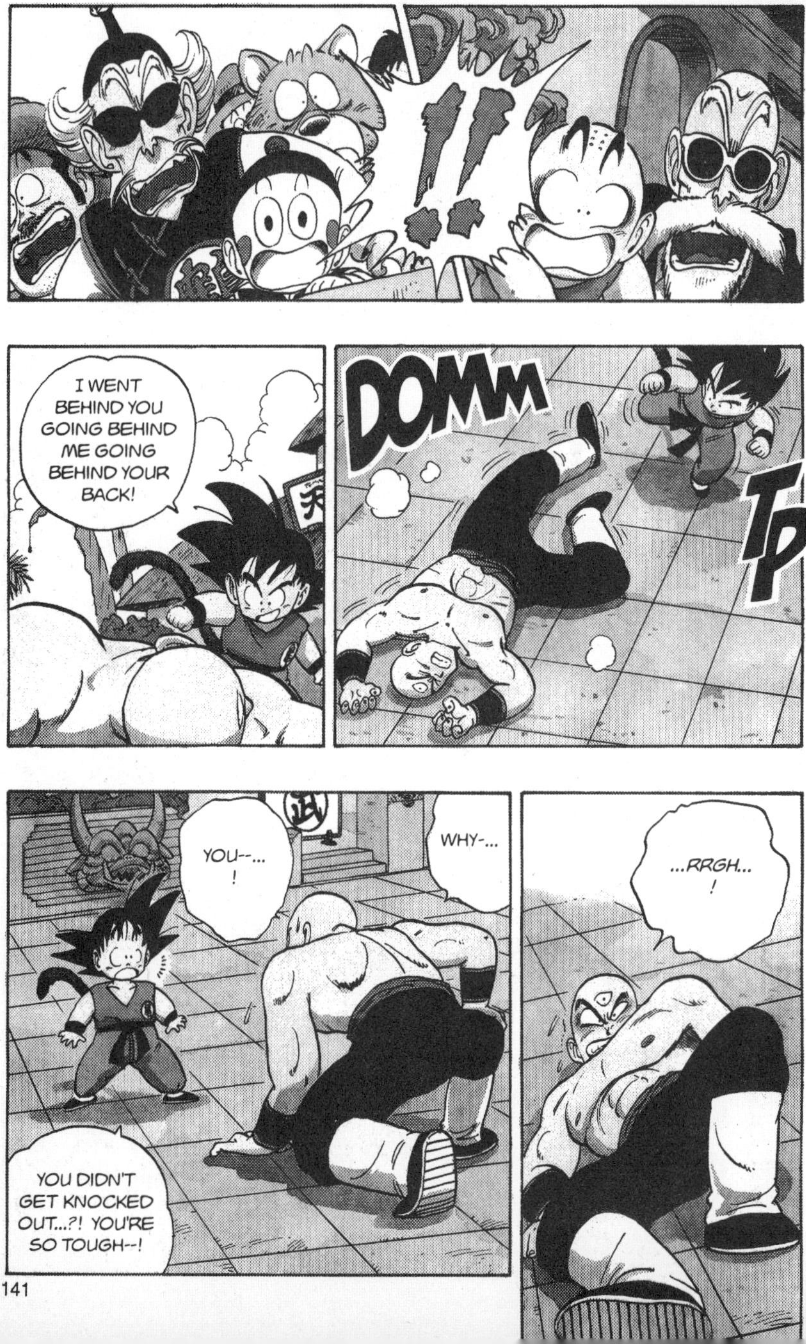
!!
DOMM
TP
I WENT BEHIND YOU GOING BEHIND ME GOING BEHIND YOUR BACK!
...RRGH...!
WHY-...
YOU--...!
YOU DIDN'T GET KNOCKED OUT...?! YOU'RE SO TOUGH--!

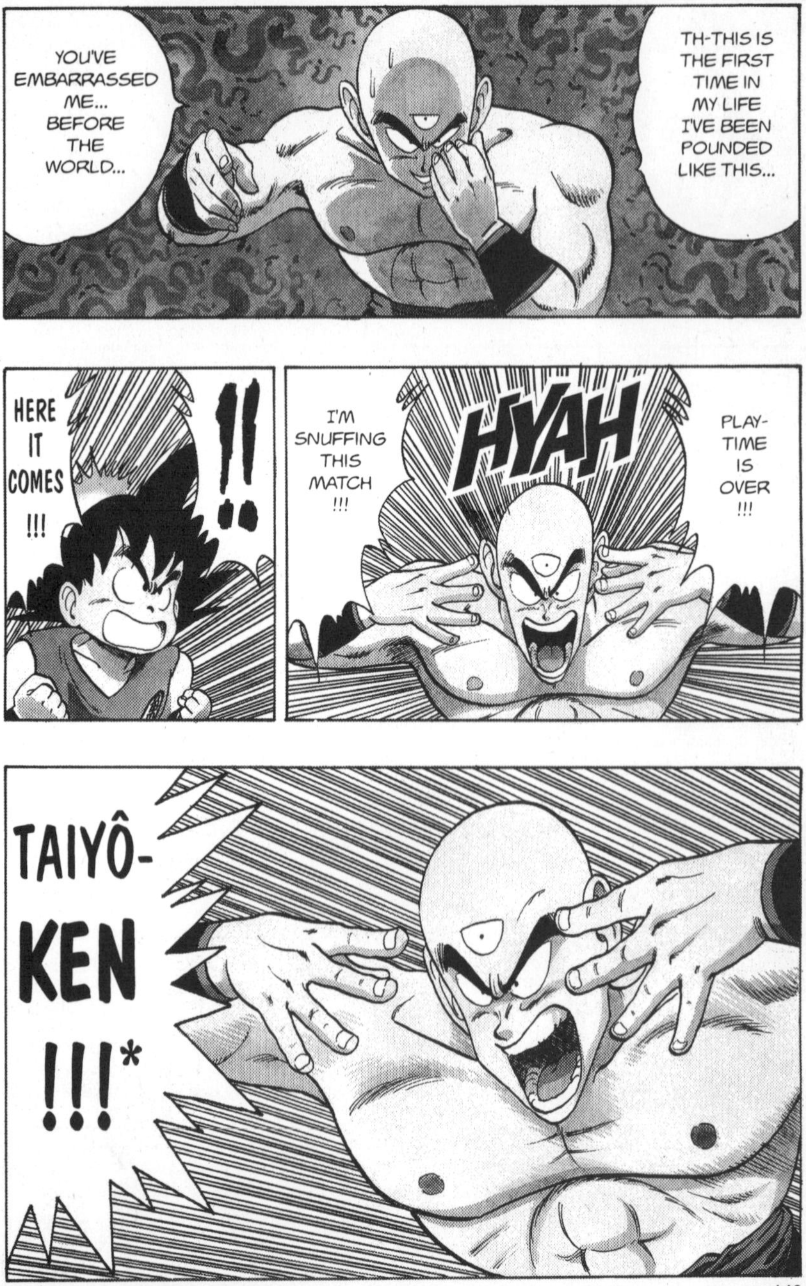
TH-THIS IS THE FIRST TIME IN MY LIFE I'VE BEEN POUNDED LIKE THIS...
YOU'VE EMBARRASSED ME... BEFORE THE WORLD...
PLAY-TIME IS OVER!!!
HYAH
I'M SNUFFING THIS MATCH!!!
!!
HERE IT COMES!!!
TAIYÔ-KEN!!!*

*A.K.A. "FIST OF THE SUN"—ED.

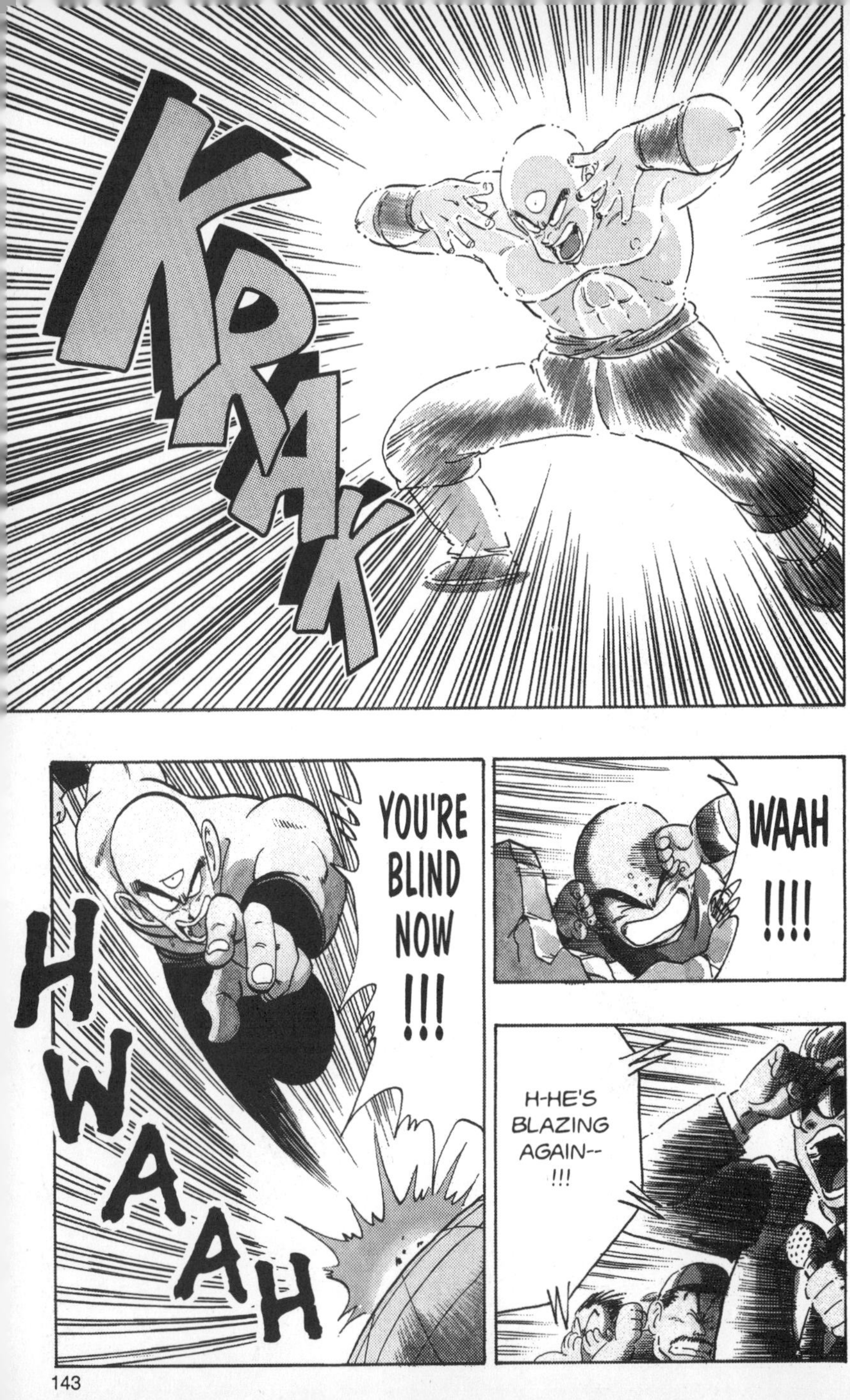
KRAKK
WAAH !!!!
H-HE'S BLAZING AGAIN-- !!!
YOU'RE BLIND NOW !!!
HWAAH

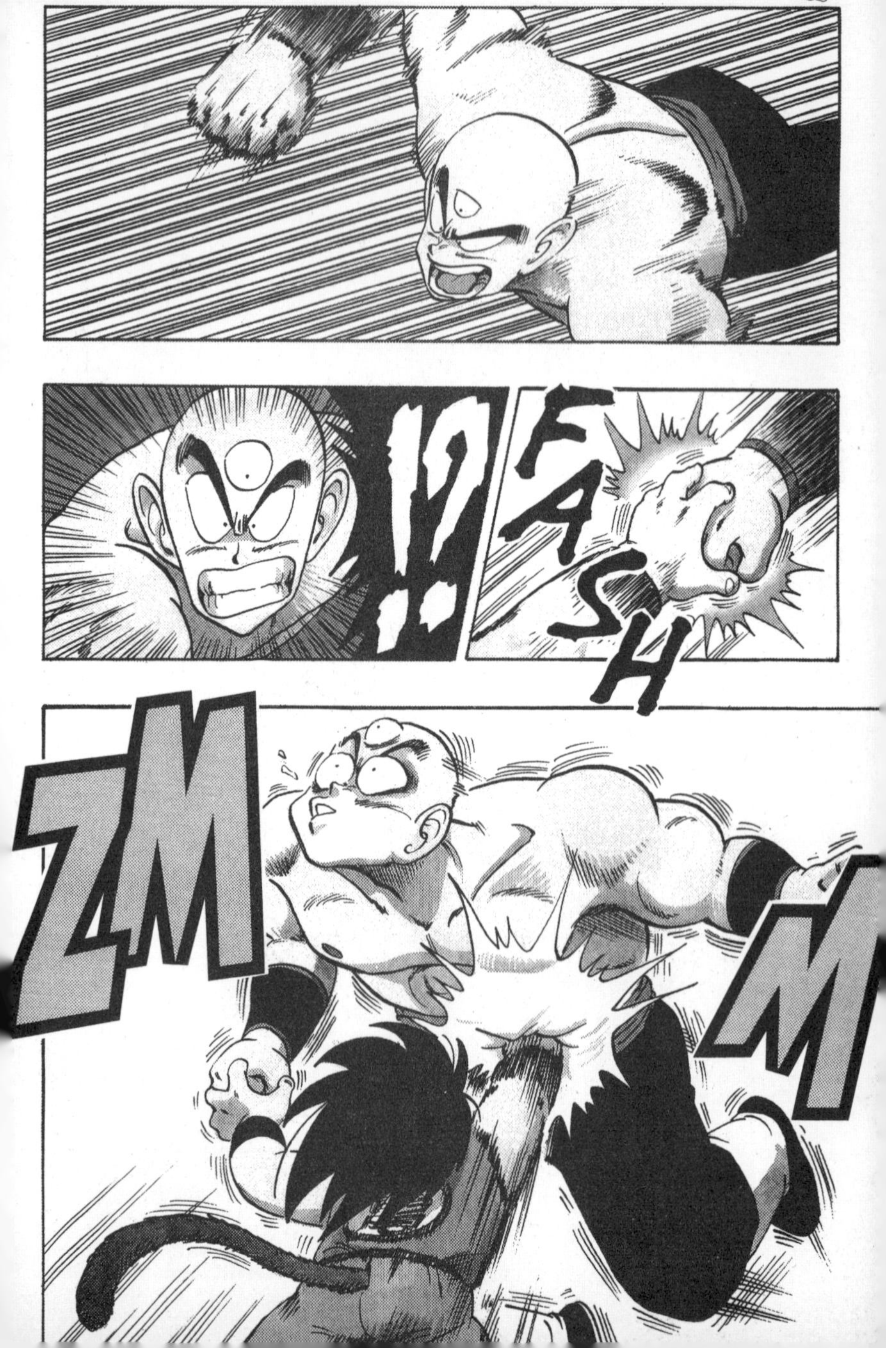
FASH
!?
ZMM

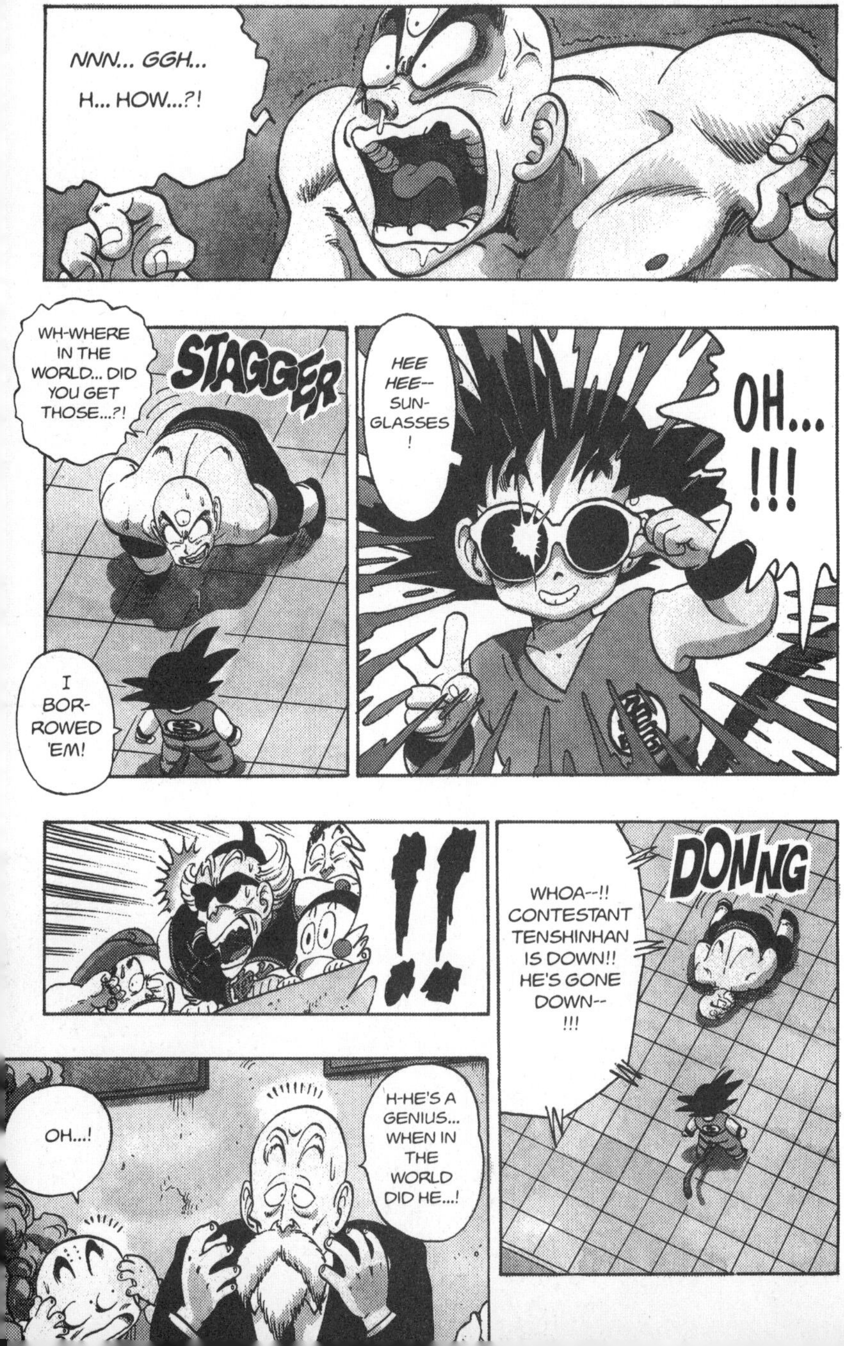
NNN... GGH...
H... HOW...?!
HEE HEE-- SUN-GLASSES!
OH... !!!
STAGGER
WH-WHERE IN THE WORLD... DID YOU GET THOSE...?!
I BOR-ROWED 'EM!
DONNG
WHOA--!! CONTESTANT TENSHINHAN IS DOWN!! HE'S GONE DOWN--!!!
!!
H-HE'S A GENIUS... WHEN IN THE WORLD DID HE...!
OH...!

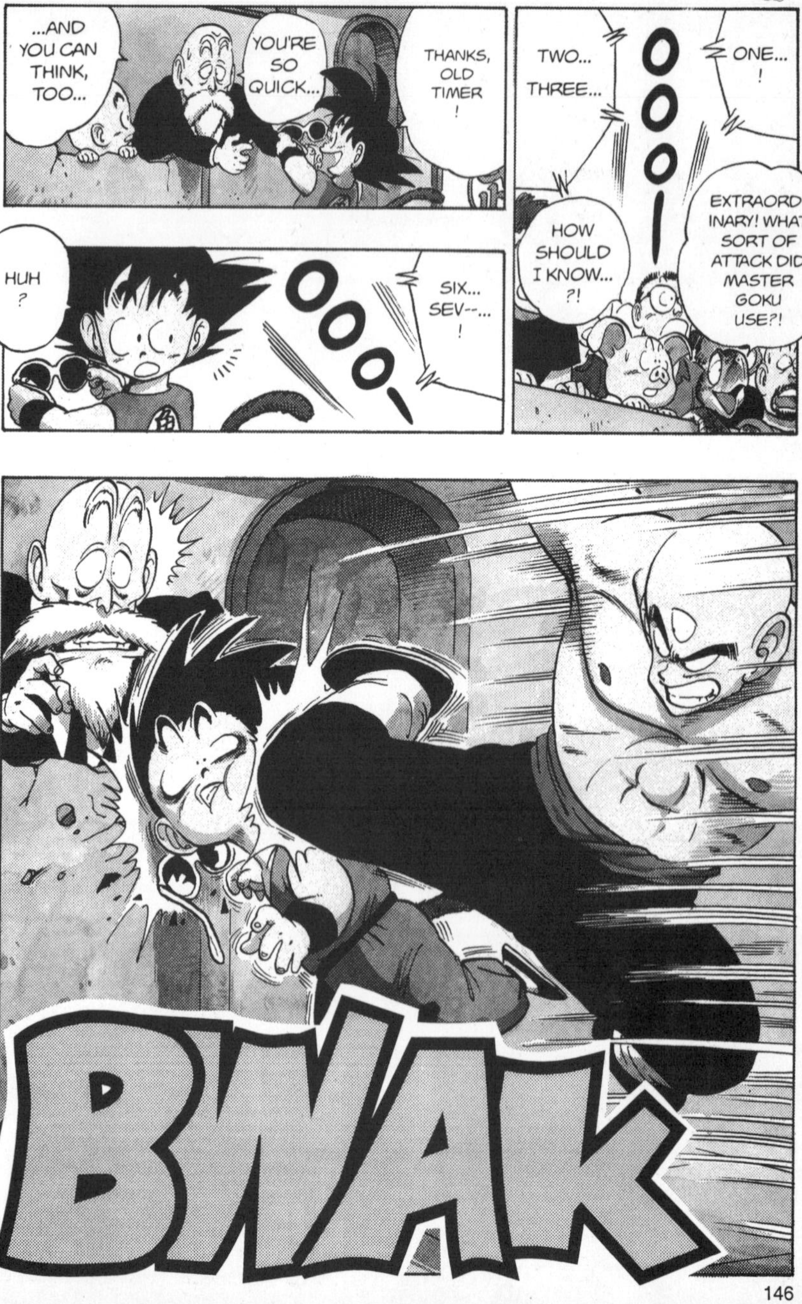
ONE...!
TWO... THREE...
OOOOI
EXTRAORD-INARY! WHAT SORT OF ATTACK DID MASTER GOKU USE?!
HOW SHOULD I KNOW...?!
THANKS, OLD TIMER!
YOU'RE SO QUICK...
...AND YOU CAN THINK, TOO...
SIX... SEV--...!
OOOOI
HUH?
BWAK

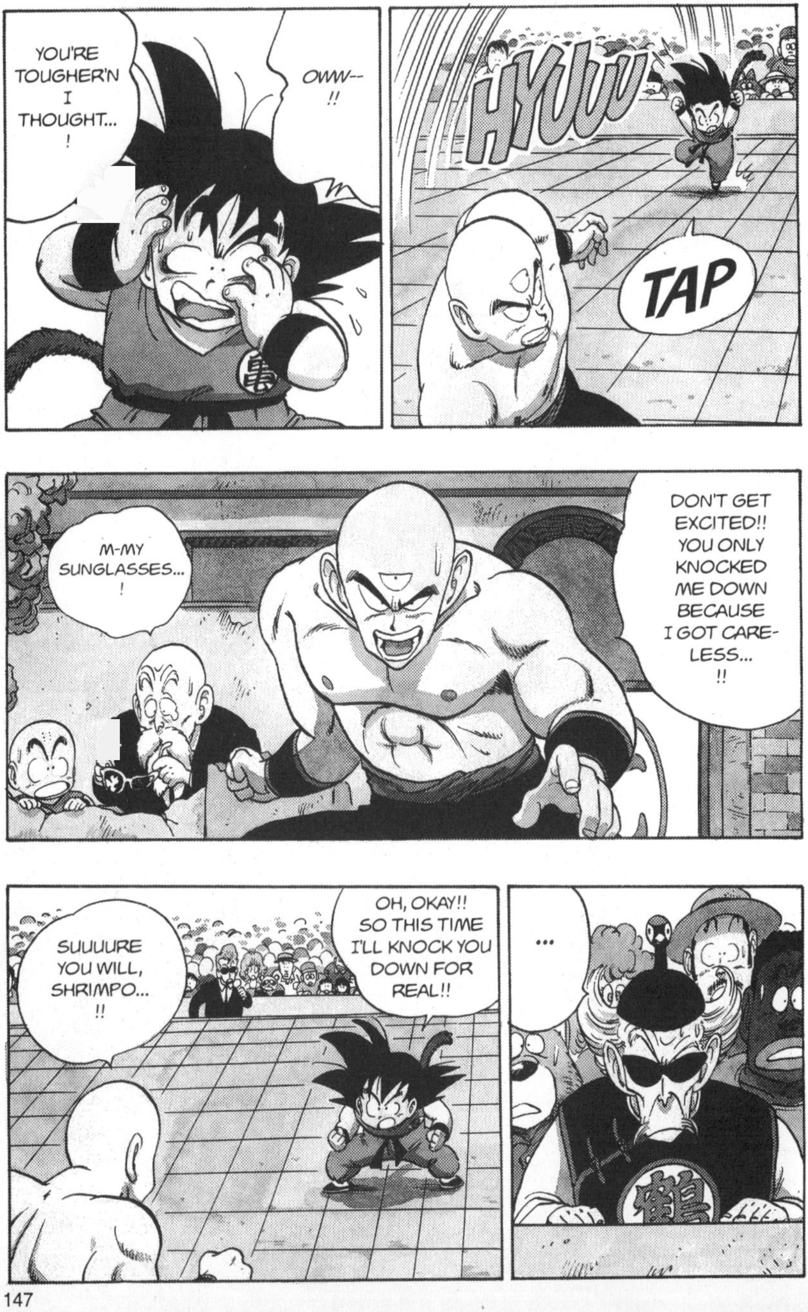
HYUUU
TAP
OWW--!!
YOU'RE TOUGHER'N I THOUGHT...!
DON'T GET EXCITED!! YOU ONLY KNOCKED ME DOWN BECAUSE I GOT CARE-LESS...!!
M-MY SUNGLASSES...!
...
OH, OKAY!! SO THIS TIME I'LL KNOCK YOU DOWN FOR REAL!!
SUUUURE YOU WILL, SHRIMPO...!!

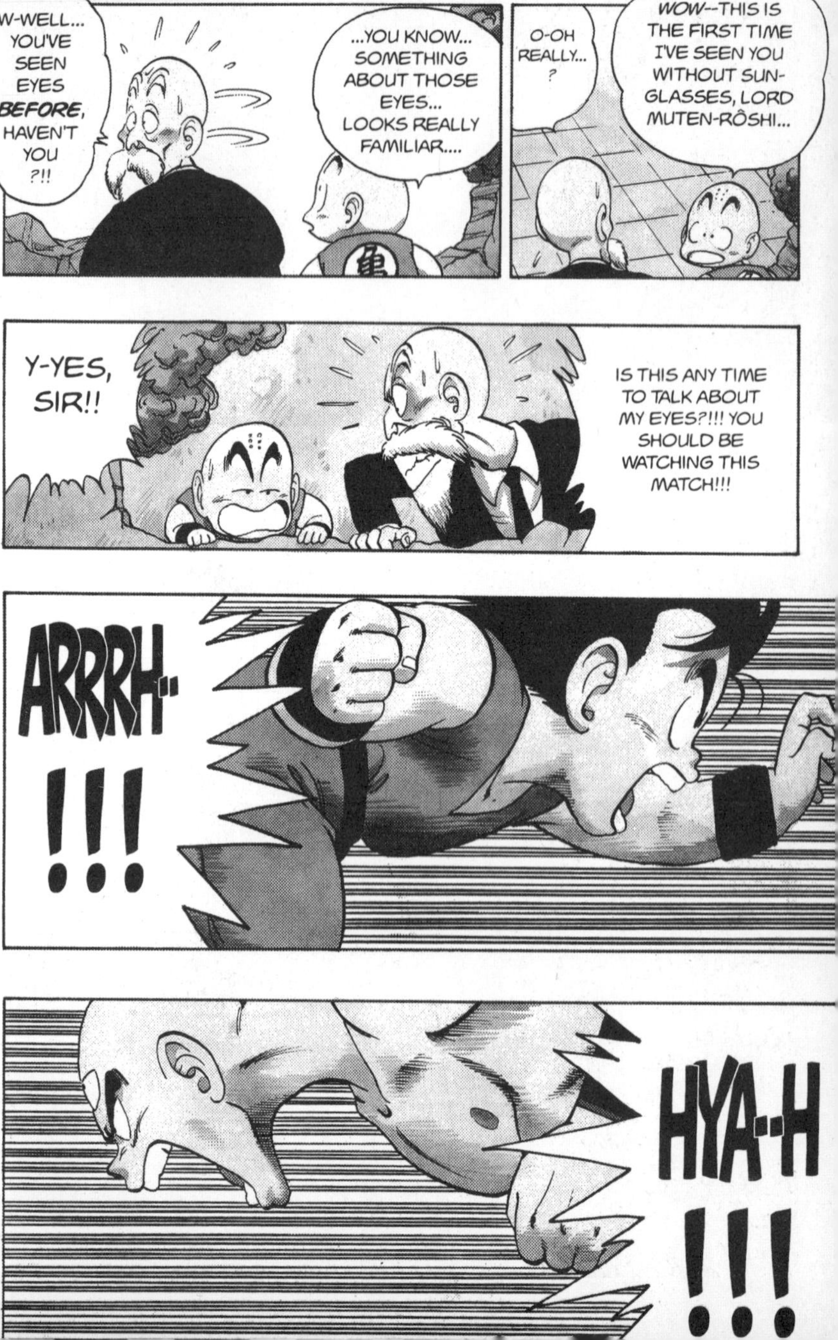
WOW--THIS IS THE FIRST TIME I'VE SEEN YOU WITHOUT SUNGLASSES, LORD MUTEN-RÔSHI...
O-OH REALLY...?
...YOU KNOW... SOMETHING ABOUT THOSE EYES... LOOKS REALLY FAMILIAR....
W-WELL... YOU'VE SEEN EYES *BEFORE*, HAVEN'T YOU?!!
IS THIS ANY TIME TO TALK ABOUT MY EYES?!!! YOU SHOULD BE WATCHING THIS MATCH!!!
Y-YES, SIR!!
ARRRH--!!!
HYA--H!!!

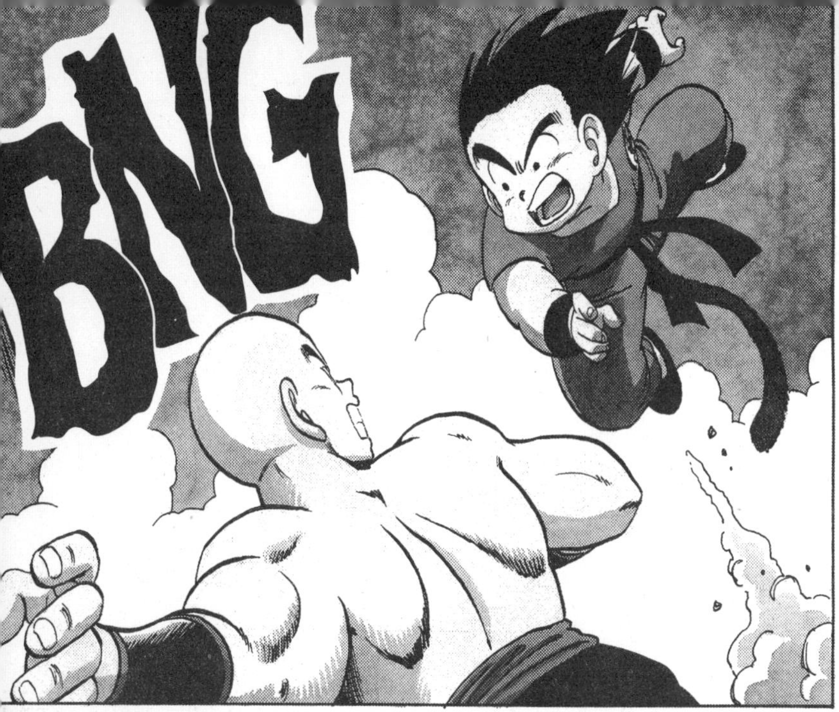
BNG

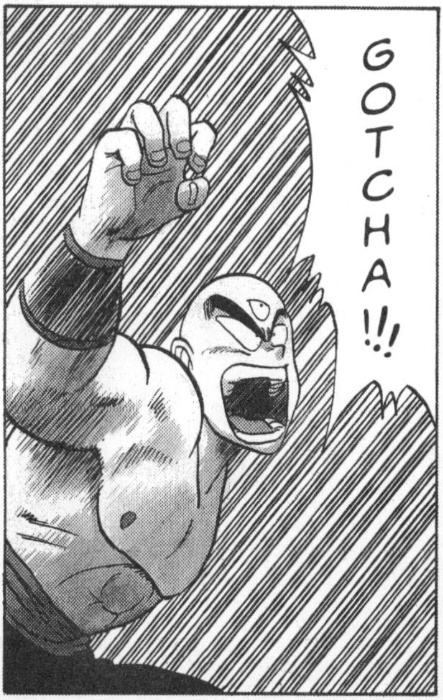
GOTCHA!!!

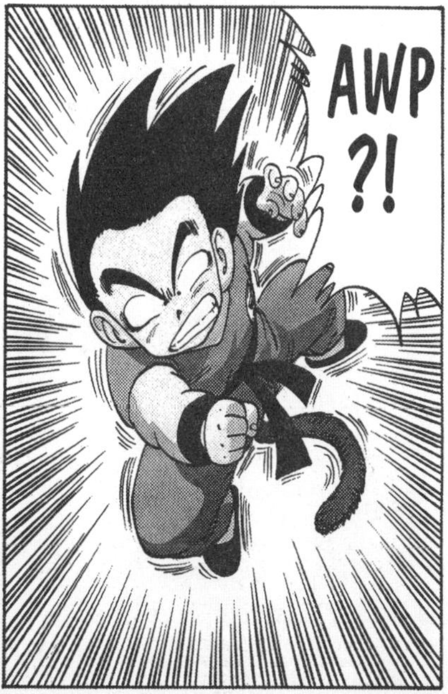
AWP ?!

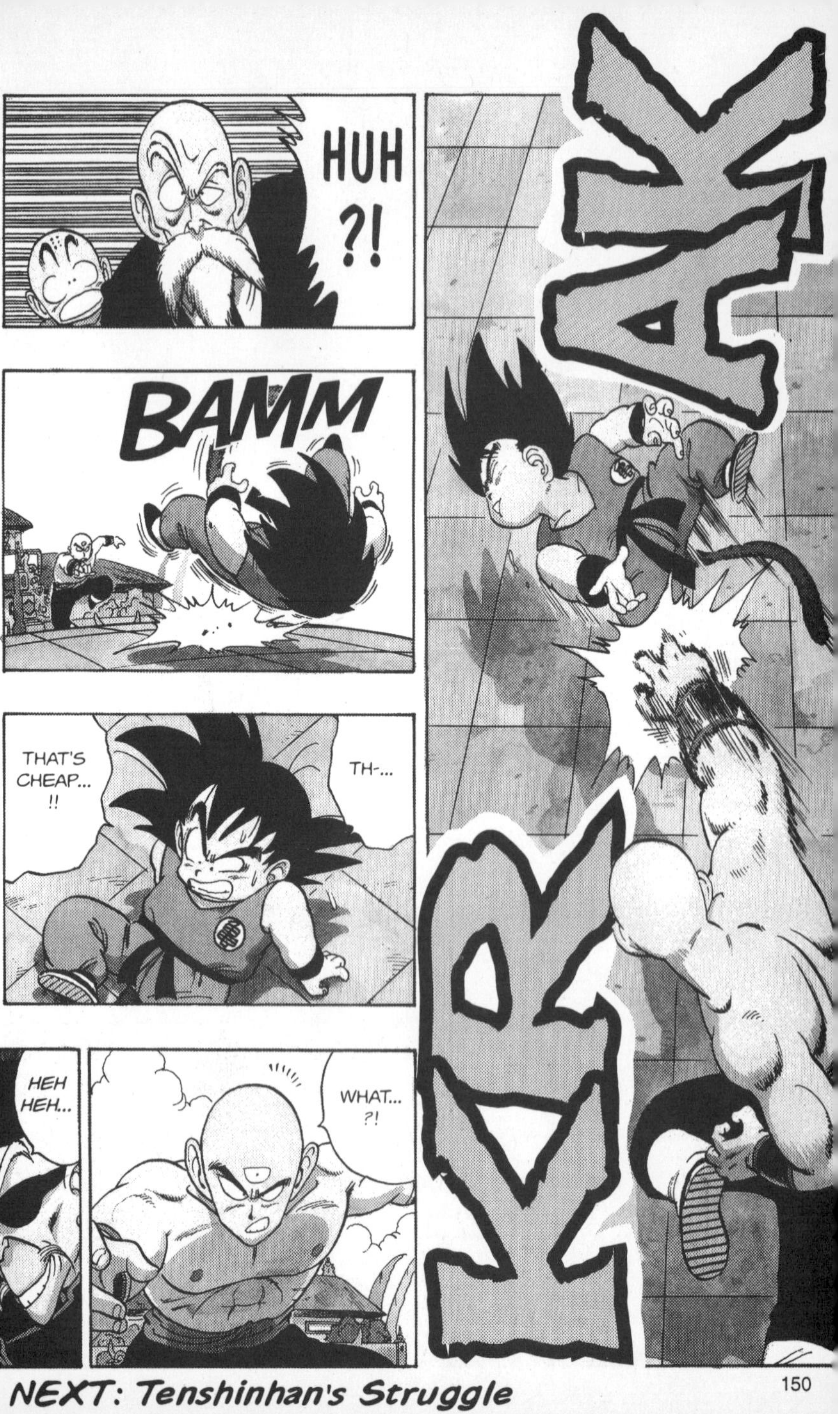

KRAK
HUH ?!
BAMM
TH-...
THAT'S CHEAP... !!
WHAT... ?!
HEH HEH...

NEXT: Tenshinhan's Struggle

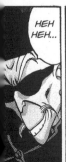

Tale 131 • Tsuru-Sen'nin

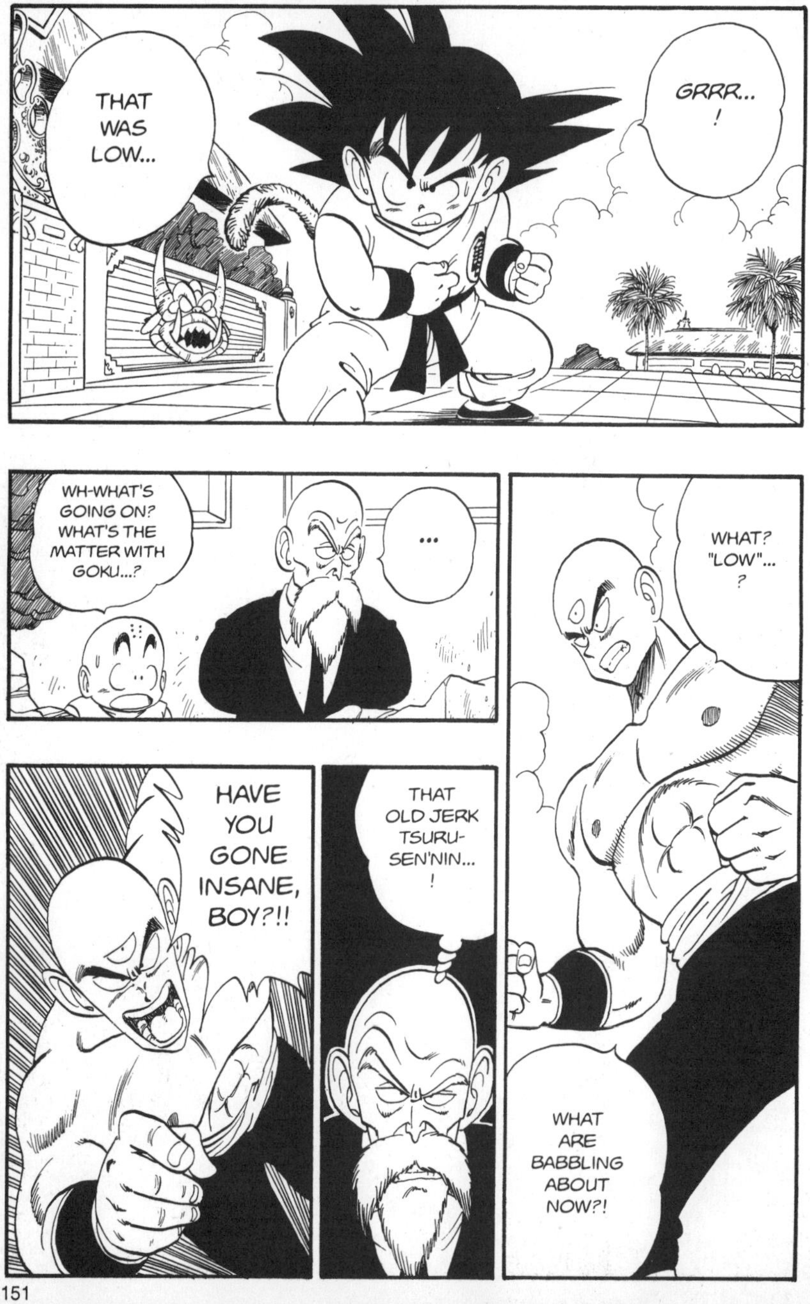
GRRR... !
THAT WAS LOW...
WHAT? "LOW"... ?
WHAT ARE BABBLING ABOUT NOW?!
...
WH-WHAT'S GOING ON? WHAT'S THE MATTER WITH GOKU...?
THAT OLD JERK TSURU-SEN'NIN... !
HAVE YOU GONE INSANE, BOY?!!

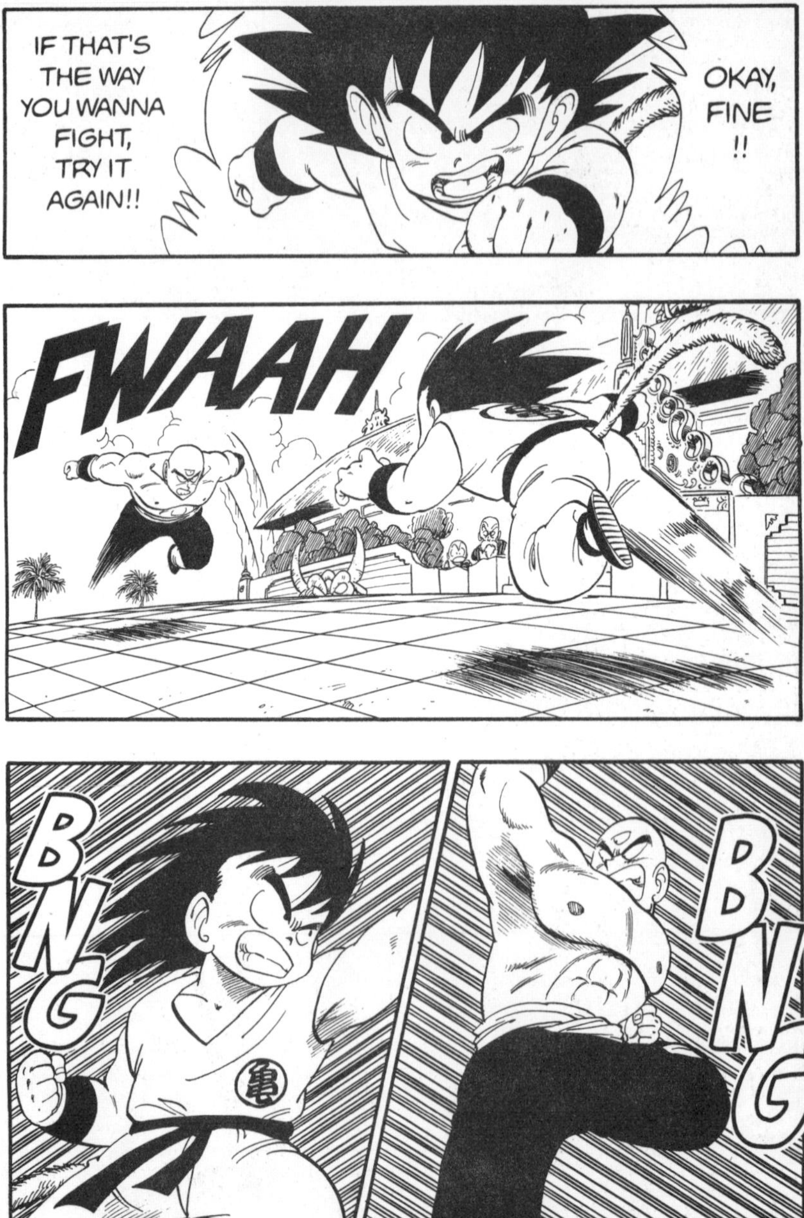
OKAY, FINE!!
IF THAT'S THE WAY YOU WANNA FIGHT, TRY IT AGAIN!!
FWAAH
BNG
BNG

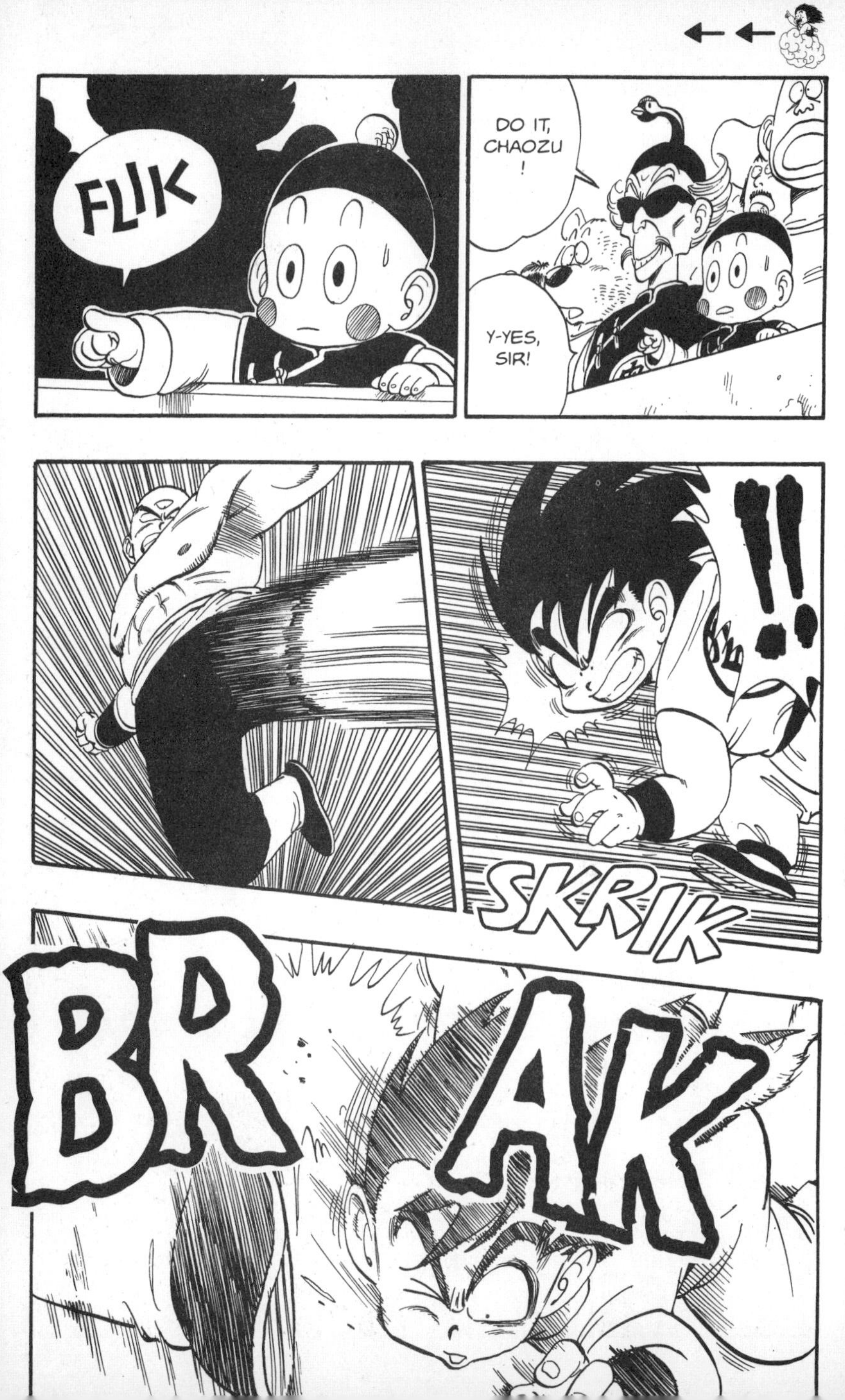

DO IT, CHAOZU!
Y-YES, SIR!
FLIK
!!
SKRIK
BRAK

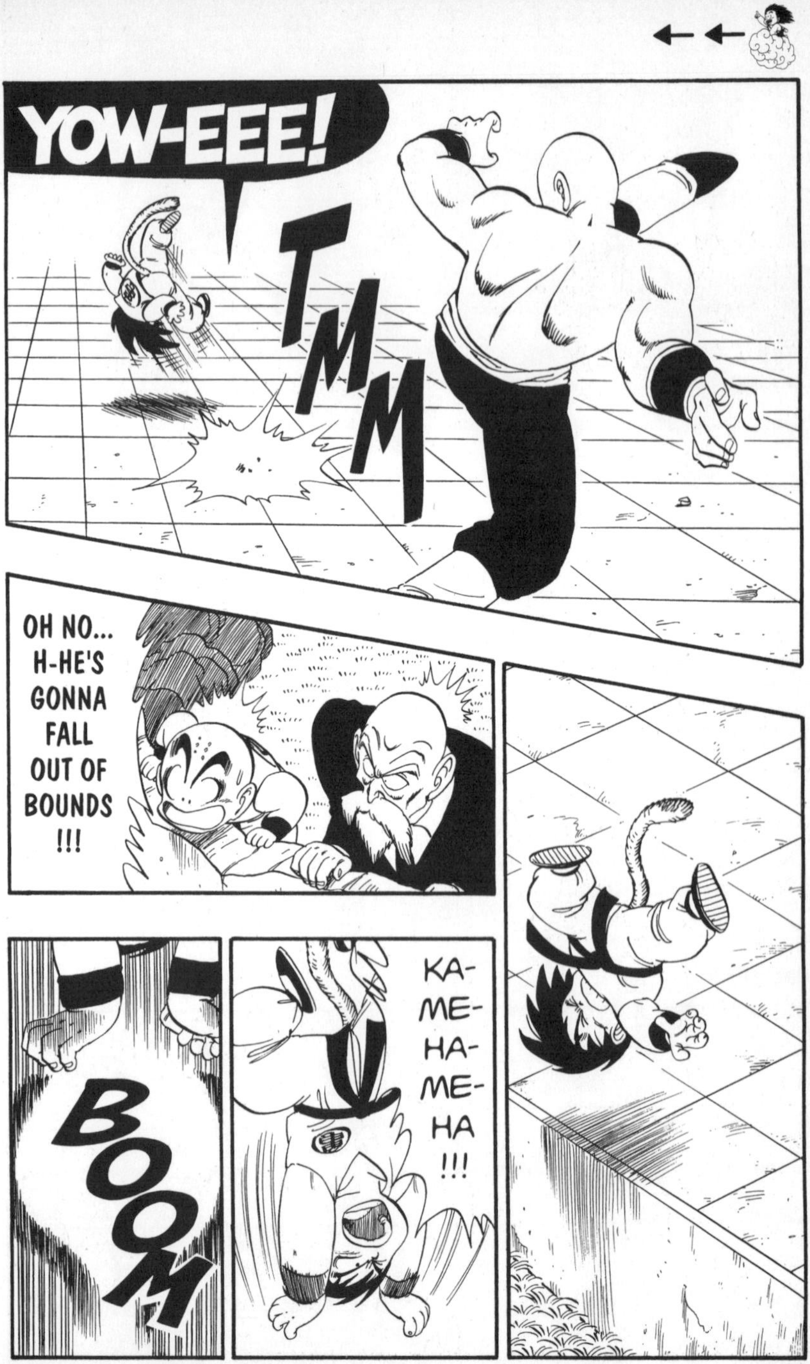
YOW-EEE!
TMM
OH NO... H-HE'S GONNA FALL OUT OF BOUNDS !!!
KA-ME-HA-ME-HA !!!
BOOM

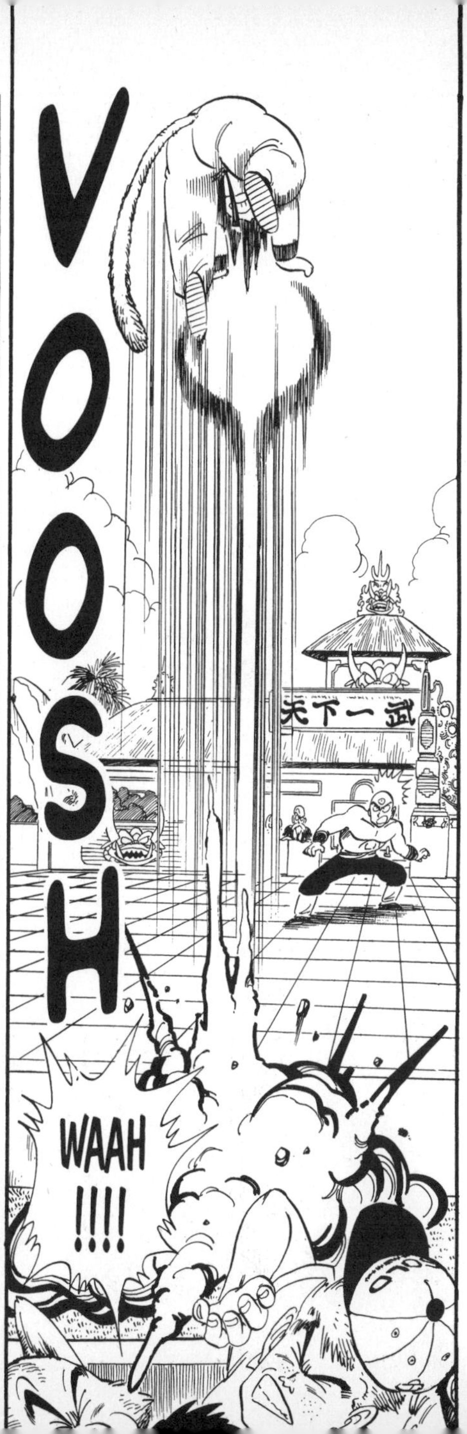
VOOSH
天下一武
WAAH !!!!

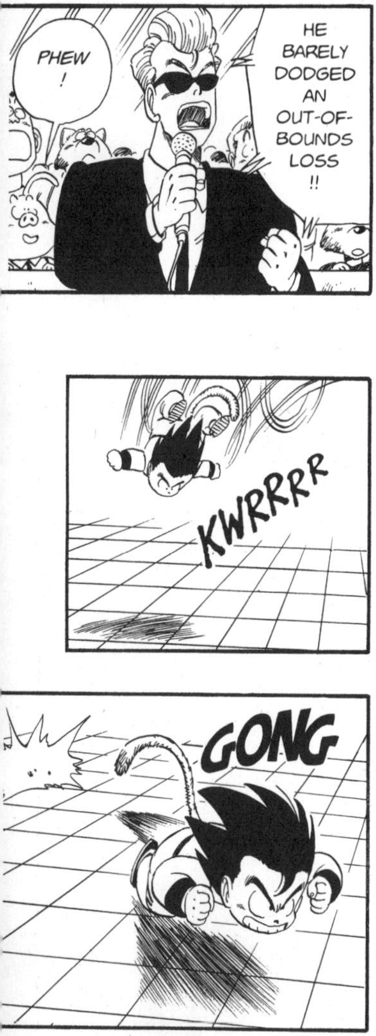
HE BARELY DODGED AN OUT-OF-BOUNDS LOSS !!
PHEW !
KWRRRR
GONG
YOU STUBBORN TWIT !!!

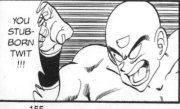

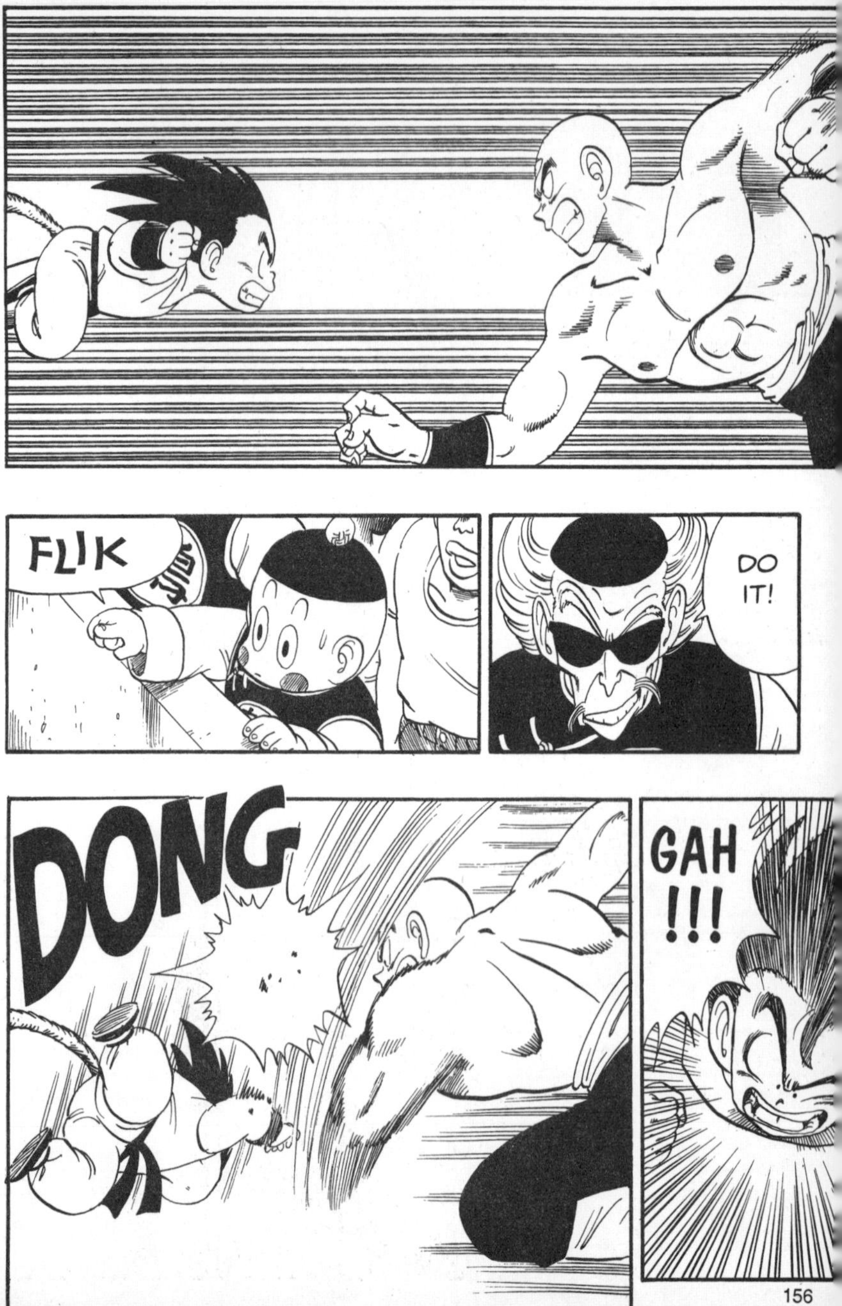
DO IT!
FLIK
GAH !!!
DONG

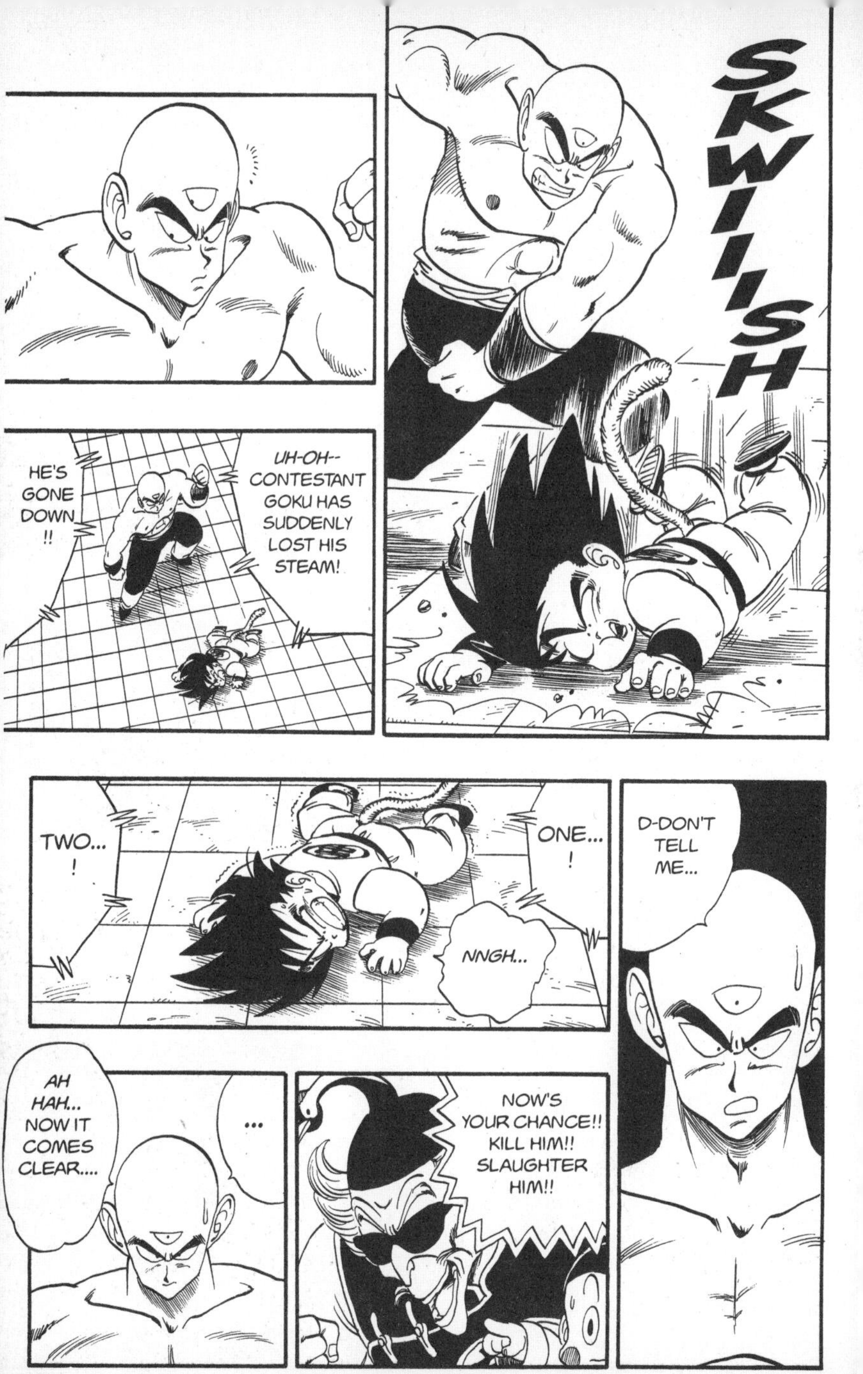
SKWIIISH
UH-OH-- CONTESTANT GOKU HAS SUDDENLY LOST HIS STEAM!
HE'S GONE DOWN !!
D-DON'T TELL ME...
ONE... !
TWO... !
NNGH...
NOW'S YOUR CHANCE!! KILL HIM!! SLAUGHTER HIM!!
...
AH HAH... NOW IT COMES CLEAR....

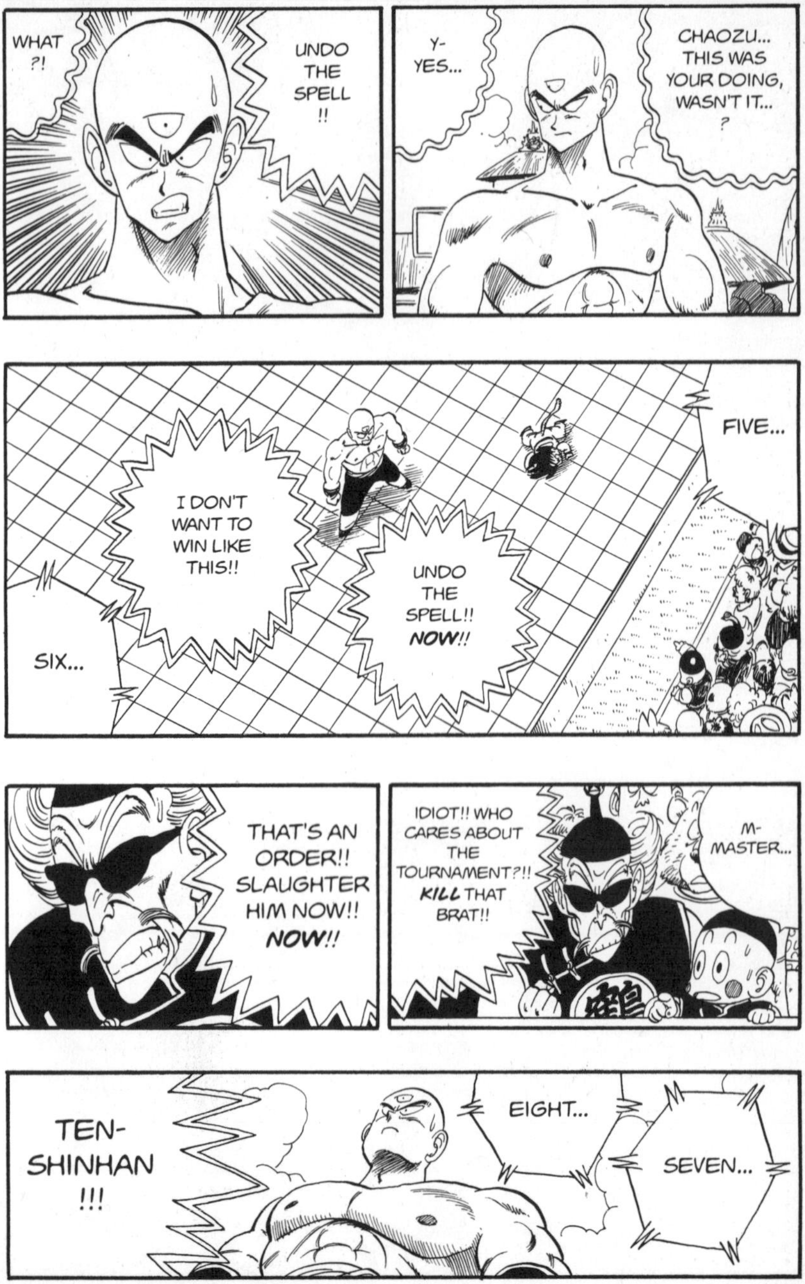
CHAOZU... THIS WAS YOUR DOING, WASN'T IT...?
Y-YES...
UNDO THE SPELL!!
WHAT?!
FIVE...
UNDO THE SPELL!! NOW!!
I DON'T WANT TO WIN LIKE THIS!!
SIX...
M-MASTER...
IDIOT!! WHO CARES ABOUT THE TOURNAMENT?!! KILL THAT BRAT!!
THAT'S AN ORDER!! SLAUGHTER HIM NOW!! NOW!!
SEVEN...
EIGHT...
TEN-SHINHAN!!!

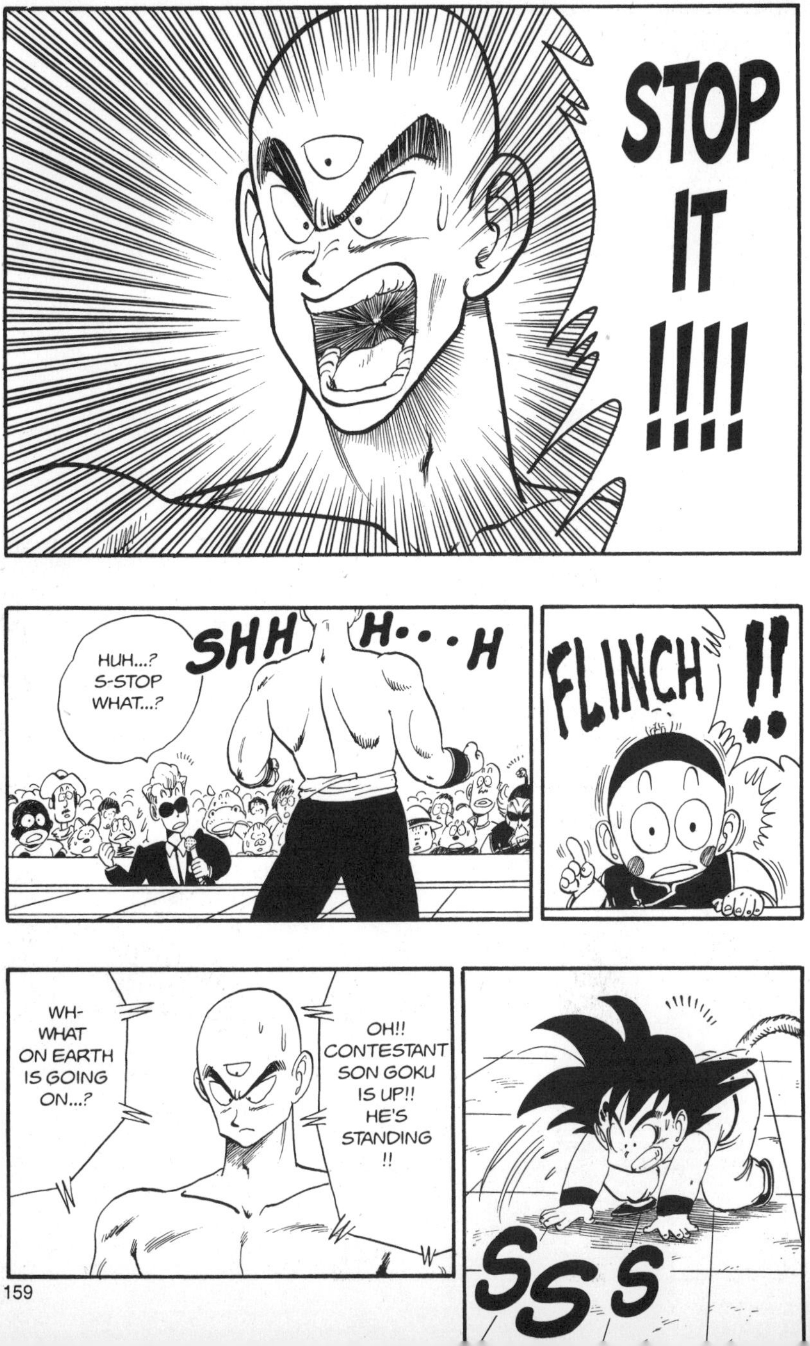
STOP IT!!!!
FLINCH!!
SHHH...H
HUH...? S-STOP WHAT...?
SSS
OH!! CONTESTANT SON GOKU IS UP!! HE'S STANDING!!
WH-WHAT ON EARTH IS GOING ON...?

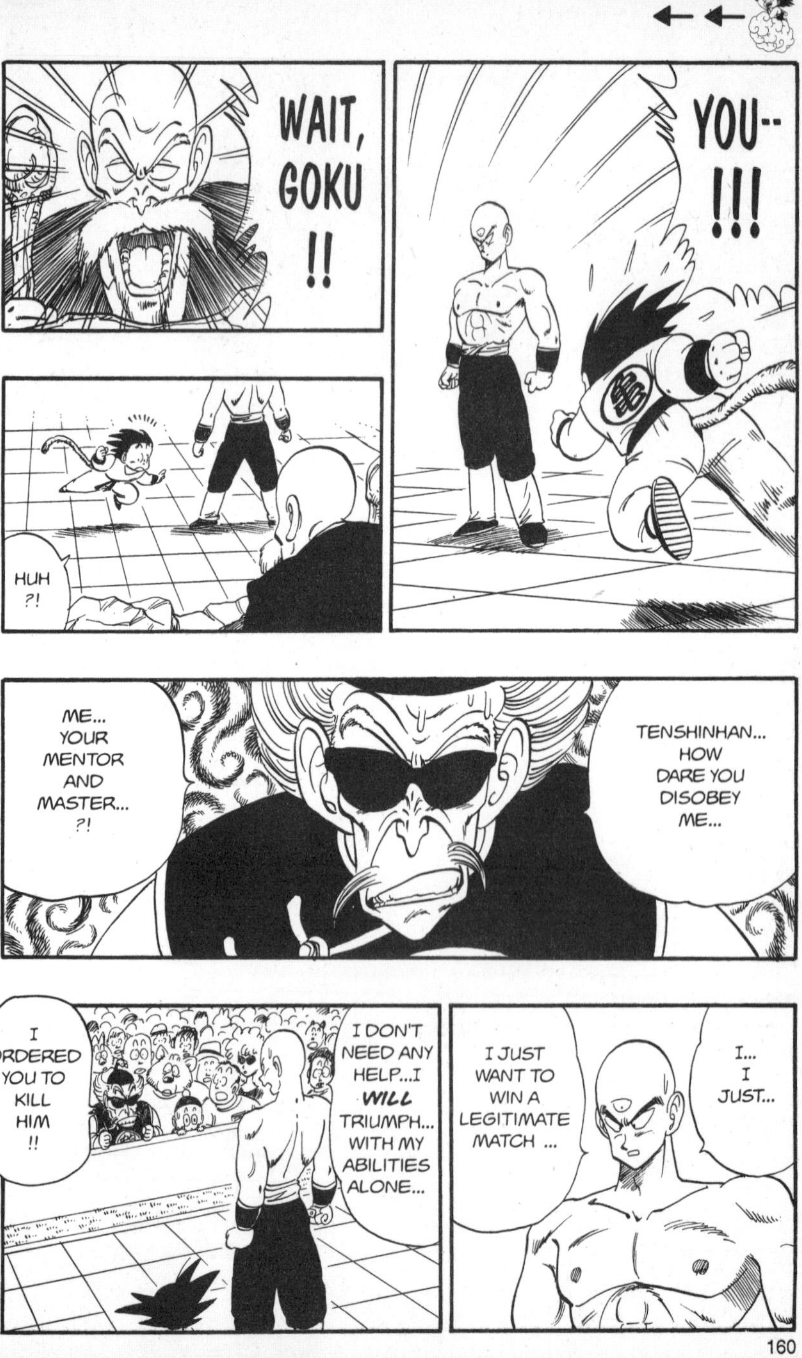
YOU-- !!!
WAIT, GOKU !!
HUH ?!
TENSHINHAN... HOW DARE YOU DISOBEY ME...
ME... YOUR MENTOR AND MASTER... ?!
I... I JUST...
I JUST WANT TO WIN A LEGITIMATE MATCH ...
I DON'T NEED ANY HELP...I *WILL* TRIUMPH... WITH MY ABILITIES ALONE...
I ORDERED YOU TO KILL HIM !!

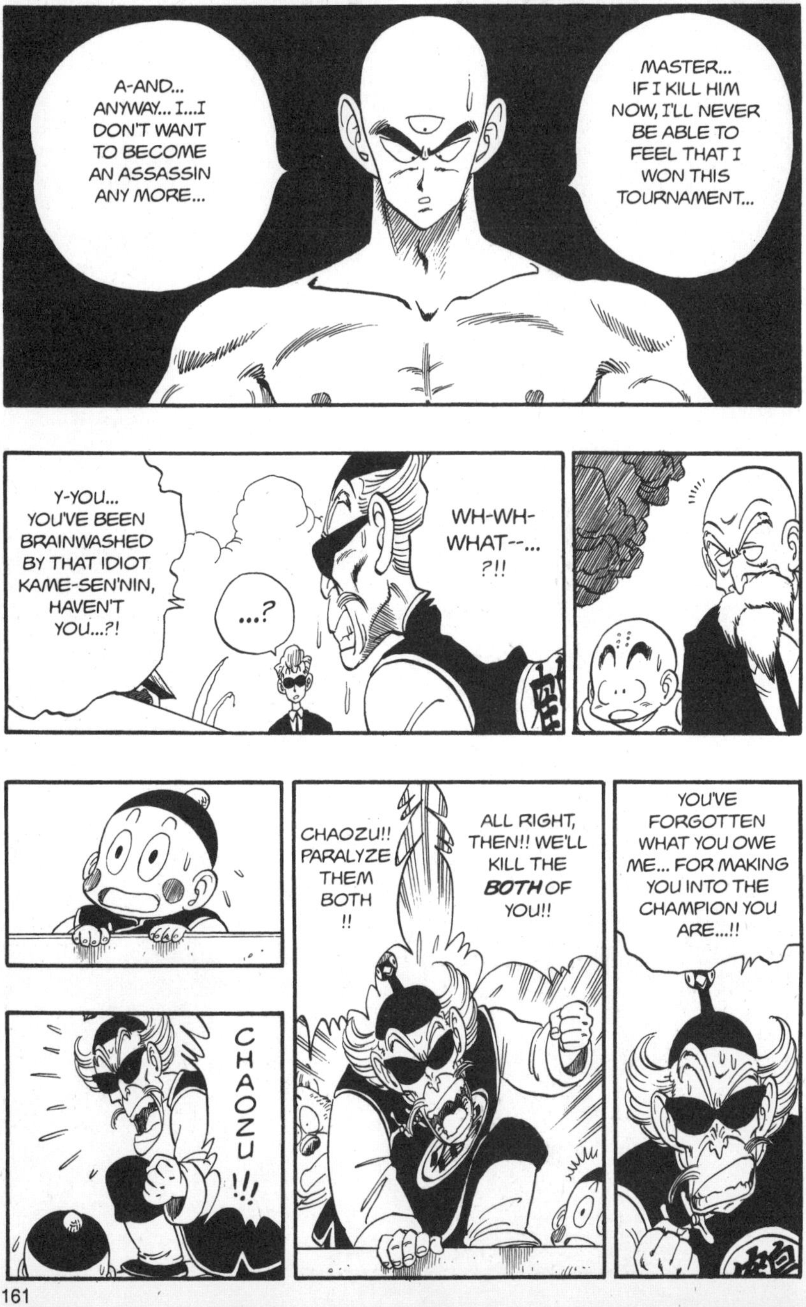
MASTER... IF I KILL HIM NOW, I'LL NEVER BE ABLE TO FEEL THAT I WON THIS TOURNAMENT...
A-AND... ANYWAY... I...I DON'T WANT TO BECOME AN ASSASSIN ANY MORE...
WH-WH-WHAT--... ?!!
...?
Y-YOU... YOU'VE BEEN BRAINWASHED BY THAT IDIOT KAME-SEN'NIN, HAVEN'T YOU...?!
YOU'VE FORGOTTEN WHAT YOU OWE ME... FOR MAKING YOU INTO THE CHAMPION YOU ARE...!!
ALL RIGHT, THEN!! WE'LL KILL THE **BOTH** OF YOU!!
CHAOZU!! PARALYZE THEM BOTH !!
CHAOZU !!!

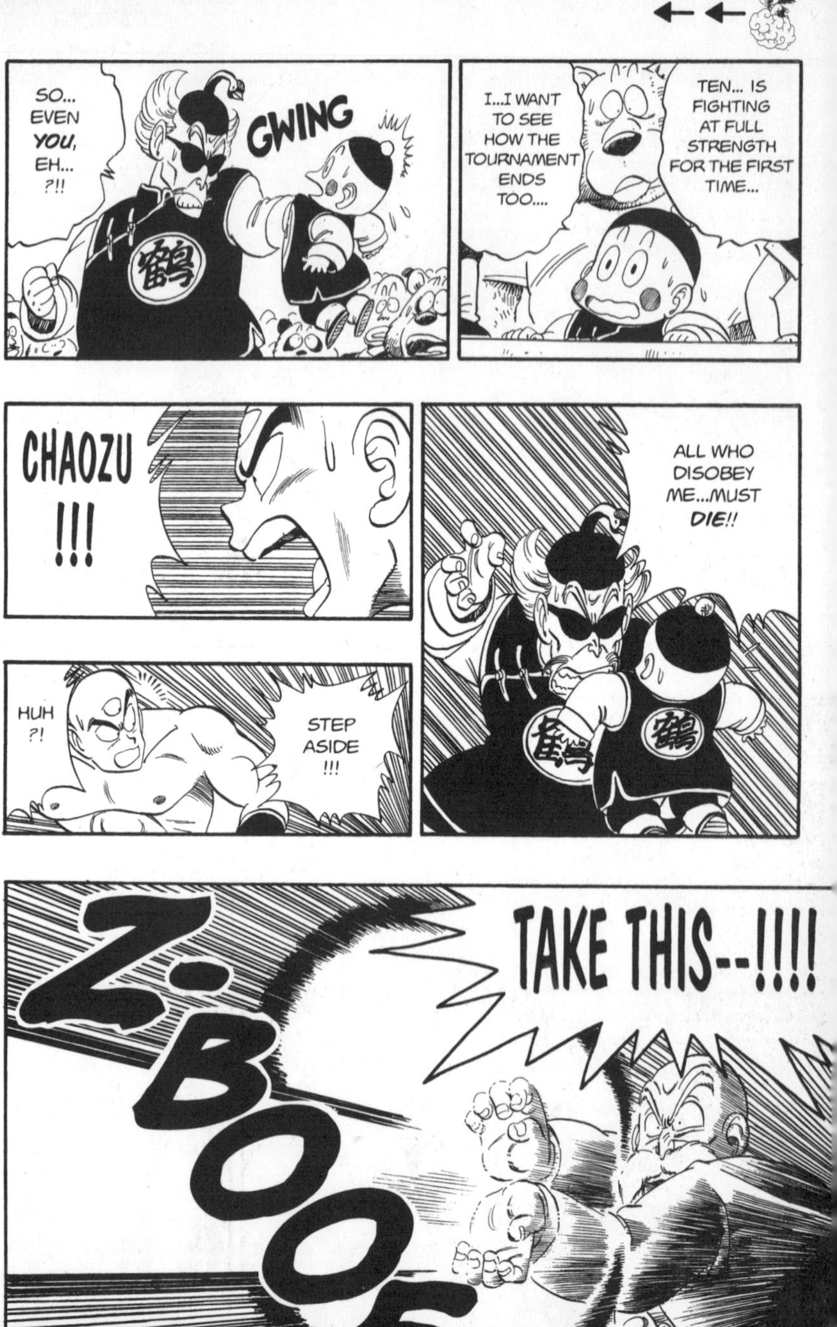
TEN... IS FIGHTING AT FULL STRENGTH FOR THE FIRST TIME...
I...I WANT TO SEE HOW THE TOURNAMENT ENDS TOO....
GWING
SO... EVEN YOU, EH... ?!!
ALL WHO DISOBEY ME...MUST DIE!!
CHAOZU !!!
STEP ASIDE !!!
HUH ?!
TAKE THIS--!!!!
Z-BOOF

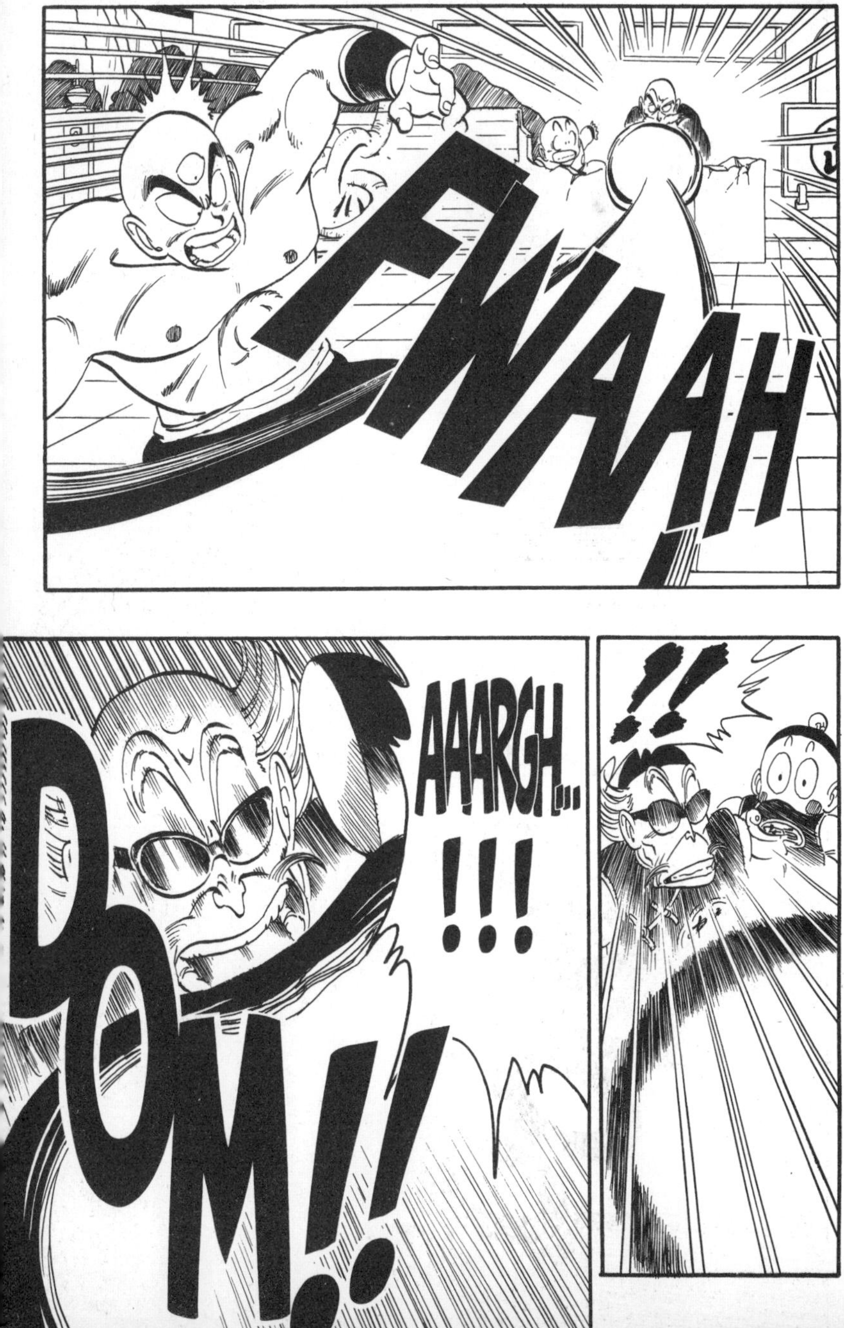
FWAAH
!!
AAARGH...
!!!
BOOM!!

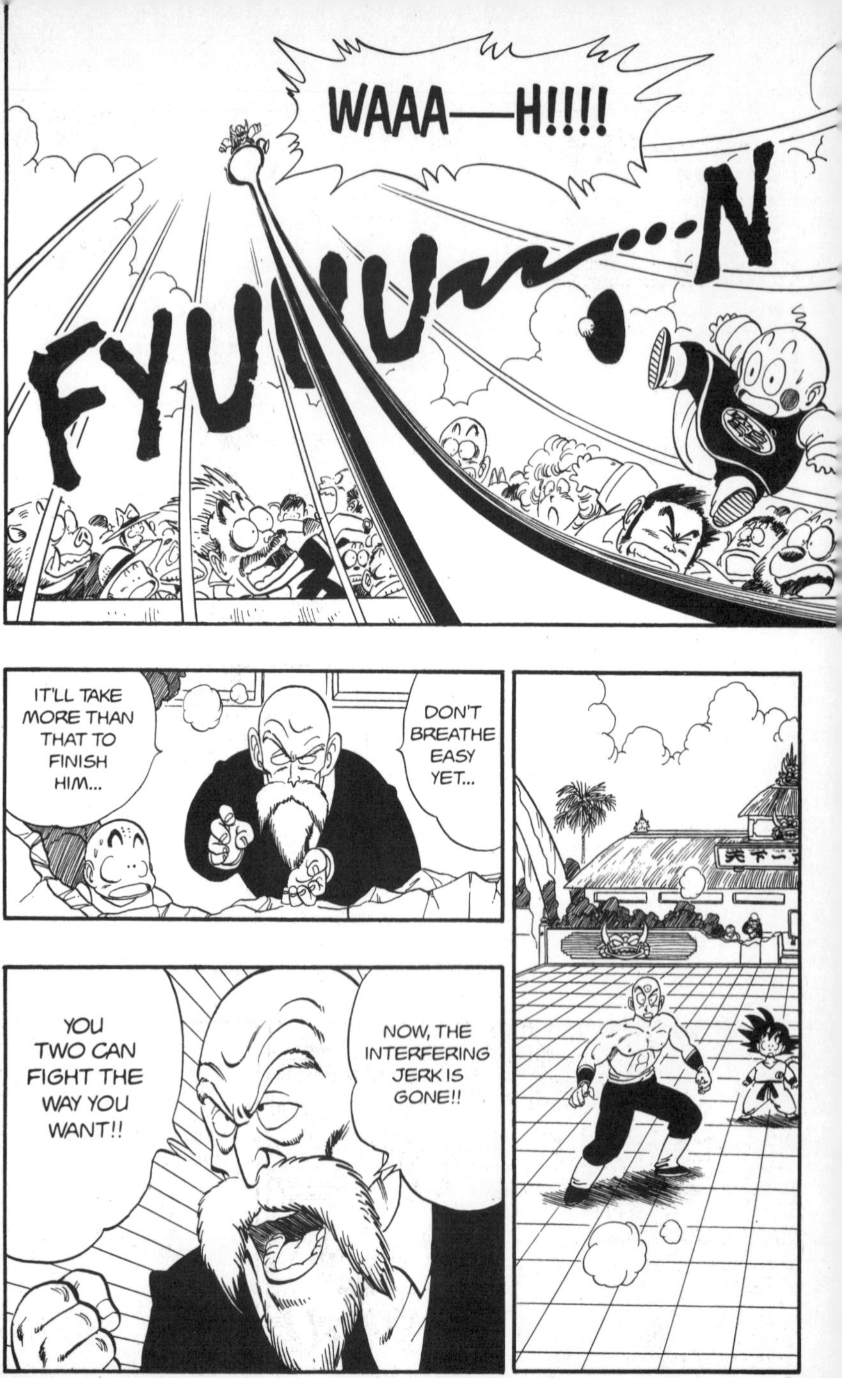
WAAA—H!!!!
FYUUUU...N
DON'T BREATHE EASY YET...
IT'LL TAKE MORE THAN THAT TO FINISH HIM...
NOW, THE INTERFERING JERK IS GONE!!
YOU TWO CAN FIGHT THE WAY YOU WANT!!

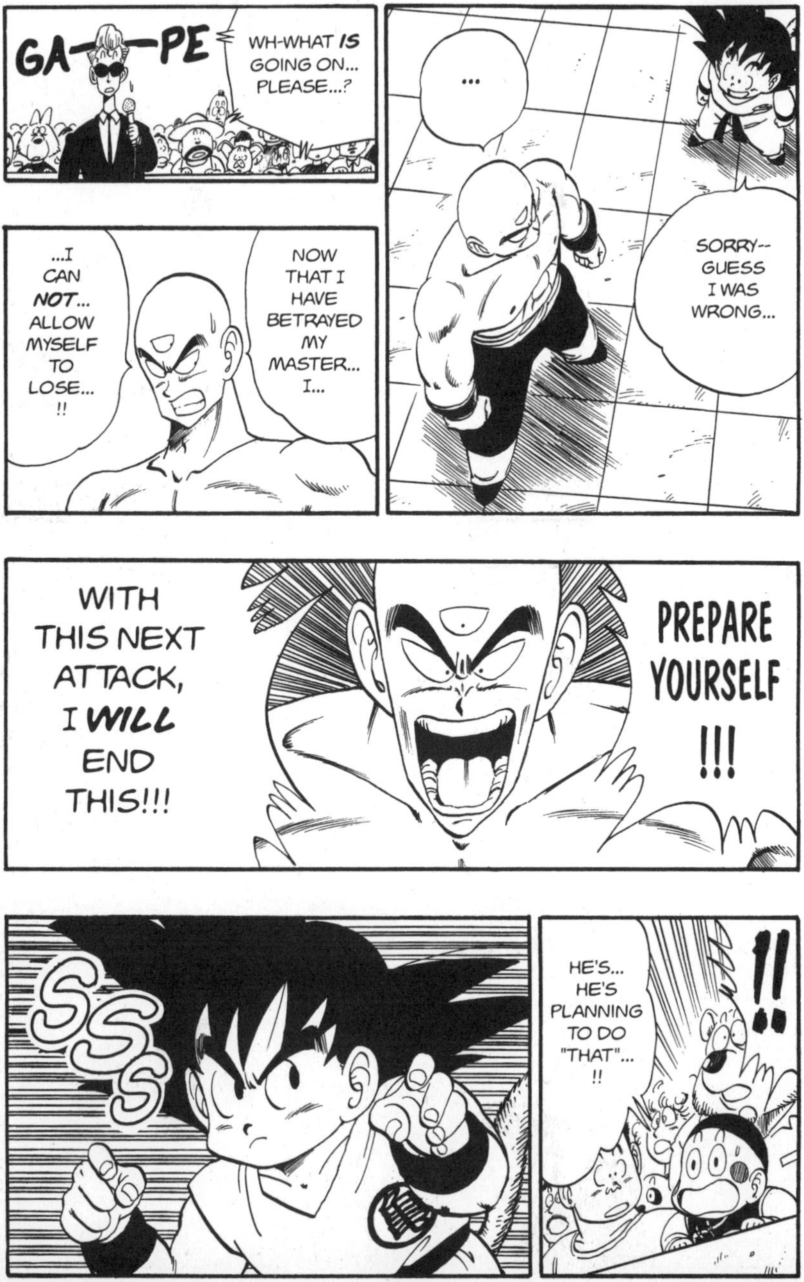
...
SORRY-- GUESS I WAS WRONG...
GA—PE
WH-WHAT IS GOING ON... PLEASE...?
NOW THAT I HAVE BETRAYED MY MASTER... I...
...I CAN NOT... ALLOW MYSELF TO LOSE... !!
PREPARE YOURSELF !!!
WITH THIS NEXT ATTACK, I WILL END THIS!!!
!!
HE'S... HE'S PLANNING TO DO "THAT"... !!
SSS

NEXT: Death Either Way

Tale 132 • The Arms Race

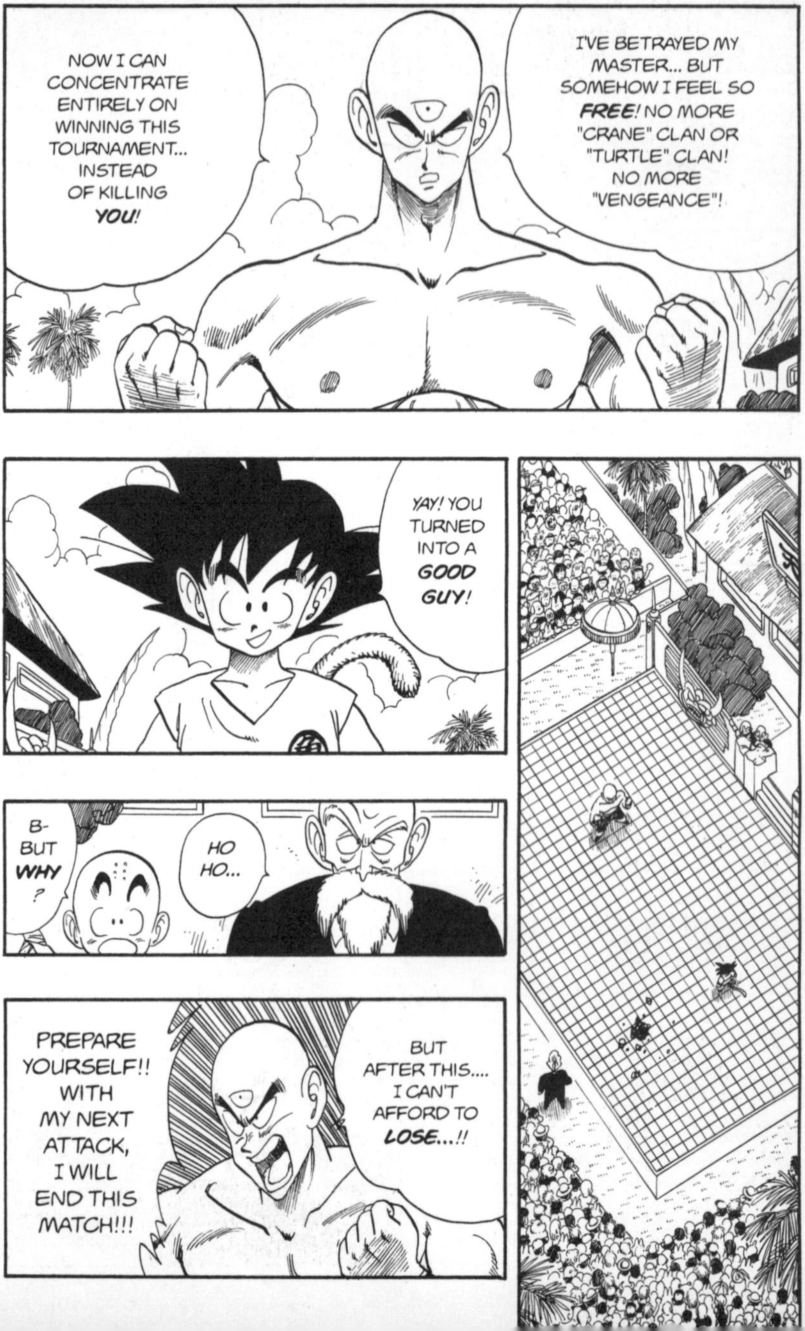
I'VE BETRAYED MY MASTER... BUT SOMEHOW I FEEL SO **FREE!** NO MORE "CRANE" CLAN OR "TURTLE" CLAN! NO MORE "VENGEANCE"!
NOW I CAN CONCENTRATE ENTIRELY ON WINNING THIS TOURNAMENT... INSTEAD OF KILLING **YOU!**
YAY! YOU TURNED INTO A **GOOD GUY!**
HO HO...
B-BUT **WHY**?
BUT AFTER THIS.... I CAN'T AFFORD TO **LOSE...!!**
PREPARE YOURSELF!! WITH MY NEXT ATTACK, I WILL END THIS MATCH!!!

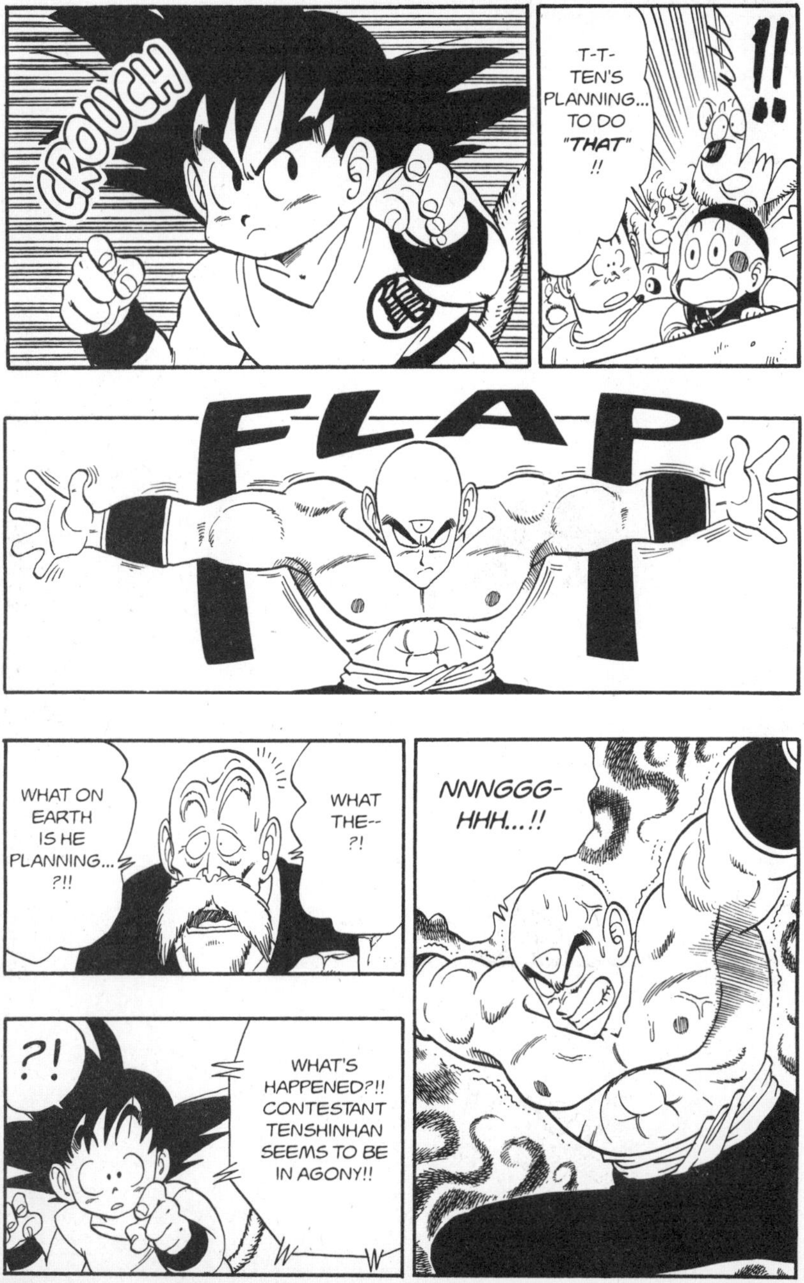
!!
T-T-TEN'S PLANNING... TO DO "THAT" !!
CROUCH
FLAP
NNNGGG-HHH...!!
WHAT THE-- ?!
WHAT ON EARTH IS HE PLANNING... ?!!
WHAT'S HAPPENED?!! CONTESTANT TENSHINHAN SEEMS TO BE IN AGONY!!
?!

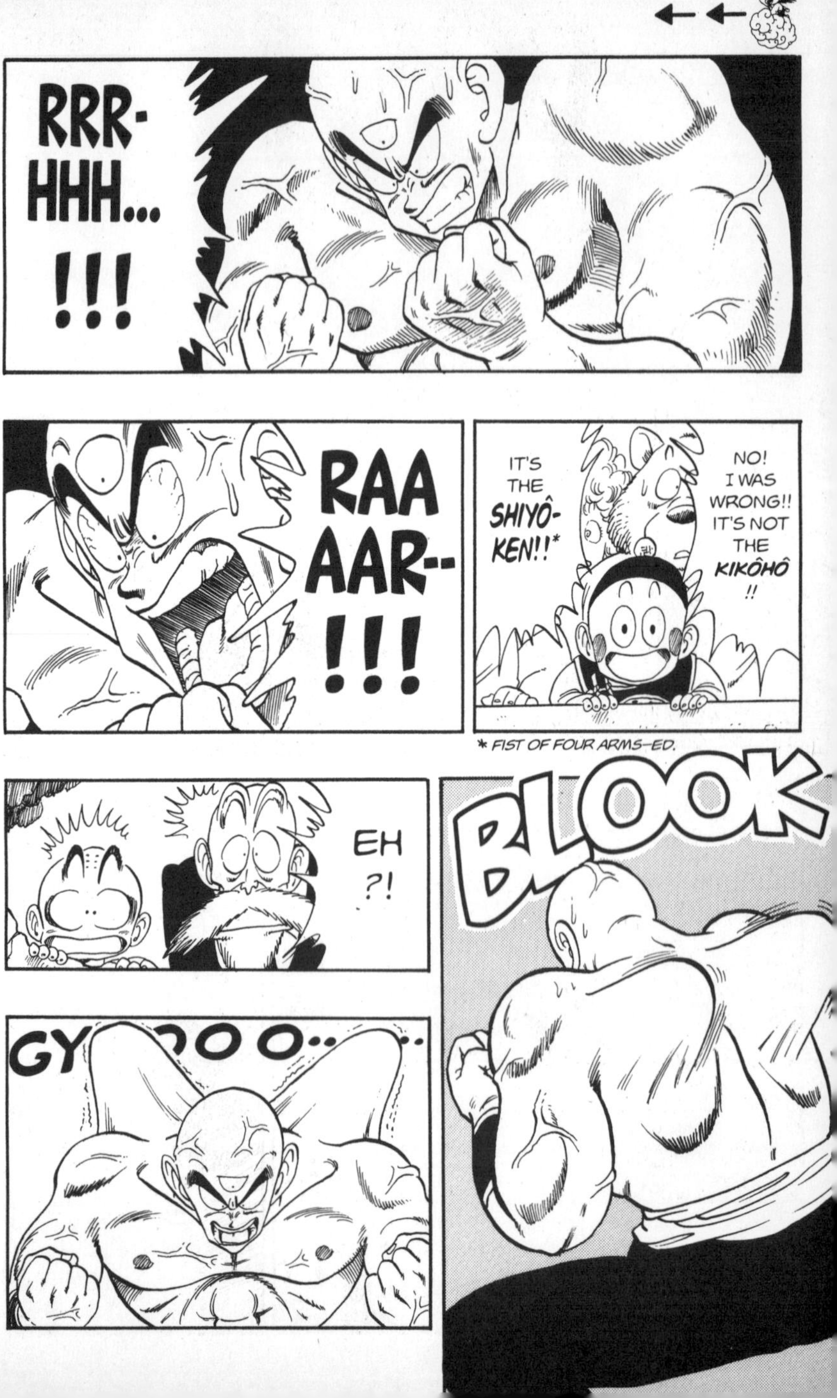
RRR-HHH... !!!
NO! I WAS WRONG!! IT'S NOT THE KIKÔHÔ!!
IT'S THE SHIYÔ-KEN!!*
RAAAAR--!!!
* FIST OF FOUR ARMS—ED.
BLOOK
EH ?!
GY OO O...

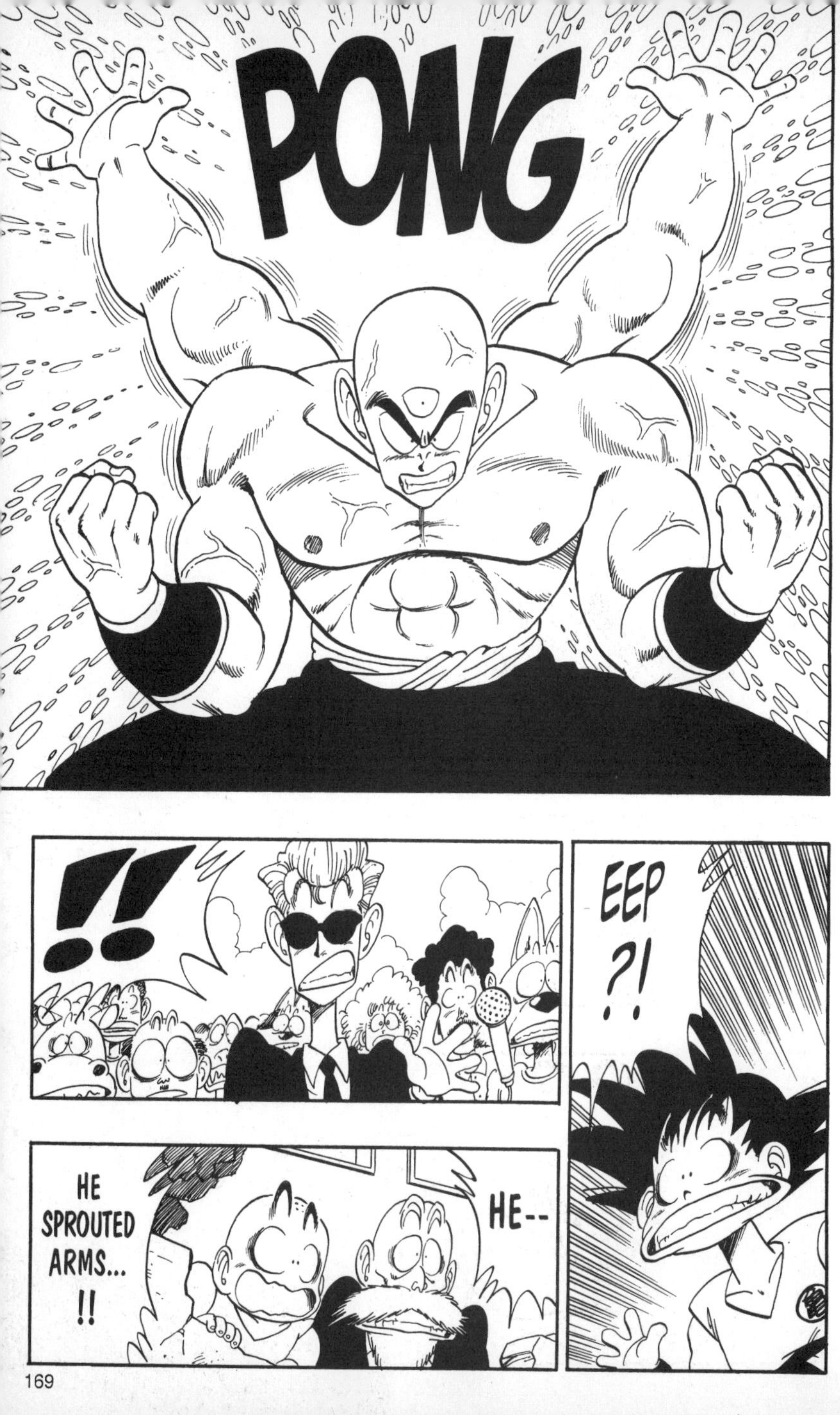
PONG
EEP ?!
!!
HE--
HE SPROUTED ARMS... !!

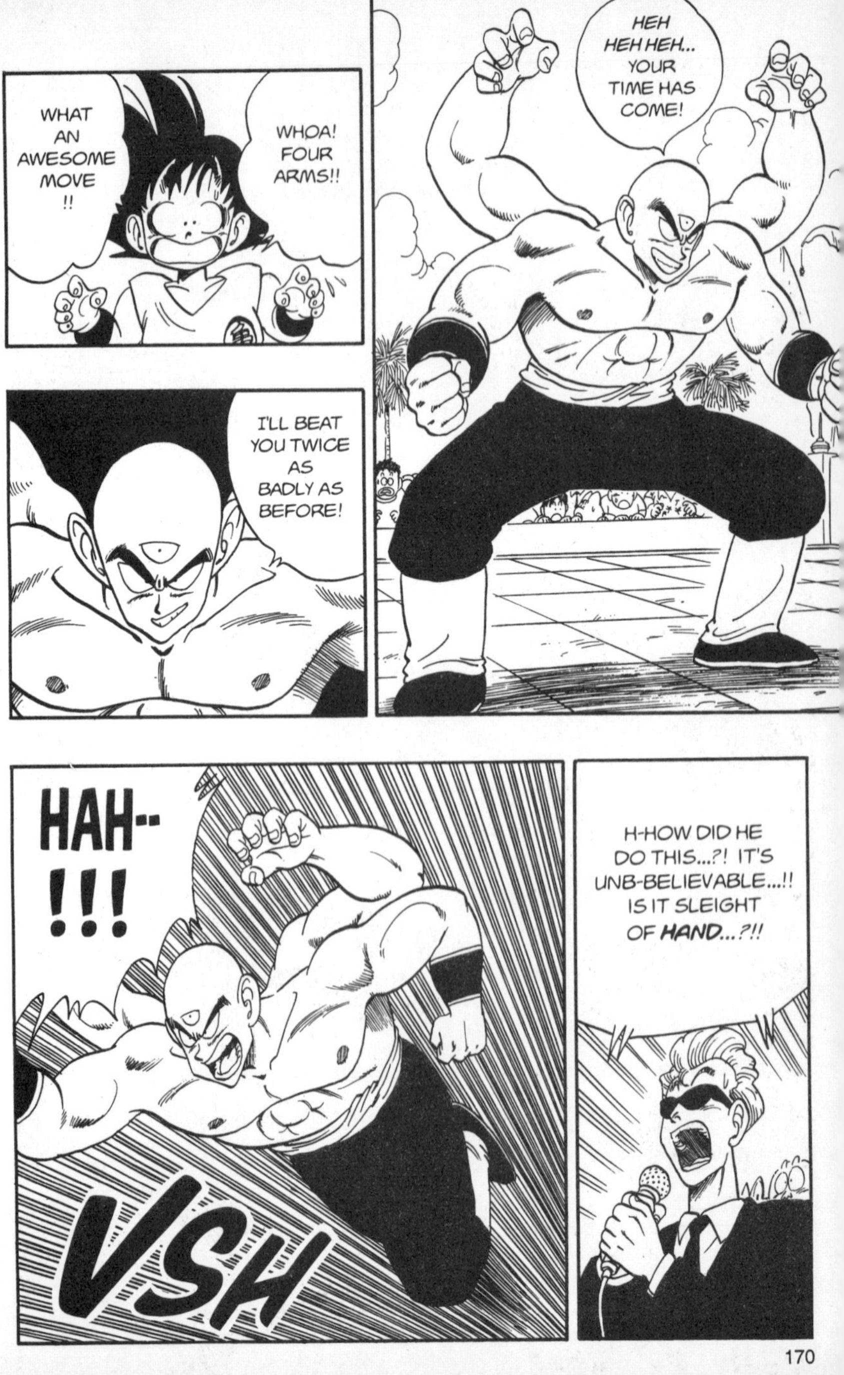
HEH HEH HEH... YOUR TIME HAS COME!
WHOA! FOUR ARMS!!
WHAT AN AWESOME MOVE !!
I'LL BEAT YOU TWICE AS BADLY AS BEFORE!
H-HOW DID HE DO THIS...?! IT'S UNB-BELIEVABLE...!! IS IT SLEIGHT OF HAND...?!!
HAH-- !!!
VSH

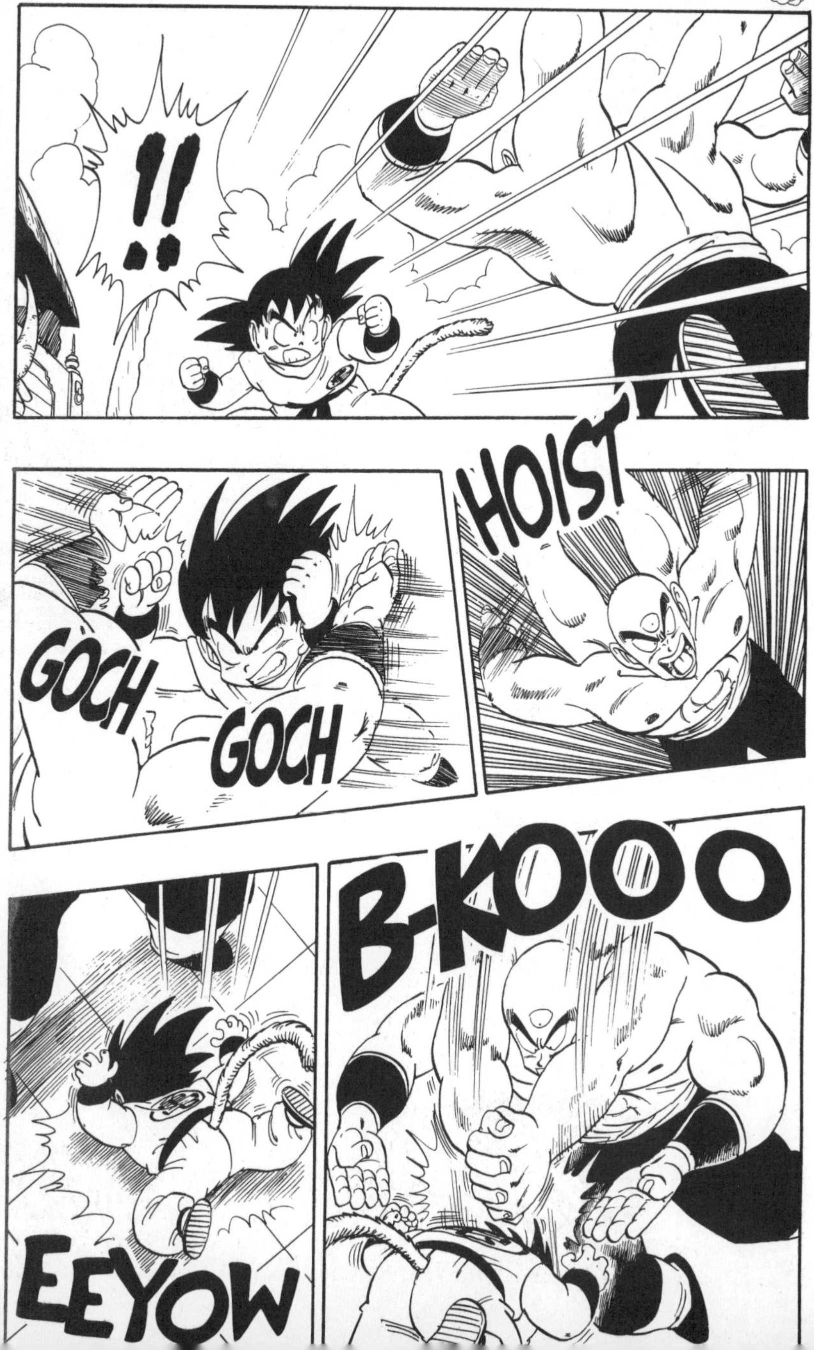
!!
HOIST
GOCH
GOCH
B-KOOO
EEYOW

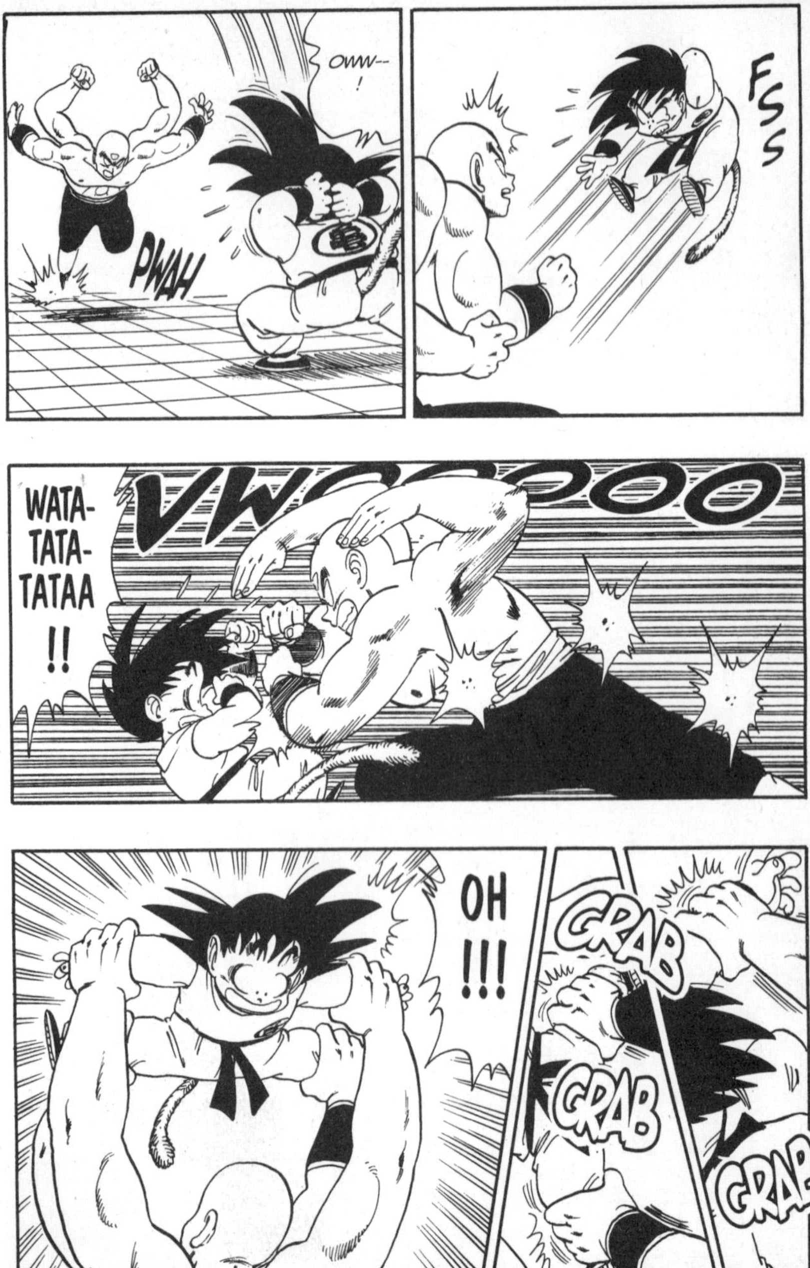
FSS
OWW--!
PWAH
VWOOOOO
WATA-TATA-TATAA!!
GRAB
GRAB
GRAB
OH!!!

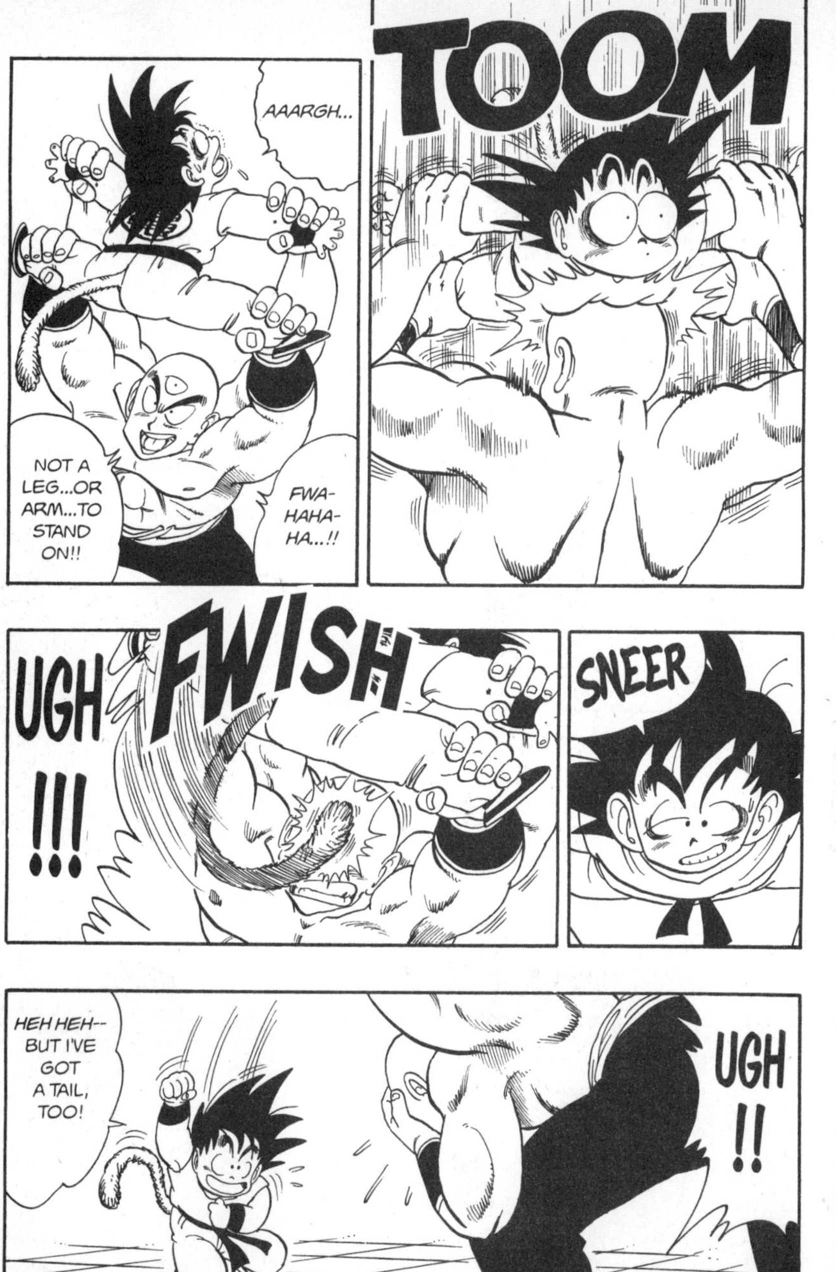
TOOM
AAARGH...
FWA-HAHA-HA...!!
NOT A LEG...OR ARM...TO STAND ON!!
SNEER
FWISH
UGH!!!
UGH!!
HEH HEH--BUT I'VE GOT A TAIL, TOO!

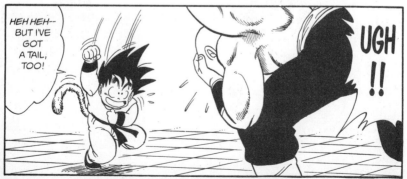

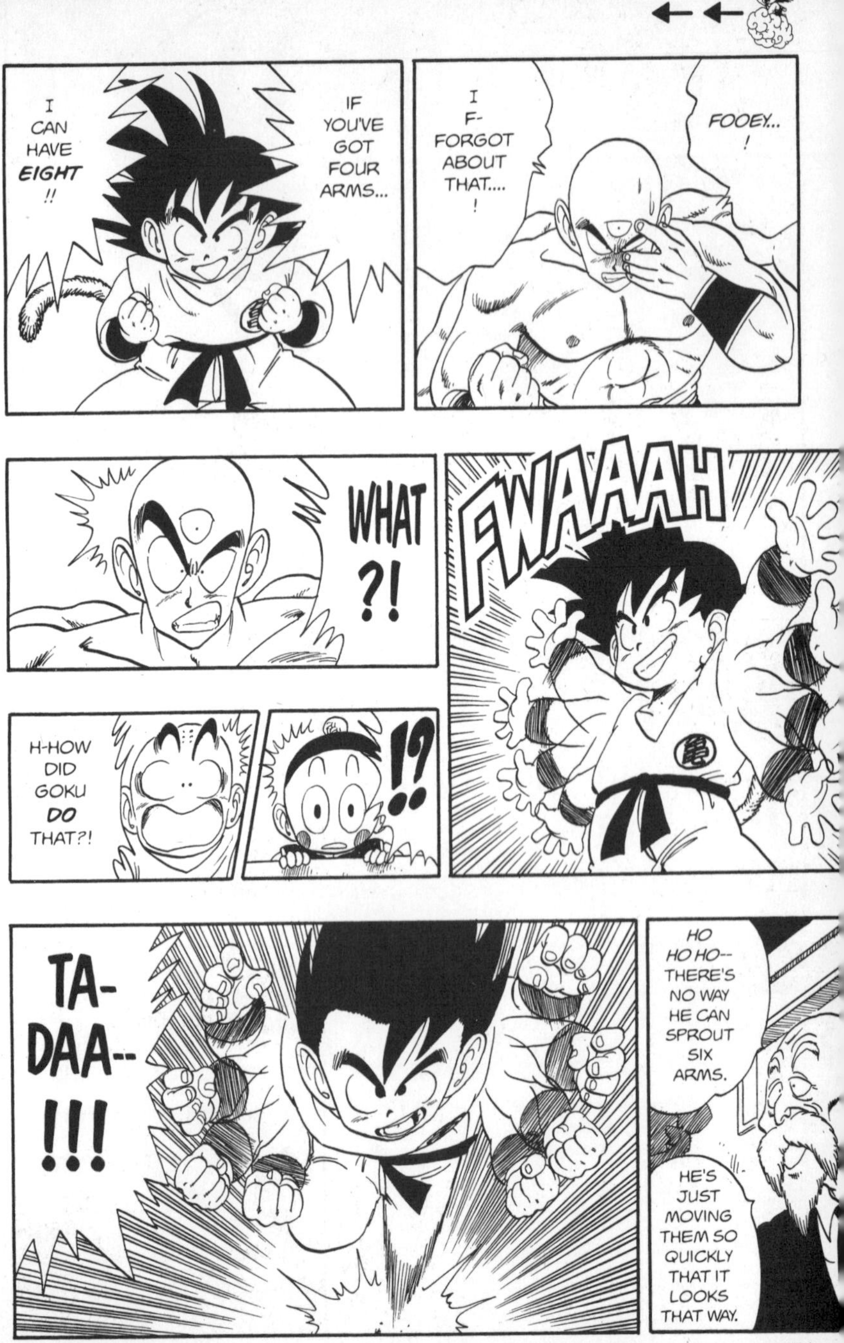
FOOEY... !
I F-FORGOT ABOUT THAT.... !
IF YOU'VE GOT FOUR ARMS...
I CAN HAVE EIGHT !!
FWAAAH
WHAT ?!
!?
H-HOW DID GOKU DO THAT?!
HO HO HO-- THERE'S NO WAY HE CAN SPROUT SIX ARMS.
HE'S JUST MOVING THEM SO QUICKLY THAT IT LOOKS THAT WAY.
TA-DAA-- !!!

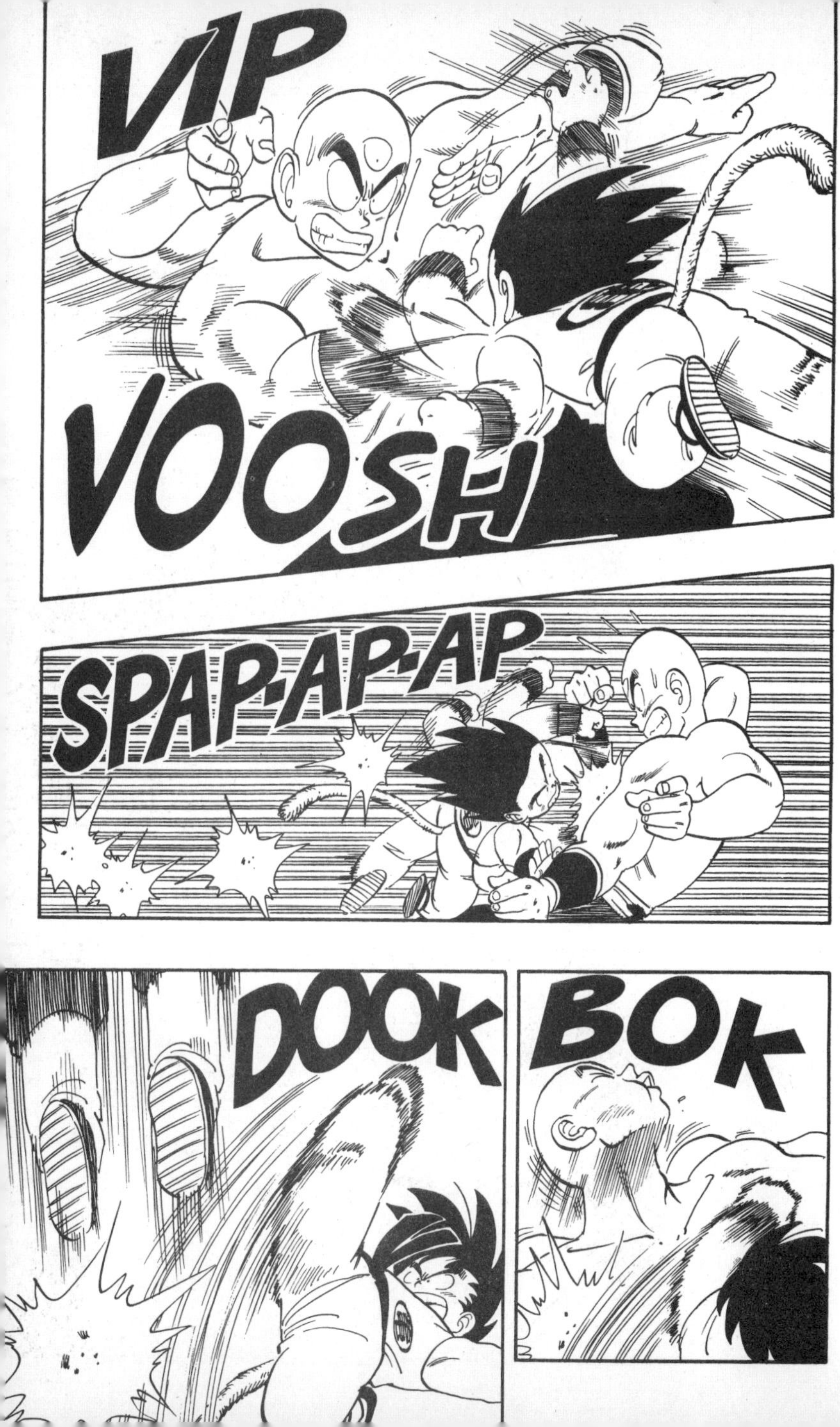
VIP
VOOSH
SPAP-AP-AP
BOK
DOOK

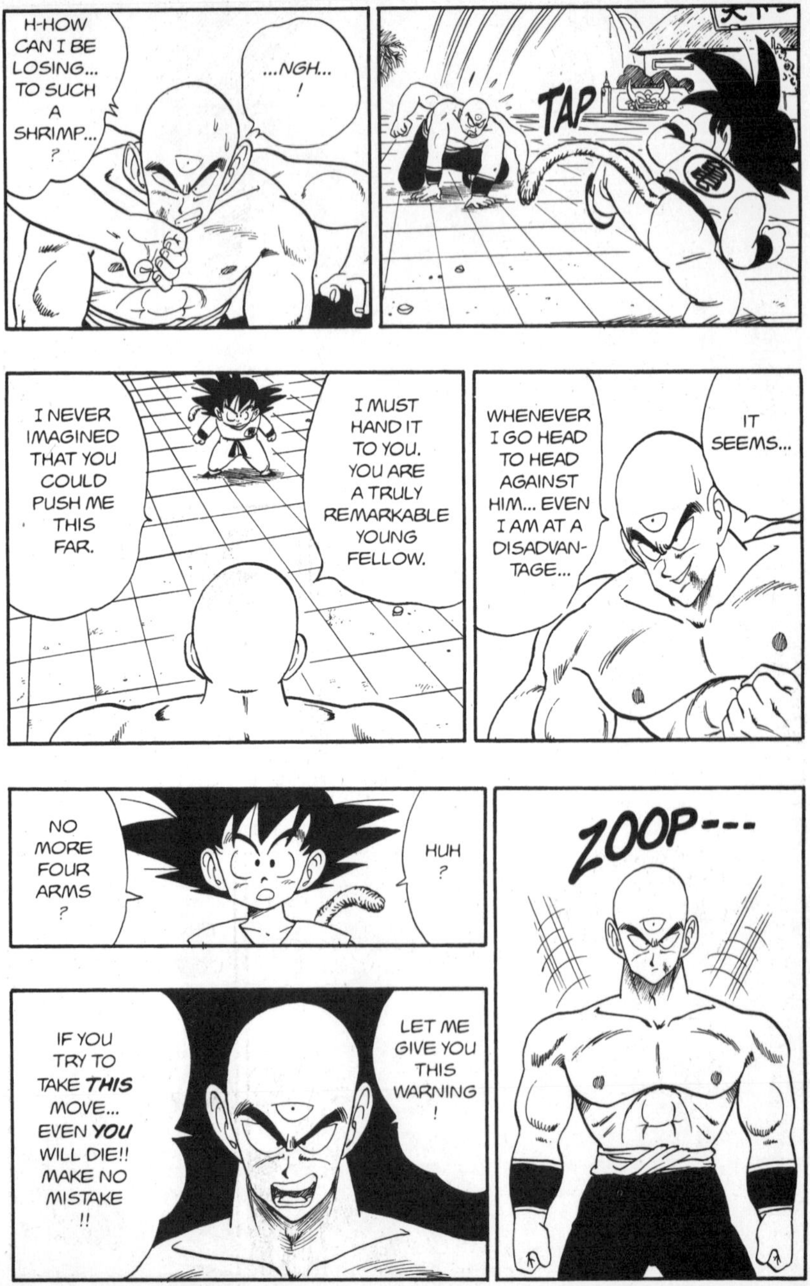
TAP
...NGH... !
H-HOW CAN I BE LOSING... TO SUCH A SHRIMP... ?
IT SEEMS...
WHENEVER I GO HEAD TO HEAD AGAINST HIM... EVEN I AM AT A DISADVAN-TAGE...
I MUST HAND IT TO YOU. YOU ARE A TRULY REMARKABLE YOUNG FELLOW.
I NEVER IMAGINED THAT YOU COULD PUSH ME THIS FAR.
ZOOP---
HUH ?
NO MORE FOUR ARMS ?
LET ME GIVE YOU THIS WARNING !
IF YOU TRY TO TAKE **THIS** MOVE... EVEN **YOU** WILL DIE!! MAKE NO MISTAKE !!

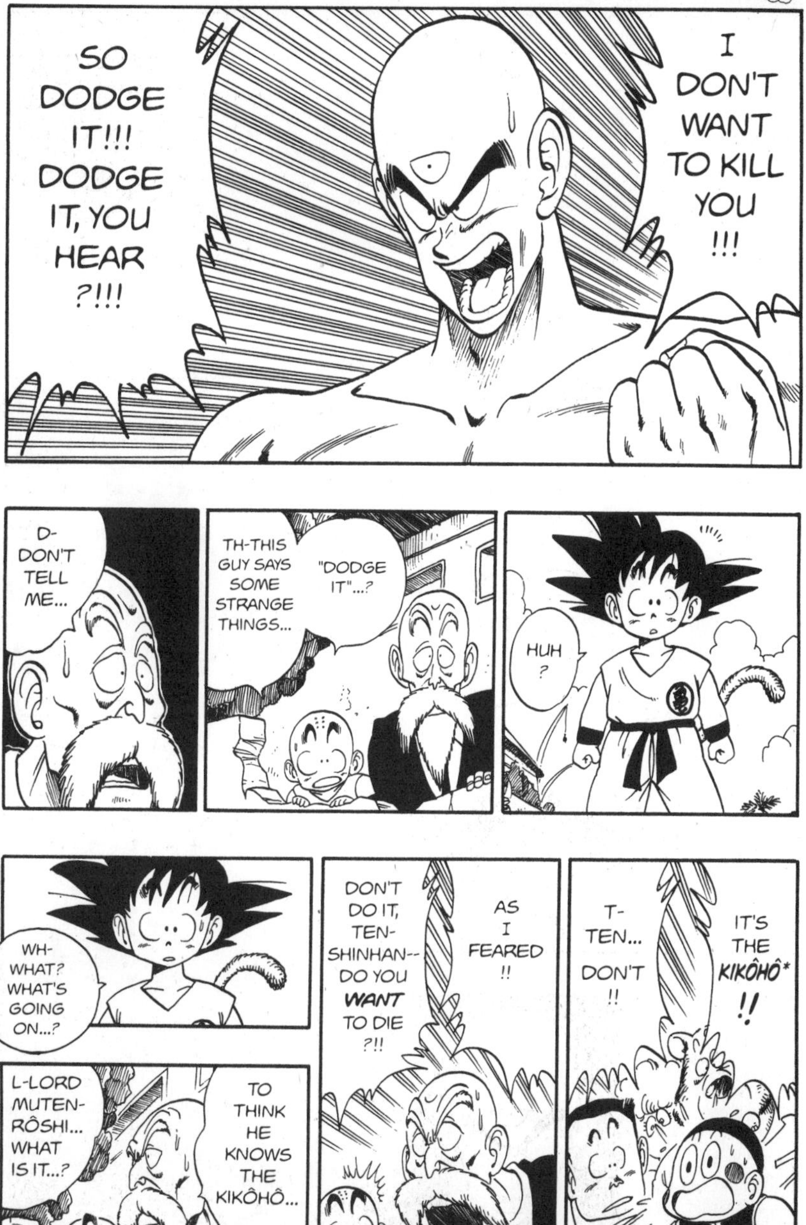
I DON'T WANT TO KILL YOU !!!
SO DODGE IT!!! DODGE IT, YOU HEAR ?!!!
HUH ?
"DODGE IT"...?
TH-THIS GUY SAYS SOME STRANGE THINGS...
D-DON'T TELL ME...
IT'S THE KIKÔHÔ* !!
T-TEN... DON'T !!
AS I FEARED !!
DON'T DO IT, TEN-SHINHAN-- DO YOU WANT TO DIE ?!!
WH-WHAT? WHAT'S GOING ON...?
TO THINK HE KNOWS THE KIKÔHÔ...
L-LORD MUTEN-RÔSHI... WHAT IS IT...?

*OR, IN CHINESE, "CHI KUNG PAO"–ED.

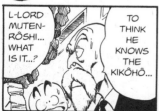

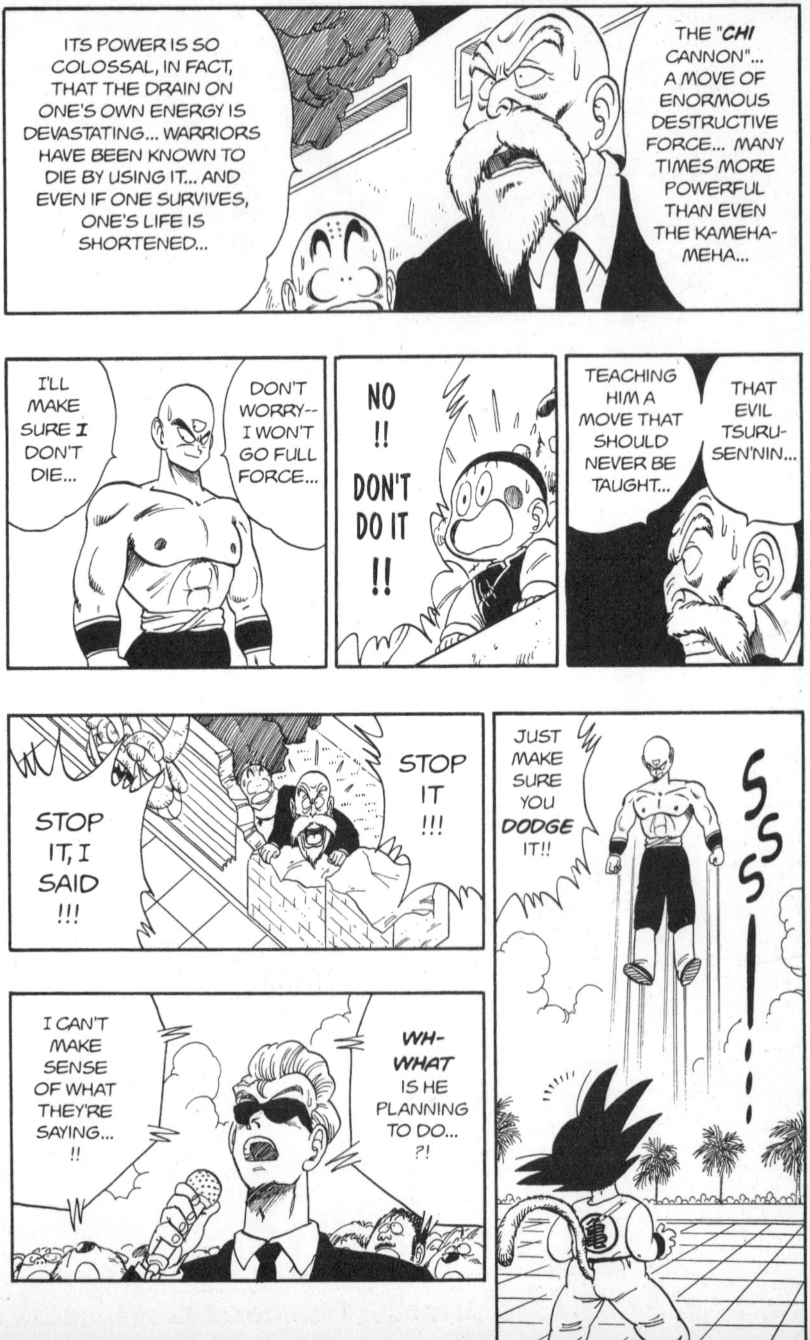
THE "CHI CANNON"... A MOVE OF ENORMOUS DESTRUCTIVE FORCE... MANY TIMES MORE POWERFUL THAN EVEN THE KAMEHA-MEHA...
ITS POWER IS SO COLOSSAL, IN FACT, THAT THE DRAIN ON ONE'S OWN ENERGY IS DEVASTATING... WARRIORS HAVE BEEN KNOWN TO DIE BY USING IT... AND EVEN IF ONE SURVIVES, ONE'S LIFE IS SHORTENED...
THAT EVIL TSURU-SEN'NIN...
TEACHING HIM A MOVE THAT SHOULD NEVER BE TAUGHT...
NO!! DON'T DO IT!!
DON'T WORRY-- I WON'T GO FULL FORCE...
I'LL MAKE SURE I DON'T DIE...
JUST MAKE SURE YOU DODGE IT!!
SSS!!!
STOP IT!!!
STOP IT, I SAID!!!
WH-WHAT IS HE PLANNING TO DO...?!
I CAN'T MAKE SENSE OF WHAT THEY'RE SAYING...!!

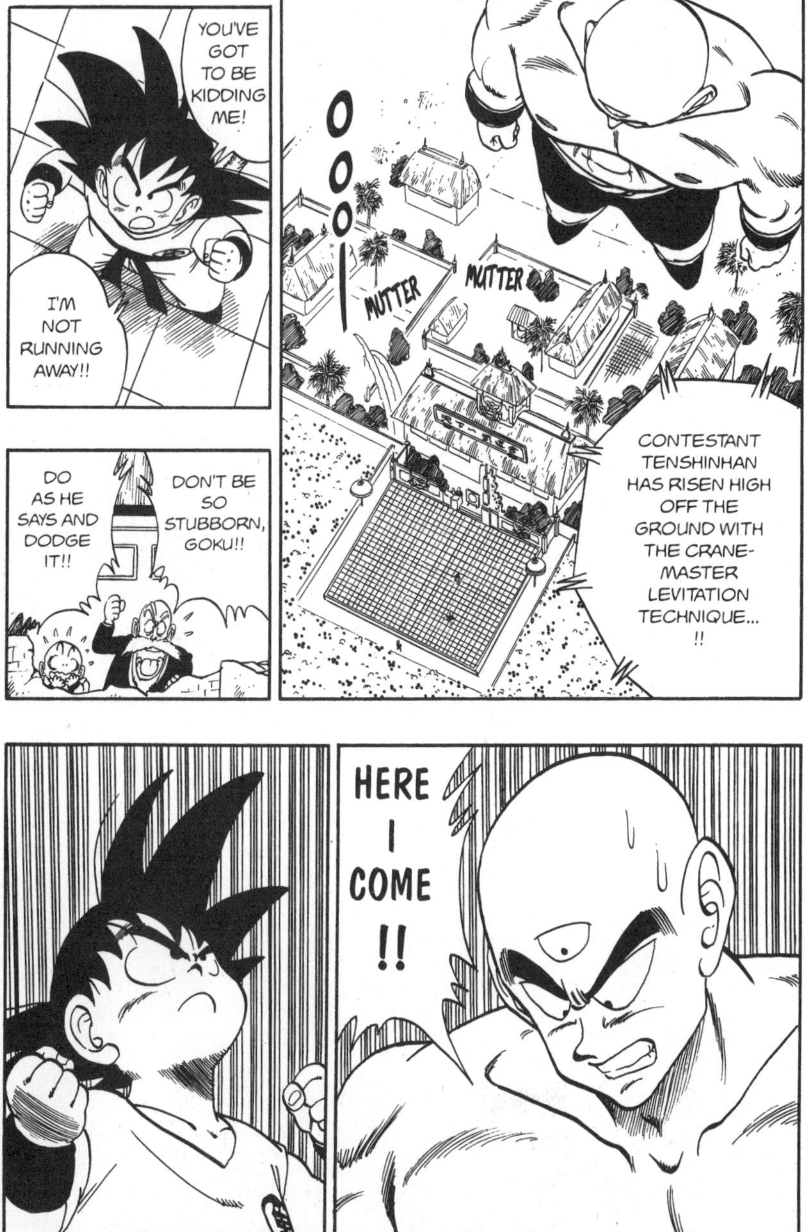
OOO—
MUTTER
MUTTER
CONTESTANT TENSHINHAN HAS RISEN HIGH OFF THE GROUND WITH THE CRANE-MASTER LEVITATION TECHNIQUE... !!
YOU'VE GOT TO BE KIDDING ME!
I'M NOT RUNNING AWAY!!
DON'T BE SO STUBBORN, GOKU!!
DO AS HE SAYS AND DODGE IT!!
HERE I COME !!

NEXT: **REALLY** the Strongest-Under-the-Heavens!!

TITLE PAGE GALLERY

These title pages were used when these **Dragon Ball** chapters were originally published in Japan from 1987 to 1988 in **Weekly Shonen Jump** magazine.

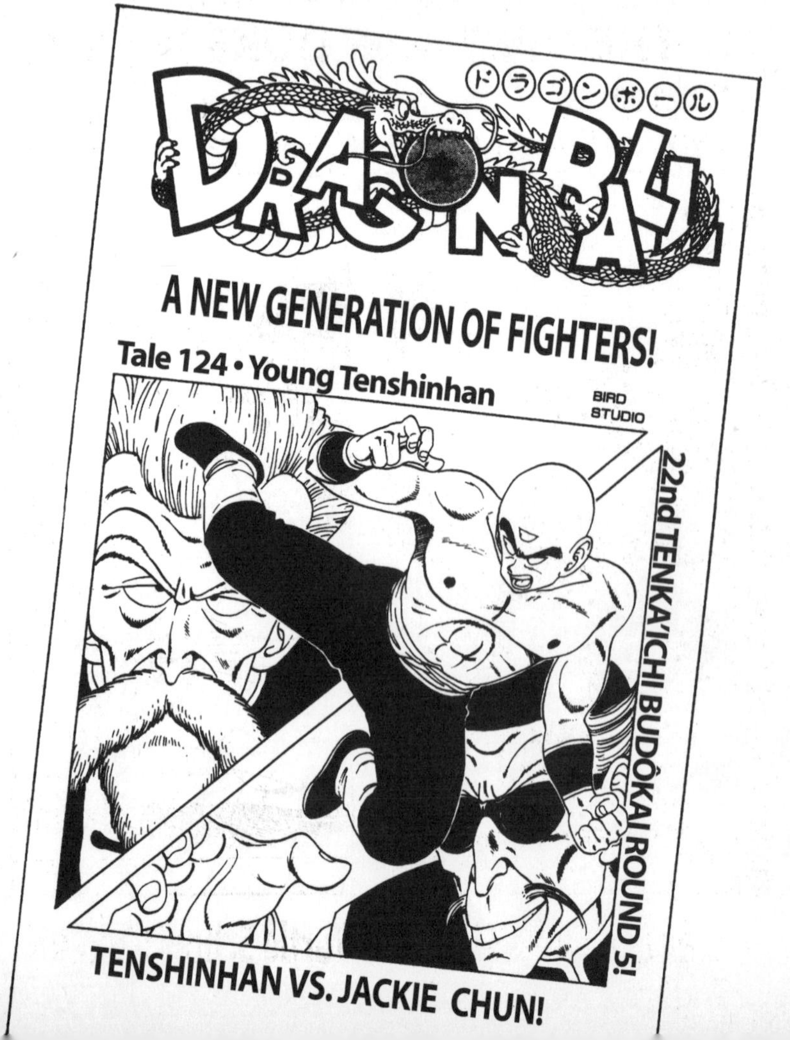

ドラゴンボール
DRAGON BALL
A NEW GENERATION OF FIGHTERS!
Tale 124 • Young Tenshinhan
BIRD STUDIO
22nd TENKA'ICHI BUDÔKAI ROUND 5!
TENSHINHAN VS. JACKIE CHUN!

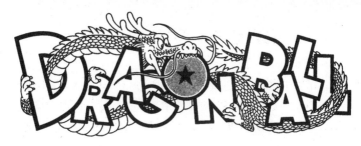

TURTLE VS. CRANE…
THE DISCIPLES DUKE IT OUT!

Tale 120
Look Out! The Dodon Blast!

Akira Toriyama
鳥山明 BIRD STUDIO

THE 22nd TENKA'ICHI BUDÔKAI: ROUND THREE

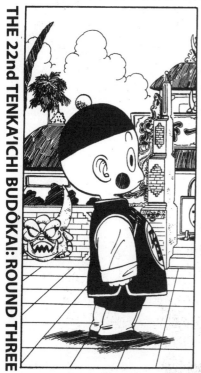

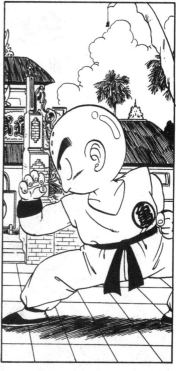

Crane School CHAOZU vs. Turtle School KURIRIN

ドラゴンボール

DRAGON BALL

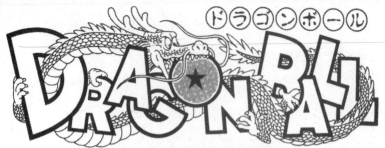

A CLOSE FIGHT? HIGH SPEED GIVE AND TAKE!

Tale 126 • Goku vs. Kuririn, Part 2

22nd TENKA'ICHI BUDÔKAI ROUND 6!

Akira Toriyama
鳥山明 BIRD STUDIO

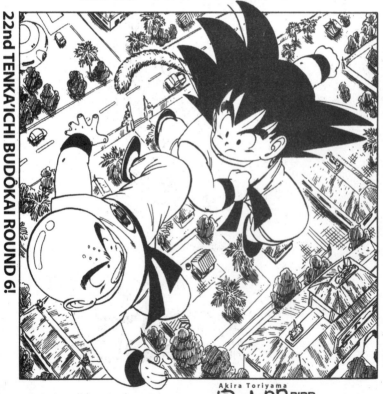

22nd TENKA'ICHI BUDÔKAI ROUND 6!

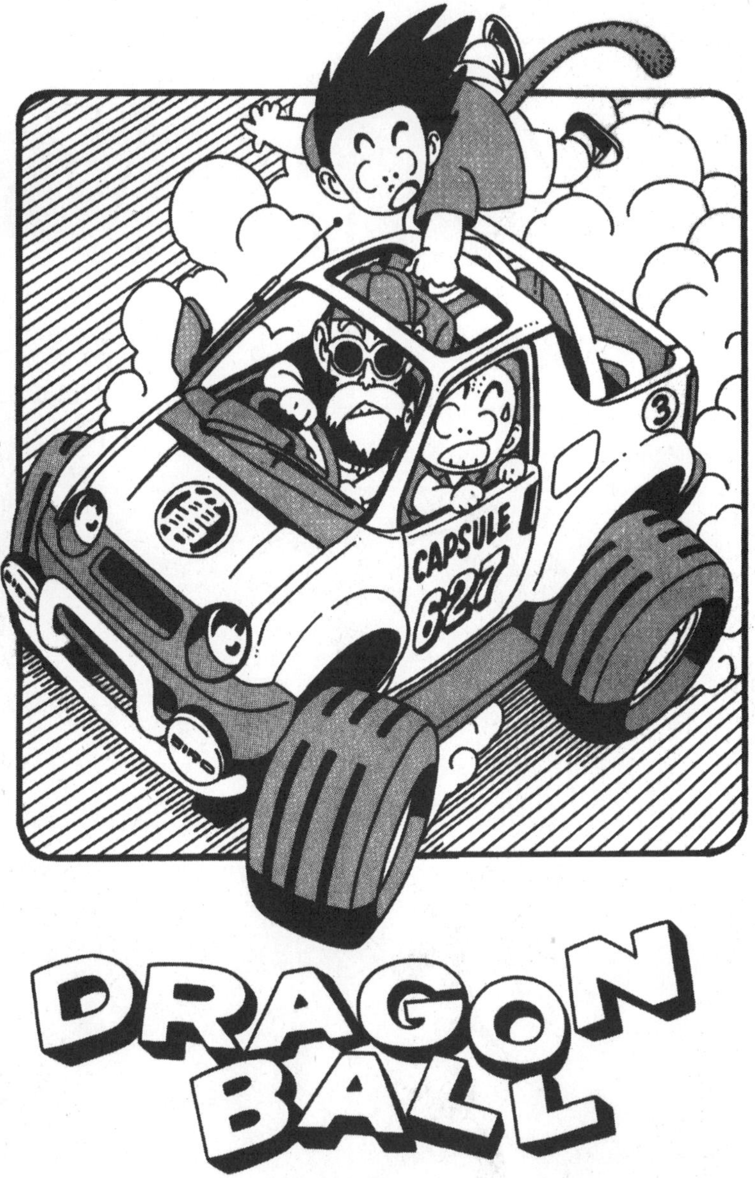
CAPSULE
627
3

DRAGON BALL

Tale 127 • Goku vs. Kuririn, Part 3

ドラゴンボール

DRAGON BALL

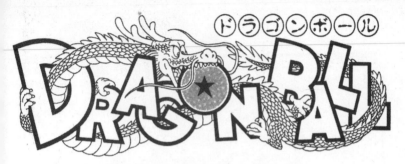

THE FINAL BATTLE OF THE STRONGEST!

Akira Toriyama
鳥山明
BIRD STUDIO

DBZ:128 • Goku vs. Tenshinhan

22nd TENKA'ICHI BUDÔKAI ROUND 7!

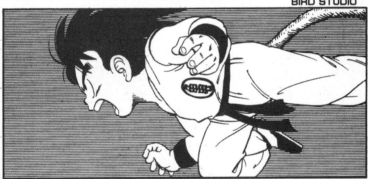

Turtle School SON GOKU

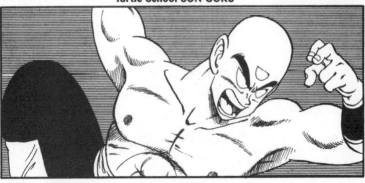

Crane School TENSHINHAN

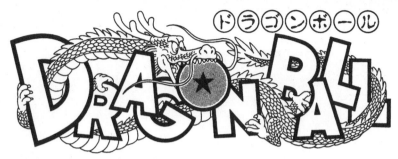

ドラゴンボール

DRAGON BALL

TENSHINHAN TRIUMPHANT???

Akira Toriyama
鳥山明
BIRD STUDIO

Tale 129 • The Volleyball Play

22nd TENKA'ICHI BUDÔKAI ROUND 7!

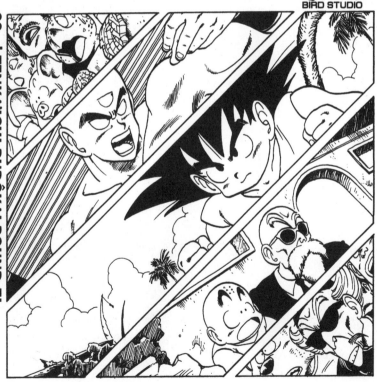

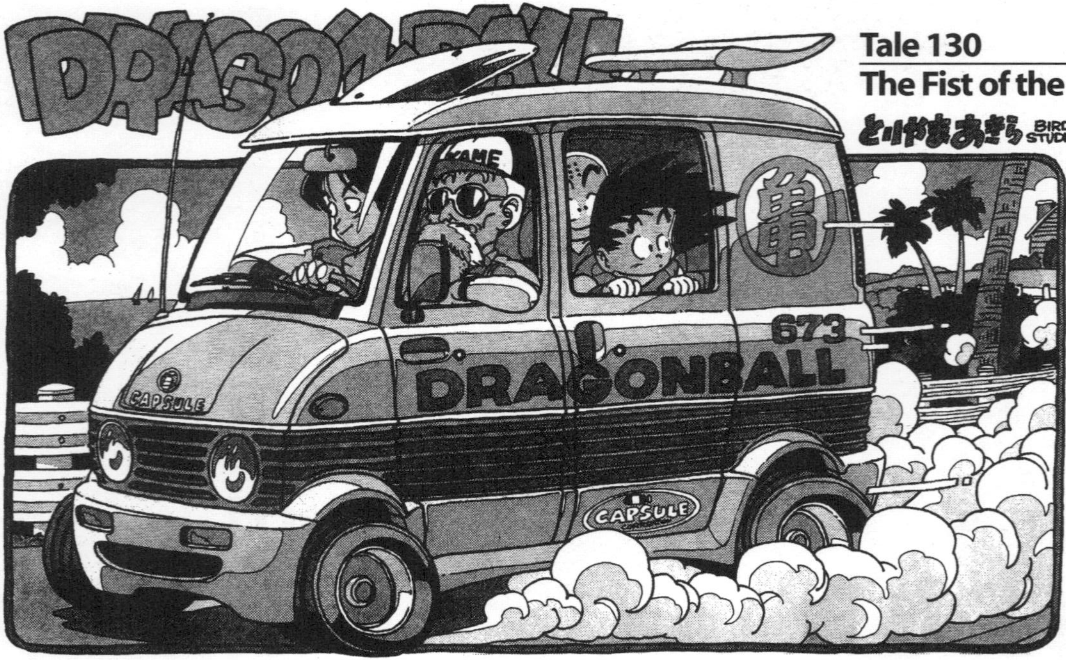
DRAGON BALL
KAME
673
DRAGONBALL
CAPSULE
CAPSULE

Tale 130
The Fist of the Sun

とりやまあきら BIRD STUDIO

GOKU STRIKES BACK AT FULL POWER!

TSURU-SEN'NIN'S FATAL TECHNIQUE!!!

Tale 132 • The Arms Race

22nd TENKA'ICHI BUDŌKAI ROUND 7!

Akira Toriyama
鳥山明 BIRD STUDIO

FREE*

DRAG★N BALL™

Collectible Display Box

FOR VOLUMES 8 THROUGH 16

Here's how you can receive a cool collectible Dragon Ball Display Box:

Purchase Dragon Ball Graphic Novels volumes 8 through 11 (purchase of volumes 12 to 16 not necessary).

1. Fill out the **Entry Form** from volume 8.

2. Enclose the following in a postage-paid envelope:

★ The *original* completed **Entry Form** (vol.8).

★ The *original* **Validation Coupons** from Dragon Ball Graphic Novels volumes 9 through 11.

★ Payment in the amount of *$4.50 for shipping and handling.* Payment must be made by enclosing a check or money order made payable to ***Dragon Ball Display Box Offer.*** (Ask your parents or legal guardian if you don't know how.)

3. Address and stuff the envelope:

ENTRY FORM (from volume 8)
+ VALIDATION COUPONS
(from volumes 9 – 11)   **Check or Money Order**

Your return address
_____

STAMP
HERE

DRAGON BALL DISPLAY BOX OFFER
P.O. Box 111238
Tacoma, WA 98411-1238

DETACH HERE ▶

DRAGON BALL © 1984 by BIRD STUDIO / SHUEISHA Inc.

COMPLETE OUR SURVEY AND LET US KNOW WHAT YOU THINK!

☐ Please check here if you DO NOT wish to receive information or future offers from VIZ

Name: _____

Address: _____

City: _____ State: _____ Zip: _____

E-mail: _____

☐ Male ☐ Female Date of Birth (mm/dd/yyyy): ___ / ___ / ___ (Under 13? Parental consent required)

What race/ethnicity do you consider yourself? (please check one)

☐ Asian/Pacific Islander   ☐ Black/African American   ☐ Hispanic/Latino

☐ Native American/Alaskan Native   ☐ White/Caucasian   ☐ Other: _____

What VIZ product did you purchase? (check all that apply and indicate title purchased)

☐ DVD/VHS _____

☐ Graphic Novel _____

☐ Magazines _____

☐ Merchandise _____

Reason for purchase: (check all that apply)

☐ Special offer   ☐ Favorite title   ☐ Gift

☐ Recommendation   ☐ Other _____

Where did you make your purchase? (please check one)

☐ Comic store   ☐ Bookstore   ☐ Mass/Grocery Store

☐ Newsstand   ☐ Video/Video Game Store ☐ Other: _____

☐ Online (site: _____)

What other VIZ properties have you purchased/own? _____

_____

How many anime and/or manga titles have you purchased in the last year? How many were VIZ titles? **(please check one from each column)**

ANIME	MANGA	VIZ
☐ None	☐ None	☐ None
☐ 1-4	☐ 1-4	☐ 1-4
☐ 5-10	☐ 5-10	☐ 5-10
☐ 11+	☐ 11+	☐ 11+

I find the pricing of VIZ products to be: **(please check one)**

☐ Cheap ☐ Reasonable ☐ Expensive

What genre of manga and anime would you like to see from VIZ? **(please check two)**

☐ Adventure ☐ Comic Strip ☐ Detective ☐ Fighting

☐ Horror ☐ Romance ☐ Sci-Fi/Fantasy ☐ Sports

What do you think of VIZ's new look?

☐ Love It ☐ It's OK ☐ Hate It ☐ Didn't Notice ☐ No Opinion

THANK YOU! Please send the completed form to:

NJW Research
42 Catharine St.
Poughkeepsie, NY 12601

All information provided will be used for internal purposes only. We promise not to sell or otherwise divulge your information.